The Salisbury Manuscript

THE SALISBURY MANUSCRIPT

Philip Gooden

CONSTABLE • LONDON

Constable & Robinson Ltd
3 The Lanchesters
162 Fulham Palace Road
London W6 9ER
www.constablerobinson.com

First published in the UK by Constable,
an imprint of Constable & Robinson, 2008

First US edition published by SohoConstable,
an imprint of Soho Press, 2008

Soho Press, Inc.
853 Broadway
New York, NY 10003
www.sohopress.com

A copy of the British Library Cataloguing in Publication
Data is available from the British Library

UK ISBN: 978-1-84529-640-7

US ISBN: 978-1-56947-5126
US Library of Congress number: 2007043758

Printed and bound in the EU

1 3 5 7 9 10 8 6 4 2

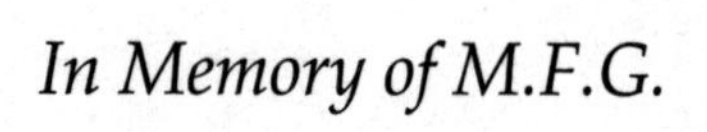

In Memory of M.F.G.

Todd's Mound

The man turned aside from the farm-track as the autumn afternoon closed in and storm clouds were scudding from the west. He was glad the light was fading. Even though he'd been careful to dress in his roughest clothes so that he might be taken for an itinerant labourer, he preferred to be moving in the gloom. Nevertheless it was going to be dark sooner than he expected. He would have to move briskly.

The man had a bag slung over his shoulder and, despite weighing little, it felt awkward on his back. He set off to his right on a path which was scarcely more than a flattened line of grass on the uphill slope. When he reached a copse of beech trees, he paused to adjust the bag so it sat more comfortably. Pulling his cap down and shrugging himself more deeply inside his coat, he left the shelter of the beeches and set off at a smart pace.

Ahead of him was the bare ridge of the slope with forlorn clumps of sheep grazing on either side. Because he was keeping his head low, the man wasn't aware of the presence of another individual making his way in the opposite direction until he saw a pair of leather leggings and great boots almost under his nose.

He nipped off the makeshift path as the shepherd – the other man striding downhill was carrying a sheep-crook – nodded and mumbled something inaudible. The man with the bag nodded in reply. He didn't speak. He couldn't see the shepherd's expression, on account of the fading light and the speed at which they passed, but he had the impression of a certain irritation, as if this hillside belonged to the shepherd. When he halted and looked back he observed that the shepherd too had stopped and was gazing uphill at him. Near the bottom of the slope the man saw what he hadn't noticed before, the roof of a simple house, more of a hut. Meanwhile the shepherd clutched his free hand to his felt hat and, using the sheep-crook as a pivot, turned away and made towards the hut.

The man wondered why he hadn't spotted the place before. Probably because it was in a small hollow and surrounded by bushes only now losing their leaves. He should have surveyed the surroundings more carefully. Not that it made any difference to his plan. His destination was well out of sight of the shepherd's hut, up and over the ridge of the hill. The shepherd did not matter. The man did not intend to return to the area after this visit. He resumed the path which now crossed an extensive ditch-like depression before climbing to the top of the ridge.

At the top he paused for a final time to catch his breath and look round. The landscape stretched away to the south and west, broken by mounds and low hills and with the glint of water. No living thing was visible, apart from the sheep waiting out the rain which had begun to fall. He could still see the corner of the roof of the hut. He wondered if he was being watched even now. Telling himself that if he was genuinely what he appeared to be – a travelling workman with his tools in a bag slung over his shoulder – then the last thing he'd be doing was stopping to take in the view, the man set his back to the wind and rain and walked down the lesser slope on the far side of the ridge.

He was entering on an oblong-shaped plateau, whose sides were high enough to obscure the view of the outside world. The wind slackened and it grew quieter. The hill was a natural feature of the landscape but there was a queer sort of design to the top of it. It even had a name: Todd's Mound, though no one knew who Todd was or why his name should have been associated with the place. The man had discovered from all his reading and researches that it had first been adapted to human use many centuries ago, long before it had become Todd's Mound. He knew that ancient people had chosen the hilltop as a secure site from which to overlook the surrounding country. They had strengthened the grassy ramparts and excavated a kind of ditch which ran almost the whole way round the base of the hill, before laying paths and constructing simple places to live and work.

At some point these people had abandoned the hilltop. Perhaps they were overrun by their enemies, perhaps it was difficult to obtain water from such chalky soil or the lowlands below became a more attractive prospect. Whatever the reason, they were long gone and forgotten. But until that point they had lived here in large numbers, and died here too. That was what interested the man. Those who had died on this fortified summit.

He walked the length of the plateau, several hundred yards. There were no trees, only shrubs and brambles. At points around the grassy rim there were small dips, even clefts, and the man was making for one of these on the south-eastern corner. Once he stopped and looked behind him, convinced that he was being followed. He was startled to see a deer shoot across an exposed area between clumps of undergrowth, a flash of brown and the white tuft of the tail showing up in the gloom. Rebuking himself for nerves, he resumed his course.

When he reached the cleft at the far edge he saw the town in the distance and the cathedral spire against the smoky clouds. He didn't spend time on the view, which was familiar to him. The man paused to readjust his bag once more, knowing that the going would become tricky from now on because of the fall of the land on this aspect of the hill. This was why he had approached the spot via the hilltop rather than making the scramble up from the eastern side. He swung through the cleft, which was like a natural gateway into the plateau, and moved slantwise down the slope, bracing himself with his right leg and keeping his arms out for balance.

He reckoned that at some time there'd been a slippage of land at this south-eastern edge. There were areas where the grass was thin and the chalk showed through. In addition, the cleft or gateway through which he'd just passed had the appearance of having once been an entrance – a kind of back entrance perhaps – to the hilltop settlement, a function it could hardly have provided given the current lie of the land. There were trees on the slope too, a few beeches but mostly clusters of yew. The man was heading for a spot just above one of these clusters, perhaps a hundred feet or so below the top of the hill and about the same number of yards to the left of the notch in the plateau.

The point was marked by an uprooted beech tree, an old and diseased one brought down by a storm sometime in the spring of that year. The man was lucky on several counts. Lucky that this side of the hill was not used for grazing and was too steep for any other purpose, including a comfortable walk. Lucky that his researches had brought him to this general area of Todd's Mound. Lucky that what he was searching for had until the springtime been concealed by the beech tree. Not intentionally concealed, for the tree was of a much later date. But the great trunk and the arm-like roots clinging to the hillside had effectively hidden the few yards of ground around its base from the casual glance of a passer-by strolling either at the bottom or at the top of Todd's Mound.

This was his third expedition to the spot. The first had been discovery. The second had been for investigation and preparation. And now came the third: the fruit of his labours.

The man with the bag on his shoulder reached the fallen beech tree. Jagged shards protruded from what remained of a base which had been half torn from the soil by the violence of the fall. The great mass of the trunk and the crown with its outflung branches, lay slantwise across the slope and provided good cover. Not that much cover was required in the growing gloom. To his left, that is on the uphill side of the tree, the man sensed rather than saw what he was looking for, a pile of mud and chalk thrown up when the tree fell. Near the centre of the mound was a darker place like the entrance to a tunnel. He experienced a tightening in his chest.

He felt his way forward in the rain until he was at a crouch and grasping a stone upright set to one side of the entrance. The stone, about four feet high, had been cut for a purpose. The work was primitive but there could be no doubt it was done by the hand of man. Resting on top of the upright was another slab of stone like the lintel to a door. The corresponding upright on the other side had fallen inwards so that the lintel was at a diagonal across the entrance. The resulting triangular aperture was small but sufficient to allow someone to worm his way inside. After his most recent expedition the man had made a rudimentary attempt to hide the spot by dragging across a severed tree branch so that it partially blocked the opening. Now he tugged at it with both hands and hefted it down the slope.

The man eased off his bag and placed it by the aperture. He glanced uphill for a last time. Seen from this crouching position, the sheer bulk of Todd's Mound seemed about to tumble down and bury him and he felt, as well as excitement, a tremor of fear. He shrugged the feeling off and pushed the bag ahead of him into the narrow entrance.

He had to crawl to make his way to the interior but, once there, the space grew bigger and he was able to kneel. His head was brushing against the low roof. There was the smell of damp and leaf-mould, and something more rank underlying it. It was pitch dark. The man unfastened his bag and brought out an oil lamp which he placed carefully between his spread knees. He took a box of matches from his coat pocket and, working by touch, struck a light. The acridity from the match filled the tiny space.

When the lamp was going the man spent some time adjusting the wick until he was satisfied with the quantity of light. The light was a warm gold. Like the smell of the match, it was oddly comforting. He squatted on his haunches and raised the oil lamp to examine the interior of the cave as if for the first time. Really he was making sure that no one had penetrated this secret space since his last visit. The fact that the tree branch outside the entrance hadn't been disturbed was not conclusive enough for him. He was a careful man who took precautions. And what he saw now did not reassure him.

The light from the lamp showed that this space, burrowed into the side of Todd's Mound, extended for about two dozen feet at right angles from the little entrance. There were pale objects piled at the end, far enough away for the lamplight not to reach fully. The tunnel-like space was wider than it was high and the roof of rock and chalky soil sloped down towards the end. If this place had once been a natural cave or fissure in the hillside, it had been enlarged and reinforced at the sides with thin slabs of stone. These stones, like the ones around the entrance, bore man-made marks.

On his second visit the man had taken some of the bones which were among the items he had discovered at the other end of the burrow. When he first picked up the bones he experienced a momentary unease. Yet he told himself, *he* won't mind, he's out of it now. Or was it a *she*, not a he? But he thought not. The bones seemed too large to be a woman's, and he was a good judge of such things. So he had placed them in a deliberate pattern a couple of yards inside the opening. The bones – shinbones and a forearm from a human skeleton – were greasy and unpleasant to the touch. Even so, handling them did not trouble him. He wanted another small guarantee that no one would disturb the burrow, 'his' burrow as he considered it.

Accordingly the man spent some time thinking of a pattern to put the bones into, a pattern that would look arbitrary but have meaning for him. He remembered the private smile he'd given as he positioned the bones in the form of an H, the initial of one of his names. It looked like an accidental arrangement yet anyone stumbling across the hidden place and worming his way into the interior could hardly avoid disturbing these carefully placed remains.

By the light of the lamp the man saw, with a thrill of fear, that that was what had happened. The shinbones which formed the uprights of the H, together with the ulna that made the cross-piece, had not merely been disturbed. They had been scattered. They were lying to one side of the burrow as though they'd been impatiently tossed there. By a human intruder? By someone trespassing on *his* burrow? The man suppressed an instinctive urge to douse his lamp as if he was being watched at that very instant, and examined the area around where he'd placed the bones.

But the ground was a mess of mud and chalk and fragments of root. There were no discernible human marks. He simply couldn't tell whether anyone else had blundered into this place. The man realized that his little precautions didn't amount to much. He recalled the shepherd striding down the hill on the far side of Todd's Mound. Was it possible that the shepherd or some other country fellow had gone poking into his burrow and pushed aside the bones which had been positioned in the shape of a letter? Had this other person found . . . what there was to be found at the far end?

There was only one way to make sure of course. To go and see. Yet the man did not move. He stayed on his haunches, surveying the space by the light of the lamp. His breath came short and fast. He heard the beating of his heart mingled with the hiss of the oil lamp. The burrow seemed to close in round him. He made a conscious effort to calm himself. When his heart slowed and his breath eased, he listened hard. The wind moaned outside and he was startled by a movement in the corner of his eye. Something small, something grey and scuttling, which disappeared into a fissure in the flank of the burrow. That was the explanation for the moving bones, no doubt. A mouse, a rat, some earth creature, had disturbed them. Yet the man was not altogether convinced by his own explanation.

Anyway there was nothing to be done except to get on with the job. He'd be making his way back in the darkness. Too late, he cursed his caution in not working by daylight. Carrying his burden away by night, he risked a broken leg or worse. Even so, he couldn't avoid the thought that there was a certain appropriateness to doing all this under the cover of night. A moonless night too. He brought a flask from his coat pocket and unscrewed the cap. He took a good swig of brandy. Its warmth reached down inside him. He stroked the flask as if in gratitude, mechanically running his fingertips over the initials incised into the surface.

Fortified, he took up his bag and the oil lamp and, with back bent, shuffled awkwardly on his knees towards the further end of the burrow. There was a collection of bones up here, including a skull and the arch of a ribcage. The skull was resting against a rock. The man himself had put it in that position. Fortunately, it remained as he had left it, lolling like a head against a pillow. The skull grinned at him as if it knew some secret. There was a hole in one side of the head although the man couldn't tell whether it was as a result of a wound inflicted before death – if so, certainly a fatal one – or whether it had been produced by the manner of his burial or even later. It was likely that this individual had died by violence or perhaps been sacrificed in some ancient, barbaric rite.

He put the lamp on the ground and lifted the skull up from its place near the ribcage. The space was cramped and airless. It would have been easier to work here if he cleared the bones but he was curiously reluctant to disturb them further. Behind the spot where the skull had been the rock was relatively smooth. Using a trowel from his bag, the man scraped away the mud which he himself had plastered there on his last visit. His arms and legs bumped against the remains of his underground companion but he was so absorbed in his work that he hardly noticed them or the small sounds behind his back – that grey scuttling creature, no doubt.

Soon his efforts revealed a low rock face. This far end of the burrow was composed of small slabs of stone, square or oblong, almost wall-like in their overall effect. They didn't fit quite snugly together but, like the entrance and the sides of the burrow, they had certainly been created by human hand.

When he had cleared a large enough area, the man used his gloved hands to grasp at the edges of a rectangular slab in the centre of the wall. It came away easily enough and he placed it on the ground. The resulting space was like the mouth of a post-box. He removed another slab. Then he reached in and groped around the recess that lay at the end of the burrow. His fingers closed round familiar objects and he breathed a sigh of relief. His secret was safe.

He brought the first of the items into the warm glow from the lamp. Its feel and weight were well known to him, likewise the dull sheen of the thing. Once again, he marvelled at the intricate workmanship. Let no one say that he was a common despoiler of graves, unable to appreciate beauty when he saw and handled it!

Swiftly he retrieved all the objects from the recess, piling them next to the bones of the skeleton. Using the lamp, he made a final examination of the recess. The light showed a roughly rectangular cavity lined with stone which had been cut to the same primitive finish as the exterior. Nothing remained inside. The cupboard was bare. He debated for an instant replacing the stone blocks but what would be the point? Anyone was welcome to visit the place now. But some instinct did cause him to return the stones to their position in the wall after all, the same instinct that had made him reluctant to disturb more of the bones than necessary.

The man, sweating from his efforts and his hunched posture and the confined space, now proceeded to wrap up the objects from the hidden recess. He had brought fragments of cloth in his bag for this purpose. Otherwise the bag had been empty, apart from the lamp and the trowel. Returning, it would be full. He loaded the bag and hefted it a few inches from the ground. It was heavier than he expected. He contemplated sitting out the hours of darkness here and sneaking back with the first glimmers of light from the east.

Dragging the bag with him, he moved into the more spacious area of the burrow near the entrance. He suddenly felt weary, not simply from the physical effort of emptying the stone cavity within the burrow but from the tension and concealment of the last few weeks.

The man had discovered the burrow revealed by the fallen beech tree in late summer. It wasn't the first time he had tramped over the area of Todd's Mound within sight of the cathedral spire, tramped without success. He persisted because his researches had shown that there should be something here on this flank of the hill. But it was only during one fine September afternoon that he observed the stone blocks above the great bole of the tree. A cursory inspection of the stones revealed that they had been shaped to serve some purpose, an entrance to an underground chamber.

Feeling slightly foolish, he crawled inside the triangular 'door' and found himself in the larger space beyond. He carried no light with him but, when his eyes adjusted to the gloom, he was just able to discern a skeleton laid out at the far end. He assumed the bones were the remains of some large animal. He crawled closer and, working by touch rather than sight, quickly established that they were human. But more than that he couldn't discover although the dark chamber seemed to offer some kind of promise. Surely it must conceal more than a pile of bones?

The very next day he returned with a lamp, pick, hammer and other tools in a leather bag. The weather had turned and the wind was gusting. He was wearing a long black coat, half as protection, half as disguise. This time he was conscious of moving more surreptitiously than on previous expeditions, conscious of playing a part. He crossed the sunken plateau on top of the hill. Anyone watching would have wondered exactly what business brought him to this isolated place. But there was no one to witness him disappear, like a rabbit wearing a greatcoat, into the hillside.

On this, his second visit, he operated methodically, lighting the lamp, unpacking the pick and the rest of the things from his bag before examining the interior of the burrow. Only to be disappointed. The sides were composed of chalky soil held back in places by stone slabs. There were no hidden recesses. It was not until he reached the area at the back of the chamber occupied by the skeleton that his straining eyes made out, beneath a veneer of muddy slime, a feature that seemed more promising. Slabs of stone arranged like large irregularly sized bricks.

The man shifted a portion of the skeleton and scraped away the mud. Soon he was prising away a block that offered the most purchase to his eager fingers. It was difficult work. He was on his knees, leaning forward, encumbered by his black coat. He raised the lamp so that it illuminated the cavity beyond. His heart banged in his chest when the lamp beams reflected off a mound of objects. He reached in and drew out the nearest. It was an elaborate neckpiece or collar, heavy and ungainly to modern eyes, perhaps, but most attractive to him. He placed it respectfully on the dirty ground and fumbled inside the recess for the next item.

Later he returned all the objects to the cavity and replaced the slab. Then he smeared mud back over the stones. He positioned the skull just below the slab against a smaller stone. He retreated to the outer part of the burrow and sat in thought. Then he gathered up three bones and arranged them near the entrance in the style of the letter H. He could not laugh at his little joke but he did smile slightly. He packed up his implements and doused the lantern.

He returned to the outside world. The wind had dropped but autumn was in the air. He looked down and observed clots of mud and streaks of chalk on his coat. He wiped them off and then used his spittle and a handkerchief to clean his hands and face as best he could. After that, he retraced his path uphill and so through the back entrance to the hill settlement, across the plateau and down the gentler slope on the western side.

For the next few weeks he remained in a fog-like state of indecision, wrestling with his conscience. Could he – or rather should he – go back and retrieve the items which he had unearthed in the burrow? The man had always regarded himself as an honest, even honourable, individual. He read widely and thought about things, even though he occupied a position where neither reading nor thinking was expected of him. He argued with himself. Didn't he have a right to goods which had been uncovered through his own ingenuity and labours? He was depriving no one else by his find. The long-dead had no use for them. If he hadn't almost stumbled across the cavity sheltered by the base of the beech tree, the objects in the burrow might have rested there until the end of time, to no one's benefit.

At one point the man set off with his bag, intending to return to the burrow and take the hoard. But his nerve failed him and he had hardly got to the halfway stage between the city and Todd's Mound when he turned back, irresolute. He attempted to bend his mind to his daily work in the cathedral and to forget about his discovery below the hill fort.

But it was in the cloisters of the cathedral that enlighten ment or guidance of a sort came to him. There was a memorial tablet on the inner wall of the covered walk of the cloisters which included a quotation from Ecclesiastes: *and if the tree fall toward the south, or toward the north, in the place where the tree falleth, there it shall be*. He'd noticed the inscription before without paying much attention to it or wondering greatly at its meaning. But, one morning, walking briskly down the cloister, he stopped and read the words on the tablet more carefully and saw how they had an odd application to his discovery.

The inscription was from Chapter 11 of Ecclesiastes. When he got back to his house, the man wrote out the inscription from memory. He stared at it for a long time. He realized that the verse provided not only a strange allusion to his discovery but an even stranger one to himself. The man wasn't especially superstitious but he'd grown into the habit of looking for little signs and markers. It was enough to determine his course. He would go back to Todd's Mound and open up the cavity in the burrow once more and bring out the objects.

As soon as he was free of duties – the next afternoon as it transpired – he slipped out of the cathedral close and, once on the edge of the city, he donned the rough coat and hat which might cause him to be mistaken for an itinerant labourer and walked rapidly into the surrounding country. The sky was overcast and he was glad that there were few people about. The only person who had taken any notice of him was the shepherd striding downhill on the western slope of Todd's Mound.

Now, a couple of hours later when it was dark outside, he sat in the stuffy burrow by the light of the oil lamp, hefting the sack which contained the treasure hoard. He took another swig from his flask. He had almost forgotten that someone, or something, had intruded on the burrow in his absence. Then the sight of the bones casually thrown to one side reminded him that the burial chamber had been visited. The idea of waiting for first light was not an appealing one.

He prepared to leave, looking round to make sure that he'd gathered up all his implements. He doused the oil lamp. He waited while his eyes adjusted to the near-absolute dark inside the burial-chamber. The entrance showed as a slightly less dark shape in the gloom. He unscrewed the flask for a final draught. Whether it was that he was no longer so absorbed in his task or whether the absence of light had somehow sharpened his senses, the man abruptly stopped in the action of returning the flask to his pocket and listened.

What was that sound from outside? A kind of rushing noise. The wind, no doubt. And that flicker of movement across the mouth of the burrow, like a curtain being drawn? The man scrabbled to get clear of the confined space as if afraid that the entrance was about to be sealed up for ever. He emerged into the open on his hands and knees, drawing in lungfuls of cold air. Still crouching, he looked from side to side. Nothing to see beyond the great bulk of the beech tree on the slope below him and the blotted shapes of the yews. The rain had stopped and the sky was clear apart from some scudding clouds and the starlight which shone stronger in the absence of the moon. He gazed up at the rapidly shifting sky and there came to him another line from Ecclesiastes, Chapter 11: *he that regardeth the clouds shall not reap*.

The man reached back into the burrow and dragged out the bag containing his spoils. He stood up, momentarily unsteady on his feet after being confined for so long. He looked out at the few scattered lights of the city and the silhouette of the cathedral spire. He put the bag over his shoulder. It was heavy. He would be exhausted by the time he got back to the security of the close. He would have to take care returning through the town even though he would be threading its streets in the dead hours of morning. And he knew its streets and alleys well.

The man was still standing near the entrance to the burial chamber. A few feet to his left was the branch which he had earlier thrown to one side. He was reluctant to leave the burrow exposed so he shuffled across to lay hold of the branch and tugged it back to conceal the entrance. Breathing deeply from the effort he turned about to begin his progress uphill, guided by starlight and the contour of the slope. He glanced at the area above the burrow. There was something up there he hadn't seen before. A darker shape squatting against the sky. For an instant he thought it was a tree with two branches splayed out in queer symmetry, one on either side. But the tree began to move. It seemed to grow higher. The branches became arms. Then it left the ground altogether and launched itself at the man. He was too shocked to move. He received the flying shape full force in his chest and tumbled backwards down the flank of Todd's Mound.

The breath was knocked out of him and an object in the bag – the trowel or an item taken from the burrow – stabbed him painfully in his back. There was another duller pain in his left leg, as though in falling down he might have injured himself. But the man was scarcely aware of any of this. Instead from where he was lying, his head lower than his feet, he saw the tree-shape once more raise itself further up the slope of the hill. Like him, the shape was breathing hard. Both of its arms were extended and it was jigging and swaying as if to keep balance. In one of the outstretched hands the man made out a metallic glint, a knife blade. If he stayed very still he might pass unnoticed. Irrelevantly, out of the depths of his mind there sprang a name, a strange name. It was that of Atropos, one of the old Greek Fates, the one who wields her shears like a blade and who cuts off the thread of life. It had all been explained to him.

Seeing the outline of the figure waver uncertainly as if it didn't know what to do next, the man remained where he was, stock still. After what seemed an interminable length of time, the black shape turned about as though it intended to make its way uphill, away from him. Yes, it was moving *away*. Without thinking, the man on the ground raised himself slightly so as to relieve the stabbing pressure from the bag at his back. As he did this, a much worse pang seized his left leg like a hot wire cutting into the flesh. He must have broken something in falling, broken an ankle, perhaps a leg-bone. He heard a suppressed groan and wondered who was making it. Another groan, louder this time, before he realized that the noise had come out of his own mouth.

Alerted by the sounds of pain, the black shape which had been starting to ascend the flank of the hill twisted back on itself. Even though the man on the ground could see nothing, he felt the eyes of the other boring into the spot where he lay. He'd betrayed himself. Now the shape started to descend the slope, almost bounding down, coming straight for him.

He put out his hands as if to ward off the figure but it continued to advance directly downhill towards the sprawling man, the knife seeming to cut a slice out of the starlit sky.

And, for the last time, another quotation from Ecclesiastes 11 passed through the man's mind: *thou knowest not what evil shall be upon the earth.*

The Side of Beef

When he changed trains at Woking, Thomas Ansell noticed that the gas lamps in the second-class compartment had recently been lit. As the train began to move, the mantles glowed orange then white and the smell of the lamps mingled with the engine-smoke that somehow penetrated even though the window was shut fast. An old woman was sitting across from him. She was reading the *Woman's Journal*. Thomas Ansell had hardly glanced at his book until then but he took it up now only to find he didn't want to concentrate. Instead he gazed out of the smeared glass at the lowering sky and the bare ridge of the horizon. Despite the fug of the compartment, he hunched his shoulders and almost shivered.

He had the compartment to himself after Andover. As they drew into the station the woman opposite glanced up at the heavy case over her head. He hefted it down from the rack and stepped out after her to place it on the platform. They hadn't spoken on the short journey. In fact he'd taken in no more than a round face and a maternal smile. She thanked him and then said some words that sounded like 'Good luck.' Aware of the train puffing impatiently at his back, Ansell might nevertheless have asked the woman why he needed luck but her attention was taken by a porter who took her case. He climbed back into the carriage, unsettled by her parting remark. Perhaps she'd noticed that half-shiver. Perhaps he'd misheard her.

The train sidled along and the gloom turned thicker. Tom Ansell abandoned the attempt to read and tucked his book into a coat pocket. At once the train jerked forward and then, seeming to fall back on itself, came to a juddering halt. There was a ledge of paler sky to the west but even as Tom looked it went out with the swiftness of a shutter. Darkness rushed at the carriage from all sides. He listened for sounds from the other compartments but there was no noise apart from the groaning and creaking of the rolling stock and the malevolent hiss of the gas lamps.

He brought his face closer to the glass. There were deep shadows under his eyes. Helen had told him that he was looking tired when he'd said goodbye to her earlier that day.

'You must take care of yourself,' she said, putting out her hand and stroking his cheek. 'You will write to me.'

'You speak as though I'm going off on some dangerous adventure for months at a time,' he said, rather wishing that that was what he was doing. Setting off on an enterprise which had a smack of danger. But a lawyer does not do that kind of thing. There are no shipwrecks or undiscovered tribes among dusty files and volumes full of precedents.

But, sitting in the railway carriage as night came down, Tom Ansell experienced exactly that, a presentiment of danger. He might have rapped on the wall of the compartment for the comfort of some response from the other side, assuming there was anyone there, but the fear of appearing foolish – more in his own eyes than another's – prevented him. Instead he made an effort to get into his book but it did not engage him. His eyes kept flicking towards the smeared reflection in the window. He imagined himself as Helen must see him. Dark-haired, long-faced, a little serious perhaps.

'You must take care of yourself,' she'd said again that

morning, as he took the hand which had touched his cheek.

'Oh, I will. And when I come back I'll have something to ask you.'

'Don't be so coy, Thomas Ansell. Surely you can say it now?'

She wasn't being serious, he could see by the mischievous twitch to her mouth.

'No,' he said. 'I won't ask now. It demands a more . . . propitious moment. The evening, and a certain dimness and glow which will suit the occasion. The conversation.'

'Very well. Though, if you want to spare my blushes, it's dim enough now.'

She withdrew her hand from his and went to stand by the window. It was drizzling and the grey sky seemed to be fixed a few yards above the roofs opposite. A man and a woman came out of a house on the other side of Athelstan Road. The man urged the woman to shelter under his wide umbrella and they walked off together.

'Is that an image of married life, do you suppose?' said Helen, beckoning Tom to join her by the window.

'How he walks on the outside to protect her from any splashes, even though there's not much traffic here, how he raises the umbrella so that the woman shall be completely covered,' said Tom. 'Yes, it could be an image.'

'But perhaps she doesn't want to be sheltered, perhaps she would like to feel the rain on her face,' said Helen. 'And I know for certain that though the woman is Mrs Montgomery that is not Mr Montgomery. *He* always leaves early in the morning to go to his work in the City. Besides, he is stouter and older than the man who is escorting Mrs Montgomery now. Today is Wednesday and every Wednesday it is the same. The gentleman you've just seen arrives at her door and the pair of them set off together for . . . who knows what or where? They always return at about the same time, in the early afternoon. What have they been up to?'

'I've no idea.'

'And no interest in speculating about our neighbours? I can see that I've surprised you, Tom, and there you were thinking this was such a – such a salubrious area.'

'You don't spy on your neighbours, Helen?'

'I do not set out to spy on them but I can't prevent the servants telling me things and then, by chance, seeing them for myself. Besides it's my duty to be curious.'

'That couple must be innocent, surely? They wouldn't appear so openly if there was anything to hide.'

'What better way of diverting suspicion than by appearing openly?' said Helen.

'Well, it's all grist to your mill,' said Tom. 'You can incorporate it into your writing. As you say, you almost have a duty to be curious.'

'Ssh,' said Helen, raising her finger to her lips. She blushed and Tom was pleased to see her lose her self-possession for a moment. 'Do not mention that again or I shall regret revealing it to you.'

Some time ago Helen had let slip that she was writing what she called a 'sensation' novel, involving an heiress who was cheated by a villain out of her property and abandoned by her husband-to-be and who was compelled to go to extreme lengths to recover both it and him. Tom was intrigued by this. He wondered just what the 'extreme lengths' would be. Yet every time he referred to the novel, Helen looked uncomfortable. In particular she did not want her mother to know what she was doing. Mrs Scott was a formidable woman, a bit dragonish. Tom could not work out how such a ferocious-looking lady was the parent of a girl like Helen. Now he said, 'So what does your mother think that you are doing up in your room when you're scribbling away?'

'*Scribbling*!'

'Composing then. Writing. But what does she think you're up to?'

'Reading, or polishing up my French, or doing embroidery or something like that, I expect. But never writing. Tom, you are on no account to breathe a word to her.'

'When will she know then?'

'When I am published in three volumes and as famous as Mrs Braddon. *Then* my mother can know.'

'Surely she ought to be aware she's harbouring a genius under her roof?'

'The time is not right, Tom, just as it isn't right for . . . whatever it was you wanted to say to me. The *conversation*.'

He was tempted to tease her some more but seeing her expression he relented and delivered some guff about sealed lips, and in reward she stretched up and put her lips to his. He drew her closer. She was soft and her breath was sweet. But they were both aware of the door, not quite closed, and the probable nearness of servants, to say nothing of Mrs Scott herself. Besides, it was a grey morning with the drizzle coming down on Athelstan Avenue and the rest of Highbury, and Tom had to be on his way to Waterloo and before that he had to visit the office in Furnival Street to pick up some papers. So he broke away and promised to call again as soon as he'd returned to town.

Now, sitting in the train compartment, he thought of Helen in her room, scribbling (or rather composing) in solitude. He was almost sorry he'd teased her that morning. He resolved to take her more seriously. The train began to shuffle forward again and then picked up speed. Tom abandoned his book altogether, put it in his coat pocket and put his thoughts of Helen to one side too, in order to concentrate instead on his forthcoming business in Salisbury. 'A strange business,' David Mackenzie had called it, one requiring 'tact and discretion'. Well, he'd see about that. Tom did not think he lacked for tact and discretion.

Fairly soon the train slowed once more and the wheels clacked over points. Looking out, Tom saw a platform gliding slowly past before coming to a complete halt. Fog-shrouded lamps were burning overhead. If it hadn't been that his compartment stopped almost opposite the sign announcing *Salisbury* with, in smaller lettering below, *Fisherton* he might have doubted where he was.

Tom Ansell hoisted his case from the rack and stepped on to the platform. It was the end of the line or, rather, anyone wishing to go further westwards had to change both trains and railway companies on account of the different gauges. Only a few people got out. A trio of porters had positioned themselves at the point where the first-class carriages drew up but none approached Tom, probably seeing that he was a youngish man and not carrying much luggage. Tom put down his suitcase and intercepted one of them. He asked whether it was far to the Poultry Cross. His inn was near the Poultry Cross, he'd been told. The porter said rapidly, 'Half a mile at least, sir,' before scurrying off to help a small elderly gentleman in a shovel-hat.

After the best part of two hours in stuffy train compartments, Tom felt his head needed clearing and would usually have chosen to walk such a short distance. But he had no idea of the layout of the city or the direction of the centre where, he presumed, the cathedral close must be. Nor, if he was being cautious, was it a very sensible notion to set off on foot during the dark and fog in a strange town in the region of a railway station, since stations were rarely built in what Helen might have called the salubrious area of a town.

He looked up and down the platform. Wisps of fog eddied under the glass roof. The platform opposite looked as distant as a foreign shore. No one lingered in the open. The windows of the waiting room and the refreshment room were fugged over. Porters and passengers were making for the ticket hall and the exit. There would be cabs outside the station to collect elderly gents and respectable matrons. Tom bent to pick up his case and noticed that the strap securing it had come undone. He crouched down and discovered that the strap had broken. It must have caught on the rack or the foot-plate. The strap was necessary because the lock was broken and the lock was broken because the case was old and battered. Good quality hide, it had belonged to his father and been made to last by Barrets, but it was showing its age now. His father had been dead many years.

Tom improvised a knot to the strap in place of the useless buckle. As he was crouching on the platform, there was a roar at his back and a flare of light and heat while the monstrous engine trundled past him, reversing out of the station. Tom straightened up and blinked as the smoke from the locomotive mingled with the fog.

When he looked around again he saw that he was alone on the platform. Well, not quite alone. About twenty yards away, as far as he could see before the fog became an impenetrable curtain, a figure suddenly materialized from an unlighted area of the station buildings and rushed to the edge of the platform. Tom thought that it was about to throw itself off the edge but the figure – no more than a black silhouette – halted just before, seeming to teeter there like a suicide on the brink of a cliff. Tom opened his mouth to call out but something prevented him. He did not want to draw attention to his presence. He glanced in the opposite direction, down the line. The train was still puffing on its backward course. And, at once, Tom realized how absurd was the notion that this individual was about to commit suicide since you'd hardly throw yourself into the path of a train which was retreating from you. Nevertheless, he wished one of the station workers would appear and take charge of matters. If there were any matters to take charge of.

He glanced again at the black shape and the skin on his scalp begin to crawl as a *second* figure detached itself from the station offices and started a diagonal approach towards the person who was at the platform's edge. This one didn't rush but nor did he move normally. There was a creeping quality to his walking like that of a stage villain. No more than half a dozen paces separated the buildings from where the silhouette stood but it seemed to take an age for the second individual to cross this space. His arms were stretched out in front of him as if he were feeling his way in the gloom – or as if he were about to give a final push to the first man teetering on the brink. This time Tom did manage to call out. Afterwards he wasn't sure exactly what he said. It might have been nothing more than a cry or a fog-strangled yelp. But it was enough.

The creeping figure stopped and turned his head in Tom's direction. The silhouetted man already on the brink also swivelled sharply to his right and then looked over his shoulder. The movement was sufficient to unbalance him and, with a wild swirl of his arms, he toppled sideways on to the track. Now Tom sensed a movement behind him, a uniformed employee coming out of the ticket hall. Calling out, 'A man's fallen on the line!' he ran to the spot. As he did so he was aware of the second figure, the one who'd been approaching slantwise, shrinking back into the darkness of the buildings.

When he reached the place where the man had plunged off the platform Tom looked down, expecting to see a black-clad figure lying on the track, injured, perhaps unconscious or even dead. But there was no one there, no one lying on or between the rails which glinted dully in the light.

'What is the trouble, sir?'

'I saw a man fall on to the line here.'

The railwayman adjusted his cap and came to stand next to Tom. Together they peered down as if a more careful scrutiny might reveal what hadn't been apparent at first glance.

'A man on the line?'

'Yes, down there.'

'You are sure now, sir?'

The porter, a lugubrious-looking fellow whose face expressed a natural scepticism before he'd even uttered a word, was standing close to Tom. He was only an inch or so less tall than the lawyer. He sniffed the air. Tom wondered if he was sniffing for drink.

'Of course I'm sure,' he said. 'I know what I saw.'

Tom spoke more sharply than he'd intended. He heard the tension in his voice and realized how much the incident had shaken him. The porter said, 'Well, whatever happened, there's no damage done, that's plain. The person you saw must've upped and scarpered.'

'He wasn't alone, the man who fell, there was someone else on this part of the platform.'

'Someone . . . else?' said the other, drawing out the words. 'This is a public place, sir. There is generally someone else.'

'But this one was about to . . .' Tom paused. He was getting nowhere. Gesturing at the closed doors and shuttered windows, he said, 'What offices are these behind us?'

'Store-rooms and the like.'

Tom had no authority to request a search of the rooms. No crime had been committed. The worst that had occurred was a minor accident, a man falling from the station platform but sufficiently unharmed to scramble up and disappear from the scene within a few seconds. And even that simple sequence of events was not credited by the railwayman.

'Will that be all, sir?' said the porter, scarcely bothering to conceal his impatience.

'Thank you,' said Tom. 'I am sorry to have troubled you.'

'No trouble is too great for an employee of the London and South Western line,' said the man, though without sounding as if he believed a word of it.

Tom Ansell walked back to where his case stood, forlorn on the platform, with the improvised repair to its strap. He picked it up and went through the ticket hall. The entire business on the platform had scarcely occupied more than a couple of minutes. Some of the individuals who'd disembarked from the London train were still milling outside by a diminished line of cabs and carriages, even a cart or two (for this was the country). Among them was the porter he'd first spoken to, who was about to assist the elderly gentleman in the shovel-hat to climb into a cab, the last in the line.

This passenger was fumbling in his coat to tip the porter before boarding but as he drew out his purse a shower of coins tumbled on to the ground. The man looked around helplessly while the porter crouched to scoop them up. The cabman surveyed the scene from his perch behind his vehicle but did not get down to assist. Tom, who was standing closest, groped for a couple of sovereigns which had rolled by his feet. He retrieved the book which had fallen from his own coat pocket as he was stooping and pressed the coins into the outstretched palm of the aged passenger, who was wearing a dog collar under a loosely tied muffler. The clergyman said, 'Thank you, thank you.'

The porter meanwhile had completed his task of gathering up the rest of the coins which he handed back to the cleric with a rather ostentatious flourish, as if to demonstrate his honesty in returning every bit of scattered money. In return the cab passenger gave the porter a large enough tip for the man to touch his cap with a soldier's smartness. Noticing Tom and wanting to do the world a favour, the porter now said, 'This gentleman wants to go in the direction of the close too, I believe, sir. The Poultry Cross.'

'Then he should share my cab,' said the cleric.

'I would be grateful,' said Tom.

'I told him it wasn't a night for walking,' said the porter, who'd said no such thing. Tom clambered in after the older man, and the porter stowed his case and the clergyman's bags. He closed the small double doors, which protected the travellers' lower limbs, at the same time calling to the cabman, 'The cathedral close, Alfred.'

The driver waited until the vehicle in front had drawn off before he rattled the reins and the cab creaked and swayed away from the lights of the railway station. The inside space was limited and even though Tom's companion was thin and small-boned with age, they were pressed together by the motion of the cab. They were surrounded by wet fog, interrupted by the occasional smudge of light from an uncurtained window. Even the clopping of the horse's hooves seemed muffled by the dankness. The animal must have known his route by instinct.

'Something is amiss?' said the old clergyman, tapping Tom Ansell on the arm. Tom was surprised at the familiarity of the gesture and only just prevented himself from giving a start. Then he realized how his posture must be giving him away. His coat was unbuttoned and he was gripping his knees tightly. His back was rigid.

'Surely a young man like you – a lawyer from London – doesn't fear a spill from a provincial carriage? You can relax.'

'No, there is nothing wrong, sir. It's merely that I saw something which . . . disturbed me on the station platform.'

As he said these last words, the scene flashed before his eyes again: the silhouette at the platform's edge, the other man sneaking up to push him over. Then his mind caught up with his companion's 'lawyer' comment. He turned to look at the individual beside him in the backwash from the carriage lights. Apart from a clean-shaven roundness to the elderly cleric's face, Tom couldn't make out much between the brim of the shovel-hat and the muffler. What he'd glimpsed moments earlier by the cab rank might have suggested a rather unworldly figure, an impression strengthened by his helplessness over the dropped money. But the impression was evidently wrong.

Without waiting to be asked how he knew about Tom's line of work, the cleric now said, 'Forgive me, I know it is impolite of me to claim a profession for you when we haven't even been introduced. I am Canon Eric Selby.'

'Thomas Ansell. And, yes, I plead guilty to being a lawyer. Is it so obvious?'

'Well, I could say that there are not so many professions open to an educated young man who must earn his living. There is the Church . . . "business" perhaps . . . the army . . . the law. I might claim, without offence I hope, that you don't appear to be cut from the same cloth which makes a clergyman. As for "business", I think not. Nor do you have a soldier's bearing. Which more or less leaves us with the law. But, my dear sir, the conclusive proof is that I noticed you clutching a copy of Baxter's *On Tort* when you were kind enough to pick up my scattered money just now. No sane man would read Baxter for pleasure.'

This was the book which had so comprehensively failed to capture Tom's interest on the journey. He could feel the bulk of the thing in his coat-pocket. He laughed and said, 'I should have packed some other reading matter for the train. *On Tort* is not very diverting at the best of times. You're obviously familiar with it, Canon Selby.'

'I had a friend who swore by it. Indeed I considered the law myself for a brief time before plumping for the Church,' said the other. 'Just as you considered the army, Mr Ansell.'

This time Tom really did start. He said nothing but waited for the cleric to explain himself. Did this man have second sight?

'No miracle, sir,' said Canon Selby, not trying to keep

the pleasure at the success of his deductions out of his voice. 'When I mentioned the army as a possible profession you gave a slight sigh and pulled away, which told me that the subject had . . . crossed your mind in some way. Not a very favourable way, perhaps.'

'Then I must be more careful of my sighs,' said Tom, feeling slightly put out and thinking how absurd it was to be having this conversation – given the oddly intimate turn it was taking – with an elderly cleric while driving in a cab through a fog-bound and unfamiliar town. 'You are right though. I did consider the army as a career.'

'I knew it!' said Canon Selby. He spoke with such delight that it was impossible to feel irritated with him.

Tom said, 'You are a loss to my profession, sir. No one in a court of law would have a chance against you.'

'If you've been listening to people for as long as I have, Mr Ansell, you learn that what is said in words is only the half of it, less than half indeed. One looks at the little movements we all make, one listens for the suppressed sighs and unexpected stresses underlying the words. Now tell me what happened on the Salisbury station platform which so disturbed you.'

There was something in the man's voice and manner which encouraged trust so Tom gave an account of what he'd witnessed. It didn't take long. To his surprise, Canon Selby accepted his story straightaway.

'You say that the railwayman didn't believe you?'

'From his attitude, no. He probably thought I'd been drinking or that the fog was making me see things.'

'It might be worth reporting this to the authorities,' said the cleric. 'The police are not up to very much in this place but there is at least one good man in the force. Inspector Foster can be relied on.'

'I am not sure there's anything to be reported,' said Tom. 'No harm has been done. There was no sign of a body on the tracks – or of any assailant either.'

'Well then, it might be better to leave it, I suppose. But remember Foster is the man to go to.'

As they'd been talking the cab had entered a more densely populated area of the town. There were passers-by, singly or in muffled groups, shifting shapes in the fog, as well as other carriages. There were glimpses of shop-fronts and chop houses and inns.

'You are going to the Poultry Cross?' said Canon Selby.

'To an inn nearby. The Side of Beef, it's called.'

'One of the town's oldest hostelries. We have had an establishment called The Haunch of Venison since medieval times and the common belief is that The Side of Beef was set up in opposition to it by a disgruntled pot-man from the Haunch. Jenkins is the proprietor now. He chatters away. Well, we are all but there.'

The old man rapped on the side of the cab and they slowed. As if on cue, an inn sign proclaimed itself as The Side of Beef in light thrown from the parlour window.

'I will not ask you your business here, Mr Ansell, but perhaps we shall meet again. Salisbury is not a large place.'

Tom was about to say that he had an appointment at a house in the close the next morning, but some lawyerly caution prevented him from doing more than returning Canon Selby's wish and thanking him for his company and advice. The cleric lifted a hand in acknowledgement before adjusting his shovel-hat and settling back into the corner of the cab. Tom climbed down, retrieved his case and paid the driver. He watched while the cab pulled away into the fog. He looked up at the inn sign as if there might be some question whether he had come to the right place. The image of a bloodied carcass of beef hanging on a frame looked more like a sacrifice than an invitation to dine. The inn was a timber-frame building with a lopsided look and first-floor windows that projected slightly over the street.

While his attention was elsewhere, a woman walking briskly along the pavement banged into him. She was of middle height, was wearing a large hat and had her head down. Taken by suprise, Tom found himself thrown into her shoulder and well-padded collar. 'Oops,' she said. The word was curiously drawn out: 'ooops'. Tom mumbled his apologies, expecting the woman to walk on, but she took a pace back. Quick dark eyes looked him up and down. She was well dressed, a little garishly too with a red band round her hat and a billow of yellow skirt showing beneath her coat, and though not young she was not so far into middle age either.

'My fault, madam,' said Tom quickly. 'I was, er, looking at the inn sign.'

'I thought perhaps you wanted to sniff at my nosegay,' said the woman. She sounded amused.

'Nosegay?'

'Yes. To sniff at it.'

She raised a gloved hand towards a bunch of flowers attached to her coat collar. Tom couldn't make out what they were, violets perhaps with a sprig of green. The woman wasn't English, had a slight accent (almost saying 'per'aps', 'sneef'), although he was unable to place it. Her voice was attractively low. Now, if such a remark about 'sniffing nosegays' had come from a woman in parts of central London – round Haymarket, say, or in Leicester Square in the early evening – Tom Ansell wouldn't have had any doubts about the nature of such a meeting. Nor would the woman's colliding with him have been an accident. But he was in a strange town on a foggy night and did not know his way round. The woman continued to assess him by the faint light from The Side of Beef. She glanced at the case he was holding and then at the inn sign. She might have been in a hurry before but seemed reluctant to move now.

'No,' he said. 'No nosegays tonight. It's too foggy.'

The woman's mouth, wide and mobile, flickered with renewed humour. 'Ah, no nosegays tonight because it is too foggy,' she said, mimicking him. She dipped her head slightly and moved off down the road. Tom wanted to watch her retreating back but he was afraid she might turn round to look at him and did not want to show that much interest. Was she a judy or what his friends might have half-mockingly called a *fille de joie*? Was that her profession? He couldn't tell. After the incident at the railway station, this encounter left him not so much unsettled as feeling a bit foolish. Why had he made such a nonsensical comment about the foggy night?

Shrugging, he climbed the steps to the porticoed entrance to the inn and pushed at the door. A small man hovering in the lobby whom he at first took for a servant turned out to be Mr Jenkins, the proprietor. Jenkins had slicked-back grey hair and a full moustache which was, incongruously, jet black. The landlord was expecting Tom, who had written on the previous day to reserve a room.

'Ah, the gentleman from Messrs Scott, Lye & Mackenzie in London,' said Jenkins, rolling the names round his tongue. 'You had a pleasant journey from London, sir? I expect you'll want to warm up. There's a good fire in your room. And there's hot water upstairs too. A bathroom with a geyser, no less. Nasty night out, isn't it. Goes to one's chest, this weather, I find. Let me show you to your quarters. Can I take your case? No, rather carry it yourself, would you? Quite understand. On business here? But then you must be on business, coming from Messrs Scott, Lye & Mackenzie in London.'

Tom regretted having made the reservation on the firm's notepaper and wondered whether the landlord was about to ask him exactly what his business was in Salisbury. But, without pausing for a reply, Jenkins continued his monologue as they ascended stairs which twisted and tilted in every direction. He prattled on about the antiquity of his hostelry and the snugness of its parlour and the quality of the food and the attentiveness of the servants until they reached a landing on the first floor. A plain young woman, a servant, stood to one side to let them pass. She sneezed and the landlord said, 'Bless you, Jenny,' sounding as though he meant the opposite. Then he led Tom along a passageway to a door which he opened with a flourish. 'There, sir!' he said, with as much pride as if he'd finished decorating the room himself that very morning.

Once he'd got rid of the landlord with the assurance that, yes, everything was fine and that, yes, he'd be down to supper as soon as he'd settled himself and unpacked, Tom surveyed the room. The walls were covered with linenfold panelling and the uncarpeted floor sloped towards an oriel window below which ran a seat so that one could watch what was happening in the street in comfort. There was a large old-fashioned bed, a four-poster with hangings, and furniture so dark and cumbersome that it might have dated from the Middle Ages. A fire was burning in an elaborate grate. It was the kind of room which should have been illuminated with candles or flaming torches but, in a concession to modernity, there was a gasolier hanging from the centre of the carved ceiling.

It would do, thought Tom, for a couple of days. In fact it was more spacious than his lodgings in Islington and, since he was here on his firm's business, he would not have to pay for his stay. He put down his case and took off his coat. He walked across to the window recess. The curtains had been drawn to keep the warmth in. Tom parted them and could almost feel the damp fog nuzzling at the diamond-shaped panes. The covered porch of The Side of Beef was to his left and the pavement where he had encountered the woman was directly below him. There was a single figure standing there now, a woman. She was gazing up at this very window. Tom drew back sharply. Despite the fog, he was almost sure that it was the same woman, unless there happened to be two females in Salisbury who were wearing large hats decorated with a band, and trolling in the same area of town.

He tugged the curtains together with more force than necessary. He wondered if she'd recognized him as he, almost certainly, had recognized her. He thought that, with the gaslight behind him, he probably appeared as no more than a shadow. He could be any newly arrived traveller at the inn. Then Tom grew irritated with himself. What did it matter if she *had* seen him? Why shouldn't he be looking out of the window in his room? And if she was what he supposed her to be, then there was nothing more natural than that she would be hanging around in the neighbourhood of the town centre looking for customers. Though, he knew, such activities in provincial towns tended to be confined to run-down areas and the lodging houses called padding-kens where less reputable travellers and even tramps would put up for the night.

Putting all such considerations to the back of his mind, Tom unpacked his case, visited the bathroom at the end of the passageway and descended the twisting, uneven stairs to the supper room on the ground floor.

The rest of the evening passed uneventfully. To Tom's slight surprise, the supper was good and the service as attentive as Jenkins the landlord had promised. He chose the lamb cutlets rather than the broiled fowl and was served by a motherly woman who fussed about him. There were a pair of clerics in close conference at a table in a corner, and a couple more men who were sitting, like Tom, with only themselves for company and reading newspapers while they ate. There was a larger group of men and women at the biggest table who, to judge by the laughter and raised voices, had already fed and drunk thoroughly. They had the plush, self-important look of burghers and burghers' wives, of the town notables.

The landlord appeared at the door of the room and

seemed to be heading in Tom's direction but he was waylaid by the large group who insisted that he help finish one of the several bottles which they'd ordered during their meal. Jenkins looked gratified. He tugged his moustache and smoothed his hair and took a spare chair from another table. At some point, Tom saw one of the diners in the large group looking at him with interest. He had arrived late, and had turned his head sharply as he passed Tom, who was sitting close to the door. Now Jenkins was whispering to this individual, a stout man who was leaning back in his chair and tapping the side of his nose.

From their glances in his direction, Tom knew they were talking about him. The landlord had probably identified him as a notary from London, and no doubt made something of Messrs Scott, Lye & Mackenzie too. It was aggravating but there was nothing he could do about it except look displeased and turn his attention back to Baxter's *On Tort*, which he'd brought down to occupy him during supper. The book was as unappetizing as it had been on the train. What had Canon Selby said? 'No sane man would read Baxter for pleasure.' Tom hoped that he'd meet Canon Selby again. He wished he'd brought a newspaper, like the other gentlemen dining by themselves. Or a novel. Though he wouldn't have been quite comfortable to be seen reading a novel. Unless it was one written by Helen, of course. If she ever finished writing her sensation novel. And if she did finish writing it, then he suppposed that he'd have to read it.

While he was eating, he noticed the same man, the nose-tapper, at the other table continuing to glance at him from time to time. The landlord had torn himself away from this elevated company but whatever he'd said had obviously been sufficient to provoke the diner's curiosity. Tom could not think that visitors from London were so unusual but he shrugged off the attention. After he had finished, he considered taking a stroll outside by the Poultry Cross – whatever that was exactly – but the thought of the dank fog and an uneasy if ridiculous sense that he might find the mysterious woman still standing outside the hotel prevented him. Besides, it was getting late.

Tom retreated up the twisty stairs to his first-floor room. He passed the plain young servant who bade him goodnight in a nasal voice. He noticed her mournful eyes. He was tired. He'd drunk more than he thought at supper. Either that or he was stupefied by Baxter. It was only as he lay in the darkness of the curtained four-poster that he remembered the scene at the railway station. The silhouette at the platform's edge, the black figure creeping up on it. He hoped there'd be no more of that kind of thing in Salisbury. He did not sleep particularly well that night, whether on account of what he'd eaten and drunk or because, having thought of it again, he could not get the station scene out of his head.

Mackenzie's Castle

If David Mackenzie hadn't got a little too well oiled after dinner at his club, he would most likely have made a safe descent from his cab after a night out and kept his leg in one piece. If he hadn't broken his leg and been laid up for several weeks, then he would never have instructed Thomas Ansell to go to Salisbury in his place. And if Tom hadn't gone to Salisbury, he would never have become involved in that fatal business over the manuscript.

But the only active partner in Scott, Lye & Mackenzie did slip and break his leg as he was leaving the cab and Tom Ansell did have to go to the city of Salisbury, with everything else that followed. It was Mr Ashley the clerk who told Tom that Mr Mackenzie's fall was probably the result of a half bottle of port too much. Tom must have looked surprised for Ashley said, 'I suppose you think I'm talking out of turn, Mr Ansell, to refer to our employer in that way. To suggest that he might have over-indulged at his club.'

'It's not my place to comment on him – or on you,' said Tom Ansell.

'Spoken with the proper caution of a fledgling lawyer,' said Ashley.

Tom grew slightly red in the face and shifted in his chair on the other side of the senior clerk's desk. Ashley continued, 'But, you see, when one has been with a firm as long as I have, one is allowed a certain latitude. I remember when Mr Lye was a young man and Mr Scott hardly grown into middle age.'

Scott, who was Helen's father, had been dead a good while now and although Mr Lye occasionally shuffled into the office his only activity was to scrawl his signature on correspondence placed in front of him. So Ashley's memory stretched back to the early years of the Queen's reign when these two men must have been in their prime. He had a fine memory too. Ansell had heard him correct Mr Mackenzie over some detail of a long-ago case. 'I think you'll find that the uncle's name was Daven*ant*, not Davenport, sir,' or, to Tom Ansell himself soon after he joined the firm and went to him with a small problem, 'If you look up *Carstairs* v. *Smith* in the archives, you will discover some helpful pointers to what you are dealing with in this situation, Mr Ansell. Carstairs was an impossible man even if he was our client. If my memory serves me right, it was the September of 1848. The early part of that month. We lost the case and I cannot say that I was altogether sorry we lost.'

Ashley was a walking archive himself. He had a high, corrugated forehead to contain all that information. Tom Ansell visualized his brain as a honeycomb of pigeon-holes, not sweet but dry as dust. It was on account of this memory combined with his long service that he had the licence to comment on everybody, the firm's clients and partners as well as junior members. Another mark of his status was that he had a separate office which no one would have dreamed of entering without tapping on the door first.

'Well, Mr Ansell, however it happened, Mr Mackenzie has broken his leg and he will be out of commission for some time. This is unfortunate because he was due to visit a client – a clerical gentleman – later this week. The client lives outside London. He lives in Salisbury. Now he, that is Mr Mackenzie, has told me that he wishes *you* to go to Salisbury in his place. But he – that is Mr Mackenzie again – wants to see you in person first. He has written to me about this and other matters.'

Tom wondered why the senior clerk couldn't have passed on Mackenzie's instructions himself. As if guessing his thoughts, Ashley picked up the top page of a letter from a neatly arranged pile on the desk. He put on his glasses and peered at it.

'He says, 'There are circumstances which are best conveyed to Ansell in conversation and not by letter. Accordingly, would you kindly request him to call on me at home this afternoon."

'Does he say anything else?'

'Not to your purpose,' said Ashley, putting the young man in his place. 'You know where Mr Mackenzie lives?'

'I have been to supper at his house.'

'He does that with all the new employees, you know, Mr Ansell, invites them to supper. Well, if you've no more questions – and if you have I am not sure I should be able to answer them – then perhaps you'd better be on your way.'

So a couple of hours later Tom Ansell was standing outside the door of David Mackenzie's ample house in Highgate village. It was a November afternoon. Lower down the basin of the city was submerged in a grey-brown fog which would not shift before evening, if then. Up here the view was clearer but everything looked the more forlorn for being exposed. A few leaves clung by threads to trees and hedges. Passers-by scurried along, muffled up against the dank air. Tom opened the gate and walked up the gravelled path past low bushes of laurel. It was the first time he'd seen the house by daylight.

There was something a touch baronial about the Mackenzies' house and he mentally contrasted it with the less ornate house where Helen Scott lived with her mother, the dragon-lady. Tom knew that David Mackenzie had had it built soon after becoming a partner in what was then Scott & Lye. The red brickwork still looked raw. Perhaps he had instructed his architect to design a building that would remind him of a Scottish stronghold, for there was a miniature turret to one side which was surmounted with battlements and covered with tendrils of ivy. The front door had a Gothic solidity while the windows on either side in the vestibule were almost as narrow as arrow-slits. Tom tugged at the bell and heard it echo inside. He waited. There was no sound except the dripping of the laurel bushes.

The door opened and a maid, sour-faced, ageless, looked at him as warily as though he was a hawker or beggar. Tom explained that he was there to see the master of the house, by invitation. The maid continued to regard him with suspicion but said nothing.

A tall woman appeared in the lobby behind the maid.

'Ah, Mr Ansell, isn't it? Mary Mackenzie. You've come to see my husband.'

Tom was gratified that Mrs Mackenzie remembered him after what had been only a single supper visit.

'That'll do, Bea. Take Mr Ansell's coat and hat and I will show our guest in.'

'Very well, ma'am,' said the servant without much grace. She took the overcoat and hat, then moved off down the hall.

Mary Mackenzie extended her hand. She had a strong, bony grasp, which suited her height and slightly masculine features.

'Mr Mackenzie'll be glad to see you. He doesn't take well to being shut up all the time.'

'I am sorry that he's laid up,' said Tom.

'Not as sorry as I am. I'm used to having the house to myself during the day.'

She gave a barking laugh so that Tom was unsure whether she was genuinely irritated. She gestured him to follow her. In keeping with the castle-like exterior of the house, the hall beyond the lobby was panelled in dark oak on which were arranged small circular shields and pairs of crossed swords which Tom recalled from his first visit and which, to his eye, had a distinctly Scottish look. They had their own special name. Claymores, was it?

'I suppose you imagine that these are all heirlooms, Mr Ansell?' she said, noticing his glance. 'These swords and shields which are all dinted and tarnished. All this military paraphernalia.'

'They certainly look, ah, well established,' he said.

'Well, I can tell you that Mr Mackenzie bought them all in one fell swoop from a Scottish gentleman who had gone bankrupt. My husband has made only one trip north of the border in his entire life and that was to purchase these items. Mr Mackenzie would like to think that he has military forebears, martial ancestors. But you can take it from me that he does not.'

Tom was faintly surprised at the disrespectful tone in Mrs Mackenzie's voice but he was accustomed enough to the way that wives talked about their husbands, and vice versa. He wondered if Helen would ever talk like that about him after they'd been married for as many years as the Mackenzies had been. He hoped not. He vowed he would never refer to her disparagingly. First of all, naturally, they had to get married. Or rather, Helen had to agree to marry him. And before that, he had to propose. The dragon-lady's acquiescence would be desirable though not essential. As for Helen, Tom thought she was on the verge of agreeing . . .

'What? I beg your pardon.'

He realized that Mrs Mackenzie had said something to him. He was so wrapped up in visions of Helen consenting to marry him that he hadn't been listening.

'I asked whether your father was a military man. He was, wasn't he?'

'Yes, he was,' said Tom. He wondered how Mrs Mackenzie was aware of this. 'But I scarcely recall my father. He died when I was small. I can remember a tall man in a blue uniform but not much more.'

'How romantic,' said Mrs Mackenzie. 'Did he die on campaign?'

'In a manner of speaking. He was on his way to the Dardanelles when he caught a fever on board ship. He was buried at sea.'

'Perhaps I should not say this but that also sounds romantic. You were not tempted to follow your father and serve your country?'

'My father's profession sometimes seems to belong to another age,' said Tom. 'The war in the Crimea was a long time ago.'

'To you perhaps. But you are young, Mr Ansell. So, the age of heroes being past, you decided to take up the dry business of law?'

'There can be blood and fury and death in the law too, Mrs Mackenzie. All the emotions of a battlefield but drawn out and buttoned up.'

'No blue uniforms though?'

'Not those, no.'

Mrs Mackenzie nodded her long face, though Tom could not tell whether it was in agreement or mild mockery. 'Well, each to his own. You will find my husband in his snuggery if you go up those stairs there at the end. The first door you come to. Knock loudly for he may be napping.'

Thanking Mrs Mackenzie, Tom went down a short passageway which led off the hall and up a flight of spiral stone steps. He was in the turreted area of the house. Gas lights set in elaborate sconces reinforced the impression of being in a corner of a cramped castle. On a landing Tom rapped at an oak door whose stout ribs and redundant ironwork might have been designed to repel a siege by a bunch of medieval marauders. If David Mackenzie had been asleep it must have been a light one for almost straightaway there was an answering 'Come in.'

At first Tom thought that a portion of the London fog

had been piped up from town and into the room since he could hardly see to the far side. As his eyes adjusted and as the pipe smoke began to eddy through the open door, he made out the figure of the only active partner in Scott, Lye & Mackenzie sitting in a wing-chair close to an open fire.

'Be quick, Ansell!' said Mackenzie. 'Shut the door. Keep the warmth in. Sit down. Have a drink.'

Tom wondered that his employer could recognize him through the fug. David Mackenzie levered himself slightly upwards on the arms of his chair. His right leg, encased in a plaster cast, was resting on a stool. He was well equipped for a prolonged siege with a pipe in one hand, a glass in the other and a newspaper on his lap, and further supplies of tobacco, brandy and water on a table next to the wing-chair. Tom made some comment about how sorry he was to see him in this state.

'It's nothing, dear boy,' said David Mackenzie, seeming pleased at Tom's concern. 'The result of a foolish accident. The ground was slippery, you know.'

The only active partner in Scott, Lye & Mackenzie looked like a favourite uncle with his broad face and monk's tonsure of white hair. But Tom knew that appearances could be deceptive. Mackenzie was sharp enough when it came to law business. He nodded benevolently but his ears missed nothing. He outlined a client's chances succinctly.

'Have a drink, I say. Help yourself to a glass from over there and then help yourself from this.'

Mr Mackenzie picked up the decanter and poured himself a generous measure. Tom would have preferred to drink tea or water or nothing at all – the debris of a pie which he'd bought at a coster's stall on the way up to Highgate sat greasily in his stomach – but it wouldn't do to refuse his employer. He fetched a glass from the sideboard and lined the bottom with brandy, adding plenty of water. He sat down on the opposite side of the fire to Mackenzie. Feeble daylight penetrated through the leaded window but a stronger illumination came from the gas jets on either side of the fireplace.

'What d'you make of this?' said Mackenzie, tapping the newspaper on his lap with the stem of his pipe. 'Of the Claimant case?'

The criminal trial of the Tichborne Claimant was drawing to a close during these autumn days. At least, it was generally believed that it must be drawing to a close soon since it had begun in the spring and had already broken records for occupying court-time with a single case. But Tom sometimes wondered why it shouldn't go on for ever. Just as things seemed to be winding down, the Claimant's counsel introduced some sensational claim or wild accusation against the presiding judge. The case was amusing to those engaged in the law, not least because the judge who was on the receiving end of counsel's accusations was the Lord Chief Justice, but it had extensive appeal beyond the law and could be relied on to sell the papers.

'Is he genuine or isn't he?' said Mackenzie.

'Surely there can be no question that he isn't,' said Tom.

'Not a *niggling* doubt?' said Tom's employer, tapping the paper for emphasis. 'Doubt is our business, you know. Doubt is the lever which can move legal mountains.'

Tom nodded. He sometimes felt that he should produce a notebook and write down David Mackenzie's little asides, or perhaps it was rather the feeling that Mackenzie would have liked him to do so.

'However, I haven't summoned you here today to chew over the Tichborne Claimant case, Tom,' said Mackenzie, folding the paper and dropping it on the carpet. While Tom was waiting to hear why he had been summoned, his employer picked up a back-scratcher from the table by his elbow. He inserted the end into the gap at the top of the plaster that encased his leg, and wiggled it around. Judging by the look of satisfaction, almost of ecstasy, that wreathed his round face, he must have succeeded in reaching the itch. He replaced the back-scratcher on the side table and said, 'How are you on the Church?'

'I, er, I . . . am not quite sure what you mean.'

'Can you tell your cope from your chasuble, and could you tell either of them from your alb?'

'No, not even if my life depended on it.'

'Let's hope it doesn't come to that,' said Mackenzie. 'In fact, I don't think you'll have much discusssion about copes and chasubles with Felix Slater. He's a canon residentiary at Salisbury Cathedral, which is where you are to go. Slater is distinctly "low". He'd probably flee at a whiff of incense. He's a stiff, somewhat cold individual, to be honest. Still, he comes from a family which has a very long association with us and we can no more choose our older clients than . . . than . . .'

'Than parents can choose their children,' completed Tom.

'Very good. Older clients can certainly be as troublesome and demanding as children. Not that Felix Slater is particularly old. And I shouldn't be too hard on him. He is a worthy and respectable man.'

'So what am I to do in Salisbury, Mr Mackenzie? Is it connected with a will?'

'Why no, not directly, though there is something to be passed on, a 'delicate' something. Let me explain, but first why don't you help yourself to another drink. And top up my glass while you're about it, Tom.'

Once Tom had refilled their glasses, David Mackenzie proceeded to explain. It appeared that Canon Felix Slater's father had died quite a few years ago at the age of ninety, died peacefully in his sleep. George Slater – also a client of Scott, Lye & Mackenzie – had not only reached a venerable age but was a venerable-looking figure too, twinkling, benign and white-haired (at this point Tom wondered whether Mackenzie was, consciously or otherwise, referring to himself). If you'd glimpsed old Mr Slater in the street, tapping his way along with a cheery greeting for his neighbours and a smile for the children, you'd have taken him for a retired clergyman. You'd have assumed that the son, Felix, was merely following in the family tradition by going into the Church. But George Slater was a far from devout individual. In fact, in his youth he'd had a reputation as a very dissolute man.

'It was a time of dissolution, of course,' said David Mackenzie, pulling complacently on his pipe. 'Not long after the beginning of a new century, the period of the Regency. Why, they got up to things we could hardly imagine these days, let alone countenance. So you might say that George Slater was doing no more than was expected of him. He mixed with writers and poets and fellows like that, and you certainly can't expect any better of *them*.'

'But he settled down later?' said Tom, wondering where all this was leading.

'In a manner of speaking. George Slater settled down, if marriage is settling. And, if it is, then presumably the more marriages, the more settled. George got through three wives – nothing sinister there, I hasten to add. He outlived them all but they died of natural causes. Felix, who is now a Salisbury canon, was one of two surviving children of these matches and he never got on with George. He was the second son by the second wife. I have always suspected that he chose the Church as a kind of reproach to his father and his father's way of life. George was a non-believer. He had a tendency to talk about his atheism as loudly as that Bradlaugh fellow does now. Father and son were opposites in other ways too. Certainly, Felix is a rather crabbed and priggish person. The name means 'happy' in Latin, you know, and I think he was called that in optimistic hope by his father. George was an expansive and good-humoured fellow – or so he seemed to me in his later days. By the time I knew him, he was married to his third wife. There was quite a difference in age. He seemed attentive enough to her while she seemed fond enough of him. But who can tell with a marriage, who can tell, eh?'

Tom pulled some vaguely sympathetic face while wondering, again, whether Mr Mackenzie was referring to himself (and Mrs Mackenzie).

'I'm telling you this, Tom, not because it has any immediate bearing on your task but because I think that you need to know something of Canon Slater's history and the history of the family. This is a strange business, one that requires tact and discretion. Normally, I'd travel down to Salisbury myself but as things are . . .'

David Mackenzie glanced down at the leg propped up on the stool. Outside it grew gloomier, or perhaps it was that the air in the room was becoming more opaque on account of smoke from the pipe.

'George Slater had an estate in Wiltshire, outside Salisbury. It's an old house, goes back earlier than the Civil War. The family money came from wool originally. Almost everybody's money in Wiltshire came originally from wool, you know. The estate has now passed to his older son, Percy, who was the older son by his second wife, the only one who produced children. Percy was a son in the mould of the father though I fear he's gone into decline. A lifetime of drinking and idling on the expectation of coming into money has done him no favours. He was a client of our firm at one time but he had a falling-out with Scott or possibly with Lye. I don't know what it was about, before my time, but he was encouraged to take his business elsewhere.

'Anyway Percy too has got through a couple of wives and it is the present one, Elizabeth, who would be the lady of the manor if she chose to spend much time down there.

But I believe she doesn't like the country and spends all the year in town.

'Felix, the younger son, the Salisbury cleric, did not receive very much after the death of father George, and almost everything which was left went to Percy. But one of the items that Felix took – or that was bequeathed to him, I am not certain which – was a trunkful of old documents and papers. I have the impression it has taken several years since their father's death for this trunk to travel the few miles to Salisbury. There was nothing of much value or importance in the trunk. I imagine that Percy Slater one day got around to glancing inside it, and decided that the contents might as well go to his younger brother, who takes an interest in history and tradition. You are with me so far, Tom? You look . . . distant.'

'Yes, sir. It's just that it's rather warm in here. And I was thinking that from what you are saying . . . there must have been an article of value inside the trunk after all.'

Tom had been thinking no such thing but felt he had to make some response. The atmosphere inside Mackenzie's snug was soporific and he wondered when his employer was going to get to the point.

'There *was* an article of value in the trunk,' said Mackenzie. 'If this was a story, it would have been a revised will bequeathing the estate to Felix. A dramatic codicil which changed everything. But instead it was a handwritten manuscript. A kind of life story.'

'Whose life story?'

'George Slater's. At some point the old man had decided to pen an account of his early days, or at any rate those days before his latter period of respectability. Now, I said that George had been friendly with writers and the like. He'd known Lord Byron and Percy Shelley and the rest of that gang. In fact, I think that Percy Slater had been christened in honour of the poet. But George Slater had mixed with other people apart from titled poets. Others less reputable, men and women both. He seems to have, er, sown quite a few wild oats in his youth, a whole field of them, as it were. Then, recollecting all this in tranquillity, he decided to write it down. It was this account which Felix Slater found among his father's effects in the trunk.'

'You've seen it, Mr Mackenzie?'

'Heavens no. So far Canon Slater is the only person to have seen it – and read it. And what he has read does not make him think any better of his late father.'

'It is scandalous, is it?' said Tom, quite awake now.

'"Bad and dangerous" was the expression used by Felix Slater in a letter to me. I'm not sure whether he was referring to his father or to the contents of the manuscript or both.'

'Surely if old Mr Slater is dead and if he lived a respectable life these many years, then there can't be much harm in an account that reaches back half a century? And if he went to the trouble of writing his early history then he must have intended it to be read or even published.'

'Do you keep a diary, Tom?'

'No.'

'That's wise. I speak as a lawyer who is cautious about what he commits to paper. Some would say it's a woman's habit, anyway. People write up their diaries every day but many would be horrified to think of them being seen by any other eyes.'

'Well then, if Canon Slater is so disturbed by this document, why doesn't he just destroy it? Burn it.'

'Here we come to the nub of the matter. Felix Slater may not have much time for his father's memory or much patience with the brother who presently lives on the family estate. But he does look on himself as the inheritor of tradition, a repository of all that's best in the Slater family. His grandfather – that is George's father – was apparently a devout and upright man, a churchman like Felix. And Felix has a nephew, the son of Percy, who is also a man of the cloth. So the Canon regards himself and his nephew as being in the family line while his father and brother are the aberrations. All this is to say that he has a respect for what is handed down to him. He would not consider destroying this legacy of his father. It may not represent the best in the Slater line, it may even be among the worst things, but Felix can't bring himself to burn it. Nor does he wish to consult his brother Percy, who should rightfully have some say in the matter.'

'So what does Canon Slater want to do with it?' said Tom, clearer now about where the conversation was heading.

'Why, he wants us to take charge of the manuscript and keep it safe in our vaults with instructions that it should remain sealed up.'

'Never to be opened?'

'This is what you have to discuss, Tom. Felix is clear that he does not wish the manuscript to stay in his house in the Salisbury close. He does not want his wife to stumble across it by chance nor his nephew, who lodges with him. However, he has hinted that the account might be made available to his descendants when he is dead and gone.'

'He has children?'

'No children but there is the nephew. I think that Felix is content that his father's history should remain under lock and key until an appropriate period of time has passed. The decision to open and read it can be left to Walter – that is his nephew and Percy's son – when he is older. What you must discuss is what is meant by an appropriate period, and of course take charge of the manuscript and bring it back to our office safe and intact. It is a mundane errand, if you like, but one that requires tact and discretion.'

'It sounds . . . interesting,' said Tom.

'You have visited Salisbury?'

'Never.'

'An attractive place. I can recommend a hostelry called The Side of Beef near Poultry Cross in the middle of town. I've stayed there on my visits. Get Mr Ashley to give you the particulars. He will also give you details of your appointment with Canon Slater. In the meantime I've written a letter which you should give Slater to smooth your way.'

He picked up an envelope from the table by his side and held it out. Tom tucked it carefully into his jacket. He wondered whether this was the sign for him to leave but Mackenzie wanted to talk. Perhaps he was missing the conviviality of work for he said, 'Now, how are things at the office?'

'I believe Mr Ashley has everything well in hand,' said Tom. 'Mr Lye was in yesterday.'

'And the Scotts? How are they?'

Tom was momentarily thrown by the question and saw David Mackenzie's grin of pleasure.

'Come on, Mr Ansell, I know that you are a regular visitor to a particular house in Highbury. Mrs Mackenzie is good friends with Mrs Scott and she hears all the news. The ladies do, you know. Helen Scott is an attractive young woman, isn't she?'

Tom considered the lie that he hadn't really noticed whether Helen was attractive then said, 'Very. I do call there from time to time, yes, and they are well. Mother and daughter are well.'

'I won't ask you your intentions. But I remember Helen when she was just so high. An imaginative and inventive young woman, too.'

Inventive? Tom remembered Helen's speculations about her neighbour Mrs Montgomery and the man who was *not* Mr Montgomery. He wondered whether Mackenzie had an inkling of Helen's attempt to write a sensation novel. But it wasn't for him to give the game away so he merely nodded.

The two continued chatting for a while until David Mackenzie signalled that the session was over by picking up the back-scratcher once more. While probing beneath the plaster cast, he wished Tom good fortune on his Salisbury errand and Tom wished him a speedy recovery.

Tom Ansell retraced his steps down the stairs to the baronial-looking hall. Mrs Mackenzie emerged from its depths.

'Ah, Mr Ansell. How is the old boy upstairs?'

'Mr Mackenzie seems well, all things considered.'

Mary Mackenzie looked at Tom quizzically and he remembered that she was friendly with Mrs Scott, Helen's mother. That must be how she had known that his father was in the army.

'Did he bend your ear about the Claimant case? I've heard of nothing but the Claimant case morning, noon and night.'

'Would you be surprised to hear, Mrs Mackenzie, that all of London hears of nothing but the Claimant case?'

She smiled in recognition of the phrase. 'Would you be surprised to hear' had been an expression frequently used by the Tichbourne family's counsel in the first trial. It had caught on with the public for no discernible reason, and was even turning up in music-hall songs.

'Good, Mr Ansell. I am pleased to see that you can make a joke. I shouldn't want to take you altogether for a dry lawyer.'

Tom should have felt condescended to but he found himself warming to Mrs Mackenzie. It crossed his mind that she was preferable to the dragonish Mrs Scott and that she might put in a good word for him in the Scott household. Then the sour-faced Bea appeared holding Tom's hat and coat and, saying goodbye to his employer's wife, he left the house.

It was almost dark outside, what with the hour and the

fog that, rather than shifting away altogether, had risen up from the London basin. Tom walked past the dripping laurels and into the street where an elderly lamp-lighter was at work causing sudden blooms of yellow to erupt through the haze. It was only when Tom had walked a couple of hundred yards that he recalled the 'errand' with which he'd been entrusted by Mr Mackenzie. Until that point his mind had been full of Helen. Collecting a 'manuscript' did not sound a very demanding task. He put it out of his mind again and thought instead of Miss Scott.

West Walk

Tom woke with a thick head the morning after his arrival in Salisbury. He'd had a restless night in the four-poster in The Side of Beef, with a dream of struggling to gather up scattered sheets of paper from a railway line that stretched across a bare plain. He was acutely aware that the longer his task took the more likely was a train to thunder down on him. He could hear a kind of rattling along the rails.

Then, in time with the rattling, came a series of knocks at the door of his room and a woman entered with a jug of warm water for him to shave and asked if she should draw the curtains. Tom recognized her nasal voice and visualized her mournful eyes. He muttered to her to leave the curtains and tried to get back to sleep. But he abandoned the attempt after a few moments, got up and went across to the window.

The fog had lifted and it was a bright, hard morning, with frost on the panes and sun glinting on the roofs opposite. The street below was bustling with people and carts and carriages. Tom washed and dressed rapidly and went down to breakfast. It was later than he thought and he was the only diner. The motherly woman who'd served him at supper the previous evening clucked around him, offering him more coffee and asking whether he was sure he'd had enough porridge and sausage and kidney and toast and marmalade. She seemed to have taken a shine to him. Making conversation, he asked the way to the cathedral close and she told him to 'follow the spire and it would be difficult to get lost, sir,' and he thought, of course, stupid question.

Conscious that he had an early appointment with Canon Slater, Tom refused second helpings of breakfast. He returned to his room to get his coat and a small despatch case, suitable for holding documents. When he was going through the lobby he saw the landlord standing on the porch. Jenkins was turning his head from side to side in a proprietorial fashion, as if he owned not merely The Side of Beef but the entire street it was situated in.

'Ah, Mr Ansell of Messrs Scott, Lye & Mackenzie. You are well rested, I hope, sir?'

'Comfortably enough, thank you.'

'And well fed?'

'That too.'

'Have you a moment, sir?'

'No more than a moment, I am on my way to meet someone.'

'It is only that I took a liberty last night and I thought I ought to tell you of it.'

Tom hesitated between annoyance and curiosity. He said nothing but stood opposite Jenkins on the porch. The landlord stroked his blackened moustache while his breath frosted in the cold air.

'You may have observed last night, sir, at supper that I was talking to some ladies and gentlemen. One of them was asking about you. He wanted to know your name.'

Tom recalled the stout individual leaning back in his chair and tapping the side of his nose, together with the frequent glances he'd cast in his direction. 'Well,' he said, 'I'm not a spy with his secrets. You are welcome to give him my name if you like. But if he can ask about me, I can ask about him. Who was it?'

'Mr Cathcart, Mr Henry Cathcart. He is one of the leading citizens of our town.'

'And why did Mr Henry Cathcart want to know the name of one of your guests?'

'He didn't say, sir.'

'Well then, there's an end of it,' said Tom, making to move off the porch. But the landlord hadn't finished.

'All he did say, was that he thought he knew you from somewhere.'

'Not from here, Mr Jenkins. I've never visited Salisbury before in my life.'

With that, Tom strode down the street, without giving Jenkins another word or look. His irritation with the proprietor of The Side of Beef was sharp enough that he didn't give much thought as to why one of last night's diners should have been enquiring after his name. Damn Jenkins! He was obviously one of those hotel-keepers who liked to insinuate himself into his guests' lives and pry out their business. Well, the man would get no more out of him, not even the time of day.

As the woman serving breakfast had said, it would be difficult to get lost on the way to Salisbury Cathedral. Wherever he turned a corner and had an uninterrupted vista down a street, the spire rose up like a needle into the clear light of the November morning. Tom pushed his way through a market and passed an elaborately crowned and buttressed landmark that he assumed was the Poultry Cross, before turning into a High Street which was lined with ancient-looking inns. It struck him that for hundreds of years people had been coming to this place, to carry on their business, to do penance, to visit one of the finest churches in the land.

There was an arched entrance at the end of the High Street, beyond which lay the close and the wide grounds of the cathedral. Once inside, the houses became both grander and somehow more sedate. There were stretches of lawn and walks overshadowed by elms and beeches. Beyond and to his left, effortlessly dominant, rose the vast bulk of the church. The little knots of visitors were easy to distinguish not just by their clothes but by their ambling gait even on this cold sunny morning. Tom was searching for Venn House, Canon Slater's dwelling, and he might have asked directions from one of the dark-garbed clerics moving as purposefully as crows among the sightseers. But he was oddly reluctant to reveal where he was going, especially after the encounter with Jenkins.

Then, out of the corner of his eye, he noticed one of the clerical figures making for him.

'Why, it's Mr Ansell.'

It was Canon Eric Selby. As last night at the railway station, he was wearing a coat and muffler and his shovel-hat. The coldness of the morning had brought a hectic colour to the cleric's smooth-shaven cheeks. Tom was pleased to see him and said as much. By the light of day Tom saw how blue the old man's eyes were, a blinking blue. He looked like an owl caught by daylight.

'Didn't I predict we'd meet again?' said the Canon. 'Salisbury is a small place. How did you find The Side of Beef and that chatterer Jenkins?'

'The landlord is certainly too curious for comfort,' said Tom. 'But the food is good and the bed isn't hard and it will more than do.'

'Good, good. Now, Mr Ansell, can I direct you somewhere?'

'How did you know I was looking?'

'For sure, you are not one of our visitors come to gawk at the spire. And you are carrying a little case which suggests that you are in the close on business, yet I noticed just now that you were pausing in your progress as if not quite certain where to go next. So ask away.'

'I am searching for Venn House. It's about here somewhere, I believe.'

Tom gestured towards the ranks of fine houses which

lay to the north and west of the cathedral. When he turned back to look at Eric Selby he observed the Canon grimacing as though he had bitten into a sour apple. There was a change in his voice when he answered too. The friendly tone was replaced by something more guarded.

'You are going to see the Slaters, Mr Ansell? Yes, well, obviously you must be if you are searching for Venn House. It's on the south-west corner of the close, near the end of West Walk. Look out for a fine wall of red brick.'

Tom thanked him and hesitated as if to give Eric Selby the chance to say more. But the Canon seemed disinclined for further conversation and merely nodded before resuming his own progress towards the north transept of the cathedral. Wondering what it was about the Slaters – about Felix Slater presumably – which caused Selby to look displeased, Tom followed the path that led to to his right. Then he turned into a tree-lined road which he took for the West Walk. There were fewer people about here, it was quieter and seemed more like a country village than a town. A carriage was waiting outside the iron gates of one of the larger mansions. The coachman was huddled up against the sharpness of the morning. A workman passed Tom, pushing an empty hand-barrow. The roadway and the grass verges were speckled with frost in places where the sun hadn't reached.

Then Tom saw someone standing outside the entrance to another of the houses, someone whose presence gave him a slight start. It wasn't that he knew the person. But his uniform showed that he was a police constable. The man was gazing right and left, but with no sense of urgency. He acknowledged Tom with a nod. Had this been his own street or town, Tom might have stopped and asked the constable what was going on. (Not that anything appeared to be going on.) But he was a stranger here. Any crime or wrongdoing was no concern of his.

Tom went a few paces further then glanced back, conscious of someone walking quickly behind him on the road in the same direction. It was a woman. The policeman was looking at her. Tom turned his head back and felt his face grow warmer. He was fairly sure it was the woman he'd met the previous evening outside The Side of Beef. The same large hat and, he thought, a flash of the same yellow skirt beneath her coat. He recalled that he'd seen her for a second time yesterday, staring up at his room through the fog.

Now the idea that she had been following him, perhaps since he'd left the inn this morning, seized his imagination. If so, to what purpose? But it was all nonsense. Why should she be following him? She could hardly be intending to proposition him in the cathedral precinct, not on a cold and frosty morning. Not with the presence of a policeman outside a neighbouring gate. He debated for a moment slowing down and allowing her to pass . . . or letting her speak to him, if that was what she wanted. But instead he quickened his pace, on the lookout for the wall which fronted Venn House. When he reached it he would allow himself one quick look behind, to check on the woman's identity.

And here, towards the end of the West Walk, was a fine red-brick wall as described by Canon Selby and, behind it, the house which belonged to Canon Slater. *Venn House* was inscribed on a plaque next to a large wooden gate set into an arch in the wall. Hearing footsteps coming closer, Tom looked over his shoulder. It *was* the same woman! She seemed to be making for him, still with the slightly mocking smile which he recalled from their last meeting. No question that she recognized him as well for she said, 'See, no nosegay now. It has withered.'

She indicated the bare collar of her coat. There was the remembered trace of foreignness in her accent ('withered' drawn out almost to three syllables).

Tom felt renewed warmth come into his face. He inclined his head slightly and said, 'Good morning, madam. A cold morning too.'

'You are coming to this house.'

It was not a question so much as a statement. Tom wondered at the intrusive curiosity of the inhabitants of Salisbury. Did they all assume that what was his business was also theirs? He nodded with a slight impatience, expecting the woman to continue on her way. But she remained standing by the gate in the wall. All at once, Tom understood that she must be calling at Venn House like him, and was waiting for him to open the gate to let her go through first. There was no bell to announce visitors. He reached forward and twisted the iron latch, indicating with his eyes that she should enter before him if that was what she wanted. Through the arch of the gate he saw a path leading to a substantial house.

The woman took a pace forward then halted as if struck by a sudden thought. She put a gloved hand on Tom's arm and looked him full in the face, not smiling now.

'You will say nothing?'

'I . . . I'm sorry, madam, I don't understand what you mean.'

'I mean, say nothing about how we have seen each other before this cold morning,' she said in the same low, slightly accented voice. When he didn't respond she showed a touch of impatience as though Tom was a slow boy who needed matters spelled out. 'I mean, last night in the town in the fog. You do remember?'

'Yes, I do remember, madam. Say nothing to who? Who am I not supposed to tell?'

The woman shivered as if from the cold and said, 'Tell nobody. Do you agree to this?'

All this time she was holding fast to Tom's arm. Her grasp was hard. He could feel her fingers through the sleeve of his coat.

'Very well,' he said, 'I will not tell anyone although I can't imagine who would be interested.'

He almost had to wrench his arm from her grip. The good humour returned to her face and she rewarded him with another smile before turning to go through the gate. Yet, once again, she paused as she was entering. 'You must wait here,' she said. 'It is best that we do not arrive together. I will send someone out. I will say that I saw a gentleman outside. Yes, I saw a gentleman searching outside.'

After passing through the arch in the wall she gave a push to the gate. She pushed at it with a flick of her heel, and some quality about the movement, something careless and unladylike, established her right to go first into Venn House and to leave Tom where he was. The gate creaked half shut, blocking off the view of the house and garden.

Tom Ansell stood outside Venn House, confused and obscurely angry, with himself rather than the woman. Her actions were incomprehensible. What right did she have to tell him to wait outside? He no longer believed that she was a woman of the town, and the fact that he had ever thought so gave him a moment's discomfort. He looked for other explanations for her arrival here. If she was a servant in the Slater household, then she was behaving in a fashion that was peculiar – and somehow improper. Tom wasn't a vindictive or sneaking individual. But had he been, he told himself, he would have made some comment to Canon Slater or Mrs Slater about the strange attitude of their servants. The trouble was that the woman had bound him into a sort of conspiracy of silence, which he could not break now. And she had given to that chance meeting outside The Side of Beef, that accidental collision, a significance which it hadn't possessed until this moment.

A different idea came to Tom as he stood, alternately watching his breath plume up in the air or looking at the sunlit spire through the bare branches of the trees without really seeing either of them. Perhaps the woman wasn't a servant in Venn House after all but a . . . a fortune-teller or gypsy clairvoyante . . . or a medium. He didn't know what had provoked these notions. The woman's faintly flamboyant appearance, maybe, that touch of foreignness about her. Even the way she had grasped at his arm. However, if she actually did follow one of these exotic trades, he didn't ask himself what she was doing calling on a cleric's house in a cathedral precinct.

By now perhaps five minutes had passed, and Tom was conscious not only of the cold but of feeling a bit of a fool into the bargain. The man who had passed earlier with the hand-barrow was returning down West Walk, his rumbling barrow now laden with sacks. The carriage which had been waiting outside the iron-gated house further up the road had disappeared. He could still see the policeman closer at hand. Tom had had enough. He wasn't going to respects the whims and fancies of a strange woman for a second longer. For all he knew, she'd forgotten about him. Or for a joke she intended to leave him loitering outside the house like some hawker or tradesman. If he did not move soon the policeman might ask him what he was doing here.

He took a couple of paces towards the almost shut door to Venn House. But before he reached it, the door opened. Swung open to reveal . . . nobody.

Venn House, Exterior

But there was someone there after all. A man emerged from the shadow on the other side of the door, holding a pair of garden shears. He was wearing a canvas apron, the pouch of which bulged with gardening implements. Sandy hair poked from under a leather cap. He gave a lopsided grin.

'You must be the gen'leman that's waitin',' he said, adding as an afterthought, 'Are you the gen'leman, sir?'

'I am a visitor to see Canon Slater,' said Tom.

The man raised the shears as if to signal that Tom should come in. He walked past the gardener, who nodded his head in the direction of the house before setting off at a diagonal across the lawn. He didn't look back. Footprints on the still frosted areas of the grass showed that he'd recently walked the same route. Tom supposed that the strange woman had alerted the first person she saw to the fact that there was a visitor by the gate. It wasn't exactly a speedy reception or a ceremonial one.

The main door to Venn House was at the end of a path lined with yew trees that had been shaped and trimmed. The effect, perhaps intentionally, was like a walk in a churchyard and so rather gloomy. But the house itself, rising above the trees, was gracious and airy-looking with plenty of windows set into light-coloured stone.

Tom reached the covered porch which had a scallop-shaped interior to the roof. He was raising his hand to the knocker when the door opened. For no reason, he half expected to see the strange woman but it was only a housemaid. He explained himself again and was shown into a hall stretching into the depths of the house. He scarcely had time to glance round – watercolour pictures, a longcase clock, a glass cabinet full of ornamental ferns against a wall – before a figure emerged from a door at the far end.

'You must be Mr Ansell. Mr Thomas Ansell of Scott, Lye & Mackenzie?'

'Canon Slater?'

Tom was surprised. The man in clerical dress who was shaking him by the hand – a warm, firm clasp – was sober-looking, certainly, but there was a spring in his step and a glint in his eye which belied the dour picture that David Mackenzie had painted of him. The mystery was instantly solved, however.

'No, sir. I am *Walter* Slater, nephew to Felix and son of Percy. I am Walter Henry Slater.'

'Of course,' said Tom. 'You are a resident of your uncle's house, I remember being told.'

'He is good enough to accommodate me rather more comfortably than I could afford for myself,' said Walter. 'I am a curate at St Luke's in the town. You have seen it perhaps?'

'I arrived only yesterday. I haven't had a chance to look round yet.'

'I hope we shall welcome you through our doors one Sunday, Mr Ansell. We are not so grand as the cathedral of course but we have a fine, strong preacher in Mr Simpson, our vicar. He enjoys a devoted following among the townspeople.'

'I would be interested to hear him,' said Tom, the half-truth coming easily enough because he would never have to listen to the Rev. Simpson. 'Unfortunately my business here will keep me only a day or so. My business with your uncle, I mean.'

Tom said this as a prompt, and Walter Slater took the hint. He led Tom to the same door from which he'd just appeared at the far end and knocked.

'Uncle, here is your London visitor.'

If Felix Slater made any reply Tom, standing to one side, didn't hear it. Walter drew back to let Tom enter and, without coming in himself, shut the door after him. The room was a study, lined with books and glass-fronted display cases. There were large, floor-length windows which doubled as doors giving a view of a garden with an orchard and, beyond that, a river and water-meadows. In front of the windows a man sat at a desk, his back to the view. Canon Slater was writing. He must have been aware of Tom's presence but he kept his head bent down and his hand moving steadily across the sheet of paper in front of him. Tom wasn't sure whether this was a deliberate ploy or whether he was too engrossed to break off. Eventually, Slater gave a little sigh, ground the nib of the pen into the paper in a gesture of finality and looked up.

'A train of thought is a delicate thing,' he said without preamble. 'Once broken, it may never be recovered.'

He placed the pen carefully in its holder and got up. He came round the desk and advanced towards Tom, holding out a hand in belated greeting. Where the nephew's handshake had been warm, the uncle's was bone-dry. Felix Slater was a tall man with a fringe of greying hair plastered close to his scalp. He was clean-shaven, with a thin mouth, a determined jaw and cheeks that were sunken.

The brief formalities done, Felix Slater said, 'You'd better sit down, Mr Ansell. Now is not the time for refreshment but I hope that you will join us for luncheon when our business is concluded.'

'Thank you, sir, I should be pleased to do that,' said Tom, taking a chair on the other side of the desk and thinking that he'd much prefer to return to The Side of

Beef. If the food and drink and company at Venn House were of a piece with his reception so far, he didn't hold out much hope for any of it.

Canon Slater resumed his place at the other side of the desk. He sat up very straight and his chair was higher than Tom's so that the younger man felt at a disadvantage. The Canon picked up the pen again then returned it to the holder. He seemed to be wondering how to begin. He said, 'How is Mr Mackenzie? He has broken his leg, I believe.'

'He is on the mend. He slipped as he was getting out of a cab. A foolish accident, he called it.'

'Then he must be looking forward to the day when "the lame man shall leap as an hart", Mr Ansell,' said Slater, his mouth twitching like a piece of string which has been given a single tug.

'Certainly he must,' said Tom, realizing that the Canon was making not only a biblical reference but also some sort of joke. He brought out the letter which David Mackenzie had given him and handed it across the desk. Felix Slater took up a paper knife and slit open the envelope. All his actions were careful and economical. The items on the desk-top – a selection of pens, blotter, ink-holder, letter-holder, paperweights – were set out in precise formation. Slater smoothed out the letter on the desk and inclined his head towards it. There was no artificial light in the study but enough came from the outside. While Felix Slater was reading, Tom saw through the window the gardener who'd appeared at the door in the wall. Like a character in a stage play, this individual strolled slowly across the view brandishing his shears. He did not look into the room as he passed.

'Mr Mackenzie says that I may have complete confidence in you . . . in your powers of judgement and in your discretion,' said Slater.

'That is good of him,' said Tom, pleased at his employer's

words even while he was thinking that Mackenzie couldn't really have written anything very different.

'He also says that you know something of the background to this situation –'

There was a rap at the door and Slater barely had time to say 'Come in' before the housemaid entered.

'Beggin' your pardon, sir, but Mrs Slater is requiring to see you now, sir.'

Felix Slater looked at the woman – she was young and red-faced – as if she were a complete stranger. Tom expected him to dismiss her straightaway by saying he was busy but his only words to her were, 'Your collar is not straight, Bessie.'

The housemaid's hand flew up to her collar and she fiddled with it, disarranging it further before retreating backwards through the door. Slater rose from his seat with a kind of practised weariness, saying, 'Excuse me, Mr Ansell, I shall not be any longer than I can help.'

He shut the door after him. Tom sat for a few moments gazing out at the sunlit garden and the bare branches of the fruit trees. He wondered what Mrs Slater was like. A formidable woman she must be, to be able to summon her husband like that. He visualized a person even more dour than her husband. He thought of Mrs Scott. And of Helen her daughter.

He continued to stare out at the garden. Other things being equal, it wouldn't be such a bad life as a canon residentiary in a cathedral close. Tom had no idea what clerical duties Felix Slater had to perform, but he supposed they weren't very onerous. To have a fine residence like Venn House and a garden that stretched down to a river. If he lived next to a river Tom would obtain a little rowing boat. He thought of Canon Slater in rolled-up sleeves and pulling on a pair of oars but the picture didn't quite work.

He listened for the sounds of Canon Slater's return but

the house was as silent as if everyone had deserted it. Or deserted him. He grew bored with sitting and got up to take a tour of Slater's study. He squinted at the spines of the books in the glassed case which almost filled a whole wall and which reminded him of the books in Mr Mackenzie's office. Taking one down would be like picking a stone off a shelf. What did these books say about the Canon? A brief inspection confirmed his suspicions. There were county histories. Indecipherable titles in Latin and Greek and German. Enough editions of the Bible to build a miniature tower of Babel. Commentaries on the Bible and commentaries on the commentaries. No sign of a novel or of a book of poems. Then Tom told himself not to be so carping. After all, for his light reading on the train journey to Salisbury hadn't he chosen Baxter's *On Tort*? What did that say about him?

Tom wandered round Slater's study. There were a few pictures clustered together in a corner above an old-fashioned wooden chest. As far as he could tell, they were engravings of scenes from the Bible. Not scenes of miracles or of a friendly smiling Jesus surrounded by disciples but dark and violent matter. There was a picture of a diminutive warrior whom Tom presumed to be David carrying a great severed head (Goliath's?) past a line of smiling women. Pictures of obscure struggles. There was a sinister image of three crones, one spinning thread from a distaff and the other two deciding where to cut it. Tom recognized the Fates and the thread of human life.

He went over to look at the display cases which were against the wall by the door. Ah, here was something different again – although at first he thought the contents were as dull as what was in the bookcase. Under sloping sheets of glass was a miscellany of objects. Wedges of stone with one end honed to a blade, pieces of flint sharpened to a point were obvious weapons or cutting implements. But other items were more baffling. Small stones cut to a circular shape and pierced so that a cord might be run through them looked to be ornaments, as did pendant-like slivers of polished rock and bone. But there were miniature tablets of plain stone that served no discernible purpose although they had undoubtedly been cut and shaped by human hand. As well, there were fragments of pottery and items made of a metal which Tom supposed to be bronze: pins and things fashioned like needles and little sickles.

It was all dry stuff but it showed another side to Canon Slater (supposing that he had collected these objects himself), as did the sinister pictures in the corner.

Out of the corner of his eye, Tom was suddenly conscious of a movement on the other side of the windows. He spun round to see the gardener looking at him. The man had his face almost pressed to one of the panes. His sandy hair poked out from under his cap. When he saw that Tom had seen him he quickly moved away. He'd never have dared to be so curious if he thought his employer was in the room. He must have assumed it was empty. Or perhaps it was merely that he was a little simple.

Just then the door to the study opened and Felix Slater came in. Tom was still standing by one of the display cases. Some words of explanation or excuse were beginning to shape themselves in his mind but they weren't needed. Far from being displeased or put out, the canon allowed a smile to fasten itself on his pinched face. A genuine smile, not a tug on a piece of string.

'Why, Mr Ansell, I am glad to see you are interested in my old artefacts.'

'You collected all these things yourself, sir?'

'I found them myself or have acquired them over the years. This is a very ancient place. I do not mean the city of Salisbury, although that is old enough. I refer to the countryside around here. Men have lived on the plain in settlements and stockades for many centuries. They have lived and died and been buried all around. There are signs of the past everywhere if you know where to look.'

Slater, standing next to Tom, stabbed a long forefinger at one of the items. It was made of bronze, with interlocking circles set in a rectangular frame. He opened the hinged lid of the case and, picking up the piece of bronze, passed it to his guest. Tom cradled it in his palm. It was unexpectedly heavy.

'You know what that is?'

'A brooch?'

'Most probably it is a belt-buckle. Admire the workmanship, Mr Ansell. Wonder at the skill of our ancestors in what we are pleased to call the Dark Ages.'

Tom examined the buckle more closely. In truth, the relics in the case did not signify much to him. The real discovery was the enthusiasm of Felix Slater, almost the passion of the man. He nodded and handed the buckle back. Slater replaced it carefully on the baize lining of the display case.

'Are they valuable?' said Tom.

'Not especially, but to me they are beyond price.'

Tom felt rebuked by the answer, which was perhaps the intention. Slater indicated a couple of other pieces: a small bone with holes bored in it so that it might be blown like a flute, and a ring with an irregular zigzag pattern which, despite its tarnish, was gold. Then, as if realizing that their real business had been delayed long enough, the churchman abruptly went back to sit behind his desk. Tom returned to his chair. Slater went through the ritual of picking up and putting down his pen once more. He glanced at the letter from Mr Mackenzie.

'Some of those things come from my father's estate at Downton,' he said, as if unwilling to leave the subject. 'It was a great pleasure in my younger days to explore the grounds and go fossicking around. There used to be stories of a torque . . . you know what a torque is, Mr Ansell?'

'An artefact?'

'It is a metal band for the neck or arm, sometimes made of gold or silver. If it is value you are looking for then such an item would be truly valuable. However, this is not much to the purpose. Now my older brother Percy lives on the estate at Downton. He is not concerned with his inheritance and is paying for a lifetime of indulgence with a premature feebleness of body and mind while the place falls round his ears. In the meantime his wife Elizabeth escapes to London when she can, which is all the time as far as I can see. I do not altogether blame her. Who would wish to spend their time immured with a sot? I am not shocking you by speaking frankly, Mr Ansell? Mr Mackenzie no doubt told you that – that I do not see eye to eye with my brother.'

'He indicated something of the sort,' said Tom.

'Fortunately, I have a nephew, Walter. He is the person who showed you in here just now. He is the . . . the son I should like to have had, Mr Ansell, I do not see any reason to conceal that from you. It was one of the happiest days of my life when Walter came to live here with me, as it was earlier when he told me that he wished to enter the Church. In due course, and with God's grace, Walter will inherit the Downton estate. Unlike his father, Walter has not disgraced himself in the expectation of plenty. Rather, he has chosen a spiritual vocation and a life of service. When he comes into his inheritance, I know that he will restore propriety to the Slater line.'

'You do not expect that to be long?'

'I do not expect what to be long?'

'The time when your nephew comes into his estate.'

'Why do you say so, Mr Ansell?'

'Because, well, from what you have been saying, Canon Slater, it does not sound as though your brother has the prospect of a long life in front of him.'

'Perhaps not. Yet we should not hasten any man's death

by expecting it too fervently. We are in God's hands after all. My brother Percy may have a few years in him still, despite his feebleness. Now, Mr Ansell, let us turn to the reason why you are here.'

Felix Slater got up and crossed to the corner of the room occupied by the Old Testament pictures. With surprising dexterity he squatted on his haunches in front of the wooden chest which Tom had noticed earlier. Retrieving a key from his pocket, he fiddled with the lock. Something about his posture, the hunched shoulders and the thin legs, reminded Tom of a heron. Slater opened the lid of the chest and reached inside. He brought out an item wrapped in cloth and, clutching it, went back to his seat behind the desk. Then, with a gesture that recalled a conjurer, he whipped off the cloth cover to reveal nothing more exciting than a large, leather-bound volume with a kind of hasp attached to it. It had the appearance of a memorandum book or a ledger.

He raised the book and seemed about to pass it to Tom. Then he hesitated and said, 'Here, Mr Ansell. You may have a brief look. This was written by my father and it is an account of a period in his life, an early period, during which he pursued an existence which it would be kind to call unrespectable and rackety. A less charitable description would be disgraceful and immoral. These are his memoirs cast in the form of a diary. I propose that they should accompany you back to London, back to the offices of Scott, Lye & Mackenzie, where they shall remain in your vault – or in your safe – or in whatever place you store important items entrusted to you by your clients. There they are to stay secure until after my death at which time Walter, my nephew, shall decide whether to read his grandfather's words or whether to dispose of them unread. The decision shall be his. That is only proper. After all, whatever my father's faults, he was a Slater, and my nephew is a Slater also.'

Tom sensed that he was listening to a well-worn explanation. Felix Slater had produced it before, not for the benefit of another human being perhaps but inside the privacy of his own head. He was justifying his decision not to destroy something which he plainly found disturbing, even dangerous. He was also putting a great deal of faith and trust in his nephew, Walter.

Tom said, 'Can I ask you, Canon Slater, whether your nephew is aware of this . . . this book? Has he actually seen it?'

'He knows of it. He may have glimpsed it, yes. He has heard that it is written by his grandfather. But more than that, no.'

'Then are you sure that *I* should be looking at it?'

'It is only for this moment, Mr Ansell. After all, since you are going to take it back to London, you should have some idea of what you are carrying with you. However, you will be able to look inside it only this once. You can see that there is a hasp here and a small lock on one side. My father wished to keep his words literally under lock and key. A wise man, in that respect at least. Now, I intend to retain the key once I have surrendered the book to Scott, Lye & Mackenzie. It wouldn't be difficult to force the hasp, but of course such a thing would never occur in a respectable law firm.'

There was a twitch of the thin mouth. Canon Slater was making another joke. Tom took the book from him and rested it on his lap. He felt the weight of it on his knees. There was the brass hasp, heavy and intricate. On one side was a raised plate into which was set a small keyhole and its apparatus. Felix Slater took up his pen and the sheet of paper which he'd been working on when Tom arrived. The signal was clear: Tom Ansell had been given a few moments to glance through the memoirs of the early life of the late George Slater, for probably as long a time as it would take his son to reach the end of the page he was writing.

Tom was baffled. He could not see why Felix Slater was permitting him to look at these memoirs, however briefly. Slater would be more than entitled to ask him to take the book to London unexamined. Nevertheless he opened it. The pages had the look and feel of a sketch pad although the paper was too thin. There were no lines or margins but only blank spaces waiting to be filled. Tom wondered whether George Slater had had the book specially made up, with the brass hasp and lock. There was a frontispiece of sorts even if it said nothing more than: *I certify the account which this volume contains to be a true and faifthful record of the years noted and dated within.* It was signed *George Henry Slater* and below the signature the date was given as the twelfth of June, 1843. The writing was neat and precise, close but easy to read, almost feminine. No sign of debauchery here. Below this, in a different hand, was a note saying: *Received from my brother Percy among other effects of my father.* This was signed by Felix Slater, followed by the address of Venn House, Salisbury and dated the fifteenth of July, 1873. Evidently, it had taken Felix a few months to decide he didn't want the book in his house.

Tom turned to a page at random. He scanned it. He was used to reading quickly, skimming through documents with their thickets of legal phraseology. But what he read now was a story, an anecdote. George Henry Slater had certainly moved in elevated circles because the story concerned that well-known and atheistical poet, Percy Bysshe Shelley. If Tom was looking for scandal, however, he was to be disappointed.

George Slater recounted how he had been walking with Shelley and another friend called Hogg by the Serpentine in Kensington Gardens. Shelley was suddenly seized with the desire to make and float a paper boat, an activity to which he was apparently addicted. He had no scrap of paper on him (and neither did his two friends) except for a bank-post bill to the tune of fifty pounds.

Tom read: *Shelley dithered for a long time but at last gave way to his obsession; with a few swift and practised movements he twisted the bank-bill into the likeness of a boat and committed it to the water, watching its progress with even more anxiety than usual. Those who throw themselves on fortune lock, stock and barrel are sometimes rewarded and so it was in this case. A breeze blowing from the north-east gently conveyed the costly craft to the south bank where, during the last part of its journey, Shelley waited for its arrival in a spirit of patience. By this exercise he gained nothing and might have lost a great deal but I saw how, mixed with his anxiety, he took pleasure not so much in the risk to his property as in the dexterity needed to build the little boat.*

This was dated June, 1811. Underneath was written another paragraph: *Everyone knows that Percy Shelley's attraction to water at last proved fatal. He, who could scarcely be dragged away from a pond or a puddle when out walking, was lost in a storm at sea off La Spezia in July, 1822. The boat which he and Williams embarked in would have been adequate on the Serpentine but it was ill fitted for the rigours of the open sea. I cannot help thinking that Shelley courted his end and took poor Williams with him. My acquaintance the poet never learned to swim.*

This section was dated May, 1843. Tom thought that George Slater had most likely transcribed his youthful diaries into this book, perhaps tidying them up and editing them. At the same time he added an extra note or commentary, reflecting his later thoughts. The first part of this entry, about the fifty-pound note, made for a charming story, if it was true. Charming if it wasn't true, come to that. And if it was typical of what was in Slater's memoirs then Tom couldn't see where the problem lay.

On the other side of the desk Felix Slater's hand moved unceasingly across the sheet of paper. The top of his head was as smooth as a billiard ball. The Canon did not once look up at Tom, who opened the father's volume at another random page. This one seemed to describe the activities of a supper club, drinking, bawdy conversation and more drinking. Towards the end he read: *Hewitt, J and I paid Jane Wilson 2 shillings. She danced nude and then lay down and posed for us. We might have had her but, in truth, she was a bad model and altogether not agreeable.*

This, like the Shelley entry, was dated (to the summer of 1812) and Slater had added an 1843 note to the effect that it was unlikely a single one of them could have had Jane Wilson, not because she was disagreeable but because they had drunk so much. They were all in a useless 'droop-like state'. Curiously, as the writer said himself, although he could remember all this he could not remember who 'J' was. As to the provenance of Jane Wilson he gave no clue. Presumably she was a servant of some kind, perhaps one waiting at table, and so beneath notice. Or perhaps a prostitute, and so even more beneath notice.

Quickly, Tom shuffled a few pages further on. Again he hit gold and he felt the blood come into his face. It was a brief description by George Slater of how he'd had a woman up against a wall in Shepherd Market. It hadn't been a very enjoyable encounter: too quick and he'd spent much time afterwards wondering whether he'd caught a 'dose'. He hadn't contracted anything, a later footnote revealed. Tom was amazed, not so much at the encounter as at the run-of-the-mill manner in which it was recounted and the fact that he'd written about it at all.

Once more he turned a few pages. Ah, respectability again. Or a sort of respectability. This time Tom encountered Lord George Gordon Byron. Mr George Henry Slater claimed to have been in the famous poet's company when the latter declared: 'Incest is no sin. It is the way the world was first peopled. The Scriptures teach us that we are all descended from one pair, and how could that be unless brothers married their sisters? If it was no sin then, it cannot be a sin now.' Underneath,

Slater had added the later comment: *There was long a rumour that Lord Byron committed incest with his half-sister, Augusta Leigh. I do not know whether the rumour was true but it is certain that the notion of incest was attractive to him because of its very forbiddenness; this was not the only time he spoke of it. I remember that he uttered these particular words in his customary style, somewhere between mischief and earnest.*

Tom glanced up at Felix Slater but the cleric appeared to be wholly absorbed in his work. Tom wondered what he was writing. For sure, the Canon's words must be more respectable than what was recounted in his father's neat hand. Tom still felt hot and – though it was ridiculous – guilty for what he was reading. He took one more dip into the book but on this occasion found nothing more dramatic than a description of a morning's hunting on the Downton estate.

By this time Slater had come to the end. He concluded in the same way, grinding the nib of the pen into the paper. He blotted what he'd written and put the sheet to one side.

'Well, Mr Ansell, you have seen enough, I dare say.'

'It is an interesting volume.'

'That is one word for it, though not the word I should have chosen. My dilemma is that I cannot now do away with this record of my father's even if I wish it had never been found or that he had never written it. Or, rather, I might wish that parts of his life had not been so very *rackety*. The volume you are holding might, I suppose, have a historical value one day.'

As Slater said this, his eyes flicked towards the cases containing the primitive artefacts. Tom realized that whatever the man's feelings about his father – unease, embarrassment, even anger or disgust – he could not bring himself to destroy what George Slater had committed to paper. The Canon had a respect amounting to reverence for old things, whether they came from a few decades before or whether they stretched back through many centuries.

'You would like me to take this now?'

'No, no. I wish you, Mr Ansell, to draw up a memo to be kept with this book of my father's. You should outline briefly the circumstances under which I came by it – that is, it was among items freely passed to me by my older brother Percy – and state that it is given for safekeeping into the hands of Scott, Lye & Mackenzie. The book is not to be opened again until after my death. Then, and only then, my nephew Walter Slater is to be entrusted with it.'

'You say, Canon Slater, that it was freely passed to you by your brother?'

'I have a letter to that effect.'

'Then that should be included with the other material. Or if not the original letter, then a notarized copy. For the record, you understand.'

'Very well.'

'And we need a name for it in the memorandum.'

'Call it . . . the Salisbury manuscript. You will see that I have formally acknowledged receipt of it at the front,' said Canon Slater.

'Very well. The Salisbury manuscript. And what if your nephew predeceases you? Who is to decide the fate of the book then?'

Felix Slater looked discomfited, as if the thought hadn't occurred to him. 'Then I suppose it should be left to his heirs and descendants. You can add a note to that effect. You are to bring the memo to me tomorrow, if you please, and I will sign it. After that, you are to take everything back to London. I need hardly add that I require you, as a representative of your firm, to keep the strictest watch over the book. Please do not let it out of your sight until you have seen it safe and secure in your vaults.'

Tom nodded and handed the volume back to Felix

Slater, who wrapped it up in the cloth once more. Tom thought Canon Slater was being over-protective of the book, treating it as though it were a truly valuable treasure rather than the private musings of a man who'd behaved disreputably from time to time when he was young. However, it is not the job of a lawyer to point out this sort of thing to a client. If Slater wanted the book guarded, then Tom would guard it and not merely because it was his job. Almost despite himself, he'd taken a kind of liking to the clergyman.

Maybe the feeling was reciprocated for Slater seemed to relax. He unfolded himself from his seat and said, 'It will be time for luncheon soon. Before that, let me show you the garden, Mr Ansell. I find that a little fresh air sharpens the appetite.'

Slater returned his father's book to the chest in the corner. Before he closed and locked it, Tom noticed that there were other items inside, sheets of paper folded or loose. He wondered if these too were prohibited material but, presumably, Slater was content to keep them in his possession.

The Canon opened the doors that led into the garden. There was a terrace that ran the length of the house, with a lawn lapping at its edge and ornamental beds, now with skeletal plants. The sun had reached this side and taken some of the chill out of the air. Slater led the way to a path that ran through an orchard and down towards the river. From their left came snipping sounds. The gardener was trimming a shrub which Tom couldn't identify.

'Eaves,' said Slater in greeting, and in response the gardener touched his shears to his cap in a kind of salute. Tom expected the man to get back to his clipping but he evidently wanted to say something for he cleared his throat. Felix Slater paused.

'Have you heard the news, sir?' said the gardener in an

odd sing-song voice as if he was uncertain whether his 'news' would be welcome.

'Until you tell me what it is, I cannot know whether I have heard it or not.'

The gardener called Eaves looked puzzled as if he was trying to work out what his employer meant. Eventually he gave up and said, 'There's been another robbery. Over at Mr Anstruther's.'

'Robbery?'

'Bobbies are there now, sir,' said the gardener, gesturing with his shears.

'It's true,' said Tom. 'I saw a constable standing outside a house further up West Walk.'

'It must be the Anstruthers then,' said Felix Slater. 'A robbery? When?'

'Last night they say, sir.'

'And do they also say what was taken, Eaves?'

'Funny things again.'

'Funny things?'

'Funny things, sir. Jelly moulds this time, I heard.'

'Very well. You may get back to your work now.'

Content with his two minutes of attention, the gardener resumed the clipping. Tom and Slater strolled on towards the river. The path wound among apple trees.

'A robbery in the close,' said Tom.

'We are not immune to crime.'

'I wonder you have not heard of it already, Canon Slater.'

'I *have* heard of it. It was what my wife wanted to tell me about earlier this morning. I was asking Eaves what he knew because the servants are sometimes aware of things that pass us by. But he merely confirmed what Mrs Slater had already told me. Someone broke into the Anstruthers' last night and stole some jelly moulds from the kitchen.'

'Why would anyone want to steal jelly moulds?' said Tom, and then with pleasure at his deduction, 'Perhaps they intended to take something more valuable and were interrupted.'

'I don't know the details but this is the second or third robbery in the close. Last time, too, only small items were taken. Toasting forks, I believe.'

'Perhaps the thief is a cook.'

'Or a crook,' said Slater, and Tom thought he detected a touch of humour. He said, 'Are you worried for your collection?'

'I might be,' said Slater. 'But to a thief, what I have collected would look like nothing more than a heap of stones and metal trinkets.'

This was not so far from Tom's initial response to the objects. He was surprised, though, by the cleric's seemingly easy attitude. By now they had reached the river bank. The water flowed fast and swollen after the autumn rains, carrying the odd tree branch or mass of green weed. Beyond the far bank there stretched meadows dotted with willows and grazing cows. A kind of timber garden-house or gazebo stood near the water's edge. It had a covered verandah on the river side and a curtain with a check pattern in the window. Nearby was a small grassy mound, with a headstone set at one end. The little grave, set out in the open, was curiously disturbing. Slater noticed Tom looking at it.

'A dog of my wife's is buried there. A little pug. She wanted him close at hand. My wife likes to sit here in the summer,' said Felix Slater.

'I would sit here too, dog or no dog' said Tom, thinking of his own lodgings in Islington and the close, stuffy air of a London summer.

'She says that it reminds her of home.'

Tom was puzzling over this remark, or rather wondering where exactly home was for Mrs Slater, when from the distance there came the sound of a gong being struck. It was the signal for lunch The two men turned back towards Venn House. Soaring above the line of the roof they could see the spire of the cathedral.

'The highest in all of England, isn't it?' said Tom, dredging the fact up from somewhere. 'It must be the pride of Salisbury.'

'It may surprise you, Mr Ansell, to know that there is not much love lost between the town and the cathedral. Hundreds of years ago the bishop owned this town, more or less, but things are different now. Oh, there is a kind of respect for this great church and the tradespeople are grateful that it brings visitors here, no doubt. Once our visitors would have been pilgrims. Now they want to look at the sights and go shopping. But the townsfolk have their business to get on with, just as we have ours. I don't suppose that more than one in a hundred of our good citizens ever considers that he is walking across the ground that his ancestors toiled on. Everywhere we go we traverse layers of the past but so few of us see beneath the soil.'

Tom glanced sideways at the tall, bird-like cleric. There was that same suppressed fire in his manner as when he had been examining the artefacts in the glass cases.

They went back inside, down the hall and past the watercolours and the case of ornamental ferns. Slater led the way through a door near the front part of the house and into the dining room. Three people, two women and a man, were already there. Tom recognized each of them. The man was Slater's nephew, Walter Henry, who smiled to see his uncle come in with Tom. One of the women was Bessie, the flustered maid – now with her collar properly straightened and waiting to serve lunch – who had appeared in Slater's study. The second woman was the mysterious personage who had told Tom to stay outside Venn House and whose existence he had almost forgotten about for the last hour or so. He had made various compromising assumptions about her: that she might be a prostitute or woman of the town, then that she was an odd visitor to Venn House (a clairvoyante or something of the kind) or possibly a servant.

But now he realized, with horror mixed with embarrassment, that she was actually Felix Slater's wife.

Venn House, Interior

The Canon introduced Amelia to Tom. They shook hands. It was a firm grasp, just as it had been when she gripped his arm outside the gate. Over her shoulder Tom could see himself in the great mirror which was set above the mantel. He was quite red in the face. His complexion made a contrast with her yellow dress. Fortunately, his confusion was not observed by Slater, who had drawn his nephew to one side and was talking in an undertone by the window. Now that everyone had arrived, the maid was busying herself by the sideboard. If Tom Ansell was flustered, Amelia Slater was calm. Her hand was warm (Tom's was sweaty) and she looked amused.

'I am pleased to meet you, Mr Ansell. You are coming from London this morning?'

'No, I got here last night,' said Tom, remembering the woman's injunction outside the gate of the house that he wasn't to mention how they'd met before. Her disingenuous question about his arrival seemed to confirm the little conspiracy between them.

'You are staying somewhere nice, I hope?'

'I have a room in The Side of Beef,' he said, almost adding, 'As you well know, Mrs Slater.' He was convinced that he had seen her hanging about outside the inn when he'd glanced out of his window on the previous evening.

She seemed about to say something else but fortunately she was cut short by Felix and Walter finishing their talk and taking their places at table. The Canon sat at one end with his nephew at the other while Tom and Amelia Slater were opposite each other. The table was large and each person seemed to be marooned in his or her seat.

After Slater had said grace, and in the pause before conversation picked up, Tom glanced round the room. It was done out in quite an old-fashioned style with mahogany furniture and dark colours. A great sideboard occupied most of the wall facing the window. No one said anything as the maid served them with oxtail soup.

The silence was prolonged while they took the first couple of sips. The maid went to stand demurely by the sideboard. Walter Slater spoke first.

'I saw Foster just now. The Inspector, you know. He has been to talk to the Anstruthers and to see what he can discover about the robbery last night. He told me that the thief gained entry from the river side. A door had been forced at the back of the house. He said that we should look to our own doors and locks.'

The name, in connection with the local police, prompted some memory in Tom's head. Foster? Where had he heard that name, and recently too? It had been while he was sitting in the cab on the way from the station. Canon Selby had said something about Inspector Foster. That he was a good man, a sound man.

'It is frightening that someone can come into a house while the people inside are asleep,' said Amelia. But she did not look frightened. Tom caught her glance; there was a gleam in her eye. 'If only Achilles was still here.'

Tom was puzzling over Achilles when he remembered the small grass mound down by the river.

'Achilles couldn't do much,' said Walter.

'He could bark and was brave,' said Amelia. 'Achilles would have protected me.'

'You do not need to fear, my dear,' said her husband. 'I am here at night and so is Walter. We shall protect you.

Did you find out what was taken, Walter? Surely it was more than a few jelly moulds?'

'Not much more, according to Foster. The cook was still going through the kitchen since it appears that the thief concentrated his attentions entirely in there. A few spoons and forks are missing. Mr Anstruther was woken by a great clattering noise while he was asleep and came downstairs. He found the back door ajar.'

'Then it is as Mr Ansell here suggested to me earlier,' said Felix Slater. 'The thief was disturbed before he could do any worse.'

'It seems an odd place to begin a robbery, in the kitchen,' said Tom 'Why not start in the more valuable rooms of a house?'

'Perhaps Mr Ansell fancies himself as a detective,' said Walter. 'If so, sir, maybe you can explain something which is odder still. When Mr Anstruther came down to inspect the kitchen together with the servants who'd also been alerted by the clatter, they found that pots and pans had been deliberately flung on to the floor. One or two items had been dented and damaged but none of them taken.'

'Wanton vandalism,' said Felix Slater.

'Inspector Foster does not think so. He said it was almost as if the thief wanted to make his presence known to the household, and that the quickest way to get everyone downstairs was to chuck some ironmongery around.'

Tom, who might have been quite pleased to be thought of as a detective, was at a loss to explain this, and said so.

'This is not the kind of crime you enjoy in London?' said Mrs Slater to him.

'I think our London thieves would be a bit more ambitious. They wouldn't be content with jelly moulds or cutlery. Of course, we have robberies by daylight in London, even murders.'

'Murders. How terrible!'

This was Amelia Slater again. She carefully placed her

soup spoon in her empty dish. 'Don't let's talk of murder,' said her husband and Tom felt faintly rebuked.

'The case which is occupying everybody at the moment is the Tichborne Claimant,' he said quickly.

'Ah, the Claimant,' said Walter.

'I do not understand the Claimant,' said Mrs Slater. 'I do not read the papers. Maybe Mr Ansell could explain the Claimant to me. You are in the law, Mr Ansell, so you know everything.'

The Claimant was safe ground. Everybody had a view – except apparently Amelia Slater – and no one would really be affected by the outcome of the case. So during the main course (cold meat from the previous day, potatoes), Tom gave an outline of the court action that was gripping London and the rest of the kingdom: how Sir Roger Tichborne, heir to a great estate in Hampshire, had been reported drowned nearly twenty years ago off the coast of Brazil; how a man from Australia had come to England in 1866 to lay claim to the inheritance, saying that he was Sir Roger; how the case had wound its way through the courts for several years before it fell apart because the Claimant couldn't show the tattoos which Sir Roger was alleged to have worn. Then a second action had been launched, this time with the Claimant as defendant. A criminal one too, alleging that the Claimant had perjured himself and issued forged bonds to pay his expenses. This was still playing itself out at the High Court. Tom Ansell had talked about it with David Mackenzie. His employer had asked him whether there wasn't still a niggling doubt over the case. Despite almost all the evidence to the contrary, perhaps the Claimant really was Sir Roger. Mrs Slater, who'd listened attentively to Tom, certainly seemed to think so.

'It would be romantic,' she said, 'romantic if this man turned out to be Sir Roger after all.'

'My dear, that has been thoroughly disproved,' said her husband. 'Everyone knows that, far from being Sir

Roger, the fellow is a butcher from Australia by the name of Orton. He is enormously fat, to judge by his pictures, while Sir Roger was thin. He cannot speak French, a language which Sir Roger was fluent in. No, Sir Roger is long dead and buried under the waves off Brazil.'

'But men grow fat with the years,' said Amelia, 'and they can change so that they are hard to recognize from how they were. People are not what they seem. Under great stress they forget what they know. Perhaps the person did speak French but now it has all slipped from his head. Whoosh!'

She gave a sweeping motion with her hand. Tom was reminded of the moment when she'd flicked at the garden door with her heel. There might have been something a touch unladylike about both gestures but there was also something attractive to them.

He'd been talking about the Claimant case so much that he was behindhand with his eating and, while he got on with his meat and potatoes, he looked from time to time at the woman across the table. She was younger than her husband but, since he looked older than he was, the gap in years was perhaps not so great. She had dark hair and mobile features, especially her mouth and her large brown eyes. He recalled that the Canon had said that his wife liked to sit in the summer-house by the river because it reminded her of home. Home? He didn't think it was England. The woman, with her faintly accented speech and spontaneous gestures, was not quite English. Yet Amelia, as far as Tom was aware, was not a foreign name.

Over the final courses (marmalade pudding followed by cheese), the talk turned to the Church, with Felix Slater asking his nephew about St Luke's and Mr Simpson, the vicar. Though neither Tom nor Mrs Slater had much to say on this topic, both uncle and nephew took the trouble to include them by glances and occasional comments. Felix

Slater might be an upright, rigorous individual, but he had unexpected turns and corners. There was the passion for ancient artefacts, and then there was the presence of Amelia Slater. Tom found himself wondering how they'd met, the circumstances under which they had married, and so on.

Though they'd been drinking nothing stronger than water fortified with a little wine, Tom felt set up by the meal and the company. Canon Slater must have enjoyed his presence too for, as he was leaving, he told Tom to come back the next evening with the memorandum which he was to draw up. 'And, Mr Ansell, you are most welcome to join us for supper, if you wish.'

Tom said he'd be glad to, though part of his gladness was the idea of seeing Amelia Slater again. He was curious about her and might discover more on a second visit.

Walter accompanied him out of Venn House, explaining that he was returning to town for an evening service at his church. Mrs Slater also came to the door. She said goodbye to Tom and to Walter. She said goodbye to Walter warmly, putting her arm about him and kissing him as though he was a valued visitor and not someone who lived in the house all the time. Tom couldn't help noticing, since there was nothing secretive or sly about Mrs Slater's actions.

It was by now early afternoon and though the sun still shone the air was chilly as the two men went up the West Walk. Tom pulled up his coat collar. He made some casual but complimentary comment about his hosts, Walter's uncle and aunt.

'My aunt?' said Walter. 'I never think of Amelia that way. She is not very aunt-like.'

This was the opening that Tom had perhaps been looking for. He was surprised that Walter so openly stated that Mrs Slater was not aunt-like. He said, 'No, she is certainly not like my aunts, my mother's sisters.'

He glanced sideways to see whether Walter was inclined

to say more. The assistant curate walked with a kind of bounce in his step but stayed silent.

Tom tried again: 'They have been married a long time, Canon and Mrs Slater?'

'Long enough,' said Walter, then as if he felt that this answer struck the wrong note, 'They met in Italy, in Florence.'

'Ah, so Mrs Slater, Amelia, is Italian.'

'On her mother's side. Her father was English. But she lived in Florence for many years as a child.'

And she thinks of it as home, thought Tom. She sits by the river at the bottom of the garden and remembers the much greater river which flows through the middle of Florence, whatever it is called. But Walter's reference to an English father explained the reason for Amelia's name, just as her many years abroad accounted for her non-Englishness.

'I think, Mr Ansell, that if you want to know any more then you should ask my uncle or *aunt*.'

Walter did not seem put out by the questions but plainly the topic was closed. Looking to turn the conversation in a different direction, Tom mentioned Canon Eric Selby since they were passing the spot near the entrance to the close where Selby had given him directions.

'I know the man,' said Walter. 'So does my uncle of course. But I am afraid there is a coolness on his side.'

He did not enlarge on this either. The coolness between the Canons must have been mutual, thought Tom, recalling the look of distaste which had crossed Selby's face when he said that he was searching for Venn House. He kept quiet now while they made their way back into the heart of the town, not certain whether any subject he raised might be unwelcome. Altogether, Walter Slater seemed less cheerful and forthcoming than earlier in the day.

Only after they'd parted company and Tom was returning to The Side of Beef did it occur to him that Walter had shown no curiosity about why he was in Salisbury. Did he know that his uncle was passing over his grandfather's memoir-book? Was he aware that he would have the responsibility of deciding what to do with it once Felix Slater was dead? In fact there was a strange aspect to Walter Slater's situation altogether. There he was, a lowly curate in a town parish, and yet he was destined to inherit a country estate. He must be a very devout man, since the Church could still be the preserve of younger sons without prospects. And what about Amelia Slater? How much did she know, beyond the fact that Tom was a representative of her husband's lawyers?

Back at the inn, Tom climbed the stairs to his room. Fortunately he did not bump into Jenkins, although he did recall the landlord mentioning that one of the guests had been asking about him the previous evening. A man who was called – he grasped for the name – Cathcart, Henry Cathcart. 'One of the leading citizens of our town,' Jenkins had called him. Well, if the fellow was curious about Tom Ansell, he knew where to find him.

Tom put all this out of his head and settled down at the small writing table in his room to draw up the memorandum which Canon Slater had requested. It was a straightforward job but he took longer over it than was necessary, partly because he wanted to satisfy Slater and partly as a way of filling up what remained of the afternoon. In appropriate legal terminology, he indicated that the volume henceforth to be known as the Salisbury manuscript was to remain sealed in the offices of Scott, Lye & Mackenzie until after the death of Canon Felix Slater. It was then left to Walter Slater (or in the event of his death to his heirs and successors) to read or otherwise dispose of as he saw fit.

By this time, it had grown dark outside and the traffic in the street had quietened. Tom made a copy of the document he had composed and put them both away in his bag. He wrote a letter to Helen Scott, outlining what he'd done that morning and describing Canon Slater and his collection of artefacts. He talked about the attractions of Salisbury and the grandeur of the cathedral. Then he remembered that Helen knew the town, for she had told him of visits here in her childhood. He made only a passing reference to Mrs Slater. When it came to signing off, he wavered between 'most affectionately yours', 'ardently', and 'with my love and affection', before settling on the last. He had brought stamps with him. Having some time in hand before supper, he went out to find a pillar-box and then wandered idly about some of the streets in the centre of town.

He must have been gone from The Side of Beef for half an hour or so. When he returned there was a welcome smell of supper wafting through the ground floor. He went upstairs to wash and change before the meal. The door to his room was slightly ajar. At first he thought the maid must be inside. But, when he pushed at the door, the room was empty. Someone had been there, however. Tom's clothes had been taken out of the wardrobe and were scattered across the bed or on the floor. His case had been upturned and the papers which it contained were strewn about the place. His initial reaction was surprise followed by anger. He gathered the papers together. They mostly related to Canon Slater's affairs. Nothing seemed to be missing. The document he'd just drawn up and its copy were still there. He was baffled. He had nothing of value, nothing worth stealing. He remembered to be glad that he hadn't yet taken possession of the Salisbury manuscript.

Without stopping to pick up any of his garments, he strode into the passage and almost collided with the landlord.

'All is well, Mr Ansell?' said Jenkins, although the man could see that it wasn't.

'Is this a den of thieves, landlord?'

They stood on the threshold of the room, gazing at the mess. Jenkins stroked his moustache furiously.

'You have lost something, Mr Ansell?'

'You mean, has anything been stolen from me? I am not sure. I do not think so. But this could be a police matter.'

'If you have lost nothing, there is no harm done and no need to summon the police, sir. This is an honest house, Mr Ansell. We've never had any trouble here.' A wheedling note had entered the landlord's voice, as he saw ways of retrieving the situation. Then, in a more calculating tone, 'Did you lock your door, sir?'

'Yes, I did – but why should I need to if this is an honest house?' said Tom, fingering the room key in his pocket. Had he locked it? He couldn't be sure. He asked, 'Who else has rooms along here?'

'You do not suspect the other guests,' said Jenkins. He sounded genuinely indignant.

'An outsider then?'

'I keep a very careful watch on things, Mr Ansell. No one gets inside or comes upstairs without me knowing it.'

'I'm sure they don't. Well then, what access is there to this floor apart from the front stairs?'

'There is a back staircase down there.'

And at that moment, as if on cue, the maid appeared at the other end of the passage. Catching sight of Tom and her employer, she halted and gave a sneeze. Seeing someone on to whom the guest's anger might be deflected, Jenkins beckoned to her.

'Still got that cold, Jenny?'

'Sorry, sir.'

'You'd better get rid of it, hadn't you,' said the landlord in a tone that suggested it was either the girl or the cold that was leaving. Having established how things stood, Jenkins waved an arm at the open door to Tom's room.

'What do you know about this, Jenny?'

She too came to inspect the room. She wrung her hands and looked mournful. Eventually she came out with, 'I don't know nothing, sir. I'm terribly sorry, sir. Do you want me to tidy up?'

'No, I'll do it,' said Tom. The irritation and bafflement had gone. He felt weary and did not want to make trouble for the harassed chambermaid. Jenkins, in contrast, looked relieved.

'When you are done, Mr Ansell, please come down and have supper and a bottle – on the house, of course.'

Tom nodded and retreated into his room. It took him only a few moments to straighten his clothes and fold and hang them up. It was disagreeable to think they'd been thrown around by a stranger but, as the landlord had said in his self-interested fashion, no harm had been done. Tom remembered the odd robberies he'd heard about at Venn House, the theft of jelly moulds and cutlery. Perhaps there was an impish thief at work in the town.

Tom took a bath in the shared bathroom at the end of the passage. The gas geyser chuntered away while Tom soaped himself and pondered the mystery of the break-in without coming to any conclusion. He changed his shirt, although it was almost as creased as the one he was replacing, and put on his spare jacket. Taking care to turn the key firmly in the lock – despite the chances of being broken into twice on the same evening being vanishingly slight – Tom turned right to the head of the stairs. A man had just reached the top. He was limping slightly and panting after the exertion of the climb. Tom recognized him, despite the dimness of the passageway. It was the gentleman who'd taken an interest in him during last night's supper. Cathcart, Henry Cathcart.

For his part, he recognized Tom for he said, 'Mr Ansell? Thomas Ansell? But you must be. You're the spit of your father. The living spit.'

The Nethers

On the eastern fringe of the city was a public house which went by the name of The Neat-herd but which was known almost universally as The Netherworld or simply The Nethers. No one remembered when the name had changed, or rather slipped, to its new form but it suited the people who frequented the place. It was a favourite with beggars and hawkers and petty thieves, together with women who were sometimes keeping them company and sometimes striking out on their own, glugging down their profits or fortifying themselves before going out on the town in search of more.

The Neat-herd, originally a straggle of low narrow cottages which had been knocked through to form a drinking area like a railway carriage without compartments, lay down a muddy lane. The lane petered out in marshy ground, adorned with the carcasses of carts and ploughshares rusting under nettles. To the rear of the public house was another dilapidated building, of wood not stone, perhaps a barn at one time.

Having safely within one basket so many bad apples (as Inspector Foster described The Nethers and its clientele) was convenient for the Salisbury police, who went to the public house in search of information or occasionally to lay hands on a convenient rogue.

At about the time that Tom Ansell was being greeted on the stairs in The Side of Beef, a police constable was leaving The Nethers. It was the same constable whom Tom had glimpsed that morning standing outside the Anstruthers' house in the cathedral close. Constable Matthew Chesney did not visit the public house in uniform. That would have been a provocation too far unless he was going to arrest someone, and then he wouldn't have gone alone. Instead he disguised himself in a working man's garb which fooled nobody. Constable Chesney knew that the disguise fooled nobody, since the male and female customers – the females especially – tended to greet him with mock salutes or pretend-expressions of terror and alarm when he walked through the door.

However, Constable Chesney's appearance at The Nethers in the guise of an artisan had this advantage: the drinkers and the landlord (a fellow called Jerry Reynolds) were aware that any visit like this was harmless. He wasn't after anybody, he was merely in quest of a bit of knowledge. And so they permitted him a few questions and even threw him a titbit from time to time. The quid pro quo for this was that Chesney and Inspector Foster left the occupants of The Nethers alone, unless they were really compelled to make an arrest in the place.

Chesney was departing The Nethers this evening in a dissatisfied frame of mind. He'd been detailed by his Inspector to see what the word was in the lower quarters of the town about the thefts from the houses in the close. The word from the Nethers drinkers was: nothing. Oh, Chesney's informants had heard that a couple of the fine drums near the cathedral had been turned over and that items, piddling items, had been snaffled. Jelly moulds, toasting forks and the like. 'Honest, Matt,' said one of the drinkers who made a point of being over-familiar with Constable Chesney when he was out of uniform, 'this will make our business a laughing stock. To break a drum and come off with swag like that'll do us no good at all, Matt.'

Chesney heard two or three other comments to this effect. Whoever was going to the trouble of breaking into the houses of the well-to-do folk should take a pride in their work, for gawd's sake, and do some proper thieving. But there was a lack of hard information, a lack of any information at all, and Constable Matthew Chesney was going to have to report to his Inspector that he had got nowhere.

The constable steered himself out of the front door of The Nethers. The cold evening air hit him full in the face, after the fuggy warmth and smell of the pub. He might have had a bit more to drink than he intended in his quest for information, and The Nethers was the third public house he had visited. Of course, you had to buy drinks for people while you were pumping them, and those people made sure they drank quick and provided their information (which they usually didn't have much of) slow. And then you had to show you had a head for drink yourself, since no one was going to give out information to a peeler who looked as though he was about to sign the pledge. In theory, Chesney disapproved of drinking, certainly drinking to excess, and as a God-fearing man he had sometimes felt like quoting to the habitués of The Nethers that verse from Proverbs about the glutton and the drunkard coming to poverty. Strangely, Constable Matthew Chesney only felt like doing this when he was himself a little the worse for wear.

The policeman went round to the side of The Nethers and unbuttoned himself to take a piss against the wall. He looked up to see the stars wheeling over the gabled end of the pub. He looked sideways in the direction of the other, barn-like edifice set further back from the lane. Gleams of light were visible through cracks and holes in the planking. There was the occasional yap of a dog and a shout or cheer from inside, which competed with the noise from the pub. Aha, thought Chesney, I know what's going on in there. It's none of my business, though.

As he was turning back towards the track which would

lead to the town, he almost collided with someone. 'Sorry, mate,' he said. The figure – it was a man – said nothing but brushed past Chesney, heading towards the wooden building. If the light had been better or Chesney less inebriated, the constable might have recognized the figure. But he didn't. Instead he staggered on his way towards the lights of the town.

The figure, however, did recognize Chesney although it took him a moment. He stopped to grin in the dark at the sozzled man's back before resuming his progress. As he drew closer to the barn, he heard a single shout which was echoed straightaway by other answering shouts. To an outsider the shouts would have been indecipherable or meaningless, for they sounded like 'Blow on 'em! Blow on 'em!', but the man was familiar with the words and quickened his step so as to be in time for the kill.

There was a person lounging by a small side door to the building. 'Evening, Jack,' said the man. The other might have been a block of wood for all the response he made but he let the man pass through the door unhindered. The interior of the barn was illuminated with a mixture of oil lamps and candles – the latter very dangerous in the event of an accidental spill although no one had given much thought to that – hanging from beams or fixed into niches and crevices in the walls. The flaring lights cast a golden glow over the proceedings, which was further softened by tobacco smoke. This, and the hush which had suddenly fallen, might have suggested a tranquil scene. All the man could see at first was an arc of backs in the centre of the beaten-earth floor and, through the huddled shoulders, glimpses of fixed countenances on the other side, seemingly looking down at the floor. There were other observers too, standing on a couple of broken-down carts and a discarded table, with the younger and more agile ones even sitting astride the rickety rafters.

Their entire attention was concentrated on an area not

much more than six feet in diameter at the centre of the barn. Here was a circular wall of stout wooden boards, rising to a little below chest height. The wood had at one time been painted white but it was now stained and flaking. The interior was well illuminated by a cluster of oil lamps hanging from a beam overhead.

Inside the ring a small dog, a terrier, was busy disposing of a pack of rats. The rats were running around the pit, some trying to get away from the terrier by squeezing into the gaps between the boards, others massing together in a kind of defensive heap against attack. But the lad who was standing in the pit, and who acted like a boxer's second in relation to the dog, prevented the rats clinging together for long either by giving them a flick with a dirty handkerchief or by puffing out his cheeks and blowing at the pile – as the shouts of 'Blow on 'em!' from the group of watchers had instructed him to do. This threw the animals into confusion, causing the the heap to collapse and giving the dog the chance to snap at one, then another, then a third, each time twisting his little body about, until he managed to seize a rat in his mouth and break its neck. Then the boy would shout at the dog: 'Drop it! Drop it!' and the terrier went searching for a new victim.

The man who'd just entered the barn jumped on to the back of one of the dilapidated carts, which stood at a little distance from the wooden ring or pit. He was nimble and reached it in a single leap. The cart swayed under his weight and the handful of other men already standing there shifted slightly to make space for him. Not one of them shifted his gaze from the pit, however.

The man was interested enough in the spectacle of rat-killing although it did not engross him as much as it did the other spectators. For one thing, he was not a betting man. For another, this was not an interesting fight between evenly matched opponents, each of them risking death or serious injury. The terrier would almost certainly come off quite unscathed after disposing of a dozen or more of the rodents. The real contest was between the dogs (and their owners) as to which of them could kill the most in an allotted period of time. So while this particular terrier was despatching fresh rats, the man cast his eyes over the company from the vantage point of the cart. There were no women in the crowd and the men were predominantly of the same type and class as those who filled the pub which stood a few dozen yards off.

The newcomer soon saw on the far side of the ring three individuals who were better dressed than the rest of the crowd. Gentlemen, perhaps, though more on account of their clothes than anything else about them. They too were absolutely absorbed by the contest, their faces tilted forward and etched by shadows, their extended arms braced on the rim of the pit.

The man waited until the match was declared over, which happened after someone called out 'Time!' as a signal to the boy who was acting as a second to catch up his dog by the scruff of the neck.

In the pause before the next bout, the man leaped down from the cart and circled round the barn. The trio of gentlemen, for want of a better word, were now standing a little away from the pit, exchanging sporadic comments among themselves but not talking to any of the others in the barn. The man tapped the shoulder of the individual he wanted to speak to.

This one spun round, instinctively raising the walking stick which he was carrying. Then, squinting through the hazier light beyond the perimeter of the ring, he relaxed and lowered his stick.

'Ah, Adam, it's you.'

'Yes, it's me,' said the man.

'What have you got to report?'

'Here?' said the man. 'Now? In front of your friends?'

'These aren't my friends,' said the gentleman, looking

over his shoulder at his companions. 'Never seen them before in my life.'

'Funny, isn't it,' said the man who'd been addressed as Adam. 'A funny thing, a queer thing. Birds of a feather and all that. Sticking together.'

'I dare say,' said the gentleman, perhaps irritated by Adam's familiarity. 'And here's another funny, queer thing, Adam. Look in the pit there. Look at the rats.'

The boy and the terrier were still inside the ring, the boy holding the dog, which hadn't yet taken its eyes off the surviving rats. The boy, meantime, was conferring with a heavy-set man leaning on the rim of the pit. Judging by the way he was looking at the terrier – with a touch of pride in his face – he was most likely its owner. For their part, the few rats which remained had started to clean themselves or to nibble the ends of their tails or even to sniff around the lad, who had prudently tied string round the bottom of his trousers to prevent them scrabbling up his legs. The rats got on with their existence despite the corpses and the fearsome face of the terrier looming only a couple of feet above them.

'They are ignorant of their fate, Adam,' said the man, gesturing at the rats with his walking stick. 'See the way they play around the feet of their destroyer. See how quickly they get back to their normal business, as if there were nothing but unclouded blue sky above them.'

'Very poetic,' said Adam.

'There's a lesson for us here.'

'Well, I am buggered if I know what that lesson is,' said Adam.

'I only say this sort of thing to you because I believe you can appreciate it,' said the man.

At this point the two men had to move out of the way while the terrier was borne off from the pit, cradled in the arms of the heavy-set individual as lovingly as if he were carrying a baby. The boy was sweeping the corpses of the rats to one side but not troubling to remove them from the little arena. Another dog was being ushered towards the ring from some dark corner of the barn, a small white bulldog this time, walking in his stumpy fashion rather than being lifted. And the proprietor of the rat-killing forum (who was a cousin to Jerry Reynolds, landlord of The Nethers) was bringing up the rear, supporting a large wicker basket on his outstretched arms. Despite the dimness of the lamplight it was possible to make out, through the hinged metal grid which formed the lid of the basket, mounds of close-packed rats. They looked like so many sweetmeats being brought to market. Moving sweetmeats.

The man called Adam said, 'I'm not staying to see more. I don't bet.'

'You don't bet?' said the other, with genuine surprise.

'It's a mug's game.'

'There is the sport too.'

'If you say so.'

'Then tell me quickly, Adam, what you found in The Side of Beef,' said the well-dressed man, glancing round to see that no one was within earshot. He was obviously eager to turn his attention back to the wooden pit, but not so eager that he didn't take time to bring out a hip flask and have a swallow from it before asking, 'What have you got to report?'

'I found nothing.'

'You were recommended to me as a man who could find things. I paid you on that understanding.'

'Can't find nothing if there's nothing to find. I turned over the room and there was nothing there, I say. Nothing we would be interested in, leastways.'

'Then why in God's name did you come to disturb me here if you had nothing to say?' said the man, letting the irritation back into his voice. Perhaps he'd picked up on the shared 'we' in Adam's answer and did not care for the implied equality.

If Adam felt rebuked by the man's tone, he didn't show it. In fact he took pleasure in saying, 'I knew I'd find you here, mister, out behind The Nethers. I wanted to track you down, that's all. I can nail you, see, as sure as any of those dogs can nail a rat.'

And with that Adam turned about and weaved his way through the men in the barn and so out of the door. Apart from Jack outside the door, no one noticed him leave for all their attention was again focused on the imminent match. The white bulldog was being held poised above the arena while the rats, whether old ones or fresh, continued to go about their oblivious business. But even if the eyes of the spectators hadn't been directed elsewhere, it is unlikely that they would have paid much attention to Adam. He had the knack of passing unseen.

Off the Dardanelles

'I knew your father,' said Henry Cathcart. 'He was a friend. We served together. He was a Thomas like you. You are very like him in looks too. I thought you seemed familiar last night. It gave me quite a start and I took the liberty of asking the landlord about you. I hope you don't mind.'

'Not at all,' said Tom, 'but why did you not make yourself known last night, Mr Cathcart?'

'I . . . I was uncertain what to do. I did not know how welcome such an intrusion would be. Besides, seeing you was quite a shock to the system. I needed time to recover. It is twenty years or more since I last saw your father. I never thought to see him again in this life and of course I will not see him. Yet last night at supper, there he was . . . or rather, there *you* were. You do not mind me saying all this, Mr Ansell? Thomas?'

Cathcart leaned across and made to grasp Tom's hand. He was visibly affected by the meeting. The two men were sitting in an empty snug off the supper room in The Side of Beef from which there came the subdued noise of diners and the clinking of cutlery and glass. A bottle of red wine was on the table between them. Tom felt almost dizzy although he had taken no more than a couple of sips from his glass.

He said, 'I am Tom. But my mother tells me that my father was always called Thomas. I was called Tom to distinguish me from him if my mother wanted my attention . . . but of course by the time it would have regularly mattered to distinguish between us . . . he was gone.'

'You do not remember him?'

'He was a – he was no more than a presence when I was small. A tall man in a blue uniform. That's all, I'm afraid,' said Tom, recalling that he'd given the same inadequate description of his father to Mrs Mackenzie a couple of days earlier.

'Ah, we did like wearing the uniform,' said Henry Cathcart. 'The women liked it too.'

Tom looked at the man sitting opposite him. Henry Cathcart was plump and well fed, every inch the leading citizen of the town as Jenkins had characterized him. Tom had some difficulty imagining him wearing a soldier's outfit. But then perhaps his father would have grown stout, had he lived. He was thinking like this in order to hold at bay other, more painful thoughts. He wanted to ask, 'My father, what was he like?' or 'Did my father ever mention me?' but these questions would have come too early in the conversation. Instead Tom Ansell said, 'Were you there when he died?'

'Not at the very moment,' said Cathcart. He paused and Tom thought that he wasn't going to say any more. But Cathcart swallowed half his glass and refilled it from the bottle then went on: 'He fell ill of a fever shortly before we reached the Dardanelles. He wasn't the only one to die on board and there was no time to put in and bury him and the others on one of the little islands in those parts. Your father was not a navy man, of course, but he had a sailor's burial. We thought he had escaped the sickness. Others had gone ahead of him and Lieutenant Thomas Ansell seemed to be on the mend. But he went in the early hours of the morning, quite suddenly. He was the last to die on the voyage and so had the distinction of being buried alone.'

'Can you describe it?' said Tom. He was curious and at the same time half ashamed of his curiosity. Yet Henry Cathcart seemed pleased enough to talk about it. He told of how Thomas Ansell had been sewn up in a hammock which was weighted with a bag of sand at the foot; of how a plank had been prepared with one end over the side of the vessel; of how the men had been paraded on deck and the colours flown at half-mast. Prayers were said over the body by the chaplain. The men stood with heads bowed. A volley was fired. The order was given to tilt the plank. Hardly an order, said Cathcart, just a small upwards gesture of the hand by the ship's captain.

Henry Cathcart paused again. Saying, 'I turned my head at that point for I could not look,' he turned his head away, in imitation of his action more than twenty years before. Still with face averted he said, 'I heard the splash as my friend's body plunged into the water. Though I heard much worse than that in battle, and in the aftermath of battle too, I will never forget that splash.'

When he turned back, his eyes were moist, and Tom felt the water gathering in his own. Both men resumed their drinking in earnest silence.

'Your mother,' said Cathcart eventually, 'is she still . . .?'

'Yes, thriving.'

'Good, good. I am glad of that. I remember Marian Ansell clearly.'

There was a wistful note to his voice and Tom wondered whether this portly middle-aged gent had been soft on his mother. He said, 'Except that she is Marian Holford now. She remarried after my father's death.'

'Your stepfather was in the army?'

'He was an attorney. Though he is dead too now. He was some years older than my mother.'

'Ah, so you have followed in your stepfather's steps, Tom. The landlord here told me that you worked for a London law firm.'

'The landlord here is altogether too curious. But, yes, I followed my stepfather. He always said that the law was a safe trade since people would never tire of litigation.'

'He was right enough there. So, tell me, you are down here on business?'

'Yes. We have a client who lives in the close. And you, sir? What happened to you after . . . after your army service?'

'I was wounded in the Russian War,' said Henry Cathcart, clasping a plump hand to his upper thigh. 'Nothing serious, though it was enough to disable me from further service and to leave me with a gammy leg. I was fortunate compared with many of my fellows. Now I own a store on one of the principal thoroughfares of this town. We sell not single things but several in different departments, clothes and drapery mostly and furnishings. I like to think that enterprises like mine are the wave of the future, places where people may buy everything they want under one roof. But owning a store is a far cry from the glory of war. Wasn't it Bonaparte who called us a nation of shopkeepers?'

'Shopkeepers who defeated an Emperor,' said Tom.

'Good, good,' said Cathcart, dividing the rest of the bottle of wine between Tom and himself. 'Shall we get another?'

'The landlord owes me a drink,' said Tom. He described how Jenkins had promised him a bottle on the house after his room had been broken into. Cathcart was all concern although Tom said that nothing seemed to have been taken. His anger and unease at the incident had dissolved under the influence of a few glasses. He was inclined to take Jenkins's view that no harm had been done. Certainly he would not be alerting the police. He felt an odd wish that Henry Cathcart should not think that he, Tom, had a low opinion of the town.

'Salisbury is a law-abiding place in general,' said Cathcart, 'although I hear there have been some robberies in the close.'

'As recently as last night,' said Tom.

'Well, here is another mystery,' said Cathcart after they'd started work on a second bottle of wine and pondered the puzzle of why a thief would want to take jelly moulds and toasting forks. The store-owner reached across to a neighbouring table and picked up a discarded copy of the *Salisbury Gazette*. After casting his eyes over the front page, he passed it to Tom, indicating a couple of paragraphs.

Under the headline *Developments in Search for Missing Sexton,* Tom read the following item: *We are assured by Inspector Foster of the Salisbury police that investigations are continuing into the mysterious disappearance of Mr Andrew North, one of the sextons at the cathedral church of St Mary. According to Inspector Foster, developments in the case are expected soon although he declined to say what they were. Our readers will recall that the sexton disappeared sometime during the night of October the fifteenth of this year. Mr North, who shared a cottage in the cathedral grounds with his widowed sister, failed to report for duty on the morning of the sixteenth although the alarm was not raised until later that day since it was assumed by his superiors that Mr North was ill at home and by his sister Mrs Banks that he had already departed for work. Mr North was last seen by Mrs Banks on the late afternoon of the previous day, telling her that he was going out for a stroll and that she was on no account to wait up for his return. We understand that Mr North had fallen into the habit of walking late and that there was nothing unusual in his request.*

There was speculation that Mr North might have suffered a serious accident or fallen victim to a sudden illness, but the absence of any report or sighting has deepened fears for the safety of the sexton. Mr North has been described as a man in good health and someone who has, in the words of his sister, 'all his wits about him'. Canon Eric Selby told the Gazette *that*

Mr North was a good worker and a valued servant of the cathedral church, adding that he very much hoped the mystery of the sexton's disappearance would soon reach a happy and satisfactory conclusion.

Tom put the local paper back on the table. The main thing of interest to him was the mention of Canon Selby.

Henry Cathcart said, 'You'll notice that they talk about developments without saying what they are. Inspector Foster probably hasn't got a clue but it gives the impression he's getting somewhere just as it provides the *Gazette* with a peg to hang the story on. A more honest headline would have been *No Developments in Search for Missing Sexton*.'

For some reason, Tom thought of the disturbing scene he'd witnessed the previous evening while he was standing on the station platform. The two dark figures, the way in which one had crept up on the other, the way both had subsequently vanished. He wondered whether to mention it to Cathcart. But he kept quiet. There could be no connection between that and the disappearance of Andrew North a month ago.

The two men chatted generally for a bit longer. They avoided talking about Tom's father, as if conscious that anything else in that line would have to wait until another meeting. Cathcart was drinking more quickly and in larger measure than Tom but he still felt woozy when the older man hoisted himself out of his chair and announced that he had to be getting back home. The store-owner enquired how much longer Tom was staying in Salisbury and expressed the earnest wish that, now he had made the acquaintance of the son of his long-lost friend, they would have another meeting before Tom's return to London. They shook hands and once again Tom saw a teariness in the other's eyes. Then Henry Cathcart, limping a little, squeezed his way through the narrow door of the snug.

Tom sat for a while longer, toying with his almost empty glass, wondering where his appetite for supper had gone, and turning over what Henry Cathcart had told him about the death of his father. He wondered whether the store-keeper had ever told the same story to his mother, not face to face but perhaps in a letter. He rather thought not. Remembering the wistful way in which the store-owner had referred to his mother, he considered it unlikely that Cathcart had seen her again after his return from the Russian War. Such a meeting might have been painful for all sorts of reasons.

Tom was about to stir himself and go to the supper room before it was too late when Jenkins entered the snug. The landlord was carrying a letter. He seemed on the verge of saying something but, maybe because of Tom's melancholy expression, he simply handed it over, giving the slightest bow as he did so.

The letter was addressed to *Thomas Ansell, esq. c/o The Side of Beef, Salisbury*. It was not stamped. He assumed it was from one of the Slater family. So it was, although not a family member whom Tom had met.

Dear Mr Ansell, I understand that you are making a professional visit to my brother Felix on matters concerning my late father, George Slater. As you are doubtless aware, I am no longer a client of Scott, Lye & Mackenzie but I would be most obliged if you would take the time to call on me tomorrow morning at Northwood House. There is a local train from Salisbury to Wimborne travelling via Downton, where you should alight. The train arrives at 11.35 a.m. My coachman will meet you at the station.

The letter was signed *Percy Slater*.

The Sick Room

Henry Cathcart let himself into his house. By instinct, he closed the door softly behind him. Inside, there was the same gloomy hush which generally lowered his spirits. But tonight Cathcart was in such a confused and unusual state of mind that he scarcely noticed it. Meeting the son of his old friend had thrown him back into the past so that, in the few minutes it had taken him to walk from The Side of Beef to his house, he had been quite unaware of the familiar streets and corners he was passing. He didn't even notice the ache from the wound in his thigh, which tended to trouble him when he walked.

Thomas – no, Tom – Ansell was pretty well the living spit of his dead father. When Henry had been chatting to him in the snug he might have been talking to the man himself. But then he would recall that more than twenty years had passed, and he would hear again that terrible splash as his comrade's body slid into the water, and so the tears came to his eyes.

The store-owner had spotted Tom at supper the previous evening and had at once been struck by the likeness to his dead friend. Surreptitious glances had been followed by outright stares and then questions to the landlord. Henry Cathcart had noticed young Ansell growing visibly uncomfortable under his scrutiny and – once Jenkins had told him the name of the new guest – he'd considered going across and introducing himself. But, as he'd explained to Tom, several things conspired to hold him back, chiefly the uncertainty over how he'd be received.

That night he slept poorly, though this was not only on account of seeing Tom but because of another encounter he'd had earlier. The following day Henry Cathcart called three times at The Side of Beef in the hope that Ansell might be there. On the third occasion, he was told that Mr Ansell had just returned and was most likely in his room. Too impatient to wait for Tom to come down to supper, Cathcart climbed the stairs and met Tom as he was about to descend.

It was extraordinary, he reflected, how similar were Thomas Ansell and Tom Ansell, the same features, the same build. Similar even down to the inflections of their voices. And then he wondered whether he was right. Did the son really look and sound so like the father, or was he wishing that on the young man?

'What did you say?'

The housemaid, having taken his coat as he walked in the front door and hung it up, now returned with a question. Standing in the gloomy hallway, Cathcart had been too wrapped up in his memories to notice anything.

'Cook asks what time you would like your supper, sir.'

'Is Mrs Cathcart awake?'

'I believe she was sleeping earlier, sir.'

'Very well, I will visit her later. Tell her maid to inform me when she is awake and is ready to see me. And tell cook that I will eat as soon as she has the food ready.'

'Very good, sir.'

'I'll be in the dining room. You do not need to sound the gong, you might disturb Mrs Cathcart.'

The maid bobbed slightly and went off to convey instructions to the cook and to Mrs Cathcart's maid. Cathcart entered the dining room and sat at the head of the table. He would be dining alone, as usual. He reached out for a decanter and filled one of the glasses which was next to the single place-setting. Henry did not usually drink much. He was a believer in sobriety and industry although without taking those virtues to excess. Yet the surprise – the shock – of encountering Tom Ansell had already caused him to drink as much as he would have consumed over several days. Perhaps that too was a reversion to his earlier life.

As he sat over his glass of wine (which eventually became several glasses) and, later, his supper (pork chops, broccoli, mash), Henry Cathcart mused over his meeting with Tom and his friendship with Tom's father. He also thought about Marian Ansell, pretty and vivacious Marian. He had been not so much soft on her as smitten with her. He had thought his friend, Thomas Ansell, a lucky dog to have found and nailed her, a very lucky dog indeed.

What was her surname now? What had Tom said? Holford, wasn't it? An attorney. So Marian had married a lawyer the second time around. Perhaps she had had enough of the alarms of a soldier's wife's life, and wanted comfort and security. And she was a widow, also for a second time. Cathcart wondered whether those slightly pert features had grown dull or coarse with age. He wondered whether, since she had chosen an attorney, she might have settled for a prosperous store-owner. Or a veteran returning from the Russian War. Cathcart wasn't to know what Tom had speculated, but the son of his old friend had been right. Seeing Marian again after he was invalided home would have been too painful. He might have called on her with the pretext of wanting to tell her about her husband's death and burial, but some scruple held him back. Even so, he couldn't help envisaging how fetching she would have looked in her widow's weeds.

Thoughts of Marian Ansell led Henry Cathcart, with a sort of inevitability, to thoughts of another attractive woman: Amelia Slater, the wife of Felix, the residentiary canon. He had first encountered Amelia in his own store, Cathcart's. She –

He was interrupted by the appearance of his wife's maid, who told him that Constance was awake and would welcome a visit from her husband.

'How is Mrs Cathcart, Grace?'

'She is not *too* bad this evening, Mr Cathcart, not too bad at all.'

Grace spoke reproachfully, as if Mrs Cathcart's condition, whether better or worse, was his fault. Wearily, Cathcart climbed the stairs. The upper part of his right leg was beginning to ache. As he approached his wife's chamber, the atmosphere seemed to grow more gloomy although the lights in the passage burned no less brightly. He tapped on the door and entered, without waiting for a response.

Constance Cathcart was sitting up in the single bed. She was reading. She looked up and smiled at her husband's arrival.

'How are you this evening, my dear?' he said.

'Oh, I am bearing up, Henry.'

She patted the bed as a sign that he should sit down at the end of it. He did so with care, knowing that he must avoid stretching the bedclothes tight over her slight body. Mrs Cathcart put down her reading matter. It was a religious pamphlet. Henry could see the name of some Reverend, followed by a string of letters, on the cover.

'It's a sharp evening,' he said.

'Yes, Grace said it was cold out.'

The room was hot and stuffy, not only because of the coal fire which radiated a steady heat from behind a screen – placed so that Constance should not be disturbed by the ministrations of the housemaid who tended it – but also because the windows were rarely opened even on the warmest days of summer. The advice of Constance's doctor was for fresh air to be admitted to the room on a regular basis so as get rid of any impurities but Constance felt the cold very easily, complained of being chilly most of the time.

'Henry, I have been thinking of something I should like to do when I am better.'

'Yes, my dear?'

'I have been reading in the papers about these Americans who have been preaching and singing in Liverpool and Edinburgh.'

'I have read about them as well. Moody and – and – somebody else.'

'Dwight Moody and Ira Sankey. Mr Moody preaches the Gospel while Mr Sankey plays the organ and sings hymns. He has a fine, strong voice. Together, they have brought many people to Christ. I would give anything to hear them preach and sing.'

'Liverpool and Edinburgh are a long way off, Constance.'

'But they are to visit London. The papers said so. London is not so far by train.'

'Well, we might consider the trip. As you say, when you are better, my dear.'

'Only *consider*.'

'We will go to London then, I promise, if this Mr Moody and Mr Sankey make an appearance there.'

Cathcart didn't remind his wife that she had barely stirred from her room for the last six months. This was a promise he was most unlikely to be required to keep. He glanced around. Apart from the narrow bed and table next to it with with a bible and a stack of tracts, the room – the sickroom – was sparsely furnished: an armchair, a washstand and a chest of drawers cluttered with little boxes and bottles, all containing the many medicines which Grace had charge of. Grace was a combination of nurse and lady's maid. She slept in a small room next door.

Constance was pleased with her husband's promise

and reached forward to pat his hand where it rested on the bed-cover. Under the white crown of a bed-cap, her large eyes fixed on his. They were the most notable feature of her pallid face. Great dark pools in which he had once taken pleasure in drowning himself.

They chatted a little more about the day. He told her that, by an extraordinary chance, he had met the son of an old friend from his campaigning days in the Crimea. He explained that Tom Ansell was in Salisbury on some legal mission. Talking about the encounter, Henry Cathcart grew lively, as Constance had been when she mentioned Moody and Sankey. She was quite interested and said, 'You must bring him here. I should like to meet this Mr Ansell if my health permits. I should like so much to glimpse someone who reminds you of your dead friend.' Then she seemed to grow tired and suppressed a yawn.

Henry stood up and leaned forward to kiss his wife on the forehead. As he was about to leave, Constance suddenly said, 'Mrs Slater called at the house yesterday. Grace told me she did. You didn't mention it to me when I saw you last evening.'

Henry Cathcart paused, his hand tight on the doorknob. He said, 'I didn't mention it because you were tired, Constance. In fact, you were almost asleep when I came up. I didn't want to bother you with unnecessary news.'

'But I always want to hear who has visited you, Henry. No news is unnecessary news. It is very tedious being isolated up here. Everyone forgets about you and the world goes on turning as if you weren't here at all. I wonder you did not mention Mrs Slater's visit.'

'She came to give me some advice on fabrics and colours,' he said. 'As she has done before. It is very useful having someone who is able to tell me about the latest fashions, useful for business.'

'But Mrs Slater is the wife of a cathedral canon, isn't

she?' said Constance. 'I don't know what she should have to do with the latest fashions.'

'Well, there it is,' said her husband. 'Goodnight, my dear.'

He closed the door quietly but firmly. In a moment Grace, always on the lookout for the welfare of her mistress, would be up to see to Constance, to prepare her for another restless night, to dose her with something or other, to turn out the gas lights, no doubt to say a final prayer.

Constance Cathcart's illness was a mystery to her husband, to her doctor and to herself as well. She'd never been strong even in the early days of their marriage but it was only in the last couple of years that she had suffered from bouts of debility and 'nerves' which were bad enough to keep her confined in her room for much of the time. And recently she had hardly emerged from there at all. The doctor was a frequent visitor, often spending longer in her room than her husband, and followed later in the day by his 'boy' bringing the prescribed medicines. Henry Cathcart left all these visits in the hands of Grace. He devoted himself to his shop business, which seemed to expand and prosper even while his wife languished and declined.

Tonight, as he made his way to his bedroom several doors away from that of his wife, his mind wasn't on Constance but on Amelia Slater. What he'd said to Constance was true enough, that he valued Mrs Slater's opinion on the latest styles and fabrics. He'd not given much thought to the idea that it was odd, or inappropriate, for the wife of a cathedral canon to have views on fashion. And, if he had, he'd probably have put it down to the fact that Amelia wasn't quite English, that she had grown up in foreign parts.

But the conversation had taken a quite different turn on her latest visit, the one that Constance had found out about from Grace. The two of them, Henry and Amelia, had been looking at a catalogue of mourning wear for women. Cathcart had been considering expanding the department in his store which sold mourning outfits. He had in mind a smaller version of Jay's or Peter Robinson's in London, a local place to which all the widows of Salisbury would naturally turn in their bereavement.

They were in the drawing room. The door was closed. Mrs Slater was an occasional visitor but she was not there often enough to excite comment from the servants. Or so Henry hoped. They were standing at a table on which the catalogue was open. On one page was an image of a child in mourning costume, on the other was small-waisted woman in a well-fitting black dress made of crape.

'I would like bombazine,' said Amelia. 'It wears better than crape.'

'Crape goes limp, true,' said Henry, 'but bombazine is more expensive.'

'Or pure silk, which is better than both,' said Amelia, smoothing her hands over her waist, which was not as slim as the woman's in the picture but still nicely shaped and graspable. Henry Cathcart was conscious of her closeness, of the movement of her hands.

'I hope it will be many years before you are faced with the choice of wearing pure silk or bombazine, Mrs Slater.'

'Every woman dreams of how she will look as a widow, Henry.'

Henry felt a little jolt at her use of his first name. He thought of his wife upstairs. It was the late afternoon, and the end of a miserable foggy day. Constance would be either resting or being attended to by Grace.

'It is not a happy dream though,' he said. 'To dream of being a widow, Amelia.'

'I think of it often,' she said, and touched him on the arm.

He didn't know what came over him, whether it was

her touch or her words, but he kissed her, at first on her cheek and then, as she did not pull back, on her lips. They stayed like that for an instant then drew apart. Amelia was slightly flushed. She smiled slightly and, more self-possessed than he was, said again, 'I think of it often, Henry. Of being a widow.'

Before Amelia Slater left, Henry gave her a little nosegay of flowers. He took them from a display in the drawing room. It was an impulsive gesture, one which he almost regretted afterwards. It was this nosegay which Amelia was wearing when she encountered Tom Ansell outside The Side of Beef later on that foggy evening. And it was inside the same hostelry that Cathcart had first seen Tom, the spit of his dead friend. Cathcart dined from time to time at The Side of Beef, when he tired of eating alone. On that evening he'd eaten little. Nor had he said a great deal, apart from quizzing the landlord. Nor did he sleep much that night, recalling Thomas Ansell, thinking of the teasing words of Amelia Slater.

Northwood House

The train journey from Salisbury to Downton was short, scarcely more than ten minutes. Tom Ansell spent the time turning over the question to which he would soon, presumably, get some sort of answer. Why did Percy Slater wish to see him? Tom would have been perfectly justified in turning down the request since the older brother was no longer a client of his firm. According to David Mackenzie, he'd had a falling-out with one of the other partners. Tom might have telegraphed to London for Mackenzie's opinion but he'd not have been certain of getting a reply by the time fixed for his meeting. Besides, Tom believed this was a matter where he could act without consulting his employer.

He wondered how Percy Slater had got to know of his visit to Salisbury. The obvious answer was through Walter Slater, whether the son had accidentally let something slip or had deliberately informed his father – though why he'd do that, Tom couldn't think. Tom was curious to meet this man who was apparently so different from his churchefied brother and son. The tone of the letter was civil enough if a bit peremptory. It didn't show any of the feebleness or decline which – according to his brother – Percy Slater was subject to.

The train chugged through the flatter landscape which lies to the south of Salisbury. An early sun had been swallowed up by clouds rolling in from the west. The train reached the small town of Downton a couple of minutes before it was scheduled to arrive. Tom got off, together with a trio of women who'd been doing some shopping in Salisbury. Shopping for drapery or clothes, he assumed, since their bags were marked *Cathcart's*. It was beginning to rain and the women made a show of opening their umbrellas.

On the stand outside the little station was a four-wheeled clarence with a bay horse in harness. The coachman nodded at Tom as a sign to approach. He was a slight man, hunching himself against the rain. He had a small, disagreeable face with a great dimple in his chin, as though someone had tried to bore a hole in it. He was wearing a billycock hat.

'Mr Ansell?'

'Yes. Mr Slater sent you?'

'Get in,' said the coachman, after a moment adding as an afterthought, 'sir.'

Tom climbed in and the carriage pulled away. They turned into a wide street and almost immediately had to halt because of a herd of cattle jostling in front of them, the animals under the control of a diminutive boy with a switch. They crossed a bridge over a river. Through the ill-fitting windows of the clarence, his nose was hit by the acrid smell of a tannery. The road began to climb slightly and the houses and cottages accompanying them petered out. Tom had no idea how far they were going. He looked out at the leafless trees which crowded the sides of the road. The window-glass was smeary with dirt and rain. The upholstery of the seats was frayed and the springs protruded so that it was difficult to find a clear patch to sit on. Whatever Percy Slater spent his money on, it wasn't to give himself a comfortable or striking means of conveyance.

After a time they began to pass a low wall on their left. Tom, by now in carping mood, noted that the wall was broken down in places. The carriage turned into an entrance and passed a single-storey lodge with blank windows and a corkscrew chimney. Though it was a cheerless morning there was no smoke coming from the chimney, no gatekeeper, no sign of life at all. Beyond the gate and on either side of the drive stretched acres of grass dotted with trees and bushes.

Tom wasn't aware they'd reached the main house until the carriage veered past its facade. He glimpsed a large covered porch, with steps and pillars. They rounded the corner and pulled up in a walled yard. The driver clambered down and stood by the coach door but didn't otherwise move. Tom opened the door himself and stood in the rain.

The driver was a head shorter than Tom. He jerked his dimpled chin in the direction of a side entrance.

'It's open. Just go inside and call. Nan'll hear you. She knows you're coming.'

Tom did as he was told while the coachman began to attend to the horse. As he'd said, the side-entrance was not locked. Tom stood in a flagstoned lobby. It struck colder and damper inside than out in the open. There was no one in the lobby. He felt slightly foolish and also irritated – after all, this visit to Northwood House was not being made at his suggestion. Perhaps he should demand to be taken back to Downton station, without troubling his host. He remembered that he hadn't thought to check the railway timetable for his return.

There was a touch at Tom's elbow. A woman was standing there. He hadn't heard her approach. She was old and tiny, all wrinkles. She was wearing a black shift-like dress, also old and creased. This was Nan, he supposed.

'I am here to call on Mr Slater.'

He had to repeat himself several times since she was hard of hearing. Eventually she said, 'Mr Slater is in the smoking room. This way.'

Her voice didn't rise much above a whisper. But she

moved decisively enough down the passageway which led from the lobby. They passed a kitchen and various store-rooms before going through the baize-covered door separating the servants' area of the house from the family rooms. On the other side of half-open doors Tom saw sheets draped over the furniture, swathed chandeliers, dust and decrepitude everywhere. What had David Mackenzie and Felix Slater said about Percy's wife, Elizabeth? That she spent her time in London. He wasn't surprised.

The door of the smoking room was ajar. Nan extended a twig-like arm as a gesture that Tom should go in. She didn't announce him but by this stage Tom wasn't expecting anything so elaborate. A man was sitting in a window-seat gazing out at the grounds, at the rain. He turned his head, reluctantly as it seemed, to look at Tom standing in the entrance to the room.

'You must be Mr Ansell,' he said, 'Well, you are welcome to Northwood.'

This was the most effusive greeting Tom had received so far this morning and he felt almost encouraged by it. Percy Slater detached himself from his place by the window. He picked up a walking stick which was resting against the cushioned seat, although Tom observed that as he made his way across the room he scarcely used it. It seemed to be more of a theatrical prop than a literal one.

The man in front of him didn't bear much resemblance to Felix, although there was the same set to the jaw. But this Slater was fuller, much fuller in his body, and more slack in the face. Where the Canon had a pale complexion, his brother was ruddy with a nose covered in broken veins. Not quite so tall as the churchman either, Tom thought, and without a trace of the bird-like characteristics of the other.

'It is a long time since I have met a representative of Scott, Lye & Mackenzie,' said Percy. 'Indeed, when they handled my affairs there was no Mackenzie in the picture. Drink, Mr Ansell?'

Tom had already caught the whiff of alcohol and seen a bottle of sherry together with some drinking glasses and a pile of magazines on a table near the window. 'Thank you,' he said, following a dictum of Mackenzie's that one should always respond positively to the hospitality of a client – or even a non-client, in this case. Leaning his stick against a convenient chair, Percy Slater poured Tom a glass and refilled his own.

Tom glanced around. The room was sparsely furnished apart from a glass-fronted cabinet containing a couple of shotguns and, opposite, a single wall which was covered in sporting prints. The prints looked fresh but everything else, the drapes, the chairs, the occasional tables, had a worn and battered appearance. Percy held out the glass of sherry and Tom went across to take it. He noticed that the magazines piled on the table by the window were a mixture of *Bell's Life* and *Sporting Life*. Percy saw where he was looking.

'You a betting man, Mr Ansell?'

'Not really, no.'

'Wise probably. I was sitting in that window-seat just now and watching the progress of two drops of rain down one of the panes. A fitful, zigzag progress but always down, down, down. They will reach the bottom eventually like all of us. I thinks to myself, if there was someone here with me, I'd lay a bet on which drop would reach the bottom of the pane first. I suppose you wouldn't care to take that bet, Mr Ansell?'

There was an almost wistful quality to the question as if he already knew what the answer would be. Tom shook his head. There were some invitations from a client, or a non-client, which you were not compelled to accept. Percy Slater settled himself into a battered armchair near a coal fire which was giving off more smoke than warmth.

He indicated that Tom should sit in an equally battered armchair on the other side of the fireplace. Slater kept his walking stick cradled between his legs.

'Yes, wise probably,' he repeated, 'wise not to be a betting man. Wise to husband your resources. Between ourselves, that was the reason that I . . . dispensed with the services of your firm. It was Alexander Lye who was responsible for my decision – is Lye still alive, by the way?'

'Though Mr Lye is getting on now, he still comes into the office,' said Tom, not elaborating on how Mr Lye turned up only to sign the papers pushed in front of him.

'Lye – always thought that was an excellent name for a man of law. Anyway, Alexander Lye made some comment to me about my betting habits. I couldn't be doing with it. I already had enough of that sort of thing from my father. Lye's words were to do with a loss which I incurred at Dwyer's. You wouldn't remember Dwyer's, Mr Ansell. Sold cigars and cheroots in St Martin's Lane but their real business was taking bets. Well, they took too much on the favourite for the Chester Cup, back in '51. A favourite isn't the favourite for nothing. The results used to come in from Chester quite late in the day so they had the leisure of a whole night to strip the place of all the movables and by the morning there was nothing left but the shell of a shop. The shell of a shop, I say.'

Percy Slater seemed half amused, half angry at the memory as he shifted in his chair. His walking stick waggled in sympathy.

'Took twenty-five thousand with them. Not all mine, of course. Fact, I got off quite lightly. But it was enough to cause Mr Alexander Lye to make a few unwelcome remarks about my betting habits – as if it was *my* fault that Dwyer's was a bunch of rogues! I did not choose to be lectured at and took my business elsewhere.'

'I'm sorry to hear it, Mr Slater,' said Tom.

'No, you're not,' said Percy sharply. 'I wasn't what you would call one of their respectable clients. No doubt they were glad to see the back of me, as you would be if this were happening today.'

His eyes narrowed as he said this and he fixed Tom with an expression that challenged the younger man to deny what he'd just said. The time for niceties seemed to be over.

'Why did you ask to see me, Mr Slater?'

'I understand that my brother Felix, the good and respectable Canon, is employing your services at the moment. What for?'

'Mr Slater, even if you were still a client of ours, I could hardly pass on that information without your brother's consent. And as you say, you ceased to be represented by my firm many years ago.'

'This is a family matter, Mr Ansell. It is not up to Felix to do exactly as he pleases.'

Percy Slater was getting agitated. He spilled some of the drink from his glass. Tom wondered about the time of the return train from Downton.

'Not so long ago I sent some stuff to my brother,' said Percy, 'old papers and the like, relating to our father George and to the history of this place. I thought he would interested in them, being a *historical* sort of person. He has had them long enough. I would like those items back.'

'I am sorry, Mr Slater, I should not even be discussing this. But – supposing such articles to exist – then I am informed that they were freely *given* to the Canon. And, furthermore, that there is a letter written by you to that effect.'

'Dammit, sir!' Percy became more agitated. There was no more drink to spill from his glass but his stick clattered to the floor. 'All this legal supposing and 'furthermores'. I can't stand it. *Furthermore,* Mr Ansell, I have no recollection of writing the letter you're talking about. Have you, by chance, seen any of these items?'

'I may have done.'

'But none of them are currently in your possession?'

'No. They are in the hands of Canon Slater.'

Tom felt uncomfortable. It wasn't merely the other man's display of anger, and the odd question as to whether he actually had any of them in his possession. There was also the fact that he himself had not seen the letter which Felix Slater had referred to, the one from Percy surrendering the papers to him. He had taken the Canon's explanation on trust. But he should have asked to see the letter, all the same. Tom made an attempt to be conciliatory.

'I am sure the material is in good hands, sir.'

'Oh, you are, are you, sir? Good hands?'

Tom tried again. He said, 'It is not as if these things have passed out of the family. There is Walter to consider as well.'

'Walter?'

'Your son, Mr Slater. The son who lodges with your brother.'

'Yes, there is always my son, isn't there?' said Percy. He spoke wearily. Plainly there wasn't much of a bond between them. Perhaps Percy considered his son to have abandoned or betrayed him by going into the Church. This seemed to be borne out by what Percy said next, 'He has turned Walter's head, has Felix.'

Tom made to get to his feet. He didn't see much point in prolonging the encounter. Mr Percy Slater didn't have to be humoured. He wasn't a client. Tom went to stand by the window, down which the raindrops were still trickling. The view beyond was one of neglect: a weed-strewn terrace, flower beds where either nothing grew or there was a profusion of unkempt plants. The parkland beyond was dotted with clumps of trees. He heard a sound behind him and turned. Percy was waving him back to his chair.

'Felix would like to have me declared incapable, no

doubt,' Percy continued. 'He would like to have me admitted to some sanatorium or asylum so that *his* Walter can come early into possession of Northwood.'

'I do not know, Mr Slater, but I don't think so.'

'Do not be taken in by that holy act, Mr Ansell. Word to the wise. I know my brother and you do not. Have you met his wife, my sister-in-law?'

'Yes, I have.'

'What impression did you form of her?'

'I – I really don't know.'

'Come on, Mr Ansell. Amelia, my sister-in-law, is an attractive woman, is she not? You can at least say that without breaking any confidences or compromising your client's privileges.'

'Yes, she is attractive,' said Tom uneasily.

'Good. We can agree on that. Can we also agree that there is, shall we say, an apparent mismatch between my brother and his attractive wife? He's a dry old stick, after all, while she is neither so dry nor so old.'

This was pretty well exactly how things had struck Tom. He shrugged and said, 'Who can tell with a marriage?'

Someone had made that remark to him recently. He remembered that it was David Mackenzie. Tom's comment might have been rhetorical but it seemed to please Percy Slater.

'True, who can tell with a marriage?' he repeated. 'The story of my brother's marriage is an odd one. You know it?'

'No,' said Tom. 'Or rather all I know is that Mrs Slater grew up in Florence and that her father was English.'

'While her mother was Italian. My brother Felix met the family when he was on a tour of Italian cities – Pisa, Florence, Lucca, Siena and the rest. He was looking at the antiquities no doubt. He was lodging with Amelia's parents in Florence. They had a single daughter, Amelia. She must have been smitten for she came over to England not so long after his return. Her own parents were dead by this time and perhaps she had no one else to turn to apart from the nice clergyman who had spoken fondly to her.'

Percy paused to take a swig from his glass. Tom noticed the edge of bitterness in his words. Perhaps he was envious of his brother, of the fact that an attractive young woman had come in search of Felix from overseas. This seemed to be confirmed by what he said next.

'Amelia threw herself on his mercy. She was a single lady in a country that was foreign to her. In due course, and after the necessary arrangements, they were married and they lived happily ever after.'

'This was a long time ago?'

'Oh, many years. Twenty or more. But Amelia has worn very well, hasn't she, while my brother has simply grown more dry and stick-like. So we've had a happy ending, no?'

'It sounds like it.'

'We'll see,' said Slater.

There was a finality to his words. Tom stood up again, explaining that he had a train to catch and an appointment in Salisbury. This was a stretch, but at the moment he simply wanted to get out of Northwood House. Percy Slater pulled out a pocket watch.

'There is no great hurry, sir. No train is due for, oh – an hour and a half at least. At two thirty to be precise. I know the train times backward. I enjoy reading my Bradshaw just as I enjoy reading the racing form. An hour and a half, I say. Plenty of time for Fawkes to take you back to Downton.'

'Fawkes?'

'My coachman. And valet. And factotum. I inherited him from my father just as I inherited Nan, who is my cook and housekeeper. Her name is Ann but I called her Nan with my childish tongue and it has stuck ever since. Fawkes is simply Fawkes, and there is no more to be said. My wife Elizabeth would like me to take on more servants but I tell her that since she is never here and I live essentially in two rooms out of the many in Northwood, Fawkes and Nan can cater to my needs quite adequately. She cooks well, if she has to. You will not stay for luncheon?'

Tom's attention was caught by this reference to the man's wife but he turned down the invitation. Turned it down with a touch of regret as well as relief. He sensed Percy Slater's loneliness. His host waved at him in dismissal.

'Very well, Mr Ansell. Go outside and find Nan or Fawkes. He will convey you back to the station. I would not have you *stuck* here.'

Slater half rose from his seat and gave Tom a perfunctory handshake. Since Tom had rejected his invitation to stay, he seemed to have lost interest in his guest.

Tom retraced his steps from the smoking room and into the servants' quarter of the house. He passed Nan. She was carrying a tray containing a plate of cheese and cold meats together with a wine bottle, presumably the lunch that he would have shared with Percy. The old, black-garbed servant could scarcely bring herself to acknowledge him with a nod. Fawkes, coachman, valet and factotum to Percy Slater, was sitting at the end of the kitchen table. He was tearing at a chunk of bread, the final item on his plate. Tom stood in the doorway.

'I need to return to the station now, Fawkes. Mr Slater said you would take me.'

Fawkes looked up at Tom. He finished chewing the bread, taking his time. Then he took a swig from a tankard beside the plate. Only after that did he get to his feet, wiping at his mouth and dimpled chin. He was still wearing the little felt hat.

'Wait in here,' he said, 'sir.'

Tom stood in the lobby while Fawkes went off to fetch the carriage. The rain dribbled down the window-panes in the door. Tom thought he'd seen Fawkes before somewhere, then reflected that he had – scarcely more than a couple of hours ago at Downton station. He thought of Percy Slater's ridiculous invitation to a wager. There was something old-fashioned about it, the kind of absurd bet that two aristocrats would have indulged in during an earlier, looser age. In fact, Percy Slater himself – drinking, idling, gaming, casting his eye over the sporting press – had an eighteenth-century flavour to him. Tom recalled that David Mackenzie had described Percy's father, George, in similar terms, an impression which was confirmed by the little he'd glimpsed of old Slater's memoirs.

Tom continued to think about the Slater family as he was being conveyed to the station by Fawkes. There was a contrast between the two brothers in almost every way: the one lean and austere, the other slack and self-indulgent; Felix's religious vocation, Percy's boredom; the Canon's passion for old artefacts and reverence for history, his older brother's devotion to gambling and the turf. It would have been interesting to have met Elizabeth and compared her to the enigmatic Amelia, to have seen whether the difference in the brothers was reflected in their wives.

Slater's carriage trundled into Downton, over the bridge and past the tannery. Fawkes drew up on the stand outside the railway station. Tom got out and looked up to thank Fawkes in the driving seat. The coachman raised a forefinger and seemed to sight down it at Tom as if his finger was the barrel of a gun. 'You have a care,' he said, 'sir.'

This might have been intended as a kindly parting remark but, coupled with the gun-sighting gesture and spoken without warmth, it sounded more like a warning. As he sat in the little waiting room (there was more than half an hour before his train was due), Tom did his best to shrug off the visit to Northwood House.

He hadn't disliked Percy Slater, in an odd way he'd felt almost sorry for the fellow, but he had not cared for the cold, neglected mansion or the two retainers. Tom still couldn't understand exactly why Percy had wanted to see him, unless he was meant to act as an intermediary between the brothers. The other puzzle was how to square the description which Felix had given of his brother with the reality. Percy might be idle and all the rest of it, but he was no fool, nor did he appear to be suffering any kind of physical decline. Tom wondered whether Felix Slater assumed that his brother must be in that condition, either because they never saw each other or because he required him to be paying some sort of price for his way of life. Perhaps that was what lay behind Percy's claim that his brother would like to have him committed to a sanatorium or an asylum. Where had he heard, and recently, someone say that people aren't always what they seem? Ah yes, it was Amelia Slater, the Canon's wife. They'd been talking about the Tichborne Claimant. Well, neither of the brothers was a fraudster but nor were they quite how they'd been painted by others.

These considerations occupied Tom during his wait at Downton station and on the short journey back to Salisbury. It was a miserable autumn afternoon, with the rain turning into a drizzly mist and then into fog, so that Tom walked back to The Side of Beef through streets where the passers-by were swathed from each other. Not yet familiar with the town, he took a couple of wrong turnings. Getting back to the inn, and even seeing Jenkins's face once more, was a relief.

The Church Porch

Walter Slater, assistant curate at St Luke's, entered the cathedral close with a spring in his step. It was out of place, perhaps, to be feeling buoyant after a funeral but he had observed this response in himself and others on several occasions, once the dear departed was tucked into the earth. It was as if the weight of the earth being piled on the coffin was simultaneously being taken off the shoulders of the mourners. Even on such a foggy, dreary late afternoon, there had been a perceptible lightening of everyone's spirits.

Walter had been helping to officiate at the service for the widow of one of the previous incumbents of the church. Mrs Parsons – that really was her name or rather the name of her late husband – had been one of the oldest and most devoted members of the St Luke's congregation. She fell asleep during the sermons and lessons, and could scarcely stand up for the hymn-singing let alone kneel down to pray, but still she came to the church as regular as clock-work on Sundays.

Mrs Parsons had always been escorted to the St Luke's services by her granddaughter, Alice Nugent. Miss Nugent did not fall asleep during the sermons or lessons but listened to them most attentively so that she could discuss their salient points afterwards with Walter.

Pleasant thoughts of Miss Nugent were filling Walter's head and he did not notice the figure emerging through the gloom on his left hand. The figure was carrying a walking stick and heading to cut him off before he could turn down West Walk. Walter was surprised, more than surprised, to see that it was his father. Percy rarely left Northwood House or Downton to come to Salisbury.

'What are you doing here, father?'

'That's a fine welcome, Walter. I have as much right to walk round the close as anyone.'

'Are you come to see Uncle Felix?''

'I am come to see you.'

Even in the half-light Walter noticed a strange, hectic cast to Percy's face. He made to resume his walk, assuming his father would accompany him. But Percy held up his stick.

'I don't want to go to Venn House. I don't want to see Felix. But I need to speak to you, Walter. Is there somewhere private we can go?'

Somewhere private? It was an odd request, thought Walter. 'We could find a corner of the cathedral,' he said. 'Evensong will be over and there will be few people inside.'

'Yes, a dark corner of the cathedral,' said his father, seeming pleased with the suggestion.

The two men began to move towards the shrouded shape of the great church. The nearest entrance was via the porch in the north-west corner. As Walter and Percy drew closer, they observed two more individuals standing in the porch, two clerics to judge by their clothes.

Percy again held up his walking stick as a sign that they should halt. He'd recognized his brother as one of the clergymen in the porch. Walter too had seen his uncle. The other man, he knew, was Canon Eric Selby.

The Canons hadn't noticed the approach of father and son, partly because of the gloom of the afternoon but more because they were embroiled in a fierce argument. Even from the distance of many yards, the sound of raised voices could be heard.

Walter and his father might have done one of two

things. They might have continued in the direction they were going and alerted the others to their presence. Or they might have tactfully turned on their heels and left the clerics to carry on their quarrel.

Instead, Percy gestured to Walter that they should get closer to one side of the porch, so that they'd be hidden from the view of the others but within earshot. Walter was at first baffled, then uncomfortable with the idea of eavesdropping on his uncle, but he'd found by experience that it was easier to humour his father than make a fuss. The two stood, wrapped in fog, and listened to the argument.

Canon Selby was saying, 'It is your fault, Slater, that Andrew North has disappeared. If you hadn't encouraged him to go poking about where he shouldn't, he'd still be doing an honest day's work here.'

'The sexton's disappearance is nothing to do with me,' said Slater in his dry, precise tones.

'He visited Venn House often enough.'

'I employed him to dig a grave in the garden. A grave for my wife's pug, I hasten to add, Selby, before your imagination runs away with you.'

'But you have a gardener – Eaves, isn't he called? Couldn't he have done the job?'

'Good grief, are all my domestic arrangements to be subject to your scrutiny?'

'I am only concerned with the missing sexton, Slater.'

'I tell you again, I have no idea where he is. I pray that no harm has come to the man.'

'You put ideas into North's head,' said Selby. 'He became obsessed with uncovering the past, with digging things up. A sexton's job is to bury, not to dig up. It is dangerous to uncover the past.'

'You refer to the poor man as if he was no more. If you know anything, Canon Selby, then you should inform the authorities, go to the police house.'

'He has been gone these several weeks. His sister is

convinced that – that a great harm has befallen him. It is a reasonable assumption.'

'Well, we must pray that he returns safe and sound. If you will excuse me, Selby, I must leave you. It is getting colder by the minute. And we have a guest for supper.'

From their position by the side of the porch Walter and Percy Slater saw Felix stride off into the mist. He was followed a short time later by Canon Selby.

'No love lost between those two, eh?' said Percy.

'Canon Selby has never liked Uncle Felix,' said Walter. 'I believe that a long time ago he wanted to live in Venn House but Uncle got his hands on it first.'

'This time they were talking about something different, the sexton who has gone missing.'

'You know about that?' said Walter, looking towards his father in surprise.

'I read the *Gazette*. I like to keep up with the news from the big city.'

Father and son entered the cathedral through the porch door. Inside there was a sepulchral gloom. The scattered lamps and candles still burning after Evensong only emphasized the great pools of shadow which filled the place and seemed to flow down from the remote ceiling. A few shapes moved through the darkness, intent on their own business.

Walter steered his father towards the left. They sat down on a stone ledge that ran along the wall.

'Is this private enough for you, Father? We are not likely to be disturbed here.'

Percy Slater sat with his walking stick between his knees.

'I had a visitor today,' he said. 'A young man from a law firm in London.'

Sitting beside him, Walter started. He said, 'I know the man, if it is Mr Ansell you mean. He has been visiting Uncle Felix.'

'And I know that too,' said Percy. 'But Walter, there is a

great deal that *you* do not know. And I feel that it is time you were told.'

'I'm all ears, Father,' said Walter with mock eagerness.

'You may not be after you've heard what I've got to say.'

Percy Slater's warning was accurate enough. If anybody had been observing the door which led out of the north-west porch some half an hour later, he or she would have seen a white-faced figure wrenching it open and almost running through it. It was Walter Slater, no longer moving with a confident bounce but heading into the evening fog with no clear destination, with no idea at all of where he was going in fact. Still sitting on the stone ledge in the side aisle was Percy Slater, tapping on the floor with the tip of his walking stick. It was too dark inside to read the expression on his face.

The Study

For a second time, Tom Ansell arrived at the gate in the fine brick wall which fronted Venn House. He peered at the plaque which announced the house. He reached out. The latch felt clammy, even through his gloved hand. In any case the gate was already unfastened. It was as well that he'd first visited the Slaters' place by day, since he doubted he'd have been able to find it on so dark and fog-shrouded a night. Not that he was the only person out and about. A couple of shapes had passed him in West Walk, moving rapidly in the opposite direction and veering to avoid him in the murk.

He walked up the garden path between the yew trees. A diffuse light came from two or three windows at the front of the house. If he'd thought about it, it might have struck him as odd that the curtains or shutters hadn't been closed against such a dank, inhospitable evening. But the first suspicion that something was wrong didn't occur to Tom until he reached the front door to Venn House. The door, like the gate, wasn't shut fast but was slightly ajar. He pushed the door open. Gas lights were burning in the lobby and in the hall and passage which stretched ahead to the interior of the house.

Tom paused in the lobby. Tendrils of mist floated in behind him. He closed the door. He listened. There was no sound. The distant smell of supper reminded him that he was hungry.

'Hello,' he said, tentatively, and then repeated himself more loudly.

No reply.

Where were the housemaids? Or his hosts, Canon and Mrs Slater? Or their nephew, Walter?

He walked into the hall and paused again, uncertain. There was no noise except for the methodical ticking of the longcase clock. He glanced to his left. The table in the dining room was laid for a meal. It was a relief to see that he was expected. Tom examined the ornamental ferns in the cabinet against the wall. He waited for someone, for anyone, to appear and acknowledge his presence. Someone to welcome him, take his coat, and usher him into the warmth of the house.

But no one came.

The last time he'd been here the talk was of various break-ins at the houses in the cathedral close. Was that what had happened tonight? Was there a thief still in the house? If there was, then Tom had alerted him by calling out.

He looked around for something with which to defend himself. He went back into the lobby. There were walking sticks and umbrellas in a cast-iron stand. He chose a walking stick with a thick, bulbous handle. Holding it at the tapered end, and feeling faintly foolish, he made his way back down the passage. The smell of roasting meat from the kitchen area grew stronger but there was no clatter of pans. Tom moved quietly, senses alert, the walking stick held up like a club. He half expected to see a dark figure dart out of one of the rooms. Unless the thief – or thieves – had already made their escape. Those two shapes he'd glimpsed in the West Walk? Except, thinking back now, he had the impression that the shapes had been female.

He reached the door of Slater's study. Unlike the other doors, this one was closed. Tom tapped on it, without result. By this stage he did not expect an answer. Some instinct told him that, if the house was occupied, then the intruder should be found in here. He twisted the knob and felt the door give a fraction. Not locked. Without giving himself time to hesitate, Tom swept the door open and almost leapt into the room, holding the walking stick high above his head and with his nerves so on edge that he would have brought it down on the skull of anyone standing in his path.

But the Canon's study was as empty as everywhere else in Venn House. It lay in darkness apart from a gas lamp burning on the nearest wall, the one on which were displayed those dark and violent pictures. Underneath them was the old chest which contained the memoirs of old George Slater and other papers. Which *had* contained them. The chest was open and its lid flung back against the wall. There was nothing remaining inside it. Felix Slater might have emptied it of its contents, in preparation for handing to Tom the Salisbury manuscript.

But Tom Ansell did not think Felix had emptied the chest. Something smelled wrong.

He cast his eyes round the study. The glass in the display cases containing what Canon Slater had called his 'old artefacts' glinted in the light from the single gas lamp. The shadows deepened on the far side of the room where large windows gave on to the foggy darkness of the garden and river. For the first time Tom's attention was caught by the fact that the curtains had not been drawn in here either. The surface of Slater's desk looked untidy and now Tom observed books and paper on the floor around the desk. Not just that. There was a strange item which Tom couldn't identify in the centre of the desk, a kind of large ball or orb with a handle sticking up from it.

He moved closer to the desk, his heart thudding away. When he saw what the ball was, his gorge rose and he turned away, feeling sick and breathless.

He took several deep breaths and steeled himself to

examine the sight more closely. Felix Slater was sitting at his desk. His head was slumped forward and resting among the pens and ink-holders so that the only part of him visible from a distance was the bare crown of his scalp, like a giant billiard ball.

Tom moved nearer still. In order to see the handle-like object which protruded from the back of Slater's neck, he had to bend forward. Canon Slater had been killed with a flint spear-head, perhaps one of those in the display cases. It had been driven forcefully into the nape of his neck. Blood had flowed down on either side of his head and formed a dark pool on the surface of the desk. His hands were splayed out on either side, as if he were prostrating himself in prayer. Tom was thankful he couldn't see the Canon's expression since the man was face downwards. He must have been taken by surprise, sitting at his desk. Whoever killed him had taken the contents of the chest.

Removing his gloves and transferring the walking stick to his left hand, Tom reached out to touch the polished stone implement before thinking better of it. He should not tamper with the scene of a violent crime. Alarm suddenly replaced queasiness as he realized that whoever had done away with Felix Slater might still be inside the house. Inside the house or outside it and nearby. He was conscious of the darkness and fog pressing against the thin glass panes behind his back. Where was Mrs Slater? Or Walter? The household servants? The dreadful idea that there might have been more killing, that there were other bodies in Venn House apart from Felix's, seized hold of Tom.

He darted back to the centre of the study, his eyes scanning the ranks of books, the pictures whose violence had been mirrored in reality, the glass cases containing what now appeared to him to be so many implements for murder. There was nothing for him here. Tom was almost out of the door, on his way to summon help, when he froze.

There were footsteps coming down the hall towards the rear of the house. Feet moving hesitantly, as if their owner didn't know his way – or didn't want to be heard.

Tom was still holding the walking stick which he'd taken from the lobby. He gripped the narrow end, holding it up like a golf club. By the single light on the wall, he glimpsed his white knuckles. By now he had blood on the back of his hands too, Felix Slater's blood.

A shadow fell across the doorway. A man whom Tom had never seen in his life planted himself on the threshold of the study. He cast his eyes up and down Tom, hardly seeming to register the stick which the other had raised to head height. He looked in the direction of the desk across which Canon Slater lay slumped. The man, who was thick-set and wearing a rain-cape, nodded his head as if in answer to an unspoken question and folded his arms across his chest. He stood blocking the way out. There was someone else standing to one side of the doorway, Tom could see another shadow.

For a time neither man moved, then the individual in the doorway said, 'Put that stick down, there's a good fellow.'

Tom was ushered out of Canon Slater's study by Inspector Foster and Constable Chesney, although at that stage he knew neither of the policemen by name. Foster had relieved him of the walking stick, deftly slipping it from Tom's hand and grasping it in his own.

They walked down the hall towards the lobby. In the lobby and around the covered porch, there was a cluster of people. Tom recognized all of them, even in his confused and distracted state. It was as if almost everyone he'd met since arriving in Salisbury two evenings ago had been gathered together to witness his capture and disgrace.

There was Amelia Slater and her nephew Walter,

together with several of the household servants, including the girl whom Slater had rebuked for having a crooked collar and Eaves the gardener. All of these might have been expected to be on the scene. But there were others whose presence was more surprising and whom Tom noted, half unawares. There was Canon Eric Selby, wearing his shovel-hat. There was Percy Slater, his ruddy face looking pale in the swirling mist. Near Percy was the odd coachman-cum-factotum, whose name Tom couldn't recall in the stress of the moment. And, oddest of all, there was Henry Cathcart, the old friend to Tom's father. What was *he* doing here?

No one spoke a word. They either looked at the ground or fastened their eyes on him in a manner that was both frightened and accusatory, so that Tom wanted to say, 'I didn't do this thing! It is a terrible mistake.'

But no one spoke and so he kept silent too.

Even though they were now outside, in the cold and misty night, Tom felt intolerably hot. His face was burning. He was suddenly conscious of the bloodstains on his hands and wanted to hide his hands in his pockets but he kept them stiff by his sides. He felt a nudge at his back.

'That way, if you please, sir. Down the path.'

Tom walked between the dripping yew trees. He was in the lead, with Inspector Foster and Constable Chesney behind him. Tom heard an outbreak of comment and whispers from the onlookers. He might have made a break for it, might have run through the gate, but the thought was dismissed as soon as it occurred. Just as well since there was a second constable stationed outside the gate of Venn House.

They moved off together, a foursome, going up West Walk. Foster walked at a steady pace beside Tom with the two constables in close attendance. He was still holding the walking stick. Tom had no idea where they were going or, rather, he struggled to suppress the idea which he did have.

'No carriage, I'm afraid, sir,' said Inspector Foster, 'but it's not too far and if we walk briskly we will soon forget about the cold. Follow my lead now, Mr Ansell, we don't want you going astray on a nasty night like this.'

The person who had murdered Canon Felix Slater watched as Tom Ansell walked down the garden path with the three policemen following at his heels, the Inspector grasping a walking stick. The young man looked stunned, as well he might. By the light of the lobby, the murderer had observed Tom's bloody hands held rigidly at his sides. Caught red-handed, the murderer thought. The poor fellow must have come too close to Felix's body and accidentally got his hands dirty. Almost involuntarily, the murderer whispered Tom's name after he'd passed by and added for good measure, 'He did it!'

Despite these signs of guilt, Felix Slater's killer did not believe that Ansell would be detained long by the Salisbury constabulary. It would soon emerge that the lawyer had arrived at Venn House after the killing. The Inspector would question him and let him go.

But that would all take time. Time which the murderer could put to good use.

Fisherton Gaol

'Well, sir, I hope you slept well.'

'I did not sleep well, Inspector. In fact, I am not sure I slept at all.'

'I told Griffiths to take good care of you, Mr Ansell. This is the best room in his establishment.'

For the hundredth time since he'd arrived at the county gaol in Fisherton Street, Tom glanced around his 'room'. It was starkly furnished, with a narrow bed, a wash-stand, a simple table and chair. In an unsuccessful attempt to soften the hard edges of the accommodation, there was a strip of thin carpet running down the centre of the room and a framed sampler on the wall. The sampler read *Bless this House*. As Inspector Foster and Griffiths the gaoler had made clear the previous evening, this was a room reserved for the most privileged of guests. It was right next to the gaoler's own lodgings and quite separate from the other prisoners. But, whatever you did to it, the place was still a cell. There was a single vertical bar in the centre of the glazed but uncurtained window, and a lock on the door which could only be opened from the outside.

'I've no complaints about Mr Griffiths,' said Tom. 'He and his wife have been all consideration. His wife brought me a cooked breakfast this morning. But it is a question of what you are used to, Inspector Foster.'

'As I said last night, sir, this is only temporary, very temporary. But you have to look at matters from my point of view. Is there any more coffee in that pot, by the way?'

Tom gestured that he should help himself to the coffee, which had been provided by Griffiths' bustling wife at the same time as she ushered the Inspector into Tom's cell. The Inspector himself had fetched another chair from outside and the two men were sitting on opposite sides of the little table. They might have been in a coffee house, apart from the hardness of the chairs and the absence of newspapers and the general grimness of Tom's situation.

Inspector Foster was a stolid man with the look of a gentleman farmer. He had the long side-whiskers known as dundrearies. He seemed fresh and alert while Tom felt crumpled and stale. He'd slept in his shirt and had only a perfunctory wash that morning. He'd been too angry and distressed to eat the previous evening and left untouched the portion of supper which Mrs Griffiths had provided, to her disappointment. Rather than eating, Tom found himself mentally circling round and round those few minutes which covered his arrival at Venn House, his discovery of Felix Slater's body in the study, the appearance of Inspector Foster on the threshold of the room, and that terrible walk out of the house and through the mist-laden streets of Salisbury. He was thankful that there weren't many people about and that, as the policeman had said, it was no great distance to the gaol. Tom remembered, fondly, his room at The Side of Beef and even the unctuous presence of Jenkins the landlord.

Tom might have been reassured by Foster's saying that his incarceration (although the policeman had used the word 'stay') in Fisherton was only temporary and that everything would soon be cleared up. But when Foster left, and Mrs Griffiths had been in to collect the untouched plate of supper, and Tom had done his best to wash the last traces of Felix Slater's blood from his hands, he lapsed into despondency. The room was still a cell, with its white-washed walls, its barred window and locked door, and he was still a prisoner. He thought of Mr Mackenzie – how would his employer react to a representative of Scott, Lye & Mackenzie spending a period of time, however short, in a county gaol? He thought of his mother.

And he thought of Helen Scott. This was the one bright spot. Not simply the thought of Helen, but the idea that she alone out of everyone he knew might be amused, even excited, by the fact that he'd spent time in chokey.

'You have to look at matters from my point of view,' repeated Inspector Foster, on this bright November morning. Tom could see the blue sky out of the window.

'I'm trying to, Inspector, but somehow my own point of view keeps getting in the way.'

'I was summoned to Venn House yesterday evening by Constable Chesney. He had been patrolling the close. We've had some robberies there recently, you know. He was alerted by the women of the house, by Mrs Slater and one of the maids.'

Tom recalled the two figures rushing past him up West Walk. Was that Amelia and one of the housemaids?

'The women are beside themselves and hardly coherent,' continued Foster, falling into the present tense to recreate the experience more vividly. 'It takes some time for Chesney to get an inkling of what has occurred. Well, sir, Constable Chesney then gives me the alert and by the time I arrive in the close there are other people – there are friends and neighbours – on the scene. They tell me that, to the best of their knowledge, there is no one left inside the house and that everyone has rushed out in terror. Notwithstanding, I approach the house cautiously. I can tell they fear that the murderer of the Canon might still be in the vicinity.'

'I thought the same thing,' said Tom. 'Not that the Canon had been murdered but that there was an intruder in the place. That's why I armed myself with one of the Canon's walking sticks.'

'Be that as it may, Mr Ansell, be that as it may. I walk into the hallway of Venn House and I know – I know – by instinct that there *is* someone inside. And my instinct is correct for now I am able to hear movements from Canon Slater's study.'

Tom said nothing. Confirming his presence again merely seemed to point the finger of blame more firmly. Besides, he did not want to interrupt Foster's narrative. The Inspector was obviously enjoying himself.

'I walk up to the door and I see – what do I see?'

'You see me.'

'I see you, Mr Ansell. And I see moreover that you are wielding a club or a stick. I see by the light from the room and the passageway that there is blood on the back of your raised hands. I stand in the doorway and wait for you to explain yourself but you say nothing. What am I to think?'

'I don't know. No, I do know, Inspector. But it's not what you think. I'm no murderer. You've just said there have been a spate of robberies in the close. Isn't it possible that the murderer of Canon Slater was the robber?'

'I've been a policeman for many years, Mr Ansell, and in my experience your thief and your murderer are like fish and fowl, quite different beasts.'

'For heaven's sake, what reason would I have to kill Canon Slater! He was a client of my firm's. I came to Venn House because I had been invited to supper by the Slaters. I had business there. I had a legal document to deliver to him.'

Tom patted his inside pocket. The letter which was there, the letter formalizing the arrangements over the Salisbury manuscript, gave a reassuring rustle. It was a reminder of Tom's real work, of his real life. But useless now, since the manuscript had disappeared and Slater was dead.

'Just so, sir,' said Inspector Foster. 'I have established these facts since. *Since*, I say. Now I understand that the maid discovered the dead body of Canon Slater and went crying to her mistress and that, together with others in the house, they ran off in all directions looking for help. I know that there were friends and family of the Canon quite close by. But at the time, I was aware of none of this. There are still a few unexplained details. I haven't yet spoken to Mrs Slater.'

Yes, Tom thought, there were a few unexplained details. Like the fact that friends and family of the Canon were close by the scene of his murder. There were Walter Slater and Amelia, their presence easily explicable. But what were Selby and Cathcart and Percy, Slater's brother, doing on the spot? If he were the Inspector, he'd be aiming his enquiries in that direction. He opened his mouth to suggest something of the sort, then thought better of it. Let the police do their own work.

But there was still a small puzzle which he wanted to put to Foster.

'You knew my name, though. You called me by it as we were leaving Venn House. Yet we'd never met before, Inspector.'

'Someone said it, I think, as we were walking by. "Mr Ansell, he did it!" They said it in a whisper, in surprise.'

'Who said those words?' said Tom, more than curious. He remembered hearing the whispering behind him as he walked down the path but had been too distracted to distinguish any words. For some reason the remark – not the giving of his name but the 'he did it!' part – caused the hairs on the back of his neck to prickle.

'I don't know.'

'A man or a woman, was it?'

'A man,' said Inspector Foster. 'But it might have been a woman, now I come to think of it. A voice coming out of the dark and the mist.'

'It's an odd thing to say.'

Inspector Foster shrugged. 'I do not see why. The person, whoever it was, was merely saying what others might have been thinking. From first impressions, you understand. You were in the study where Canon Slater was found dead, you were standing there wielding a stick, you had bloodied hands.'

Tom shivered and looked down at the backs of his hands. He thought he detected a speck of blood on one, still. There was a sort of sense to what the Inspector said, though no one had seen him, Tom, in the Canon's study apart from Foster. Or had they? Had someone glimpsed him through the uncurtained windows? If so that person might justifiably have assumed Tom was the killer. Unless that very person was the killer.

'Anyway,' continued the Inspector, 'I was not paying close attention to people's words, sir. My concern was to get you away from the vicinity of Venn House before anyone could come to harm.'

'I suppose you thought I was going to take a swing at somebody with that walking stick.'

'I was just as concerned that harm might come to *you*, Mr Ansell. It seemed best to get you to a place of safety.'

'To the county gaol,' said Tom, gazing round the room once more.

'This is a secure place out of the public eye. Best to keep you in here while tempers got cooler and minds got clearer and I could ask a few questions.'

'So I can go now?'

'In a few hours you can go. There are a handful of queries I have to make and then you can return to your room at The Side of Beef.'

'I do not think I'll be staying in Salisbury, Inspector. My business here is terminated with the death of my client.'

'But I must request you prolong your visit by two or three days.'

'Why?'

'Because although my immediate enquiries concerning you, Mr Ansell, may be nearly finished, there is no saying whether you won't be called to contribute to the investigation in future. If so, it would be handier to have you on the spot rather than sending to London.'

Foster looked genial enough as he said these words but he tugged at his side-whiskers as if in emphasis. Tom sensed that he might be prevented if he tried to leave the city. And, in fairness, he might have some work to do in attending to Felix Slater's estate.

'Did you find any documents in the study, Inspector?' he said. 'Or, to be more exact, did you see a volume rather like a diary with a hasp and a lock?'

'I don't think so. Why, is it important?'

'Not especially,' said Tom.

Foster looked as though he didn't quite believe Tom but he said nothing. Instead he drained his coffee cup and stood up. He stretched out his hand and shook Tom's, saying, 'An hour or two, sir, and we shall have you out of here.' The gesture and words were reassuring.

But once Foster had left the prison apartment, Tom couldn't be certain whether or not he had turned the key after him. If he had, it had been done in a discreet fashion. Tom was reluctant to try the door in case it was locked, which would indicate that the policeman still regarded him as a prisoner. Nevertheless, he did get up and test the door. It was locked. He sat down again and picked up his cup. The coffee was cold. He tried to steer his mind on a different course, away from himself, now that the first shock of Slater's murder and his own incarceration had worn off.

Tom started to wonder why Slater had been killed. Was it connected to the disappearance of the Salisbury manuscript? Or something different altogether? More important, who had done it? Who had felt sufficient coldness or fury towards Felix Slater to take a flint spear-head from the display case and plunge it into the nape of the man's neck? The Canon had surely been taken off his guard. That suggested that whoever was in the study with him was someone he knew, someone he was not expecting to harm him. Therefore, not a stranger or an outsider, which tended to confirm what the Inspector believed: that this was not the individual who'd been breaking into other houses in the close. So, a friend or a fellow cleric, a member of the family, a servant?

Tom ran his mind back over the group gathered in and around the entrance to Venn House. Leaving aside Bessie, the maid with the crooked collar, and Eaves the gardener, together with some other servants he didn't know, there were Felix's wife and his nephew and his brother, as well as Canon Eric Selby and the store-owner Henry Cathcart.

He remembered what Inspector Foster had said, the words whispered into the air, the words which had enabled Foster to call Tom by name. 'Mr Ansell, he did it!'

Tom had shivered when Foster said that. Why? Some sixth sense? He was seized by the feeling that it was the murderer himself who'd spoken, in an attempt perhaps to imprint his guilt on the minds of those standing around. The murderer himself. Or the murderer *herself* since the Inspector hadn't even been sure whether the voice was male or female.

The only woman in question, Amelia Slater, she had quite a deep voice. And her behaviour on their only two previous encounters was definitely odd. That teasing meeting near The Side of Beef and then her plea to him outside the gate of Venn House next morning that he should say nothing of that first, chance event, her pretence the next day that they'd never met at all. She'd pretended well, better than he managed to pretend. Had Amelia Slater got something to hide? Was she afraid of her husband or was she merely tired of him? Was she conducting some kind of liaison with another man? But it was a leap from that to murder.

Out of the various men who'd been on the scene, he had little knowledge of their relations with Canon Slater. True,

Percy hadn't cared for his clerical brother, had told Tom not to be taken in by his 'holy act'. And he'd demanded that Tom get back the papers which had been passed over to Felix. And now the papers, their father's memoirs, were gone. Did Percy travel to Salisbury to recover them in person? Had he confronted his brother and killed him following an argument?

Too many questions and absolutely no answers.

There was Walter, Felix's nephew. The curate seemed on friendly enough terms with his uncle, the two had talked easily at the lunch table a couple of days before. There could be no motive there, surely?

Tom was aware that Eric Selby did not like his fellow Canon. He recalled the look of distaste which crossed Selby's face when he was asking directions to Venn House. Walter Slater had said that there was a coolness between the two men, although without enlarging on the reason. He found it hard to believe that old Selby could have plunged a flint into the bare neck of a fellow churchman. Yet, though it was hard to believe Selby was capable of such a deed, it was strangely easy to visualize him doing it.

As to the next man on the scene, Henry Cathcart, Tom didn't know what to think. His impression was of a kindly man who, at their only meeting, had been deeply affected by memories of Tom's father. Yet this prosperous storekeeper and citizen of the town had once been a soldier. He must be familiar with killing at first hand. But what was his link, if any, to Felix Slater?

And then Tom recalled that there had been another individual standing near the porch at Venn House as he was being so ignominiously escorted away by the police. A fifth man. It was Fawkes, the servant to Percy Slater. There was something unsettling about Fawkes. 'You have a care, sir,' he'd said to Tom at Downton station the previous day, as if issuing a warning. But he knew nothing further about the fellow. Fawkes was on the spot because he was with Percy Slater, his master from Northwood House.

Tom spent an hour or more on speculations about who might have murdered Felix Slater, and why. He got nowhere. His mind wandered in other directions. He suddenly remembered the old woman who'd been travelling in his compartment on the Basingstoke train. She'd said something, wished him 'Good luck' perhaps. He searched for other portents to this ill-fated trip. He wondered when the moment of his release would arrive. If Foster required him to stay in Salisbury, would the policeman take the easiest course and keep him clapped up in Fisherton Gaol as a potential suspect? The next time Griffiths or the gaoler's wife appeared, Tom would ask for pen and paper and write to David Mackenzie with a full account of what had happened. An intervention by Mackenzie might have some effect on the provincial police. Yet Foster hadn't seemed the kind of person to be swayed like that.

Tom's thoughts were interrupted by the sound of the door opening. Mrs Griffiths stood there.

'A visitor, Mr Ansell,' she said.

Tom resigned himself to another interview with Foster.

'A lady, it is,' added the gaoler's wife, glancing to one side before moving away from the cell door.

And he thought, for no good reason, that the visitor was that new widow, Mrs Felix Slater.

But when the person who'd been standing next to Mrs Griffiths appeared in the doorway, he gasped. A younger woman stood there.

It was Helen.

Canon Selby's House

It was easily enough explained, once Tom had got over his first surprise at seeing Helen – his surprise and delight. For it was Canon Eric Selby who had, indirectly, caused Helen to come down from London on a morning train. He was aware that Tom worked for a London firm but hadn't known that the firm was called Scott, Lye & Mackenzie. Many years ago, as Selby hinted to Tom on their cab ride from Salisbury station, he had considered the law as a career before deciding to go into the Church. He was a friend of Alfred Scott, Helen's father, a good enough friend to have become godfather to Helen. Indeed, she had spent some of her childhood time in Salisbury.

When Canon Selby discovered that Tom was an employee of his late friend's firm, and apparently distressed at the young man's predicament, he had telegraphed to his only contact, the formidable Mrs Scott, although without being aware of Helen Scott's friendship with Tom.

Tom didn't know – nor did he spend time trying to find out in the first confusion of his meeting with Helen – exactly how events had unfolded when the telegram had arrived at the house in Athelstan Road, Highbury. Whether Helen had informed her mother that she intended to travel down to Salisbury by the first available train, whether she had left with Mrs Scott's blessing, whether she had slipped out of the house undetected by her mother (a more romantic idea, surely), none of this mattered much.

What was important was that Helen was here with him, in Fisherton Gaol.

She sat, upright, slim, bright-eyed and fresh-faced, on the chair which had so recently been occupied by the solid form of Inspector Foster. Mrs Griffiths produced further supplies of coffee as well as some home-made cakes and generally fussed over their lady visitor. A red-letter day for her, it must be, with a lady and a gentleman from London brought together in the prime apartment of Fisherton Gaol.

Once they'd got the preliminaries out of the way, the circumstances under which Helen had discovered what was happening to Tom and her speedy journey from Waterloo to Salisbury, Helen gazed appreciatively round the sparsely furnished room with its whitewashed walls. Her gaze suggested she was visiting a grand house, even a palace. As Tom had half foreseen, she seemed excited by his incarceration. Not, he hoped, the fact that he was languishing in prison under temporary suspicion of a murder but that he was here with her and she was here with him, and wasn't this all a new experience, a dramatic experience for them both. She said as much.

'Except that you can leave at any time,' he said.

'Oh, Tom, don't,' she said, reaching out to grasp his hand.

'I don't know why I'm here.'

'They say that a man was murdered.'

'There was a murder but I had nothing to do with it.'

'Dear Tom, of course you didn't. But you must tell me all about it. Tell me now.'

So Tom described to Helen almost everything which had happened since his arrival nearly three days ago in Salisbury. He talked about his meetings with Felix Slater and the discussion of the Salisbury manuscript. He described his trip to see Percy Slater. He recounted the events of the previous evening at Venn House. How the place had seemed to be eerily empty. How he'd suspected that something was wrong because of the open front door, how he'd discovered Slater's body, how a policeman called Foster had materialized at the entrance to the study and taken him for a murderer and how it was all an absurd mistake and Foster knew this and promised Tom he'd soon be released from this gaol, to which he'd been taken for his own safety rather than because Foster genuinely suspected him of a crime.

He left out a few details. He didn't mention, for example, his conversation with Henry Cathcart and the man's connection with his father. This didn't seem relevant to the death of Canon Slater. Nor did he say much about Amelia Slater, beyond a reference or two. This was probably relevant but Tom was oddly reluctant to talk of the Canon's wife, now a widow.

He was gratified when Helen made appropriate responses. She sighed and looked aghast at frequent points in his story. She wiped away what looked like a tear. She rose from her hard prison chair a couple of times and came round the table to hug him as he sat on his hard prison chair. Tom began to see that there were advantages to being an innocent victim.

Things were taking a turn for the better. And they took a better turn still when Inspector Foster came back to announce that Tom was now free to leave the prison. The Inspector looked admiringly at Helen, who swiftly explained why she was there. Tom asked the policeman whether he'd made any progress.

'You asked before, Mr Ansell, about some papers belonging to Canon Slater. I have now established that they were kept in a chest in his study. The chest is empty. What did it contain, sir? Your attitude earlier today suggested to me that you knew something about it.'

'There was a memoir written by George Slater, Felix's father,' said Tom, 'and I think there were other items in the chest, loose papers maybe. I had only a brief glimpse of the memoir-book. It is of interest to the Slaters but I don't believe it would mean much to anyone outside the family.'

Tom didn't add that the book was the principal reason why he'd come to Salisbury. But he couldn't resist saying, 'If things have been taken, doesn't that show the murderer is the same thief who's been working in other houses?'

'Possibly, possibly. Though there was no sign the house had been broken into.'

'Anyway, I haven't got any papers. You are welcome to search my room at The Side of Beef,' said Tom, reflecting that Foster had probably done just that already.

'I have been taking formal testimony from some of the household, Mr Ansell,' said Foster, not responding directly to Tom's invitation. 'You were seen making your way to Venn House by Mrs Slater and by Bessie the maid *after* they had found the body of Canon Slater. They passed you in West Walk going in the opposite direction.'

'A pity they did not say so earlier.'

'They were understandably too distressed to speak last night. You should be grateful to Mrs Slater for positively identifying you, for all that it was dark and foggy. Besides, it is always possible that a murderer may return to the scene of his crime. I am giving you the benefit of the doubt, Mr Ansell. And, as you said, you had no motive to kill Canon Slater. Nevertheless I must still request you remain in Salisbury for a few days more.'

'How is Mrs Slater?' said Tom, feeling guilty that he'd criticized her. It was her witness that she'd seen him yesterday evening going *towards* (rather than away from) the house that had apparently exonerated him. That, and the absence of any motive.

'Under the circumstances, she is quite composed,' said Foster. 'Now I suggest that you leave with this delightful young lady. Where are you lodging, Miss Scott?'

'With my godfather, Canon Selby. I have already left my luggage there. He told me where Tom was, ah, staying. I too will remain in Salisbury for a time. I have pleasant memories of the town, Inspector, from when I was young. It must be nice to live here.'

This was the right remark to make. Foster tugged at his side-whiskers and beamed. He ushered them through the door. Tom and Helen were seen out of Fisherton Gaol by Mr and Mrs Griffiths as if they'd been regular visitors. The only thing missing was the hope that they might return again soon.

The day was clear and bright. They were not far from the town centre and The Side of Beef. Tom's first wish was to go back to his hotel room and change his shirt. He might have spent only a short time in the best apartment of Fisherton Gaol but he still felt the prison taint clinging to him.

So, while Helen sat in the lobby, Tom quickly washed and changed upstairs. Jenkins seemed surprised to see the couple. The landlord knew what had happened – hardly surprising, everyone in the town must know of the brutal murder of one of the residentiary canons – but he avoided referring to it directly, instead wringing his hands and saying, 'Terrible, sir, terrible, that event in the close last night,' while casting sidelong glances at Helen. Jenkins was presumably aware of the fact that Tom had spent the night elsewhere (and in the county gaol) but, if so, was too tactful to mention it.

Before they left The Side of Beef to go to Canon Selby's house, Tom told Jenkins that he'd be requiring the room for a few days longer. He was going to add that he was staying in Salisbury to assist the police with their enquiries – which was true, more or less – but decided against giving the landlord that pleasure.

Eric Selby did not live in the cathedral close but nearby in New Street. It was the afternoon and the town was bustling. Helen was pleased to be back in a town she remembered from childhood. She was pleased to be with Tom. She was pleased with life because she was hearing about a murder at a safe remove. She looped her arm through his, and he kissed her cheek, glad and grateful that she'd left London to see him in gaol.

'Riding to the rescue like a knight on a white charger,' she said. 'Only that is the wrong way round, since it should be you, Thomas Ansell, who comes to my rescue.'

'We'll see,' he said, more cheerful than he'd been for several days.

'Tom, I have an idea.'

'Anything.'

'Inspector Foster did not seem very glad to be releasing you.'

'Perhaps no policeman likes seeing a man go from gaol before he's caught the real culprit. Or perhaps he doesn't think I am innocent of Canon Slater's murder and it's more that he doesn't have enough evidence to hold me any longer.'

'Well, in that case,' said Helen, 'we should be helping him to track down the person who actually did it. That would put you absolutely in the clear and we would also be bringing an evildoer to justice.'

'Helen, you are not reading – or writing – one of your sensation novels now. This is real life. A man has been killed. A household has been turned upside down. I've spent my first and, I hope, last night incarcerated in a gaol. I'm not sure I want to get any more involved.'

'You are involved, Tom, like it or not. Canon Slater was a client of your firm – *our* firm, I should say, since my father was one of the partners. And the book you came to Salisbury to collect has been stolen, most likely by the same person who murdered the unfortunate Canon. So I say you are involved in this affair.'

'This isn't like spying on your neighbours,' said Tom, thinking of Helen's speculations about the woman who lived across the road on Athelstan Avenue, and trying to shift the argument in a different direction. 'There are dangers here.'

'Telling me there are dangers will have the opposite effect to the one you intend. And I don't *spy*, Mr Ansell, I observe and draw conclusions.'

'Or make up stories.'

Helen uncoupled her arm from Tom's.

'If that's how you feel, I begin to regret that I came racing down to Salisbury.'

'No, no, it's a good idea in principle, Helen. But I'm not sure how we can proceed in practice with tracking down a murderer or helping the police.'

'We can begin by talking to my uncle, Canon Eric Selby. He has lived here forever and he knows what goes on in the town.'

'Uncle? I thought he was your godfather.'

'He is my godfather. But he told me to call him Uncle when I was little and asked him one day how I should address him. He said he hadn't any nieces while for my part I hadn't any uncles, so it all seemed to fit. He is quite avuncular, don't you think?'

The avuncular Canon Selby seemed genuinely pleased to see Tom Ansell in company with his god-daughter. He commented on the coincidence that he should have been friends with a partner in the firm of which Tom was now a member, and the greater coincidence that Tom should be 'paying his addresses' (as he put it) to Helen. He passed lightly over the circumstances under which he'd last seen Tom as he was being escorted away from Venn House, and said, 'I don't expect you slept much last night, Tom, if I may call you that now. I know that I did not. It is dreadful to think of what happened to Felix. It is frightening to think there is a madman on the loose.'

'A madman?'

'Why yes. Who but a madman could have done this?'

The three of them – Eric Selby, Tom and Helen – were sitting in the drawing room of the Canon's trim house in New Street. There was a Mrs Selby, a small woman who had made a single appearance to say hello and then disappeared with a bird-like rapidity. A maid served them tea. Talk of a madman went oddly with the tea. Tom hadn't eaten since breakfast at Fisherton Gaol and his appetite wasn't really satisfied by sandwiches (cucumber or anchovy) and little cakes. He promised himself a good meal that evening at The Side of Beef. Now Helen, in between delicate bites at her cucumber sandwich, started to quiz her godfather about Felix Slater.

'I am sorry for his death although it is no secret that I did not see eye to eye with Felix,' said Selby. 'In fact, we had an argument of sorts on the day of his death.'

Helen asked him why they'd argued. It was the sort of question which Tom could not have put, or at least not so directly.

'Lay people often assume that men of the cloth are cut from the same cloth,' said Selby, 'but we are not. We're as different as men are from one another in any other walk of life, and although we may be obliged to love our neighbours, there is no verse in the Bible that says we have to get on with them. Felix seemed to be a spare, dry man. But like a lot of men with that appearance, he had passions. One of them was for digging into the past, for disturbing the dust of centuries. There is nothing wrong with that although I fear he sometimes neglected his duties in pursuit of his passion, his obsession I might say. Felix's example and encouragement had turned the mind of one of the cathedral sextons, so that the poor fellow spent every spare moment looking for buried treasure or relics.'

Tom recalled the newspaper article which Henry

Cathcart had shown him. About a sexton who'd disappeared. Canon Selby himself had been quoted in the article.

'Now this man North has vanished, gone goodness knows where. And I held Felix partly to blame, not for the disappearance of course but for the mania which seized him beforehand. The fellow was a good and honest worker until Canon Slater infected him with his notions of disinterring the past. I am afraid that I taxed Felix with this very subject on the day he died. Of course, I must now regret that I spoke so directly to him.'

He didn't sound very regretful. Tom wondered whether there had been more to the argument than Eric Selby was claiming. He said, 'Canon Selby, do you remember yesterday evening when Inspector Foster arrived at Venn House and I was being put under – when I was being escorted away by him, do you remember hearing someone whisper my name and then "he did it"?'

Selby brushed some cake crumbs off his front. He thought before speaking. 'I might have heard that.'

'Was it a man or a woman?'

'I'm not sure. Did I even hear those words, now I come to think about it? Or was it just an idea hanging in the air, as it were? It did look bad for you, Tom.'

Tom didn't need any reminding of how bad it looked.

'So you have no idea who might have committed this murder, sir?' he said.

'Even if I did, I would not say. It is not for me to go passing on suspicions, supposing I have any. But I have no idea. A madman, it must have been. Or a burglar surprised in the act and resorting to violence.'

And that seemed to be the general conclusion in the town: that Canon Felix Slater had been killed by an intruder, who was either bent on robbery or, more simply, a homicidal maniac. Certainly, this was the version reported on the front page of the *Gazette,* which Tom saw on his return to the hotel. Under the headline in large type *Dreadful Murder in Cathedral Close* was a story which was long on speculation but short on fact. There was a description of how the body of the distinguished cleric had been found by the housemaid and the alarm raised by Mrs Amelia Slater. Death had been produced by a single blow to the back of the neck. The weapon was a flint spear-head, ironically (the newspaper's word) one of the primitive implements which Canon Slater collected as a pastime. Then there was a paragraph about a burglar or a madman or a combination of the two, necessarily brief because it was all speculation. There was a reference to the other, unexplained robberies in the close. Apart from Mrs Slater, the only people named in the piece were Walter, nephew to the deceased and assistant curate at St Luke's, and Percy Slater, brother of Felix and owner of the Slater family home at Downton. Of the others on the scene, including Tom, there was no mention.

Inspector Foster was quoted as claiming that the Salisbury constabulary were actively searching for the intruder, for 'the person or persons who have done this terrible deed', as if the police could or should be doing anything else. Foster was a shrewd, experienced man. Tom had learned to respect him after a couple of encounters. Tom recalled that Foster had been sceptical about the idea of an intruder. There'd been no sign of a break-in at Venn House, he said, chiming with Tom's conclusion that Slater was attacked by someone he knew. But, for the newspaper, had Foster deliberately spread the story of an outsider so as to lull the fears of the real killer? A killer who came from within Slater's own circle of family or neighbours?

Tom left Helen at her godfather's house. Selby had pressed him to stay for supper but Tom was tired and, besides, he sensed that the Canon was looking forward to having his god-daughter to himself. He and Helen were to meet the next morning. So Tom enjoyed a good supper at The Side of Beef and retired early to his room. After the excitements of the previous day and the restless night he'd spent at Fisherton Gaol, he slept well, surprisingly.

As for the others involved in this case, those in Felix Slater's circle of family and acquaintances, how did they sleep on this second night after the murder?

Henry Cathcart, as usual, went to visit Constance in her sick room during the evening. He might have been distracted but she scarcely noticed. She had spent much of the day poring over the news of the terrible murder with Grace, who read and reread the front page of the *Gazette* to her invalid patient. Constance's normally pallid complexion was flushed, more from the excitement of the murder than the stuffiness of the room. Her large dark eyes were wider than ever. She was too caught up in the drama and outrage over the death of a cleric to make any disparaging comment about Amelia Slater. She was more lively than Henry had seen her for a long time.

Cathcart did not reveal to his wife that he had actually been on the scene when the police arrived at Venn House. If that news had come to light – it might have done, you never knew, Salisbury was not a large town and gossip was rife – then he was ready with a story. A story which was half true: that he had gone to the Canon's residence on the night of the murder so as to return to Amelia Slater some designs and catalogues which they had been discussing. But the subject didn't come up. Constance was more concerned about their safety, or rather *her* safety, with a madman on the loose. Henry did his best to reassure her.

He would personally make sure the doors and windows in the house were fast before going to bed. And Grace slept in the next room, didn't she?

Then he withdrew to his own bedroom. He could not help thinking of Felix Slater's death nor of the fact that Amelia was now a widow. By coincidence, the pair of them had been looking at pictures of mourning outfits very recently. What was it Amelia had said? (But he didn't have to struggle to remember, her words were imprinted on his brain.) *Every woman dreams of how she will look as a widow, Henry.* How had Henry Cathcart interpreted Amelia's remark? Had he asked himself whether Amelia meant a 'dream'in the sense of an idle fantasy or speculation, or a 'dream' in the sense of longing?

Amelia Slater really was dreaming. She saw her husband slumped forward over his desk, the spear-head protruding from the back of his neck. She groaned and moved uneasily in her sleep. The doctor had given her something to soothe her nerves and something else to help her sleep. But she could not escape her dreams, which swirled with light and ghastly colour. In the dream, her husband's study was illuminated not by gaslight but by the unforgiving glare of day. The blood from his wound flowed across the surface of the desk, soaking into papers and blotters, running down the sides and pooling on the carpet. Trying to keep clear of the blood, Amelia reached out to finger the sharp flint. Her fingers touched the makeshift weapon. For an instant, she was undecided whether to pluck it out or even to push it further in so as to seal up the wound. But the flint-head was fixed deep, the damage was already done.

There was no going back. And there was no more time either. The blood was lapping at her shoes and then at the hem of her skirt. She was wearing a dark fabric – crape, bombazine, she couldn't remember – and the blood did not show at first. But she felt the added weight of it dragging her down as if she was wading in water. She must escape before she was pulled under by the tide of blood. She turned towards the door. Before she could reach it, the door opened. She wanted to shout out a warning to whoever was coming in, that they should beware of what they might see, beware of the taint of blood. But it was too late. A figure stood just outside the doorway. To her surprise she recognized the outline of Walter. She could not make out his expression, could not see whether he was angry or sad or happy at the scene in front of him.

There were other individuals in Venn House too. The maids Bessie and Mary, for example, and Eaves the gardener (although he did not sleep inside the house but in a little store-house where his tools and other gardening equipment were kept). But as for how they slept and whether they suffered from bad dreams, as for what they thought and felt about the murder of their employer, Canon Felix Slater, none of these things is really any of our concern. They were only servants, after all.

Walter Slater was sleeping as uneasily as Amelia. He was not in his comfortable bedroom in Venn House. He had not slept there on the night of the murder and he was not sleeping there now. Instead, Walter had retreated to his church, St Luke's. He was in the bell-tower. He had made himself a kind of nest out of old vestments and pieces of curtain and he was curled up in a corner of the ringing room, which was reached by a spiral staircase running up from the corner of the transept. It was a comfortless spot. The loops of the bell-ropes dangled down like so many nooses. The room was cold despite having only slit windows. But it was a place where Walter Slater knew he should not be disturbed at least until the Sunday morning. There was a creaking door at the bottom of the spiral stairs, so Walter would be alerted if anyone was coming up to the ringing room. No one knew he was sleeping in the church. Walter had managed to carry on with his usual duties during the day following the murder of Felix, and anyone observing his battered, unshaven look and his crumpled clothes would have attributed them to the shock of what had occurred at Venn House. Walter might have been capable of attending to his work during the day but he could not face sleeping under the dead man's roof.

Percy Slater had now returned to Northwood House. He had remained in Salisbury on the night of his brother's murder, staying in Venn House. Percy had stayed not so much because there was anything he could do – had he been so minded – in terms of comforting the widow or consoling others in the household or helping in any investigation, but because the fog was too thick to allow him and his driver Fawkes to get back to Downton. Now he was back and sitting in the smoking room where he had greeted Tom Ansell a couple of days earlier. It was nearly midnight, the fireplace was full of ash, the bottle in front of him all but empty, and the house cold and clammy. The rest of his establishment – if it wasn't absurd to call two people, Fawkes and Nan, an establishment – had long since retired for the night. Percy knew that he too would have to stir himself sooner or later and plod along the flagged passageway to his room. But he did not shift from the armchair by the dead fire.

Instead, he thought of his late brother. He had never liked Felix, regarding him as a sanctimonious hypocrite. He asked himself what he felt now that the holy Felix was no more. The answer was, he did not feel a great deal.

There was no point in pretending to a piety that didn't exist in him. He was, however, sorry about Walter. Not so much that Walter should have, like him, been so violently bereaved, but that he had gone to see the young man on the afternoon before Felix's death. The visit had been the result of an impulse, a disastrous impulse. He recalled the look of shock on Walter's face after they'd had their quiet chat in the gloom of the cathedral, the way Walter had gripped his knee as if he could not believe the other's words, the way that Walter had sprung to his feet and rushed off into the gloom of the aisle. Percy hadn't seen him again, or rather he had had only a brief glimpse of him when they were all crowding about the porch of Venn House, watching the lawyer fellow being taken away by the police. Walter had not looked well but sick and pale. Hardly surprising. Percy supposed that none of them looked any different.

Percy wondered about the circumstances leading up to Felix's murder. He thought about his own involvement. He reached for the bottle and poured out the last bitter dregs.

Canon Eric Selby was the final person to have been present at the entrance to Venn House when Tom Ansell had been brought out like a man under arrest. Selby recalled the words which Tom claimed to have heard. The exclamation, surely involuntary, 'He did it!' Selby might even have uttered those words himself. It was, as he'd said, an idea which was in the air. Seeing a man with bloody hands escorted out of a house where a murder had occurred, anyone might have reached the same conclusion.

But none of this affected Eric Selby's comfort. He had dined and drunk well in the company of his god-daughter or 'niece' Helen (and his wife, of course). They had talked about Helen's father, Alfred, and recalled childhood holidays in Salisbury. When Helen had gone to bed, Eric Selby stayed up, musing on the death of Felix Slater. A terrible event, needless to say. But he could not find it in himself to summon up much grief for the man.

Mrs Banks's House

It was Helen who came up with the idea that she and Tom should go off and see Mrs Banks, the sister of Andrew North, the sexton. From their conversation with Eric Selby, it was evident that North's strange behaviour before his disappearance was being laid at Felix Slater's door. There'd also been Selby's mention of buried treasure and relics. This had gripped Helen's imagination. She referred to it several times as the couple were walking through the close in search of the row of artisan cottages which lay tucked away out of sight of the cathedral and the grander houses. Tom thought of reminding Helen, again, that she wasn't composing a melodramatic novel but in fact the words had pricked his curiosity too.

They found North's dwelling in the middle of a neatly kept terrace. Here lived some of those who did manual work, both menial and skilled, in the cathedral and its precincts. Mrs Banks was a widowed woman who kept house for her brother and who, according to Selby, eked out a meagre income by taking in needlework. She had the look of a withered apple, red and wrinkled in the face. Once Helen had explained that they'd been directed there by Canon Selby, Mrs Banks's attitude towards these well-dressed visitors shifted from wariness to welcome.

She invited them into a tiny parlour which doubled as a dining room. She apologized for the absence of a fire but it was early in the day and she was not expecting visitors. Tom and Helen were directed to sit on what was obviously her best bit of furniture, an old chaise, while Mrs Banks prepared the tea. Tom looked round. The room was spotless, the dining table polished like a mirror. By the sofa there were a few books on a shelf, more volumes than the Bible and a prayer book. Tom picked one up. He was slightly surprised to see that it was a history of Salisbury. Surprised that a cathedral sexton should possess such a thing. Yet who was to say that a man who earned his living with his hands shouldn't also use his head? The book certainly belonged to the man for he had written his name in full – Andrew Herbert North – on the fly-leaf. The handwriting was neat and fluent, not that of an uneducated individual.

Hearing Mrs Banks returning, Tom quickly put the book back on the shelf. The sexton's sister came into the parlour with a tray, on which was a teapot and china cups. She served Tom and Helen and perched on a wooden chair facing them. Tom explained that he was acting for the lawyers who had represented Canon Felix Slater. He implied that he was looking into the Canon's affairs, which was true enough, and that they'd been told that Mrs Banks might be able to help them, particularly over the link between her brother and the Canon. Mrs Banks's face wrinkled still further at the mention of Felix Slater – by now Tom was getting used to this response to Slater's name – but she just about managed to express regret and horror over the terrible murder.

'None of us have slept safe and sound in our beds since it happened,' she said. 'Mind you, I haven't slept sound neither after my brother Andrew went off. It is over four weeks since he left here saying he was going for a walk, and he has never come back and I do not know that he ever will come back. I missed my husband Banks when he was gone but, truth be told, I miss my brother more.'

She was close to tears. Helen got up and put her arm round the older woman and produced a handkerchief.

Mrs Banks put aside her teacup on the dining table. She dabbed at her eyes and then admired the stitching on the handkerchief while she composed herself and Helen sat down again next to Tom.

'Thank you, my dear,' she said, and then to Tom, 'Forgive me, sir, but sometimes it is all too much to bear. Inspector Foster has been kind in his official way and says that he is still making enquiries about my brother, but in the next breath he will say that Andrew is a grown man and he cannot have come to much harm and no one bears a grudge against him and he is no one's enemy and he will surely turn up one day and walk through that door there.'

She glanced towards the tiny hallway beyond the parlour, as if she expected her brother to appear at that instant. Once Mrs Banks had overcome her initial reserve, she started talking in long breathless stretches. Tom thought it was a relief for her to have sympathetic listeners.

'Your brother was not in any kind of trouble?' said Helen.

'No, miss, he is an honest workman. Everyone speaks well of him.'

Tom said, 'We have heard that Mr North used to do some work for Canon Slater.'

'The Canon employed him to do odd jobs. Mrs Slater's dog died not very long ago and Andrew dug a grave for him in the garden. But he did other things as well.'

'Other things?'

'Canon Slater is – no, he was, I should say the Canon *was* – a man who went digging and delving in the country around here. He was looking for old arty – arty somethings.'

'Artefacts,' prompted Tom.

'That's the word. Being a gentleman, Canon Slater didn't do much of the digging and delving himself but got my brother to do it instead.'

'What did they find?' said Helen. 'They must have found things.'

'It didn't look like much to me, miss, but then I expect the Canon took the best pieces for himself.'

'So you saw items which your brother dug up,' said Tom. 'Maybe he showed them to you.'

'I remember an evening, last spring it would have been, when Andrew came in like a blast of cold air, all high-coloured in the face and excited. He and Canon Slater had been out somewhere beyond the city and they had uncovered . . .'

Mrs Banks hesitated. Helen, with her cup lifted halfway to her lips, smiled in encouragement. 'Please tell us, Mrs Banks.'

'. . . an old grave or tomb, Andrew said. It seems awful to go disturbing people who'd been minding their own business underground for hundreds of years, but my brother said they weren't people with flesh and feelings but no more than a pile of old bones and anyway he was used to dealing with dead bodies, wasn't he? They didn't mean much to him. Canon Slater would say a quick prayer over them and the two of them never carried anybody's bones off but allowed the people to go on resting in peace, so it was all right.'

'On this particular evening you said your brother showed you something?' said Tom when Mrs Banks paused for breath.

'It was a bracelet which he said was gold. It might have been, I don't know, Mr Ansell. To me, it looked like a circle of muddy yellow, tarnished and dented. But Andrew said that when it was cleaned up, it would fetch a few quid.'

Mrs Banks's free hand flew to her mouth, as if she'd said more than she intended. She added quickly, 'I do not mean my brother was after money. It was more that he was trying to show me that he wasn't wasting his time. In fact, it was the excitement of finding buried things which he really liked.'

Tom recalled the passion with which Canon Slater had spoken about the subject. The effect on Andrew North had obviously gone deep, becoming an obsession and even the 'infection' mentioned by Selby. But he trusted Mrs Banks's view of her brother even if it was biased. There were simpler ways of making money than fossicking around old tomb sites with the distant expectation of coming across brooches and rings. Those who did such things must be motivated more by the excitement of the hunt rather than by any idea of profit.

'Did your brother sell the bracelet?' he said.

Mrs Banks answered more confidently. 'I don't believe so. It is probably still up in his room. I have not been to Andrew's room since he – since he left – except to dust it and sweep it and air it. I would not dream of disturbing his things. He would be angry when he comes back.'

Once again, she looked towards the little hall with a forlorn expression.

'Before Andrew . . . disappeared . . . did he give any indication of what he was doing?' said Helen. 'Still searching for hidden things, buried things?'

'I dare say, miss. But if he was, he had stopped telling me about it. He knew I didn't approve for all that Canon Slater said it was all right. Andrew turned a bit peculiar in the summer. He went off for long walks in the evening, after he'd done a full day's work. He wouldn't tell me where he was going but I think he was up to his old tricks because his clothes were sometimes dusty or muddy afterwards. He tried to pass it off as dirt from his ordinary work, but I knew better. The clothes had a fusty smell, not like you get from fresh, honest-turned soil. And *he* smelled of drink sometimes.'

'Perhaps he was out getting oiled with some of his fellows,' said Tom.

'My brother did not get "oiled", as you put it, Mr Ansell, with anyone. He preferred to drink by himself. He had a little flask containing brandy.'

There was an awkward silence after Tom was put in his place over the 'oiled' remark, before Helen said, 'Was Canon Slater with him when he went out on these summer evenings?'

'I do not think so, miss. My brother turned in on himself and got impatient with the company of others, not that he'd ever been much of a one for company in the first place. Andrew made one or two remarks about Canon Slater which seemed to say the two weren't as friendly any more. Andrew spent time poring over old books too – he was always a good reader, unlike me. In the old days, he used to read the Bible. He could recite it off by heart. But lately he has not seem so bothered with the scriptures. Instead he has been taken up by big books with maps and such inside. I came in here once to see him with a great volume open on his knees, his nose as close to it as if his life depended on it. He was making notes, always the methodical man. He glared at me so I left.'

'Did you have a glance at the book?'

'Like I say, it was maps and writing together on one page, but I could not see clearly.'

'Where would he get such a book?' said Helen.

'There are books in the cathedral,' said Mrs Banks, as if the question was a surprising one. 'There is a whole library of old books in the cathedral somewhere.'

And there are old books in Felix Slater's study, thought Tom. Perhaps North had borrowed from the Canon – or stolen – some volume which might lead him to more tombs and artefacts.

There seemed to be little more that Mrs Banks could tell them. Tom and Helen might have asked to look at North's bedroom but, if the sexton's sister was reluctant to do more than sweep in there, she certainly wouldn't have allowed strangers to poke around the place.

Mrs Banks handed the handkerchief back to Helen, who said, 'Thank you for seeing us, Mrs Banks. By the way, you said that your brother and Canon Slater had been somewhere near the city when they discovered a burial place. Do you know what direction it was in? North of here? South?'

'I can't tell you exactly where that was, miss. But I do know where Andrew was going more recently, at the end of the summer. He let it slip. It's Todd's Mound, outside the city.'

'Did you tell the police?' said Tom

'Inspector Foster said he would send one of his men to look round up there, but I do not know whether he was speaking just to soothe me.'

'We'll have a look,' said Helen, 'and we will tell you what we have found. Even if it is nothing.'

'Oh, I hope it is nothing,' said Mrs Banks, tears forming afresh in her eyes. 'I hope it is nothing!'

The Burial Chamber

Helen was dressed for rambling, with thick skirts and stout boots and a sensible hat. She had equipped herself with one of her godfather's sticks and taken one for Tom as well. Less practically, Tom was wearing his hat and a smart overcoat, which, Helen joked, made him look fit only for the city street. They hired a cab to take them the mile or so north of the city boundary in the direction of Todd's Mound. The pretence, which wasn't altogether a pretence, was that they were out for a stroll. However, this was no brisk spring day or a balmy one in summer, but an overcast morning in late autumn.

They paid off the driver, explaining that he need not wait since they'd return to Salisbury on foot. The town was at their backs. Ahead of them rose the steep sides of the landscape feature known as Todd's Mound, drab under the grey sky. There were, unsurprisingly, no other walkers in sight.

Access on the eastern side looked difficult since the land fell away steeply there. The couple set off on a rough track which ran in a westerly direction round the base of the mound.

'Tom,' said Helen, 'you are a lawyer. I have a question but let me phrase it in a lawyerly way. If one were to stumble over treasure, would one have the right to take it?'

'In principle, no. One has no right to take anything that is not one's own property.'

'Not even under the law of finder's keepers?'

'I'm not sure that law has ever been enacted in Parliament.'

'So this man Andrew North and Canon Slater, they would not have been acting legally in taking items from a burial place?'

'Probably not. On the other hand, if they picked up something which had been dropped on the way to a burial place and which had lain there over the centuries, then they would have been entitled to keep it.'

'A clear distinction,' said Helen. 'I am so glad you are a lawyer, Tom, though others might consider it a rather dry profession.'

Thinking that this was more or less what Mrs Mackenzie had said to him, Tom pointed out, 'The law was good enough for your father, Helen.'

'Oh, he was a dry man. But we've wandered from the point. Did North and Canon Slater commit a crime in taking things from a burial chamber?'

'Strictly speaking, they probably did. But the wronged party here is the Crown rather than the original owner of the property, and the Crown will not be very vigorous in pursuing a few bits of metal and flint, even assuming they have any value. Felix Slater for one wasn't interested in these things because they might have been valuable but because they were evidence of past ages.'

'Which is more or less what Mrs Banks said about her brother.'

'Except in North's case hunting hidden items had become a kind of obsession.'

By this time Tom and Helen had arrived at the western flank of Todd's Mound. From here another path led off at right angles to the summit of the mound. They began the slightly steeper ascent, pausing for breath under a copse of beeches.

It was the sharp-eyed Helen who saw it. Something

with a dullish glint which was not quite concealed under a pile of leaves below where they were standing. She bent forward and extracted a hip flask from the leaves. She turned it over several times.

'It must be his.'

'Whose?'

'Andrew North's. See here, Tom.'

On one side of the pewter flask a small set of initials had been inscribed, not professionally but neatly enough to suggest a careful hand.

'A.H.N.,' said Helen. 'Who else can it be?'

'This flask is North's all right,' said Tom, unscrewing the cap and sniffing at the contents. 'He was called Andrew Herbert, I saw the names in one of the books at his sister's. And she said that he carried a flask of brandy. There's a little left in here.'

'You said he "was" Andrew Herbert. You think he's dead, don't you, Tom?'

'Most likely. A workman with a good reputation who starts to behave oddly, who absents himself for a long period without anyone catching a whiff of his whereabouts, one associated in some way with a churchman who has recently been murdered. Yes, Andrew North is dead.'

'Murdered?' said Helen.

Overhead the remaining leaves rattled in a sudden gust. Tom shivered but managed to turn it into a shrug. 'I don't know. Yes, maybe murdered.'

'So if North's hip flask is here, where is North?'

'He could be anywhere. The flask might have fallen from his pocket as he was climbing up or down the hill.'

'But it tells us he was here at Todd's Mound.'

'Or that someone was here. It might not have been North who dropped the flask.'

'His murderer, you mean?'

Tom noted the controlled excitement in the way Helen

referred to the 'murderer'. He glanced sideways. She was still holding the pewter flask. There was colour in her cheeks. He leant across and kissed her.

'Tom,' she said half jokingly and only after a little time had passed, 'what if someone is watching!'

And, as if on cue, they heard a heavy tread behind them, the sound of a person descending the hill. A person who was wearing leather leggings and great boots. In surprise, Tom and Helen sprang apart.

There was another watcher to this encounter. One who was – not by chance – in the vicinity of Todd's Mound and who had seen the approach of two figures with a familiar outline. This individual took shelter behind a patch of bare brambles and observed the girl pick up an object from the ground. The flask was not easily identifiable from such a distance but the watcher knew what it was straightaway, since the flask had been taken from a dead man's body and a swig taken from its contents. It must have dropped out of a coat pocket as the watcher was going downhill those few weeks before. And now, in the present moment, a third person was added to the scene as the shepherd swung downhill and almost collided with the couple who'd just been spooning and were oblivious to the newcomer. The threesome, the shepherd, Ansell and the girl, exchanged a few words, more than a few words, quite a regular session in fact. After a time the couple turned away and continued their uphill progress while the shepherd kept going at a downhill diagonal, fortunately in a direction away from the observer. This person waited until Ansell and the girl were almost out of sight over the skyline before slipping from the cover of the brambles.

* * *

Tom and Helen didn't speak again until they were inside the embankment at the top of the hill. It took them a moment to catch their breath and they rested, leaning on the walking sticks which belonged to Eric Selby. While they were climbing each was thinking of what the shepherd had said: that few people came to visit Todd's Mound for pleasure and certainly not at this time of year. But that he had seen someone coming up this same path a few weeks ago, towards the end of the afternoon, and that he had particularly taken notice of the man on account of his shifty, uncomfortable look. The man had a bag slung over his shoulder and might have been an itinerant labourer, but the shepherd did not think so. The man struck a false note, as it were.

The shepherd, whose name was Gabriel as Helen quickly established, did not say all of this in quite such a coherent form or using exactly these words but rather the gist was teased out of him by Helen. To begin with, she smiled at Gabriel and showed him the pewter flask and wondered aloud whose it might be – those mysterious initials A.H.N. – and whether it would be possible to find the owner so as to return the flask, obviously a treasured item as the initials showed. And, by the way, had Gabriel seen anyone recently on these slopes? Tom noticed again what an assured touch Helen had with people. How she was able to speak naturally with them and gain their trust and find out what she wanted to find out. How she could be evasive with the truth (for example, she already knew whose the flask was). She didn't even seem embarrassed that Gabriel had almost run into them while they were embracing. Of course, reflected Tom, the blonde tendrils of hair which curled down from under her sensible hat and the wide blue eyes might have something to do with it, especially where men were concerned. But the effect worked on women too. Mrs Banks had revealed things to Helen which she might not have done to Tom alone.

'It must have been Andrew North,' said Helen. 'We know that he was in the habit of visiting Todd's Mound after he worked with Canon Slater. And he disappeared from the house he shared with his sister at about the same time that Gabriel saw someone walking up here, someone looking shifty and uncomfortable. North the sexton?'

'The shepherd has a good memory for the people he encounters.'

'So would you, Tom, if you saw more sheep than people. Well, now we are here, what do we do next?'

They looked round at the bare interior of the plateau. It had a roughly rectangular shape, protected by ramparts of grass which had crumbled in places. There were a few shrubs and patches of bramble but no signs of human occupation, whether ancient or modern.

Helen and Tom hadn't come out to Todd's Mound totally unprepared. Helen had found a book in her godfather's library which detailed the locations of some of the tumuli and other ancient remains to be found in the region around Salisbury. Little was known about Todd's Mound (not even who the eponymous Todd had been) but it seemed there had most likely been entrances or gateways at both ends of the plateau, although a land-fall in the east had made access almost impossible from that side.

Tom pointed to the opposite end, the eastern one.

'If there's anything to be found,' he said, 'it should be over there.'

'Why?'

'Look around, there are no signs of disturbance to the earth here. And there weren't any marks either near the path we've just come by. If North was poking around and digging things up, it must have been somewhere different.'

They began to pace the length of the hilltop. There was a rustling in a patch of bushes as they passed and they turned to see a deer start from shelter and scamper back towards the western side of the mound. Helen paused and held her hand to her breast.

'That startled me, Tom.'

Tom Ansell, also, had been startled but he wasn't displeased to see the effect on Helen since it was an excuse to put his free arm round her for a moment. Then they resumed their progress towards the far embankment, in which there was a kind of larger dip or notch. Through this, as they walked, they caught glimpses of the city and the cathedral spire.

'This is where one of the entrances to the settlement – or whatever it was – must have been,' said Tom, as they stood on the lip of ground below which the land fell away steeply. The slope was studded with clumps of yew and to one side lay the great carcass of a fallen tree. Helen turned her back on the view and surveyed the grassy basin they had just crossed.

'It's strange to think that our ancestors once lived up here. I wonder why they moved away.'

'Perhaps they were driven out and had no choice over moving,' said Tom. 'Or they got bored with life on this cold hilltop and wanted the comfort of the lowlands.'

'They have left no traces.'

'Except their burial places.'

'They would not be buried here, inside this place,' said Helen gesturing at the area bounded by the earth ramparts.

'But not far outside either. On the slopes around this hill maybe.'

They moved back to the entrance or gateway to Todd's Mound. Tom looked downhill in the direction of the fallen tree. A tattered black shape seemed to unfold itself from the tangle of branches and Tom felt a thrill of horror until he realized that it was nothing more than a crow, a great crow which rose into the air and clattered out of sight round the slope of the hill. Tom wrinkled his nose. He glanced at Helen standing beside him but, though she too had observed the bird, she was now gazing out at the city and the countryside beyond.

'What are you doing?' she said. 'Wait for me.'

'Stay there, Helen. It's probably nothing.'

He was already several yards below and to one side of the embankment gateway. The slope was steeper than it seemed from above. To keep his balance, Tom used his walking stick. The hem of his coat brushed against the chalky soil. He edged towards the fallen tree. That was where the crow had been. That was where the smell seemed to be coming from.

He halted to get his bearings. But if he'd expected to see anything he was disappointed. The flank of the hill-side rose sharply on his left. The bulk of the fallen tree – a beech, he thought – lay a little below where he was standing. The crown of the tree was further down, although a number of severed branches were strewn casually across the slope. Where the roots had been was a gaping black hole with only tooth-like shards remaining. Nothing more. But not quite, because Tom noticed that just above the root-hole was another gap, a yet darker space, partly obscured by a branch to which withered leaves still clung.

Afterwards he didn't know what had drawn his attention to that darker spot on the slant of Todd's Mound. Whether it was the suspicion of something man-made in the arrangement of stones around a hole in the ground. Or the way the severed tree branch almost seemed to have been positioned so as to obscure the hole. Or the sense that, if the smell – a sharp, unpleasant smell – on the hill-side had a source, then it was from here.

Tom covered the few dozen feet to the place. He was right. It was an entrance, of sorts, into the hillside. There were three slabs of stone forming a primitive door, although one of the uprights had fallen. He tugged at the branch laid across the entrance.

'What *are* you doing down there, Tom? Are you all right?'

By now, Tom was on his hands and knees, oblivious to the mud on his coat. Oblivious too to Helen's call. A strong smell emanated from the mouth of the cave or chamber or whatever it was. Something dead lay in there. Of course something dead lay in there! It must be a burial chamber. But this was a recent death, not one from thousands of years ago.

Two things prevented Tom Ansell from rising to his feet and scrambling back to where Helen stood, and then calling for attention and help. The first was the fear of looking a fool. Whatever was inside the chamber might be animal, not human. He did not want to summon a rescue party to pull out a dead sheep. The other reason was that Tom felt he ought to see this through himself. It was up to him to have a first sight of whatever lay inside this hole in the hillside.

Clutching his stick with one hand, he got out a handkerchief and held it tight against his nose and mouth as he edged his way inside the aperture. The smell was almost overpowering. He paused. There were small sounds, scuffling sounds, which he could just detect over the banging of his heart. He coughed, and the scuffling stopped. Using the walking stick as a probe he pushed forward and it tapped against a hard object. He picked it up. A bone, a human bone he thought. But not recent, because it was white and dry and stripped of everything.

The day was overcast but there was enough light seeping into the entrance of the hole for Tom to get an impression of what was lying deeper inside. More scattered bones, it seemed, and something else in among the bones, not white and sterile like them, but an object which was wrapped up and foul-smelling and too large to be a sheep. An object with shod feet. He prodded at the soles of the feet with his stick. Then he crawled as fast as he could out of the hole, going in reverse. He sat on the chalky slope, gulping in draughts of fresh air, even if that air was still tainted by the scent from the burial chamber. A movement startled him. It was Helen. Worried by Tom's absence, she had half walked, half scrambled down the slope. Her hair was tumbling out from under her sensible cap and her face was flushed. Seeing Tom, she shrieked because of his appearance. He'd turned a touch green. But Tom hardly noticed her arrival or her shriek. Instead, he was trying to keep his gorge from rising and he was thinking: two bodies in three days. It's a bit steep.

Somewhere below Tom and Helen, near the eastern base of Todd's Mound, was a third figure. The discovery of the body – it must have been discovered, judging by the woman's shriek, sharp as a bird-call – was no surprise to this person, who had been responsible for putting the body in the burial chamber. Well, it would have been found sooner or later. No great harm done.

Canon Selby's House, Again

Tom Ansell's thoughts were echoed by Inspector Foster that evening as he sat with Tom and Helen in the drawing room of Canon Selby's house. They were all sipping brandy, courtesy of the owner.

'You mustn't make a habit of this body-finding, Mr Ansell. First Canon Slater and now, well, now whoever the unfortunate individual was out at Todd's Mound . . .'

'We think it was Mr North,' said Helen.

'Possibly, possibly,' said the policeman with all his professional caution. 'But there's no way of telling, is there? Not until we get some of those clothes cleaned up and give Mrs Banks a sight of them.'

This was true enough. The process of recovering the corpse from the flank of the hill had taken up most of the day. Tom and Helen returned to the town on foot and entered the police house, muddy and bedraggled and breathless. Inspector Foster had to be found and their story told several times over. A trio of constables was gathered and, together with the Inspector and Tom and Helen, they were driven back to Todd's Mound in a carriage and a cart. A carriage for Foster and the two young people, the cart for the three constables. There was a purpose to the cart, as they realized later. Tom urged Helen to stay behind – he could lead the group to the place by himself – but she insisted on being 'in at the kill' (as she said, before clapping her hand over her mouth in horrified amusement).

Tom and she had been content to do no more than guide Foster and his men towards the point above the fallen beech on the eastern side of the hill. They did not see Gabriel the shepherd again. Perhaps he was alarmed by the crowd of police. Tom and Helen watched from the embankment gateway while the constables did what was literally the dirty work down below under Foster's direction. The first constable to go in, Chesney, came out almost straightaway. He said, 'There's two of 'em in there, guv.' Foster explained that they weren't interested in bare bones, which might have lain there for centuries, but in fresh (or fresh-ish) corpses. Chesney should go back inside and concentrate on that.

The burial chamber was too small to hold more than a single person at a time so first Constable Chesney and then the other policemen entered one by one, holding their breath and tugging at the corpse until it was brought out, inch by inch, from the interior of the burrow and laid out on the hillside. One of the constables turned away to be sick. Even from a distance the sight was unpleasant. Tom instinctively put up his hand to shield Helen but she had already averted her gaze.

The body was still clothed but the garments were stained and discoloured, and rents in the material showed grey-green flesh underneath. The head, which was the same colour, had little hair left and the face was shapeless and pitted with myriad tiny holes. It was apparent too that small animals must have been feeding on the whole body.

The police had brought with them ropes and a canvas sheet in which they tied the body, and a makeshift stretcher to carry it away on. Foster ordered them to lug their burden to the other side of Todd's Mound and dump it in the cart. He slapped down the frivolous suggestion of one of his men that it might be quicker to roll the body down the steep incline on this side and collect it at the bottom. After their initial shock and surprise, Tom and Helen had become fascinated by the process, almost against their will. Helen, in particular, had started hanging over the shrouded body in a manner that Tom considered pretty unhealthy. He put it down to her novelist's sensibility.

While his men were dealing with the corpse, the Inspector and the others returned to Salisbury. By now it was growing dark. Foster promised he would call on them at Canon Selby's to give them his news.

Foster was as good as his word even if he didn't have much to convey. Identification of the corpse was almost impossible, said the Inspector, and in any case it would have to be cremated as soon as possible in the interests of public health. Identification could only be done through the dead man's garments which, when cleaned up, would be shown to Mrs Banks in the hope (or rather the fear) that she might recognize some article belonging to her brother. He thought it likely that the corpse was North. The Inspector had already informed Mrs Banks of this because, chancing to meet him in the street, she had badgered him with questions. He had no choice but to tell her they had unearthed a body which was probably Andrew's.

'Mrs Banks is naturally distressed,' said Foster, 'but when she found that it was you two, Mr Ansell and Miss Scott, who had made the discovery, she was grateful you had gone to such trouble after you visited her. I didn't know you had called on Mrs Banks.'

'It's not against the law, Inspector,' said Tom.

'Of course it's not, sir, but I must say that we do not much approve in this part of the country of members of the public involving themselves in police business. Asking questions, finding corpses and the like.'

'Is there evidence of foul play on the body, Inspector?' said Tom quickly.

'Foul play?' said Foster, pulling at his great side-whiskers and gazing into space as if the words were spelled out there in capital letters. 'You mean murder, Mr Ansell. There's no evidence one way or the other, I'm afraid, not on the body itself. It's in far too decomposed a state for us to tell anything from it, whether the chap was throttled or bashed over the head or stabbed in the back. But I don't think that Mr Whoever-he-was crawled inside that burial place by himself. Someone pushed and shoved him inside so that he was lying next to the remains of some other gent, who is none of our concern since he died long before the Salisbury police was a gleam in anyone's eye. But the pushing and the shoving to Mr Whoever-he-was suggests to me that *he* was done away with.'

'Not Mr Whoever-he-was but Mr North. We know that North was in the habit of visiting Todd's Mound, Inspector,' said Helen, repeating what she'd said to Tom earlier that day. Helen was back on an even keel. A hot bath, a change of clothes, a light supper and some of her godfather's brandy (taken by Helen against Eric Selby's advice), together with the basic excitements of the day recollected in tranquillity, had brought her back to her usual self.

'Just because we've found a body in a solitary place which a man was accustomed to visit doesn't mean that body and man are one and the same, Miss Scott. After all, it could be that a second individual had an interest in that burial place. In fact, we know a second individual had an interest because one of them had to kill the other in order to leave the first one there. If you see what I mean.'

'You mean that Andrew North might be the murderer himself,' said Tom, 'and that the body which isn't yet identified could be someone else?'

'I am not going to start accusing people of murder, Mr Ansell, without a little more evidence. You should be glad I follow that policy. Remember, sir?'

And of course Tom did remember his treatment at Foster's hands, fair treatment on the whole, when he'd been put in Fisherton Gaol.

'Has either of you seen Walter Slater?' said Foster, in an unexpected change of subject.

'No,' said Tom. 'He lives at Venn House, doesn't he, with his aunt and uncle?'

'He does normally,' said the Inspector. 'But he hasn't been there since the night of his uncle's murder.'

'Perhaps he has gone back to his father's house in Downton,' said Tom.

'No. I have established that Walter Slater is not at Northwood either.'

'His church? He is a curate in the town.'

'Yes, at St Luke's. He was seen there the morning after his uncle's murder but he has not been sighted since.'

Despite the warmth of the Selbys' drawing room, and the sense of having eaten and drunk well at the end of a long and anxious day, Tom Ansell experienced a sudden chill. He had liked Walter Slater on the strength of a single meeting. He hoped nothing had happened to the fellow. Of course, there was another explanation why the curate might have gone missing after Felix's murder but Tom was reluctant to give it house room.

'By the way, Miss Scott,' said Foster, 'where is your godfather? Here we are sitting in his house and warming ourselves by his fire and drinking his brandy, but there is no Canon Selby.'

'He had to go out on business, I believe,' said Helen. 'Church business, that is.'

'Just as long as he hasn't disappeared too,' said the Inspector. 'Well, I'd better be making myself disappear. I will keep you informed of any discoveries we make about the body from Todd's Mound. But don't go tripping over any more remains, Mr Ansell.'

After Foster had gone, Tom and Helen remained sitting

near the fire, sipping at their brandy and musing over the events of the day.

'How do you suppose this second murder of Mr North is connected to the murder of Canon Slater, Tom?'

'Perhaps it isn't.'

'It must be.'

'It's only in a story that deaths and murders have to be tied together.'

'So you think there are two different murderers wandering about Salisbury, Tom? That makes things worse.'

'No, I don't really think there are two murderers. The law of chance and probability would argue against it.'

'But as a certain lawyer said to me this afternoon, "I'm not sure that law has ever been enacted in Parliament."'

'Oh dear,' said Tom. 'Tell me I don't really sound so pompous.'

'You don't. Not very often anyway. Now you tell me something. You said you had a look inside this book, this memoir, which Canon Slater wanted to entrust to the firm. Now the book has gone, taken by whoever killed him, I suppose. So the book must have contained something valuable, some secret maybe. What did you see in it?'

Tom recalled glancing through the Salisbury manuscript, reading the anecdotes about Byron and Shelley, the other little item about the woman who'd danced in the nude and posed for George Slater and his friend. The reference to the prostitute in Shepherd Market and George's fears that he'd contracted some disease from her.

Tom said, 'It was an interesting book.'

'I can see from your expression, Tom, what "interesting" means. It means scandalous and compromising, doesn't it?'

'Well, there were some stories in the memoir about meeting famous poets and the like. There was a story about Shelley sailing a boat on a pond made out of a fifty-pound note. The boat, I mean, not the pond.'

'But there were other, less respectable things too, Tom. Was the Canon's father's book like the kind of thing they sell in Holywell Street?'

Tom might have asked Helen how she knew about the type of books which were for sale, on the sly and under the counter, in a particular stretch of Holywell Street near Exeter Hall in the Strand, but he saw the look on her face – somewhere between amusement and determination – and said, 'Yes, there were some details in George Slater's memoir which would not be publishable. Adventures with women of a certain sort, and so on.'

Helen put down her brandy glass and clapped her hands in delight.

'Why, Tom Ansell, I wish I had had a sight of the – whatd'youcallit? – the Salisbury manuscript!'

'That's as may be, Helen, but a brief glance was enough to tell me why the Canon wanted the book out of his house and in safekeeping in our vaults.'

'He could have destroyed it without going to all the trouble of summoning you to Salisbury.'

'He would not destroy it because he had too much respect for the past, but neither did he wish to keep it. He wanted it to be seen by no one except his nephew Walter. Walter was to have the final decision on what happened to it, but only after his uncle's death.'

'And now his uncle's dead and the book is gone.'

'I don't see how the book gives a motive for his murder though.'

'And I don't understand,' said Helen. 'Everything you've said suggests that the Salisbury manuscript was somehow dangerous. Why, it might have contained something about the Canon himself.'

'Then why did he allow me to look at it? Anyway I don't think old George Slater would have had much to say about a son who went into the Church, except a few words of dismissal or contempt.'

They were silent for a moment, trying to work their way through the tangle of confusion and doubt.

'No, no one would have killed to get it,' said Tom. 'What it contained was compromising, true, but the writer was dead and the events he referred to took place many years ago. But I can see it the other way round. Felix Slater might have resorted to – to extreme measures to keep the book.'

'Even murder?'

'Yes,' said Tom, surprising himself as he said it. The residentiary canon might have looked like a venerable churchman but he had been tough and wiry as an old bird. Perhaps ruthless underneath it. 'But there's a problem. *He* didn't murder anyone. He was the victim.'

'So perhaps Canon Slater was murdered after a tussle,' said Helen. 'Perhaps he was killed by someone who wanted the book.'

'Which wouldn't be of much concern to anyone outside the family. Who didn't know what was in it. Walter had never seen it while Felix Slater told me that his brother Percy passed it over to him as part of his father's effects, though some years after old George Slater died. I got the impression that Percy hadn't been interested.'

'You said you went to see Percy and that he wanted the stuff back.'

'That's true. But I think he was saying it out of a general dislike of his brother and the wish to cause trouble.'

'Couldn't this Percy Slater have gone to the Canon's house and demanded the manuscript back? Couldn't there have been a fight and so on?'

'Possibly,' said Tom, sounding to himself like Inspector Foster in a cautious mood. 'Only there were no signs of a fight or a struggle in his study. He was taken by surprise. Someone he trusted, or someone he knew at any rate.'

'What about Mrs Slater?'

'Amelia? I don't think so.'

'Because she's a woman, Tom? And because we all

know that the gentle sex cannot plunge the knife in any more than they can be familiar with the books for sale in Holywell Street. So is Mrs Slater some pious clergyman's companion, retiring and docile, like my godfather's wife, Mrs Selby?'

'Not at all,' said Tom carefully. He recalled that Helen hadn't yet caught a glimpse of Mrs Slater. 'It's a strange kind of union. Mrs Slater is half Italian. Apparently Felix met her when he was travelling on the Continent. Met her in Florence where she lived with her parents. When they died she came to England and she . . . she . . .'

'Yes?'

'Well, how Percy Slater put it was that she threw herself on Felix Slater's mercy since she had no one else to turn to. And so they married and have lived in Salisbury ever since.'

'Happily ever after?' said Helen.

'That's what Percy said. Only he spoke the words with a kind of sneer. I thought perhaps he was envious of his brother. Mrs Slater is an attractive woman, Helen.'

'I can tell that by the way you refer to her. But isn't it odd, Tom, that she should have travelled from Florence to "throw herself on the mercy" of a cathedral canon?'

'Maybe they had some kind of understanding. But we'll never know, since I'm not going to ask her and he is dead.'

'We're going round in circles here,' said Helen. 'Talking of understandings, Tom, we were having a conversation before you left London . . .'

Tom got up and went over to where Helen was sitting on the other side of the fire. He knelt down and took both her hands in his. Her hands were warm.

'Shouldn't you be on one knee though?' she said.

Tom was about to say that this wasn't, perhaps, the most propitious moment to be talking about marriage and that he merely wanted to be near her when they heard the front door closing quietly as someone came into the house. Before Tom could rise to his feet again, the door to the drawing room opened. It was Eric Selby. If he saw anything strange in the sight of the young lawyer kneeling before his god-daughter, her didn't say so.

In fact, he said nothing, but simply stood in the doorway with a peculiar, abstracted look in his eyes. Underneath his shovel-hat, his white hair stuck out in disordered tufts as though he'd jammed the hat on in a hurry.

Eventually Helen said, 'What is it, Uncle? What's wrong?'

The Drawing Room

Earlier that evening Henry Cathcart had had a visitor. It was Bessie from Venn House. She was wearing a black armband and a doleful face. She carried a letter from Mrs Slater. Henry had of course written a note of condolence to the widow. Now he had a reply on black-lined note-paper, asking him to call on her straightaway. She did not have to say that she was not free to leave her home. A new widow is not at liberty to come and go as she wishes, not without exciting comment.

It was the early evening. Cathcart waited a short while to allow Bessie to get well on the way back to Venn House before setting off there himself. It was the first time he had been to West Walk since the night of the murder. He was admitted by Bessie, who put on a mild show of being surprised to see him. Mrs Slater was sitting in the drawing room. She was dressed in mourning and reading a book. She looked quite composed. She closed the book and put it on the arm of her chair.

'Mr Cathcart, how good of you to come.'

'How are you, Mrs Slater?' he said, noting that she had not called him by his first name.

'I am – how do they say it? – bearing up.'

'Bearing up' was his wife's expression, he thought. He went to stand opposite her but took care not to come too close. He debated for an instant leaning forward to take her hand, which was covered with a thin black lace glove, and kissing it. But now did not seem the moment. He was conscious of how warm the room was, even warmer than Constance liked her sick room.

'It must be terrible to have to stay in this house,' he said.

'It is my home,' Amelia said. 'I feel quite safe with the servants. And there is Eaves.'

'Eaves?'

'The gardener.'

'But forgive me, Mrs Slater, the gardener does not sleep in the house, does he?'

'Oh no. But he is within call. It is only a shame that Achilles is not still alive. He would have been company for me.'

Cathcart remembered that Achilles was her little pug. It had died some time in the beginning of the year. If he thought it strange she should be regretting the death of her dog rather than her husband, he did not say so. There was no doubt that she looked good, that she looked very good, in mourning clothes.

'You haven't seen Walter, have you, Henry?'

'Walter? Oh, your nephew.'

'Yes, my nephew.'

For the first time, Cathcart observed marks of pain on the woman's face. Amelia's wide, mobile mouth was set in a rigid line. Her forehead, which was partly concealed by the black trimmings to a little hat, was creased as if she were trying to remember something.

'No, I haven't seen Walter, not since the night, the terrible night when . . . when . . .'

'When it all happened,' she completed his sentence.

'Do you think something has happened now?' he said. 'To Walter?'

'I pray not. It is simply that no one has seen him for a day or more. His bedroom has not been slept in.'

'You have informed the police?'

'Inspector Foster knows. I believe he has been looking for Walter too.'

'I expect he'll turn up soon.'

'I don't want him to turn up soon,' she said, her hands suddenly bunching into fists on the arms of the chair. 'I want to see him now.'

'You should not worry,' said Cathcart. 'Walter is a fine young man.'

She looked at him and smiled.

'You are right. I should not worry. Walter is a fine young man.'

Amelia rose from her chair. She moved closer to Henry and said, 'But, my dear Henry, I think it is *you* who should worry.'

Cathcart was aware again of the heat of the room. He was so struck by the way she had addressed him – *my dear Henry* – that he scarcely noticed the rest of her words. Eventually he said, 'I? Why should I be worried?'

'Because you left something behind on your last visit here, on the very evening when poor Felix was killed.'

'What did I leave?'

'This,' said Amelia Slater, moving away and reaching for a little reticule lying on a nearby table. 'I put it here for safekeeping.' She opened the beaded bag and brought out a pale silk handkerchief, a man's one.

'Is that mine?' said Cathcart.

'It must be,' she said, making a show of scrutinizing the handkerchief. 'There are some letters embroidered on it. Ah, here they are. 'H.G.C.' I do not know of anyone else with the initials H.G.C. Do you know of anyone else?'

She held up the handkerchief by a single corner.

'And now I look more carefully, Henry, I see that there are some specks of colour on the handkerchief. They look like specks of blood.'

'It is blood,' he said quickly. 'I remember that I nicked myself while I was shaving that morning. Some of the blood must have got itself on the handkerchief.'

'Tut,' said Amelia Slater. 'And you, one of the leading

citizens of the town and one of the most prosperous too, could not afford to provide yourself with a fresh handkerchief for the day ahead?'

'I meant to, I expect,' he said. ' But I probably just stuffed it in my pocket and forgot about it.'

'Ah well,' she said, continuing to watch the handkerchief sway gently a foot from her face. It was as if she was conducting a hypnotic experiment on herself. 'No doubt you have had a lot on your mind, Henry.'

Was he supposed to cross the few feet separating them and retrieve the handkerchief? Cathcart was reminded of a child playing a game. Suddenly he'd had enough. Something about the situation – whether it was the heat of the room or Amelia's high-handed treatment of him or something less specific – reminded him of his wife Constance. He made to snatch at the handkerchief but at the last instant Amelia let it fall from her fingers so that it appeared she had surrendered it. He stuffed it into his coat pocket.

'I must have dropped it,' he said.

'Ah, but where?'

'Outside Venn House somewhere. In the porch.'

'No, Henry. It was found inside, quite close to the door of Felix's room. Bessie saw it but was too frightened to pick it up. She told me instead. So I picked it up – and now I have dropped it again – into your hand.'

'Amelia . . . Mrs Slater . . . I am not sure what you are saying.'

'I am saying nothing, Henry. I am too busy thinking of the death of poor Felix and of how I require another mourning outfit.'

'What you are wearing now looks – looks fine to me. Sober and dignified and in the fashion, if I may say so.'

'No, no,' said Amelia, making an up-and-down motion with her hands from the top of her black-bonneted head to the tips of her black shoes, 'no, no, all of this I am wearing is – how do they say it? – "cobbled together". Yes, cobbled together.'

'Then you would like to come to my shop and select something more *à la mode*?' he said.

'I should like nothing better than to visit your delightful shop, Henry. But, as you know, a widow is barely allowed to move a step outside her own room after the death of her spouse. She is as good as walled up like a bad person in a fairy story. As if she were the one guilty of his death! So, no, I cannot visit your shop. But I would be grateful, more grateful than I can show you at the moment, if you could send some of your people here to Venn House to see to my needs. No, do not send your people but come yourself.'

'Of course,' he said. 'It would be my pleasure.'

Now, despite the heat of the drawing room, Henry Cathcart felt cold. Cold and angry. Amelia put out her black-gloved right hand as a sign that he might kiss it, also that their interview was over. He kissed her hand, but automatically, without thought.

She said, 'What does it stand for, the G?'

It took him a moment to understand what she was talking about then he said, 'George. It stands for George. Good evening, Mrs Slater.'

Walking back to his house, his leg causing him trouble, Henry Cathcart felt, paradoxically, not the damp chills of a November evening but a renewed warmth, the result of a temper which was turning from cold to heat. He was angry not so much with Amelia Slater – though some resentment in that quarter would surely be justified, he considered – as with himself. Angry in general for having allowed himself to be led so far astray, so very far, by the wife who was now a widow. Angry in particular that he had dropped the monogrammed, blood-speckled handkerchief which

Bessie the maid had found. The handkerchief placed him inside Venn House on the evening of Felix Slater's murder. Not much evidence by itself perhaps, although the blood speckles might have been awkward to explain away, but Cathcart was reluctant it should come to the attention of Inspector Foster. He had a high respect for Foster. No, the handkerchief now tucked into his coat pocket was not much evidence by itself, but it provided sufficient pressure for him to fall in straightaway with Amelia Slater's request that he should provide her with fresh mourning outfits.

Yet, even as he turned these matters over in his head, he thought again of how fine she looked in mourning, how very fine.

Then he wondered whether he should get rid of the handkerchief or whether it was safe to have it laundered at home. If he got rid of it, he would have to burn or bury it. Otherwise the monogrammed initials were too revealing. If he did get rid of it, who was to say that it had ever existed, or rather who could say that it had been found, blood-speckled, near the site of a murder? But there were two people who might testify to that, he reflected. There was Amelia Slater and Bessie the housemaid. Mustn't forget the housemaid.

The Ringing Room

While this was going on, while Inspector Foster was giving the news to Tom Ansell and Helen Scott, while Cathcart was seeing Amelia Slater, Canon Eric Selby had been talking to Walter Slater.

The two men were in the ringing room of the bell-tower of St Luke's. It was cold and damp and poorly illuminated by a few candles. Selby was concerned for the young man's physical welfare. He was gaunt and unshaven. It could not be healthy to spend so long up here in this stone-walled, cheerless chamber, whatever one's reasons. But Selby was still more concerned for Walter's mental state. He was not speaking much, but what he did say was distracted and hardly coherent.

When Selby had first been alerted to Walter's whereabouts by Miss Annabel Nugent, he had not believed it. But the young woman had been insistent. She was gathering up some dead flowers from the church – one of her little, self-imposed duties – in the hush and dark of late afternoon when she saw her friend, the curate, going up the stairs to the bell-tower. He was clutching a bottle and something else to his chest in the manner of a fugitive or thief. He had not noticed her standing in a side aisle. There was such a fixed, almost desperate look on Walter's face that he had not noticed anything at all but seemed to be moving like an automaton.

Annabel made to move towards him but he had already disappeared up the spiral staircase, pushing the door to behind him. She half opened it again but the door gave a great creak and she heard the shuffle of climbing feet halt above her. She looked down and observed some crumbs on the floor. He had been carrying a loaf of bread as well as the bottle, clutching the items to him as though he feared someone might seize them. She didn't know whether to be more surprised at this or at the queer, fixed expression on his face. Was he feeding someone up in the tower? Was he feeding himself? Suddenly frightened, Annabel turned and walked quickly out of the church. She spent some time waiting outside for Walter to appear again. It was late in the day, there was no church service. What could he be doing up there in the bell-tower? She asked herself whether his mind had been turned by the murder of his uncle.

Wondering what to do next she then remembered not the vicar of St Luke's, Mr Simpson (who, in truth, she did not like very much), but an old friend of her grandfather, the late Rev. Parsons. So she called on Canon Eric Selby and, haltingly, explained what she'd seen. And Selby had surprised her by the speed with which, after his initial doubts, he had put on his coat and shovel-hat and accompanied her back to St Luke's. He might have been an old man, very old in Annabel's eyes, but he walked with vigour and purpose. On the way, Annabel tried out her idea that Walter had become disturbed on account of the dreadful murder of his uncle, Felix Slater, which was the talk of the whole town. It's possible, said Selby, without revealing that he had been present at the aftermath of the murder himself.

Once they were inside St Luke's, Annabel grew reluctant. She wished she hadn't summoned the nice old gent now. For sure, Walter would be nowhere to be found (certainly not up in the bell-tower), and she'd look a fool. On the other hand, part of her hoped that Walter was all right and not skulking in the tower anyway. She was a little frightened too, and allowed Canon Selby, old as he was, to go first through the creaky door and up the spiral stairs. It was almost completely dark and they had to feel their way up.

They reached the little, stone-flagged landing outside the ringing room and Annabel got a terrible shock because there was a figure standing in the doorway, waiting for them. It was Walter Slater. She would have known him in any case but a little light leaked out from the room, a couple of flickering candles which outlined his shape.

'I heard the door,' he said, his voice sounding strange to Annabel's ears. 'Miss Nugent, I recognize you but what are you doing here?'

'I was worried about you.'

'Who is that with you?'

'This is Eric Selby, Walter. You know me, do you not?'

'Yes, sir. I know you. What do you want?'

'I think, Miss Nugent, that it would be best if you left me to speak to Walter by myself.'

Annabel was half sorry, half glad to get her dismissal. She walked back down the stairs. She thought of poor Walter up in the ringing room, and felt curious. A little frightened still. Walter wouldn't do anything to the old man, would he? He was a churchman. They were both churchmen. Then she recalled the murder of another churchman only a few days before.

In the ringing room, Canon Selby was saying, 'Shall we go and get something to eat?'

'I'm not hungry.'

'You aren't sleeping up here surely, Walter?'

But Selby saw against the wall a pile of material, old vestments and the like, which seemed to bear the marks of a body. There was, too, a kind of fustiness to the chamber for all its chill.

'What if I am? This is my church – I mean, I am curate here. I can sleep here if I want.'

'Most curates of my acquaintance would expect to be

better accommodated than this. Does Reverend Simpson know you are here?'

'Of course he doesn't. No one knows I am here. Except you and Miss Annabel now.'

'Well, well,' said Selby, 'never mind the fact that you are here for the time being. The question is why you are here when you have a home to go to. I am sure that your aunt needs your comfort and protection.'

'Who?'

'Mrs Slater. Amelia.'

'Oh, my aunt. Yes, perhaps she does.'

Both men were standing face to face. Selby was almost a head shorter than Walter but the authority seemed to lie with him. He spoke the last words softly and put his hand on the other's shoulder. Walter irritably shook off his grasp.

'Is this to do with your uncle's murder?'

'My uncle's murder,' said Walter as if the thought had just occurred to him. He took a step or two backwards. 'You were there when – when Canon Slater was killed, weren't you?'

'Not *when* he was killed,' said Selby carefully. 'But I did arrive on the scene shortly afterwards.'

'What were you doing?'

'I do not know that I have to answer your questions, Walter, but I was out for a walk.'

'On such a cold and miserable night?'

'I have always enjoyed walking in the cathedral close whatever the weather. I was out walking that evening as on so many others and I noticed a noise and disturbance coming from your uncle's place, from Venn House. I wondered if anything was wrong.'

'You did not like Canon Slater,' said Walter. It was a statement rather than a question. 'I heard you two arguing on the day that he died.'

Eric Selby looked surprised at this but he did not ask

how Walter had discovered the argument. Instead he said, 'It is no secret that there was not a great deal of love lost between your uncle and myself but I regret his passing as much as any honest citizen of Salisbury must regret it, especially as it occurred in such terrible circumstances. Does that satisfy you, Walter? I had nothing to do with his murder.'

Without giving any sign that he'd listened to these last words, Walter Slater turned away. He sat down on the makeshift bedding and buried his head in his hands. When he looked up again he seemed taken aback to find Selby still there. Selby was tired of standing. He went to sit on one of a handful of chairs placed in the room for the benefit of the bell-ringers.

'You are a man of the cloth, Walter, as I am. We talk about the sins of others but less often of our own. Something has occurred to make you act in this very uncharacteristic way. You must either be sinning or sinned against. Which is it? Won't you tell me?'

'Oh, you want me to tell you, do you?' said Walter Slater. 'You want me to confess? Very well, I shall.'

Hogg's Corner

Several miles away, in Northwood House, Fawkes was awakened by a shuffling and snorting from the horses. Fawkes – the coachman and valet and factotum to Percy Slater – chose to sleep in a loft above the stables rather than in the cold and cavernous main house. His master made no objection. Percy Slater ran an odd establishment, or more accurately he didn't run it at all but let it fall to slow ruin about his ears. Fawkes might sleep where he pleased as long as he was available when required to convey his master about the place and for other odd jobs. So Fawkes had fashioned for himself quite a cosy area at the gable end which was once used for storage. He had equipped it with a simple bed and a chair and a little table. He liked the way he could look down on the world, even if it was no more than the world of the stables. It gave him the same feeling of apartness as driving a coach. He liked the privacy of the stables, the absence of visitors, not that anyone visited the main house. He probably preferred the company of horses to people. Percy Slater had once told him that he was like Lemuel Gulliver in the story but Fawkes did not know what the man was talking about.

Now Fawkes heard stealthy movements from down below and was wide awake at once. It was that sound which had disturbed the horses. Fawkes was used to the stable noises, the sound of exhaled breath, the creak of the wooden stalls during the night. But this was a human being.

He took hold of an iron bar which lay beside the bed, kept there for just these eventualities. A ladder led up from ground level to rest against one of a pair of cross-beams that supported the planks or flooring of Fawkes's quarters. There was no light in the stables but Fawkes's eyes were used to the dark, and he could just make out the uprights of the ladder from where he lay on his bed, snugged against the end wall. He listened as a first, experimental foot was placed on the bottom rung, then a second foot on the second rung, and so on. The ladder creaked slightly.

Fawkes waited, lying on his back, his head turned sideways to watch the top of the ladder, his right hand gripping the iron bar. Fawkes was not frightened. He did not scare easily. The advantage lay with him, since he was awake and the intruder did not know he was awake. Besides, he had an idea who it might be. In due course, a cap and a head appeared at the top of the ladder.

'Stop right there, mate,' he said. 'I can crack you over the nut before you get a foot higher in the world.'

'Why'd you want to do that, Seth Fawkes?' said the head. 'I mean you no harm.'

'I know you and your games.'

'Well, I'm a-coming up now.'

The head grew to a pair of shoulders, then added arms, torso and legs. There was something monkey-like about the figure which now drew itself over the edge of Fawkes's living quarters. Meantime, Fawkes had swung from his bed and was fiddling with an oil lamp. But he kept the iron bar within reach just as he kept an eye on the new arrival until he had got the lamp hissing and glowing.

'How'd you get in here?' he said.

'Through the door. And, before that, over the wall, Seth.'

'It's a high wall,' said Fawkes. He was so unused to being called by his first name, rather than the more customary

Fawkes, that to hear it was as odd as being addressed by a stranger. Yet the man sharing his little eyrie in the stables was, regrettably, no stranger.

'Leaped it, didn't I,' said the intruder, referring to the wall.

'Regular spring-heeled Jack, aren't you, Adam?'

'Enough of the complimenting. It's a bloody cold night out. Got anything warm to drink?'

Fawkes had a bottle of port, filched from his master. Reluctantly, he uncorked it and passed it to the other man. He watched as Adam swung himself round so that he was sitting with his legs dangling into space. He observed that Adam was wearing a kind of knapsack, which gave him a hunched appearance. The other man threw back his head and tilted the bottle to swallow, exposing his neck and his Adam's apple. A single blow there would do it, thought Fawkes.

Adam put down the bottle. He wiped his mouth. He looked slyly at Fawkes as he handed back the bottle.

'I can guess what you're thinking,' he said.

'Guess away.'

'One quick push and I'd topple off here, wouldn't I?'

Almost right, thought Fawkes, though it was more of a blow than a push that he was considering.

'Why would I want to do that?' he said, aloud.

'To pay me back for that little joke on Salisbury station,' said Adam.

'Joke? Oh, *that* little joke. You pushed me on to the line.'

'You were not pushed but fell. Just toppled off the platform when you saw me coming.'

'You speak as if you was out strolling. Saw you *sneaking* up rather.'

'Anyway, there was no danger, no train coming. You got up and vanished. No harm done. Just my bit of mischief after a good day out.'

Fawkes recalled that recent day out. He'd come in by train from Downton to visit a certain padding-ken or low boarding house run by a Mrs Mitchell. Fawkes had an understanding with Mrs Mitchell which went back many years. After their session together he'd ended up in the pub called The Neat-Herd (but universally known as The Nethers). There he had encountered Adam, not for the first time. They'd drunk quite a bit before Fawkes had to leave for the Downton train. Adam had been in an especially sprightly mood and had accompanied Fawkes to the station, darting around in the black garb he favoured. He was like a devil on wheels. Fawkes thought he'd got rid of him finally but his shadow had played that last trick on him on the station platform, bursting out to surprise him like some silly kid. Fawkes had been pissed enough to topple on to the track but retained enough of his wits to scramble out of the way pretty damned quick.

'You do like mischief and games, don't you, Adam?' said Fawkes now, squinting down his forefinger as if he were aiming a gun. 'You always have liked a spot of mischief.'

'Keeps me going,' said the other happily.

There was an irritating bounce to Adam, as if he was never going to be troubled or put down by anything. Seth Fawkes knew that bounce only too well. He said, 'What do you want here?'

'Your master asleep?'

''Spect so. Most honest people are at this hour.'

'Your master honest? Ha!'

'Beware of your tongue.'

'I know Mr Percy Slater and his honesty. Didn't he commission me to do a little job of breaking and entering a man's room in a hotel because he wanted to know what documents that man was carrying? Letters and such to do with the *honest* Slaters.'

'You should thank me for that commission, Adam. It was me as put your name forward to my master, knowing he wanted a spot of dirty work done.'

'Well, thank you, Seth Fawkes. I am forever obligated to you. That shows you don't bear me any hard feelings for that bit of larking about at Salisbury station. Your mistress now, is she at Northwood House tonight?'

'Mrs Slater is not here from one year's end to another, as you know. She stays in London.'

'What about the old woman?'

'You mean Nan? You can say her name.'

'Does she sleep tight?'

'Don't know, Adam. She don't sleep here in the stables anyway.'

'We won't be disturbed then.'

'Disturbed in what?'

'We're going on a little search,' said Adam.

He shrugged the knapsack off his shoulders and unstrapped it. He drew some sheets of paper from it and began to study them.

'Pardon me,' said Fawkes. 'You may be going searching, but I am staying here. For I have noticed that it is the middle of the night.'

'Then we shan't be seen.'

'We won't be able to *see* neither.'

'We shall. The night is clear. No mist, no fog. There is a little moon to light our way.'

'Whatever you want to do you can do by daylight.'

'Too much risk. Besides, you know I like the dark. I work better then.'

'I'm staying here,' said Fawkes, but he spoke without conviction.

'Pardon me but you are not staying here. I need your head. You know the way to Hogg's Corner?'

'It's not a corner but a few oak trees behind the house. I don't know why it's called Hogg's Corner.'

'Doesn't matter,' said the other. 'That's where we're going.'

'Why?'

'I've got a little scent that's a-tickling my nostrils, a scent coming from Hogg's Corner. You can bring that lamp with you.'

'Don't need a light. I know this place like the back of my hand.'

'But I don't after all this time,' said Adam. 'Besides I may want to do a spot of reading later. You got a spade in here?'

'There's a shovel for mucking out with,' said Fawkes.

'That'll have to do. Get it as we go. And give me a swig from that bottle again. Have one yourself while you're about it.'

Fawkes handed over the bottle of port, marvelling at the cheek of the man. Offering him to drink out of his own store! Once again, as Adam tilted back his head to swallow, he was tempted – very tempted – by the idea of striking him on the exposed throat. But he did nothing apart from take a draught from the bottle after Adam had returned it, in his own good time. Adam stuffed the papers back into the knapsack and slung it over his shoulder as a sign that he was ready. Then he shot out his arm and did something odd. He pressed his thumb into the great dimple on Fawkes's chin.

'There,' he said, 'been wanting to do that for a long time, brother.'

'Keep your dirty hands to yourself,' said Fawkes. 'Don't be so familiar.'

The two men clambered down the ladder to the ground floor of the stable and made their way past the stalls. The horses – there were only three of them since Percy Slater kept as reduced an establishment in here as he did elsewhere – moved uneasily at the presence of a stranger.

Fawkes found the shovel. He was quite glad to be

holding something which might double as a weapon even if it was awkward carrying both shovel and lamp. He took care to walk behind Adam, holding up the lamp to throw some illumination ahead of them both. They entered the yard and Fawkes paused before unlatching the gate, wondering whether Adam had really come over the wall of the stable yard. They stepped out into the open.

'What now?' he said.

'Kill that light,' said Adam.

'There's no one to see,' said Fawkes, though he'd earlier claimed not to need a light.

'Even so.'

Fawkes obediently doused the light. They waited for a few moments until their eyes grew used to the dark. As Adam had said, the night was for once free of mist or fog. A quarter moon hung in the sky. The bulk of Northwood House was to one side, beyond the wall of the stable yard.

'Lead the way, my friend,' said Adam. 'Take us to Hogg's Corner.'

This was what usually happened when Fawkes was in company with Adam. He disliked and sometimes feared the other, but he tended to comply with his suggestions or orders.

They rounded the house and skirted the terrace and the planted beds which extended beyond it. The area was as neglected as the rest of the estate. Weeds sprouted between the flagstones of the terrace and the flower beds were barren or bedraggled. Fawkes looked back at the house. No lights in any of the windows but then there were rarely lights in Northwood House.

There had once been a clear division between the parkland beyond the terrace and the flower beds and lawn, marked by a ha-ha as the land dropped away. But the grass had grown up on both sides and the stone of the hidden retaining wall had been allowed to crumble, so the division was no longer clear even by daylight. All that was left was an abrupt drop between the two levels.

Fawkes knew it was coming and he knew that the drop wasn't much more than four feet or so. Placing shovel and light on the edge, he leaped off into the dark. He half hoped Adam might leap after him and sprain his ankle or worse. Adam did jump but he was so light and limber that he seemed to bounce back up as he hit the ground, like a jack-in-the-box.

'See there,' said Fawkes, once he'd retrieved the shovel and the lamp. He was pointing ahead of him. 'Those trees there, that's Hogg's Corner.'

The two men set off across the rough ground in the direction of a cluster of trees which stood in isolation on a kind of knoll about two hundred yards away. The little hillock stuck up oddly, as if a great head adorned with a few wild tufts had abruptly thrust itself up through the ground. An owl hooted. The men's breath frosted in the air. The grass underfoot was so thick and tussocky that they were almost wading through it. The moon gave off a feeble glow. As they approached the oaks the ground began to rise slightly. It was obvious that the trees were old from their outlines alone. The trunks were thick and the branches twisted like ropes. The trees were grouped in a rough circle on the fringes of the knoll but it was so ragged and incomplete that it did not seem as though they had been planted deliberately in that way. There was a cleared space in the middle like a bald patch.

As Fawkes and Adam moved under the low-lying branches, their feet crunched on the nuts and mast strewn on the ground. Adam halted in the centre of the approximate circle.

'Now light the lamp again,' he instructed his companion.

When Fawkes had done as he was told, Adam crouched down and loosened the knapsack from his back. By the light from the lamp, he examined a sheet of paper which he drew from the bag and laid flat on the ground. He stabbed his finger at a point on the sheet. Fawkes stood behind him, holding the shovel. He might have brought it down on the other's head. But he didn't. Instead he followed the next lot of instructions.

There was a reason why Seth Fawkes did nothing to Adam, despite the provocation and the opportunities. There was a reason he did not strike him across his exposed throat or whack him over the head with a spade. It was because the two men were brothers and because the fraternal bond still held, frayed as it was. Seth Fawkes was the older by a little more than a year. Until recently, they had not seen each other since childhood. Both had been born to a couple who worked on the Northwood estate in old George Slater's time. They came from a large family in which all the children were given Old Testament names. Discipline was strong but there was also some attempt at education by the mother. The children had been taught to read and write, in a rudimentary fashion. Despite the mother's care, though, Seth and Adam were the only survivors.

In fact, Fawkes had long believed his brother Adam to be as dead as the rest of his siblings. Adam had got into frequent scrapes as a youngster, then the scrapes turned to petty crime. He drifted to the city of Salisbury, became involved with the law when acting as a 'crow' or lookout for robberies and, before long, disappeared into the smoke and anonymity of London. After a few years with no word or sign, Seth Fawkes assumed that his brother was dead or in gaol or transported. If he ever thought about it – which he didn't much – then he was relieved rather than sorry. He'd always regarded himself as the respectable one, growing up on the Northwood estate when George Slater lived there with his various wives and continuing to work there even as the place decayed further under Slater's son. Eventually there were only the two of them left, him and Nan (and Percy Slater of course), to occupy a great echo-y house.

So you could have knocked Seth Fawkes down with a feather when, one evening in The Nethers scarcely a year before, he noticed a weathered individual eyeing him. The moment Seth caught his glance, the other moved towards him though he was plainly sitting and drinking and minding his own business in a corner. Seth wasn't a great one for company but he did enjoy a jar or two after he'd been to visit Mrs Mitchell. He liked to wet his whistle and sink himself in memories of Mrs Mitchell's frowsty bed before it was time to return to Northwood House and the stables.

'Mind if I join you?' said the weather-beaten man with a crooked grin.

Seth Fawkes looked round. The place was full of laughter and smoke. There were other empty seats and benches. He shrugged, although when the other sat next to him on the bench Fawkes instinctively shifted a few inches away. He would have moved further but he was wedged into a corner.

'You don't know me, do you?' said the man, placing his pint carefully on the table before tapping his fingers on the battered surface.

'No.'

'I know you though . . . Seth.'

Fawkes looked at the other man properly. 'Mr Fawkes to you,' he said. His companion wore an expression that wasn't so much cheerful as filled with glee. He said, 'It's like a birthmark on you, that hole. Can't get rid of it this side of the grave.'

Automatically, Seth Fawkes's hand flew to his shaven chin, to the great dimple that sat in the centre of it.

'Mind you, you could grow a beard to disguise it,' said

the other. 'I have found that small things are the best disguise, Seth. Even a change of name can work a trick. Spectacles now, they're good. When people look at a face, see, they notice the spectacles but they don't take notice of what lies beneath 'em. Or you can change the colour of the hair with a dye. I recommend a touch of rastik, comes from the East and gives a reddish tinge to the hair. Women of a certain sort use it but I always say why should we be denied the benefits available to the fairer sex, eh? Then, afterwards, you wash it out, see –'

'Why are you talking to me?' said Fawkes. But there was a sinking in his guts even as he said the words.

'I haven't finished yet, Mr Fawkes. Let me finish and the answer to your question will be clear. And you might learn something useful. The point of using this dye on your bonce, this rastik, is that people remember reddish hair just like they remember spectacles. And that will be how you're described afterwards if there've been any witnesses, described as 'a fellow with red hair', see. By that time naturally you'll have washed all the red out and, well, nobody is going to know you from Adam. From *Adam,* I say. Do you know who I am yet, Seth?'

As if to reinforce what he'd just said about dyes, the man took off his cap and ran his hand through his short, sandy-coloured hair.

'Jesus,' said Fawkes. 'It can't be.'

'You're right there, mate. It's not Jesus.'

'You bugger,' said Fawkes.

'Closer,' said the weather-beaten man, replacing his cap. 'I've been called worse in our own tongue and in many other tongues besides.'

'Adam, it's you,' said Fawkes. 'Jesus.'

The man called Adam made to stretch out his hand towards Seth's face. He seemed to want to touch the dimple in his bare chin, the mark by which he'd been able to identify him, although it was more of a mocking gesture than an affectionate one. But Seth jerked his head away and rammed himself further into the corner.

'Aren't you pleased to see your long-lost brother, *Mr* Fawkes?'

'I'd rather you'd stayed lost.'

'Well, there I cannot oblige you. Fact is, I have decided after a lifetime of wandering round this great globe of ours to return to the land of my birth, to the very town where I first saw the light of day.'

'How can I be sure you're who you say you are?' said Fawkes. He knew the truth well enough but was desperate to pick holes in it.

'Oh-ho, like the Claimant, is it? You think I mightn't be who I say I am?'

'Don't know what you're talking about,' said Fawkes. He had an inkling, though. Like the rest of England he had heard of the Tichborne Claimant but he did not read the papers and was not interested in long-running law cases.

'This geezer who everyone thought went down with his ship off South America somewhere but, lo and behold, he turns up in England after many years trying to claim a fortune. Lord, Seth, I have been away many years and I'm better informed than you are. But if you want to be certain I am Adam, then let me tell you this . . . and this . . . '

And he went on to reel out a string of family details about their dead parents and their dead siblings (Abel and Shem and Abigail and so on) – details of which any trace or memory, apart from with these two, had long since dropped off the face of the earth. Seth Fawkes admitted defeat. He took a long draught from his pint and, sighing, screwed himself further into his corner. Adam grew more cheerful or gleeful and went off to get their pots refilled.

When he came back, Seth said, 'What do you want here, Adam Fawkes?'

'I admit to Adam but not to *Fawkes*, no, it's . . . something else instead. I have enjoyed a variety of surnames. Let me see. I have been called Farmer in Australia and Quarles in Canada and Leigh-Smith in the United States and other things in other places. But I've always kept the name of Adam through thick and thin, 'cept once when I passed as a woman. Wasn't Adam then, oh no.'

'None of that tells me what you're doing back here,' said his brother, both disturbed and faintly disgusted by the other's account of his false identities.

'Now, Seth, the way you say those words tells *me* you think I'm up to something.'

'You're always up to something, Adam. Mischief and the like.'

'Nothing could be further from my mind,' said Adam with a twinkle in his eye. 'I wanted to breathe my native air, return to the bosom of my family or all the family that's left me. By the way, I hear you're not married, Seth, you've got no woman, no little nippers to trouble your slumbers.'

'Suits me,' said Seth Fawkes, realizing with irritation that his brother must have been asking questions about him.

'I heard old George Slater had died quite a while ago and that Percy lives in Northwood now. I always had a soft spot for Percy. He comes here sometimes for the ratting in the barn, doesn't he?'

Seth said nothing. He wanted to keep Adam out of his life even though the younger man had only just elbowed his way back into it. He certainly did not want his brother returning to Northwood House and attempting to strike up some sort of acquaintance with Percy Slater. Perhaps he feared they might hit it off.

'What happened to that holy joe brother of his?'

'He's in the Church,' said Seth, squinting down his finger at Adam as though he was sighting a gun and half wishing that he was holding an actual weapon. 'He's what they call a canon in the cathedral.'

'Is he now?'

'There's no place for you here, Adam,' Seth suddenly declared. 'Northwood isn't like it was when – when you last saw it. The place has gone downhill. There's only me and Nan left now –'

'Nan? That old bat. She must be a hundred and six if she's a day.'

'Percy's wife is never there but passes her time in London.'

'Do not trouble yourself, brother,' said Adam, patting his neighbour on the shoulder. Again, the gesture was more mocking than reassuring. 'I haven't come back to go and bury myself at Northwood. The place was a country hole all those years ago and I don't suppose it's any different now. Although there was one thing . . .'

He fell silent for a moment and, to cover whatever he'd been about to say, sank his face in his pint-pot. Then he went on, 'Tell the truth, I've come back to these parts for a bit of peace and quiet. Last place I was in I had to get out of a bit smartish for reasons we needn't go into. So now I'll just find myself a cosy billet in town and won't trouble you at all. Though it would be nice to meet sometimes, wouldn't it, brother? Talk about the old times.'

'I've got to be going to the railway station now, Adam,' said Seth, pushing himself out of the corner and waiting for Adam to shift himself. 'Got to be getting the train back to Downton.'

'I'll keep you company,' said Adam.

And so he did, jigging and skipping and jawing while they made their way through the outskirts of the town and Seth wondered how he could shake him off. Fortunately, he left Seth before they reached the station. Adam asked his brother if he could recommend a good bed-house in the town or – as he said they called it in the United States – a cat-house. Seth pretended not to know what his brother was talking about.

If Seth had hoped not to see Adam again he was to be disappointed. However, his brother did not cause any overt trouble – at least, not to his knowledge – and he assumed that he must have found his cosy billet. Seth didn't ask him where and Adam didn't volunteer any information.

They encountered each other from time to time in The Nethers and Seth's animosity towards Adam started to fade. He had no wife or children or friends apart from Mrs Mitchell (who was a *paid* friend), he preferred the company of the horses in his master's stable if he was honest. Nevertheless he had a brother.

Adam let slip little hints of how he'd passed the intervening years, not honestly it seemed. He'd done his share of thieving and he hinted at darker business. Occasionally at their meetings Adam would pass over an item as a kind of peace offering. It would be a thing of such small value, like a toasting fork, that if Adam had stolen it Seth wondered why he went to the trouble. Nevertheless he accepted it because, in part, he was slightly afraid of Adam and this seemed the best way of keeping him quiet.

And so when he learned that his master Percy Slater wanted to find out what was in the personal luggage of a certain young lawyer from London, Seth indicated to his brother that there could be a little job for him. Now he regretted that closer involvement with Adam. For it seemed to have led to this moment now when the two of them were crouching by moonlight in Hogg's Corner.

Back in Northwood House, Percy Slater was not asleep although it was well after midnight. He was not even in his bedroom. Instead he had been slumbering in his smoking room, over the dying fire, the guttering candles and a couple of near-empty bottles. Slumbering until some sound awoke him. His hearing was good, whatever else about him had decayed. It was a sound from outside. He hoisted himself to his feet and moved unsteadily towards the window. There was a little moonlight. By it, he could just see, pressing his gaze to the pane and screwing up his eyes, the silhouette of a figure standing on the untended ground beyond the terrace and by the ha-ha. For an instant the figure was poised there and then it dropped out of sight. Percy rubbed a hand over his eyes. When he looked again a second shape was wavering against the darkness before it too fell from view. Slater stared out into the night for several more bleary minutes, not quite sure of what he'd seen or whether, indeed, he'd seen anything at all.

Then his attention was caught by a spark of light, a tiny flicker that appeared from amid a circle of trees in the park. Percy began paying attention now. He knew the location of the light. It was coming from the little knoll known as Hogg's Corner. The flicker went out for an instant and Percy realized that it was someone passing in front of it.

Without troubling to light a candle, Percy crossed the smoking room and unlocked the glass cabinet which contained a pair of shotguns. He took one from its resting place and hefted it in his hand. He opened a drawer and, again working by touch, drew a handful of cartridges from a box and slipped them into his trouser pocket. Then he left the smoking room and went down the flagged passage to the kitchen quarters. He found his way with the merest brush of his free hand against the wall.

In the lobby he took a coat from a peg and let himself out of the side door of the house. The night air blew away the fustiness in his drink-fuddled head. He paused for an instant then loaded the shotgun, knowing that if he delayed until he was closer to his quarry the sound of the action would carry across a still night. 'Quarry.' The word amused him but it also stirred something within.

Slater crossed the yard and made a circuit round the side of the house. Like his man Fawkes, he was very familiar with the house and grounds. It was where he'd grown up and although he'd never had his brother Felix's taste for rummaging about the estate, he could still have found his way about blindfold – or after dark.

Percy Slater stood on the weed-encrusted terrace and stared into the night. The light on top of the hillock known as Hogg's Corner glowed with a fire-fly's persistence. Percy considered for a moment summoning Fawkes from his snug in the stables to deal with these trespassers. But he was fairly sure that one of the shapes he'd seen dropping over the ha-ha was Fawkes himself. Something about the angle of the body, its outline, caused Percy to think that one of the night wanderers was indeed his own man.

Percy trusted Fawkes. Or, perhaps more accurately, he had never had any reason to distrust him. Fawkes had worked for his father, as had Nan, and on George's death he had inherited the old retainers along with the estate. Fawkes was of a similar age to himself but whereas Percy had grown slow and was running to fat, the coachman had kept a youthful slightness even as his face had become more aged and disagreeable.

If it was Fawkes out there in the cold and dark, on top of Hogg's Corner, then the question was, who was his companion? At once Percy remembered that odd and unsettling fellow who Fawkes had claimed could get into that lawyer's room in The Side of Beef, the fellow who'd popped up out of nowhere at the dog-fight the other night. Not only had Percy taken against him personally, the fellow hadn't even discovered anything in Ansell's room. But if it was Fawkes together with Adam creeping about the edges of Northwood, what were they doing there?

There was only one way to find out. Percy Slater felt some old instinct uncoil inside him, the instinct to follow a trail, to track down its source, to . . . kill.

Moving lightly on his feet, for all his bulk, and wide awake now, Percy Slater reached the boundary between the garden and parkland. He placed the shotgun carefully on the upper ground and slipped, almost tumbled, on to the rougher grass beneath. When he'd recovered his breath and smoothed his clothes down, he retrieved the gun and set off.

The light in the centre of Hogg's Corner vanished as he drew nearer, since the lie of the land got in the way. But there could be no doubt that there was someone up there. Scraping and scrabbling sounds alternated with subdued grunts or curses. Percy Slater gripped the shotgun in both hands and moved closer still, his breath coming shorter with the exertion and anticipation. He heard a hissing, and the sounds of scraping ceased. Something about the hissing enraged him. If it was his man Fawkes up there, he'd soon sort him out. Him and his companion. Let them know what was coming to them.

'Fawkes!' he said. He was almost shouting. Why shouldn't he shout? This was his house, his land.

If, a few minutes after this, you had been standing on the terrace of Northwood House, you would have heard the sounds of voices raised in threat or anger. It was a still night and the sound travelled easily from Hogg's Corner. The next sound you would have heard from inside or outside the house, since it was the boom of a shotgun going off. Would have heard, unless you were Nan, whose hearing was poor and who slumbered on undisturbed in her room.

A House by the Arno

'It's a very extraordinary story,' said Eric Selby. He'd already given a brief account of how he'd been summoned by Miss Nugent to see Walter, intimating that he had a great deal more to say. 'What I have to say is quite shocking in its way, especially for you, Helen.'

'I am not a little girl any longer, Uncle.'

'Well, I would normally have some doubts about telling either of you, but Walter Slater said that he does not care now who knows his secret. His confession. He told me I might as well shout it from the rooftops. Once I had persuaded him to talk, it poured out of him like – well, like water from a breached dam, like blood from a wound. The poor fellow.'

'Where is he now?' said Helen. 'He is not still in the bell-tower at St Luke's surely?'

'I accompanied him on his way back to Venn House though I didn't see him right to the front gate. Nevertheless he promised me that he would return home and sleep in his own bed, not in the damp and discomfort of the ringing chamber.'

Canon Selby was sitting with his god-daughter and Tom in the seclusion of his drawing room. The rest of the household had long since gone to bed. Selby no longer looked so distracted as when he'd first appeared at the door. A good measure of brandy and Helen's solicitous words had restored him to his usual humour.

'Walter Slater has made a confession, you say?' said Tom.

'Yes, but it was not what you might think. Nothing to do with Felix's death. At least I do not think so. It wasn't even *Walter's* confession in a sense but another's. All I can say is that his father behaved very badly, his uncle too.'

'Percy and Felix Slater?'

'The pair of them,' said Selby, shaking his head. 'Mind you, I had had my suspicions once upon a time. There'd been rumours around the close many years ago. I'd put them to one side though.'

If all this had been designed to sharpen the curiosity of his listeners, it was succeeding. Both sat on the edge of their chairs, while the Canon leaned back in his and took another sip from his glass.

'It appears that Walter Slater is not the nephew of Felix,' he continued. 'He is not the nephew but the *son*.'

'What?' said Tom.

'There is more. Nor is Amelia the aunt of Walter. Rather, she is his *mother*.' He paused to let this sink in. 'Walter was in complete ignorance of his real parentage until the other day, the day of Felix's death in fact. Percy travelled to Salisbury to tell him. It seems that something had prompted Percy to do this, to put the record straight once and for all.'

Helen said nothing. Tom felt himself go cold.

'I called on Percy Slater that day,' he said. 'He invited me to go to Northwood House. I don't really know why. He talked about his brother in quite bitter and sarcastic terms, venting his feelings. He told me not to be taken in by his holy act.'

'Implying that Felix was a hypocrite,' said Canon Selby. 'Well, there'a a grain of truth in that. But we should not judge the dead too harshly.'

'My God,' said Tom, 'do you suppose it was something I said which caused Percy to go off and reveal the truth to Walter?'

He struggled to remember in detail what had passed between him and Percy Slater. There'd been talk about gambling and an argument about the material which had been transferred to Felix, together with some general aspersions on the character of the Canon. Had Tom said something which caused the Canon's brother to go straight to Walter and tell all? If so, Tom realized with dismay, then he must bear a share of the consequences. Whatever those consequences had been, exactly. He put that disturbing thought to one side.

Selby noticed his agitation and said, 'Don't worry, Tom. If you did make some remark – *if*, I say – then it was surely unintended. Like a man walking along a mountain path who idly kicks a stone over the edge and starts a landslide.'

'Thank you, sir, but that's not a very comforting reflection,' said Tom.

'I mean that someone would have kicked the stone over sooner or later. It was bound to happen. From what Walter told me, his father – his uncle, I should say – had been on the verge of informing him of his true parentage on several occasions. He was merely waiting for the right provocation.'

'Which I provided.'

'We don't know that, Tom,' said Helen.

'It is enough to say that Percy acted rashly, even dangerously, by telling this story when he did,' said Eric Selby. 'Yet he cannot be altogether bad, for he brought up Walter as if he were truly his son.'

'What is the story?' asked Helen. 'Tom was only just now describing to me the Slaters' marriage. How they met in Florence and so on. A "strange union", you said.'

'That was no secret,' said Tom. 'Both Walter and Percy said as much.'

'It seems that Felix not only met Amelia when he was visiting Florence many years ago. Her parents had a house by the Arno. It seems that they became – well . . . that they became . . .'

'Lovers,' said Helen.

'Thank you, my dear. Yes, they became lovers. Shortly after Felix returned to England, Amelia suffered a double shock. Her parents died in an outbreak of cholera. No sooner had she lost them than she discovered that she was with child. Having no one else to turn to, she eventually travelled to England to find Felix Slater.'

'To throw herself on his mercy,' said Helen.

'Why, yes, that is how it must have been. We can have no idea of what words passed between Felix and Amelia, but we do know the result. Felix was a rising churchman in the town, fixed on a respectable course of life after all his – his gadding about on the Continent. Of course, he'd been a clergyman when he went abroad but possibly the warmer air – or the looser customs of foreigners – or something else, I don't know what – caused him to forget his vows and his vocation. But he paid the price after he returned for here was a woman, half English, half Italian, on his doorstep, pleading for his protection.'

'Couldn't they simply have married and have done with it?' said Tom. 'If Amelia was expecting a child then, when it came, they could have claimed . . . they might have pretended . . .'

'That the baby was premature,' said Helen.

Both men looked at her, Tom with new respect, Eric Selby with a kind of relief at his god-daughter's plain speaking.

'Amelia was not precisely with child when she arrived in Salisbury,' said the Canon. 'You might say that the child was with her. By this time, Walter had already come into the world. She turned up with a three-month-old baby. Or six months old. Walter can't be quite sure. You understand that he was in a distressed and confused state when he was telling me all this. What he knows, from Percy, is that his mother travelled through Italy and France by herself, a baby son in her arms.

'Though he might agree to marry Amelia, Felix could not – or would not – acknowledge the child as his. At least he did not do so publicly, no doubt thinking of his position. Instead he turned to his brother for help. Percy and his wife had recently lost their own son in infancy. Whether the idea came from Felix or from Percy doesn't matter, but it was the older man who offered or was persuaded to take Walter as if he were his own child. As you've discovered, Tom, Percy isn't a man who has much time for convention. Perhaps he was pleased by this evidence that his clerical brother was – how should I put it? – capable of being a sinner. Perhaps he was moved to pity by the sight of the baby. Perhaps his wife, his first wife, was eager to adopt little Walter as her own. But, whatever the reason, it was an act of kindness that they took the boy. Took him quietly and without fuss and brought him up as if he were truly their own child. At the time they lived in London, far enough away from Salisbury for gossip and rumour not to travel. Though, as I've said, there had been a little whispering in Salisbury itself. He could not keep everything concealed. Felix and Amelia were married in due course. Percy soon afterwards lost his first wife, the woman whom Walter had always been led to believe was his mother. Later Percy married again. I do not know whether Percy's second wife is aware of the truth – that she is a step-aunt rather than a stepmother.'

'And meanwhile Walter grew up believing that Felix was his uncle and Amelia was his aunt?' said Tom.

'It is an extraordinary situation, is it not?'

But there had been little signs and pointers, thought Tom, there'd been puzzling moments which were now explained.

Such as the affectionate way that Amelia had bade farewell to Walter in the porch of Venn House the first time he'd encountered them, or the young man's reference to her as not being especially 'aunt-like', which Tom had taken as being no more than a comment on her age and manner. Then there had been Percy Slater's odd attitude to his 'son', the dismissive way he'd talked about him. Tom had put it down to disapproval of Walter's decision to go into the Church and to lodge with Felix.

But, regarded in this new light, the situation suddenly became plain. Felix's saying that Walter was just the son he would like to have was the nearest he had come to admitting the truth. There was a kind of daring hypocrisy in the statement. Similarly, hadn't Canon Slater mentioned his happiness when Walter came to live with him? With *them*, of course, with the unacknowledged father and mother. What was Amelia Slater's attitude to all this? She must surely have been delighted to have her son under her own roof for the first time. What was her part in all of this? How easy or hard had she found it to remain silent all these years? Was it part of the understanding between the couple that she should never refer to Walter's true parentage?

He was suddenly aware that a silence had fallen and that Helen and Eric Selby were looking at him curiously. Rapidly, he explained how the story they'd just heard had thrown light on several small incidents or remarks which he'd noticed since his involvement with the tangled affairs of the Slater family. He had one final question for Canon Selby.

'Do you think that George Slater, the father, was in on the secret?'

'Who can tell, Tom? It is possible he was kept in ignorance. His older son lived in London while George did not, by all account, have much to do with the younger one. Perhaps he also took Walter for the son of Percy.'

'Why do you ask, Tom?' said Helen.

'Because if George Slater did know, then he might have made some reference to it in his manuscript, his memoir.'

And, Tom thought without saying it out loud, that might have been a motive for the theft of the Salisbury manuscript and the murder of Felix.

Running over the events of this dramatic day as he lay, restless, in his bed at The Side of Beef, Tom Ansell realized how the revelation of Walter's parentage had shaken everything up. It was like looking through a kaleidoscope. New patterns emerged. But they were ugly patterns, with a bloody red and a jealous green the predominant colours.

Canon Slater emerged in a new light. Tom wasn't sure whether it was a flattering light or not. The passion that had run in his veins hadn't simply been for the artefacts of the past. He had once, in his younger days, been the lover of a woman – a girl, in fact, for Amelia could have been little more than that when they met in Florence by the Arno – a girl whom he had got with child, as the expression goes. Tom wondered whether the Canon's preoccupation with the past, with digging up remains, was somehow related to his having buried the scandalous part of life, if only as a kind of reverse image of it. Then he recalled Slater saying that he'd always been interested in disinterring the past from his earliest days, that he'd enjoyed fossicking round the Downton estate as a child. Well, Felix Slater was dead now and there'd be no more fossicking.

If there'd been a shortage of suspects or motives for the murder of Canon Slater before, there were now several to be drawn directly from Felix's own family.

Tom had scarcely known his father – not much more than a tall man in a blue uniform, as he'd described him recently to Henry Cathcart – but at least he could recognize him as a father. He tried to put himself inside the mind of a man of about the same age as himself who, with brutal suddenness, discovers that the gentleman and lady he's been brought up to treat as his uncle and aunt are his actual parents. It was as if he'd discovered that the man his mother had taken for a second husband – Martin Holford, a kindly but somewhat aloof figure who'd steered Tom into his career in law – was revealed to be his actual father. How would he, Tom, respond? Disbelief at first, yes. And then . . . what? The effect would surely be overwhelming.

Walter's reaction had been a compound of anger and dismay. His immediate instinct had been to run away from Venn House and hide himself in the comforting surroundings of St Luke's. But had that really been his immediate instinct? Had he rather been driven by fury or distraction to go straight to Venn House and confront the man now revealed as his father? Did he kill the cleric while his mind was turned by the news, and then flee to the shelter of the bell-tower?

Tom thought again. If Walter Slater had endured a distraught encounter with Felix, then there would have been the sounds of it reverberating round the household on the evening of Felix's death. Raised voices and angry tones would have been overheard by the servants. And by Mrs Slater too, surely. Unless she was somehow involved in her husband's death, an accomplice to his murder. Tom had a vision of Walter storming into the house and confronting his mother. Of tears and embraces coupled with garbled explanations and infinite regrets, while anger bubbled away underneath. Had they together gone to see Felix? Together brought about his death?

The strain on Amelia over the years must have been immense too. If Walter had been subject to a violent shock, she had had to endure many years of pain. To have surrendered her son all those years before and then to have him return home as a kind of guest, but without being able to acknowledge him for who he was, must have added to an almost intolerable burden.

But even as Tom's imagination painted the picture of an anguished mother, he wondered whether it was so after all. What he'd seen of Amelia Slater suggested a coolness, a detached and half-amused attitude to things. She didn't look as though she might be carried away by a sudden rage. Yet one of the things that Tom had learned even in his brief time as a lawyer was that there was no predicting human responses. The most passionate and vehement person might take an insult or shock with equanimity, while the meekest of individuals could suddenly lash out in fury.

If Amelia Slater hadn't herself been the murderer, however, that did not mean she might not be covering up for her son's action. For the first time in her life she might have acted in truly maternal, protective fashion. Another picture: Amelia entering Felix's study and seeing Walter standing over her husband's body and – understanding and forgiving everything in an instant – giving him the time to make his escape before she ran out with her maid into the fog and darkness of the West Walk to raise the alarm.

There was a third member of the Slater family to consider. Percy Slater had travelled from Downton to Salisbury on the day of his brother's murder – and shortly after Tom had called on him – to find Walter and to put the record straight, as Eric Selby had expressed it. If Walter had indeed gone on to kill his father, then Percy bore part of the blame for the manner in which he had revealed the truth to his nephew. He, too, must have lived for years with the weight of deception, with the pretence that the boy who'd known him as a father was no son to him. All that time, his resentment at his pious and holy brother must have been simmering. According to Canon Selby, Percy had on several occasions come close to revealing the truth. That he had finally done so without warning, on a fog-bound afternoon, was perhaps the least surprising thing of all.

To go to the son instead of having it out with his brother perhaps showed a kind of vindictiveness – or cowardice – on Percy's part. He intended to wound the young man who had betrayed him by going to live in his father's house and following his father's priestly vocation. *He has turned Walter's head,* Percy had said of Felix. It must have looked like gross ingratitude for Percy's having taken on Felix and Amelia's young child all those years before.

Had Percy taken a further step though? Perhaps he hadn't been content to wound with mere words but had resorted to force. Was it Percy who'd been the unknown visitor to Felix's study and who, while his brother was occupied about some business at his desk, had taken the flint from the display case and plunged it into the exposed neck of the man he despised?

One thing seemed certain. That Felix Slater had been killed by someone he knew. The evidence showed Felix was taken off guard when he was sitting at his desk. That argued for someone close to him, a member of his family. Yet, by the same token, it suggested there'd been no violent argument or furious confrontation beforehand. Which, in turn, indicated that if it had been Walter or Amelia or Percy – or some combination of the three – who had killed him, then the murder had occurred at a composed moment, when the sound and fury had died down. Which, by another turn, tended to exonerate Walter and Amelia and Percy, since Tom couldn't believe in a 'composed moment' with all these family secrets being dug up, such old and rotting secrets smelling to high heaven.

They'd discussed how much of this should be conveyed to Inspector Foster, since it might alter the way he treated the murder investigation. Eric Selby's view was that the secret was primarily Walter's and that it was his to tell to Foster if he chose. At the least he should have another day or so to come to that decision.

Tom's mind had chased in circles and he settled to sleep

with nothing resolved. Nor did he sleep soundly. It was perhaps the thought of rotting secrets which caused Tom to dream of the other part of this long day, the part before he and Helen had heard Selby's revelation.

He was once again on the slope of Todd's Mound, gazing into a dark hole bored straight into the hillside. He recognized it as the burial chamber. Standing above him was Canon Selby, sermonizing, jabbing with his forefinger, holding forth like an old-time preacher. Behind him and over the ridge of the hill there gathered black clouds while the wind scattered a few brown leaves. The owlish, benevolent look had vanished from Selby's face. In its place was a rigid contempt. He was denouncing Felix Slater for hypocrisy and immorality. Denouncing him by name. Around him were the members of the Slater family, Amelia his wife and Percy his brother and Walter his son. They were nodding in agreement with every fervent word.

But there were others present as well. It was a jumbled reprise of the scene outside Venn House when Tom had been escorted away by Inspector Foster and the constables. In Tom's dream there was Fawkes the coachman-cum-valet to Percy, there was Henry Cathcart, there was a gaggle of servants, including Bessie the housemaid and Eaves the gardener. They too were nodding their heads vigorously. Someone said, 'I did it.' Tom struggled to identify the speaker but he could not. Could not even say whether it was a man's or a woman's voice. The words were blown about on the wind like dead leaves.

Eric Selby stretched out his arm and pointed down the hill. Tom turned to look. He expected to see Felix Slater, the object of Selby's vitriol. But there was a different dead man making his way up the hill. It was Andrew North. Although he had never seen him alive Tom recognized the sexton, on account of his worm-eaten countenance and the rents in his raggedy clothes through which his flesh glowed grey and green. Lower down the steep slope stood North's sister, Mrs Banks. She was wringing her hands. Dead as he was, North was moving up the slope with vigour. To his alarm, Tom observed that he seemed to be making in his direction. But North veered away from Tom, merely turning his gaunt and eroded head as he passed. Then the dead sexton fell on to his hands and knees in front of the entrance to the hole and, like some animal, scuttled inside without a backwards glance.

Tom shivered, not because of the chill from the rising wind, but because he knew that North was never going to come out alive from that hole again. Except that he was already dead. So, if he was dead, would he emerge alive after all? In search of some solution to this conundrum, Tom looked uphill towards where Selby was orating. But there was no one there at all. The slope of Todd's Mound was quite bare.

Mrs Banks's House, Again

The next morning Tom was surprised by the early arrival of Helen at the hotel with Inspector Foster. He was in the middle of breakfast when he saw Helen beckoning to him from the door of the dining room, the policeman at her shoulder.

'Tom, you've finished?' she said and then, while he was still swallowing a mouthful of egg and bacon, 'You must come with us.'

'Why? Where?'

'Better if we explain outside, Mr Ansell,' said Foster. 'We're raising folks'curiosity by standing here.'

This was true. The handful of other diners were staring at the trio in the doorway. Tom got his coat and accompanied Helen and the Inspector into the street outside the porch of The Side of Beef. It was a more promising day with the sun breaking through.

Inspector Foster explained that they had identified the body extracted from Todd's Mound as being almost certainly that of Andrew North. Not from the body itself since that was decayed beyond recognition but because of an item discovered in a pocket of the trousers which the corpse was wearing. From within a pocket in his own coat the policeman withdrew a crumpled, discoloured sheet of paper and passed it to Tom.

Tom unfolded it. There were a couple of lines of writing in a neat hand: *And if the tree fall toward the south, or toward the north, in the place where the tree falleth, there it shall be.*

'See,' said Helen, who had obviously studied the paper already and grasped some point which was eluding Tom.

'The writing looks like Andrew North's from what I remember of an inscription in a book of his,' said Tom. 'And I do see these words have something to do with where his body was found, in a place near a fallen tree, but even so –'

'It's from the Bible,' said the Inspector. 'From Ecclesiastes, Chapter 11, verse 3, to be precise.'

Tom looked at Foster who was tugging at his great side-whiskers in pleasure. 'Not that I'm a great Bible reader, Mr Ansell, but Constable Chesney knows the Good Book backwards and he identified it straightaway. I always say we are able to find out everything we need to know from within the force.'

'Look at the words the writer has underlined, Tom,' said Helen impatiently. 'He has underlined the 'And' at the beginning and 'north' in the middle. He must have taken the words to apply to himself, as a kind of message to *Andrew North* that he should search that spot under Todd's Mound.'

'I suppose so,' said Tom, peering more closely at the grubby, creased piece of paper and asking himself whether Helen wasn't letting her imagination run away with her. The fact that Inspector Foster appeared to believe it, however, made the idea more plausible.

'I have asked Miss Scott to come with me, Mr Ansell, when I visit Mrs Banks to break the news to her of her brother's death. Now that he is officially dead, as it were, I must ask to examine his effects to see whether they contain any clue. I have already prepared the way and it cannot come as a great surprise to her, but such news is always shocking, you know, however braced you are against it. To be the bearer of bad tidings is perhaps the worst part of a policeman's lot – a lot which is generally a happy one, in my experience. Mrs Banks was very complimentary about Miss Scott on account of your visit yesterday and I thought it would be helpful to have a feminine touch in this business.'

'And I thought you should come as well, Tom,' said Helen, 'considering that you were the one who actually found the body of this unfortunate man.'

Tom wondered whether all this wasn't a bit irregular but he was willing to do what he could, which shouldn't amount to much since it was the Inspector who would have to deliver the message while Helen supplied the 'feminine touch'. On their way to the artisans' dwellings which lay beyond the great cathedral, Foster explained how the day would surely come when women would be recruited into the police alongside men, a notion to which Helen responded with enthusiasm, provided, she said, 'we are not expected merely to dry tears and mop brows.'

'Have you seen Walter Slater?' said the Inspector.

Tom was taken aback by the direct question. He hesitated before replying. 'No, I haven't seen him, but I've heard he is back at home.'

'Home?'

'In Venn House, I mean.'

'Is he now?' said Foster while Tom wondered whether he'd betrayed a confidence and whether the curate had actually returned to Venn House after his meeting with Eric Selby the previous night.

They reached the terrace of workers' cottages. Mrs Banks had noticed them passing the window of her parlour for the front door was opened before Foster could knock. She must have been cleaning out the grate for there were traces of ash on her hands, which she was wiping on her apron. One look at Foster's face was enough to tell her the news. Water welled into her eyes. The Inspector did not have to say a word. Helen stepped forward and embraced the older woman. She had to bend down to do so. Foster and Tom stood by, feeling both uncomfortable and relieved.

'I am forgetting my manners,' said Mrs Banks after a few moments. Her voice was, surprisingly, under control. 'We should not be standing out here like this for neighbours to see. Come inside and I will make you a pot of tea.'

They crowded into the small parlour. There was a neat mound of ash beneath the grate. Tom observed a pile of folded clothes together with needles and thread on the chaise, all of which Mrs Banks carefully removed to a corner. When the tea had been made and they were all sitting down, the three visitors crowded side by side, the Inspector showed Mrs Banks the tattered bit of paper containing the Ecclesiastes verse.

'Yes, that is Andrew's hand,' she said. 'He always wrote a neat hand. But what do the words mean?'

'It is part of a verse from the Bible,' said Foster. 'I am not sure the words mean a great deal in themselves but they seem to have confirmed to your brother that he was on the right track when he went searching out at Todd's Mound.'

'The right track!' said Mrs Banks. 'He was never on the right track since he caught the illness and went about sniffing and digging in the earth to take things out.'

Rather than putting things in, thought Tom, which would have been his proper job as a sexton. At that moment a shadow fell across the window followed by a clattering outside the front door and then the same noise in the hallway. Constable Chesney almost fell into the small room. He looked about in confusion.

'What is it?' said Foster sharply.

'Guv, I need to speak to you urgent,' said the policeman before looking at the other three and, obviously considering that his abrupt appearance might be disrespectful, adding, 'sir and ladies.'

Foster ushered Chesney out of the room and the two held a whispered conversation in the hall. Tom and Helen, and probably Mrs Banks as well, didn't even attempt not to overhear. Not much more emerged than the words 'dead', 'murder', 'suicide' and 'shot', which was enough. Hearing the whispers, Tom turned cold. He at once thought of Walter Slater.

Inspector Foster entered the parlour once more.

'You will have to excuse me, Mrs Banks. A – a circumstance has arisen which requires my immediate attention. Please accept my condolences on the loss of your brother Mr Andrew North and be assured that, if he has been the victim of a crime, then we will leave no stone unturned in the pursuit of the perpetrator.'

Tom and Helen turned to watch as Foster and Chesney passed the window outside. Besides curiosity, Tom felt a faint sense of frustration. What was the urgent circumstance? Who was dead? Were they murdered or had they committed suicide? Was it to do with the death of Felix Slater? Why weren't he and Helen being invited along to assist the authorities? After all, they had some expertise by now in the matter of dead bodies found in suspicious surroundings.

'What is happening?' said Mrs Banks. 'Did I hear that policeman use the word murder?'

'I heard it too,' said Tom.

'Not to do with my brother?'

'I don't believe so.'

'What is happening?' repeated the woman, in confusion, almost anguish. 'All these murders in a small place. Has there ever been such a thing before?'

'Mrs Banks,' said Helen, 'I know that Inspector Foster was going to ask whether he might examine your brother's room for any evidence about his . . . his unexplained death. Now that he has been called away so suddenly, could we have a look instead? Like the police, we have an interest in finding out who is doing these deeds.'

'You may do as you please, Miss Scott. If my Andrew

was still here, I would not have allowed anyone to disturb his things . . . but now that he isn't here . . . well, I . . . '

Her already creased face grew more wrinkled and she struggled to hold back her tears.

'We found this,' said Helen. 'It is your brother's, I think.'

From her bag she produced the pewter flask which they'd picked up on the flank of Todd's Mound.

Mrs Banks took the flask and angled it so that the initials incised into the surface caught the light.

'Yes, this is his. "A.H.N."' She recognized the shape of the initials rather than spelling them out. 'Where did you . . .?'

'Close to where he was found,' said Tom, concealing his surprise that Helen had kept the flask. 'It must have fallen from your brother's pocket.'

'Thank you for this,' said Mrs Banks. 'You want to look at Andrew's room, you say? There is nothing to see there but you may go upstairs. His is the door on the right.'

Tom followed Helen up the narrow stairs which led off the hall. There was a cramped landing at the top with two doors giving on to rooms that made up the entire first floor of the cottage. Helen opened the right-hand door, paused on the threshold for a moment and then in a couple of paces crossed to the window and drew back the curtain. The sexton's room was plain, with furniture made out of deal and faded wallpaper depicting some unidentifiable yellow flowers against a brown background. In addition to the single bed there was a chest of drawers, a kind of cabinet and a wash-stand. The place was very clean but the subdued light of a November morning only served to strengthen the melancholy feel of somewhere which was unlived-in or abandoned.

'What do you hope to find, Helen?'

Tom stood uneasily just inside the doorway. He quite admired her manner of treating the place as if it were her own – really, a confident young woman could get away with a great deal these days which would cause a man to be slapped down! – but he didn't see what they could expect to discover in Andrew North's room.

'I don't know, Tom. We're investigating.'

'Like the police.'

'Inspector Ansell has a certain ring to it, don't you think, Tom?'

'Or Inspector Scott. After all, Foster was looking forward to the day when women might join the force. Perhaps he was joking.'

'No, he wasn't. Seriously, Tom, we've heard that the cathedral sexton was a man who spent his time poring over books and maps after he caught this infection for digging things up. He made notes, he wrote things down. His sister called him a methodical man, just as she is an orderly woman. As well, Andrew North seemed to be looking for guidance, for signs that he was on the right track. He copied down that Bible verse about the fallen tree and underlined the words that he imagined applied to himself. Perhaps he wrote down something which might help to identify his murderer. Perhaps he has concealed something valuable in this room.'

It didn't seem very likely. While Helen slid open the drawers in the chest to see nothing more than a few items of clothing, clean and neatly folded, Tom got down on hands and knees and peered under the bed. Peered at a chamber-pot which was decorated with a frieze of pink roses. It was the same pattern as the china ware on the wash-stand. Tom detected the neat and womanly taste of Mrs Banks.

The only item of furniture still to be examined was the cabinet. It had a triple function, as a writing desk, book-case and medicine chest. There was shallow ledge for writing on, a shelf immediately above it which contained a few books and on top of the shelf a closed case in which to store potions and pills for when the occupant of the bedroom was sick.

Tom looked at the books. He was already aware that

there were hidden depths to Andrew North but he was surprised to see volumes of poetry, including *Palgrave's Treasury*, as well as *A Children's Guide to Classical Myths* and histories of Salisbury and Wiltshire. He tugged at the handle on the miniature double doors of the medicine chest but they wouldn't budge.

'It's locked.'

'Then try this,' said Helen, holding up another object which she'd retrieved from her bag. It was a small, dull-looking key.

She couldn't help smiling while she waited for Tom to ask the inevitable question. Which he did.

'You remember when they brought the body out of that chamber in the hillside,' said Helen, 'and the policemen were wrapping it up in canvas and I was standing close by –'

'Too close, I thought,' said Tom, 'but I told myself it was just your way. After all, you have a duty to be curious about everything, Helen, since you intend to write a sensation novel.'

Helen drew herself up and said, 'Curiosity brings its own rewards, sometimes. I looked down and saw this key on the ground. It must have fallen out of Mr North's pocket as the constables were manhandling his body.'

'You should have given it to the Inspector.'

'But the key might not have been the dead man's. It could have belonged to anyone who chanced to have been wandering over the hillside with a hole in his trouser pocket. Anyway, what does it matter, Thomas?'

'Why didn't you tell me you'd found a key?'

'How was I to know exactly when we might need a key? Maybe we weren't going to need one at all. I was waiting for the right moment, the appropriate moment, to produce it, just as I waited for the right moment to return her brother's flask to Mrs Banks. Now are you going to see whether *this* key will open *that* chest, or shall I?'

Tom took the key and inserted it in the lock in the chest. It worked, of course, as he had somehow known it would. He felt the thrill of discovery when the key turned. There were no medicine bottles or pill-boxes inside. Instead four cardboard boxes were neatly arranged. Helen took out the topmost one, which was about the size of a shoe-box. On it was a label, half torn off. In ornamental capitals was printed, *Adler's Ointment: Suitable for all Types of.* While Tom was wondering about the application of Adler's Ointment, Helen unfastened the lid. Inside was a mass of items individually wrapped in brown paper. She placed the box on the ledge of the cabinet. They unfolded a couple of the items. Then all of them, arraying them on the ledge. The result was a jumble of objects, made of stone and metal and baked earth.

Helen looked a bit disappointed but Tom thought of how, when he was a child, he'd collected bric-a-brac and stored it away in just this fashion, not wrapped up in brown paper but kept in secret in a cigar box belonging to his dead father: a broken bit of clay pipe, an empty snail shell, an old and tarnished coin.

But he was also reminded of the more formal display in the glass cases in Felix Slater's study, for here too in Andrew North's collection were flint arrow-heads and bronze buckles and decorative pins, together with tiny shards of pottery. It seemed to be conclusive proof that the sexton, encouraged perhaps by Slater, had become possessed by the desire to dig up the past and hoard the little treasures which he had found. But this was no trove. The items here didn't look as though they could be worth much more than the objects in Tom's childhood box, even assuming anyone had been willing to purchase them.

While he was picking over the contents of the box, Helen had reached for a black-bound book which was also inside the cabinet.

'What's that?'

'A kind of diary,' she said after a moment. 'At least it has dates and brief entries and some sketches too. The diary of a dead sexton. It is the same writing as on the note which the Inspector showed us.'

Tom peered over her shoulder as she riffled through a few pages. As Helen had said, there were dates followed by a couple of handwritten lines or a short paragraph, sometimes with a drawing or two.

'It seems to be more of a record or a catalogue of what he'd found, and where and when,' said Tom, pointing at an entry and reading aloud, '"8th March – Glyde Field – 4 arrow-heads and a copper pin. 29th March – Saddler's Farm pasture – stone axe-head and bronze buckle."'

Underneath or alongside some of the comments were simple impressions of the objects. Tom imagined Andrew North, sitting up here in the solitude of his room, and sketching the little artefacts as a way of confirming his ownership of them before he deposited them in the cardboard boxes. As well as pictures of the buckles and flint-heads there were diagrams of squares and circles with shaded areas and crosses, occasionally with initials (G.F., T.B.) next to them. It took Tom and Helen a minute to work out that these were plans of the fields and mounds where Andrew North had made his discoveries or where he hoped to make them.

'Isn't it extraordinary, Tom? Not this diary or whatever you want to call it, but that someone can go out into the countryside and just dig up long-lost items wherever he plants a spade.'

'I dare say there was some research involved. You'd have to know where to dig in the first place. And there was something which Felix Slater said to me when we met. He said that people have lived on the plain for centuries. There are signs of the past everywhere if you know where to look. It must be true but maybe not all the time.

See here: "9th April – FS and I to Hobb's ditch – came back empty-handed."'

'FS is surely Felix Slater.'

'I thought Mrs Banks said that her brother and the Canon fell out. Yet he is still going off exploring with him.'

'These entries refer to last year, Tom. Here is more writing with dates, during October and November but with nothing at all for December and then beginning again this year in, let me see, February. Oh! Hear this: "Buried dog at request of FS today – ground hard – She fussed about and rolled her eyes – FS and I had words." Who is this "she"?'

'Mrs Slater. Her pet dog died and was buried in the garden,' said Tom, easily able to imagine Amelia Slater fussing and rolling her eyes. 'I have seen the spot by the river. Perhaps this was when the bad feeling started between North and Slater.'

'The last dated entry is for 3rd October this year, and then just blank pages.'

There was a silence while they both contemplated the significance of those blank pages.

'When did Mrs Banks say that her brother found the bracelet?'

'In the spring, wasn't it?'

Helen turned a few pages back and almost straightaway found the place. She read aloud: '"Eureka! – I do better by myself – out by the old road and south of the Martins house – golden bracelet." He was so excited or distracted that he forgot to put the date but the previous entry is early April.'

'We'd better look through these other boxes.'

'In case there's a gold bracelet,' said Helen.

'For the purpose of our investigation.'

'Of course.'

The other cardboard boxes, hastily examined, proved to contain much the same assortment as the first one. They discovered the bracelet, however. Gold it might have been but it did not look especially attractive or valuable. The discovery proved that North had been a hoarder, not a thief, otherwise he would surely have attempted to sell the thing. No, judging by these remains, Andrew North had been a magpie even if a knowledgeable and methodical one.

Then Tom and Helen sat down side by side on the narrow bed and looked through the rest of the sketchpad or diary for any hint to the dead man's fate. Closer to the final entry, the handwriting grew less tidy and the comments seemed to become more personal but less easy to follow. There was the same quotation from Ecclesiastes – *And if the tree fall toward the south, or toward the north, in the place where the tree falleth, there it shall be* – but without the underlining. There were references to an unnamed person who was surely his sister, Mrs Banks. (*A good woman but she does not approve. Would like to ask but I glare at her and she dare not.*) There were even brief descriptions of what might have been dreams (*dark yews – shadowed places – Atropos, beware of Atropos.*).

Helen noticed this last entry and said, 'Tom, what's Atropos?'

'I don't know.'

But he did know, couldn't quite bring it to the surface. Something was lurking in his brain, a story he'd heard once, a picture he'd seen somewhere.

They discussed whether they should take the the black-bound diary but decided against it. It did not seem to reveal anything significant about the circumstances leading to the man's death, after all. Similarly, the contents of the cardboard boxes, though valuable to the late sexton, didn't appear to provide a sufficient motive for his murder and should remain with his other effects.

They replaced the items in the boxes and restored everything to the cabinet. Helen left the key to the cabinet on the wash-stand, in the place where North could have put it if he'd taken it out of his pocket. Inspector Foster might chance across it when he searched the room. As a competent investigator, he would test it on the locked cabinet and come to his own conclusions.

Tom and Helen went downstairs to say goodbye to Mrs Banks, who was furiously sewing in the little parlour. She was making a repair to a man's coat. Needle in one hand, a frayed portion of cloth in the other, she was bent forward over the coat, tugging at a thread with her teeth. Tom remembered that she took in neighbour's clothes to repair. She looked up, dry-eyed, and folded her hands over her work. She said, 'Work is good. It takes your mind off things. Have you seen enough?'

'Yes, thank you, Mrs Banks,' said Tom. 'We have left the room as we found it.'

'We are sorry for your loss,' said Helen.

'Thank you, my dear.'

The couple went out into the lane that ran outside the terraced cottages. It was mid-morning by now and the light was stronger. Helen made to loop her arm through Tom's but he was preoccupied. Before they'd gone more than a few yards he stopped and clicked his fingers. Helen almost laughed, it was so like a man acting badly, acting out the pretence of suddenly recalling something.

'Atropos!'

He walked a few feet further.

'Well, are you going to tell me?'

'It was the sight of Mrs Banks sewing that did it. That and the book on the shelf in her brother's room.'

'Yes, you may tell me, Tom. You've had enough pleasure at my ignorance and slowness by now.'

'Atropos was one of the Fates in Greek legend. There were two others – Clotho was one and the third I forgot the name of. The first unreeled the thread of life, the second decided where it should be severed and the third – that was Atropos – she actually did the deed.'

Tom mimed snipping a dangling piece of thread with a pair of scissors.

'Andrew North was an enquiring man, self-educated. There was a book about Greek myths in his room, a children's guide. So it would come naturally to him to make that kind of reference – to talk about Atropos with her shears snipping off the thread of life. And there is more. One of the pictures that Felix Slater had in his study was of the three Fates. North probably saw it on the wall, perhaps the Canon explained to him what it meant.'

Tom could hear the excitement in his own voice. He felt elated to have deduced this. To have forged the link between a one-word entry in Andrew North's diary, a classical picture, a children's guide and a woman bent over her sewing in her parlour. But Helen looked not so much baffled as disbelieving. He waited, eager to explain more. But his love had already understood and was not impressed.

'Very good, Tom, but it doesn't get us any further. I can see what you're saying but, for all we know, the sexton was doing no more than expressing a sense of doom. Perhaps he had a feeling that someone was after him, and his feeling was right. But Atropos isn't a real person. Unless . . .'

Now it was Helen's turn to grow excited. Rather than click her fingers she clapped her gloved hands though she was encumbered by her bag.

'Unless it is the Canon's wife. The mysterious Mrs Slater who I have yet to meet. Atropos is a woman, you say. We saw that entry in the diary about the day Mrs Slater's dog was buried in the garden. She was upset, rolling her eyes, didn't he say?'

This time it was Tom's chance to be sceptical.

'I don't think so. I can't see Mrs Slater killing someone because she didn't like the way he'd buried her dog. Besides it was months ago, back in the winter.'

Tom and Helen stood facing each other in the lane, silent. A couple of passers-by stared at them, wondering whether they were having a pause in an argument. Eventually the two resumed their progress back towards the cathedral close and the city beyond. There was no more to say for the time being. They'd exhausted the possibilities of Atropos and even Tom had to admit that his insight had provided more sound than light.

As they were walking along the West Walk and coming closer to Venn House, they saw a gaggle of individuals standing just outside the gate, several men and a couple of women. Tom recognized all of them. There was Inspector Foster and Constable Chesney in company with Henry Cathcart, the store-owner and his father's old comrade, and Mrs Slater. To one side were Eaves the gardener and Bessie the maid. Eaves sneezed violently, wiped his nose with the back of a grimy hand and gave Tom and Helen a lopsided grin, with his gardening tools clanking in the kangaroo-like pouch he wore. Bessie seemed to be imitating her mistress. She was rubbing at tear-filled eyes. Her collar was definitely askew. Tom wondered what Canon Slater would have said, if he were still alive.

Inspector Foster and Mr Cathcart were trying to calm Amelia Slater, who was garbed in black. She was alternating between sobs and gesticulation, oblivious to her surroundings. Cathcart put a hand on her shoulder, only for it to be shrugged impatiently off. The Inspector and his constable stood at a slight distance, not attempting to intervene, though Foster was making futile shoving motions with his hands as if to urge everyone to step back inside, out of public view.

Seeing Tom and Helen, he broke away from the group and met them as they approached. There was relief on his bewhiskered face that he had someone normal to talk to.

'What is happening, Inspector?' said Tom.

'Peculiar developments,' he said.

And they were peculiar, Tom and Helen decided, talking it over later in the calm and comfort of the snug in The Side of Beef. In fact, the news was so disturbing that Helen forgot to make more than a passing reference to her first sight of Mrs Slater and Mr Cathcart. For the news which Constable Chesney had brought to Mrs Banks's cottage, the news which had to be whispered in the hallway and which caused the Inspector to rush off, concerned the death by shooting of Mr Percy Slater, Felix's brother. His body had been discovered early that morning by Seth Fawkes and an old woman who lived and worked at Northwood House ('She is called Nan,' Tom explained to Helen. 'She has lived in that place since the time of Percy's father. She and Fawkes.')

Percy Slater had been found in a clump of trees a few hundred yards from the main building, apparently a victim of his own shotgun. But killed by his own hand or by another's? Who could say? After stumbling across the body in the early morning mist, Seth Fawkes had taken the carriage to Downton and then, finding that there were no trains leaving for Salisbury, had driven on to the city to report the death of his master at the police house. He appeared wild-eyed and dishevelled.

There was no further information at this stage, according to Inspector Foster. No one – that is to say, neither the aged Nan nor Fawkes (who slept in the stables for some obscure reason of his own) – could shed any light on the matter.

It might have been assumed to be a suicide since Percy was known to be somewhat reclusive. He had a reputation for drinking and gambling. His wife spent her time not at Northwood but in London. But, with the recent death of Felix Slater, the Inspector's mind had inevitably turned to thoughts of murder. The task of finding Walter Slater, whom he believed to be Percy's son, became more urgent. At the very least, there was the obligation to inform him of his father's death. Tom Ansell and Helen Scott knew the truth of the matter, that Walter was in fact the son of Felix, but to raise this at the moment would only have muddied the waters. Inspector Foster had gone to Venn House because Tom had told him that that was where Walter was. However, apart from the servants, the only occupants he found inside were a fresh widow and a regular visitor, Mr Henry Cathcart, who had apparently come to discuss mourning clothes with Mrs Slater. There was no sign of Walter.

Hearing that he was looking for the man he described as her nephew, and pressing the Inspector for the reason, Mrs Slater flew into a great state, not so much on account of the violent death of her brother-in-law but because of the continued absence of Walter. She broke down in tears and as the Inspector tried to leave – seeing that there was no more information for him to gain in Venn House – she pursued him through the garden and out into the West Walk where Constable Chesney was stationed. Chesney was rocking on his heels and no doubt wondering how much longer his guv'nor was going to be inside the big house. Henry Cathcart, meanwhile, was chasing up the garden path after the widow in the attempt not so much to console her as to get her to return inside.

While Foster recounted all this to Tom and Helen, they exchanged slightly uncomfortable glances. Both of them could guess why Amelia Slater had reacted so hysterically. But if the Inspector noticed their discomfort, he didn't mention it. Instead he said, 'Mr Ansell, you mentioned that you hadn't actually seen Walter Slater but that you heard he had returned to Venn House. How did you hear?'

'I can answer that, Inspector,' said Helen confidently. 'My godfather Canon Selby saw Mr Slater yesterday evening, saw Walter that is. They met . . . somewhere in the town. My godfather said that they talked together and when they parted company, Walter was making his way back to Venn House.'

'He was going home?'

'I suppose you could say that.'

'What would *you* say?' said the Inspector, picking up on Helen's qualified reply.

'Venn House isn't Walter's home, in a sense,' said Tom.

'Well, whether you call it his home or not, Walter is no longer there,' said Foster with a touch of impatience. 'Hasn't been seen in the place since the night of Canon Slater's murder.'

'You must ask my godfather. He met him last,' said Helen.

'I intend to. It is a matter of urgency to trace the young man.'

After the Inspector had departed to question Eric Selby, Helen said, 'The truth will come out now. My godfather will be bound to tell that policeman what Walter told him.'

'Which will point the finger of suspicion at Walter. It must do. Do you think he is involved in Percy's death?'

'I don't know, Tom, I haven't even met him. Is it likely that a man could kill both his father and his uncle? Can any man feel so strongly and violently against his own kin?'

Such crimes seemed to be fit only for the most sensational pages of a newspaper or a shocker of a novel, not connected to a curate in a cathedral city. But Tom, who had no uncles and only the most distant memories of his father, could only sigh.

'I don't know either. Walter seemed a very . . . pleasant, easy-going individual – for a churchman. But who is to say how he or anyone might respond? He discovers the man he thought was his father is his uncle, and vice versa.

He might be so furious with both of them that, in his distraction, he does something dreadful. If the Inspector were here, he'd probably tell us not to jump to conclusions. And if I were the Inspector, I'd question Percy Slater's man Fawkes very carefully.'

'Why?'

'I didn't trust him or his looks,' said Tom, recalling Fawkes's gesture of squinting along his finger like a man looking down a gun barrel. 'He is supposed to have discovered the body of his master early this morning and then come racing into Salisbury to inform the police.'

'Supposed? If he'd had a hand in the business, he'd hardly have rushed off for help,' said Helen. 'And what has all this to do with the death of that sexton? And your Atropos?'

Tom confessed ignorance. They were no further forward. It was only when Tom went upstairs to his room that he came a step closer to a solution to the mystery.

Hogg's Corner, Again

If Tom and Helen had been able to have a glimpse of Seth Fawkes at that moment, they might have been surprised. He was striding up and down the overgrown terrace at the back of Northwood House, his face contorted and his mouth working as he gave vent to his feelings. His grief and anger at the death of his employer were quite genuine and growing stronger.

He had, as Inspector Foster described, driven at first to Downton and afterwards to Salisbury to report the mysterious demise of Percy Slater to the proper authorities. Seth Fawkes had then returned to Northwood House with a sergeant and a constable. Together, they removed the body from where it lay inside the ring of trees which fringed Hogg's Corner. They carried it into the house where, after some debate, it was taken to Percy's bedroom. Nan did her best to arrange the corpse decently. A local doctor was summoned from Downton not so much to pronounce on the cause of death, which was apparent enough, as to confirm the sergeant's opinion that this was no suicide.

Percy Slater had died as a result of a chest wound. His shotgun had been found lying nearby. Even a layman could see it would be difficult if not impossible for a man to inflict that kind of damage in that kind of place by his own hand. Seth Fawkes did not dispute this. He merely said that he had no knowledge of how Mr Slater met his end. His story was that soon after first light he had been alerted by a flock of crows circling above the early mist which covered Hogg's Corner. Also, he had a sense that all was not well. Furthermore, there was no sign of his employer. (He neglected to say that Percy Slater didn't usually emerge from his room until mid-morning.)

Fawkes went on to describe how he'd at first gone out alone, to almost stumble over Percy's body in the clearing at the top of the knoll. He returned to the house and told Nan before taking the carriage and driving to Downton. All this and it was not yet nine o'clock on a November day. He was wild-eyed and dishevelled when he reached the Salisbury police house. Whether it had been suicide or murder, there was no immediate reason to suspect him of having a hand in the death of Percy Slater.

Yet there was much which Seth Fawkes left unsaid both on his visit to the Salisbury police house and in subsequent answers to the sergeant's questions – and Fawkes was not a voluble man at the best of times. He had indeed gone out early in the morning to find Percy's body. There *was* a flock of crows in the air and on the tree branches round Hogg's Corner, and Seth *did* feel that all was not well. But he found his master's body because he knew it was there, having first seen it some six hours before by the glow of an oil lamp which he had carried from the stables. He had been witness to the events which led up to the fatal wounding of Percy Slater. He knew that it was not suicide but murder.

That gap of six hours had been to allow his brother to make his get-away.

What happened was this. After consulting the drawing which he laid out on the bare ground, brother Adam had fixed on a particular spot where there was a tiny hollow, three or four feet wide, roughly in the centre of Hogg's Corner. If the knoll had really been a balding human head, then the hollow would have been the impress of a finger-tip in the topmost point of that head. Adam instructed his brother to start digging, telling him that he would take over after the first couple of feet down, reassuring him that they would not have to dig far.

'How'd you know this is the right place?' said Seth, unwilling even to begin.

'Because, brother, this here tells me so –'Adam waved the sheet of paper which he had taken out of his rucksack – 'and because any fool can see that this here mound is hollow in the middle and the earth has fallen in at just the point where you're about to start a-digging.'

'Any fool can see that this is a wild goose chase,' said Seth. 'It's a mare's nest.'

Adam put down the lamp and crossed the distance between himself and his brother. He closed the space with a kind of caper. The two men were about the same build and height, and Seth was the older, though not by much. Yet Seth felt intimidated by the nearness of the other. He always did, whether Adam was in a mischievous mood (screwing a thumb into his chin) or a more malevolent one (jumping out at him on a station platform).

'It is not a wild goose chase or a mare's nest or any other silly animal lurking in that head of yours. I know what I'm doing. Leave the brain-work to me. You can do the other. And what you are doing, brother of mine, is digging here.'

To indicate the place, Adam stamped his foot in the middle of the hollow like a petulant child.

'Do it yourself,' Seth wanted to say but he did not. Instead he scraped at the surface of the ground to clear it. The edge of the spade clattered against some small stones and pebbles as he flicked them out of the earthen hollow. The sound would carry a distance on the almost windless night, thought Seth. As he worked, he allowed himself to grunt and curse. There was no law against showing Adam he was unhappy. He almost hoped that they would be interrupted. Yet there was no one to interrupt them apart from Percy Slater. And, if he knew Percy, his employer would be lolling drunk in his smoking room or snoring in his bedroom.

At that moment there was an urgent hissing sound from Adam, who'd been crouching on the ground and, with the aid of the lamp, poring over the wretched plan which he'd weighed down with a couple of stones. Seth stopped, his spade poised to cut into the ground. He listened.

There was no mistaking it. Noises of breathing, of panting and wheezing. Seth recognized the approach of his master, Percy. Despite wanting to be interrupted a moment ago, he now grew alarmed. What was the old devil doing up and about at this time of night? Then a shout rang out. 'Fawkes!'

Seth did not move, did not reply. There was more wheezing as Percy Slater began to climb the short slope to the crown of Hogg's Corner. Adam moved the few paces which separated him from Seth and took hold of the spade. Seth was holding on to it so tight that his brother had to prise his fingers from the handle. At first Seth thought, why does he need the spade when I have already started doing the digging for him?

The light cast a subdued circle in the immediate area of the plan while everything beyond was in shadow. Seth could not see clearly what his brother was up to as he scampered towards the ring of trees at the approximate point where Percy would appear. But he could guess.

Time passed. There was a pause in the heavy breathing and then a sigh. Again came the call 'Fawkes?' but it was less a shout, more of a question. It crossed Seth's mind that he might cry out a warning to Percy but even as he opened his mouth, there was a clang and clatter from the edge of the knoll. Seth stumbled towards the spot.

Under a tangle of low branches stood Adam. He was holding the spade which he had just used as a weapon. On the ground lay Percy. Seth got down on his hands and knees. His master was still breathing, breathing steadily, all things considered. It didn't sound as though there was anything much wrong with him. He might have been asleep. A great fury seized Seth but, when he clambered to his feet, he spoke calmly enough.

'What have you done, brother?'

'Didn't want us to be disturbed. I gave him a rap on the noddle.'

'And now you give me that spade.'

Adam surrendered the spade. It was a heavy, old-fashioned implement, with a wooden handle and shaft around the bottom of which an iron blade was fitted like a kind of tunic. Adam must have hit Percy with considerable force because the blade was loose. As if divining his thoughts, Adam said, 'He's a tough 'un with a thick noddle. Only gave him a tap. Keep him out long enough for us to finish the business.'

For almost the first time in his life, Seth detected a note of apology or justification in his brother's voice. It gave him heart for what he did next.

Flinging the spade behind him, where it would be out of his brother's reach, he said, 'I've had enough. No more business here. You will help me take Mr Slater back inside and you had better hope, Adam, that he keeps breathing steady.'

Adam stooped down and picked up something from the ground.

'To be honest, brother, I don't care whether Mr Slater keeps breathing steady or whether he keeps breathing at all. I came here to get a job done and I'm not going until it's finished. Now, pick up the spade and get back to it.'

There was only the little light of the quarter moon and the trio was in the shadow of the trees. More by outline than because he could see clearly, Seth realized that Adam was holding a shotgun. Seth knew it belonged to Percy. His master must have taken it from the cabinet in the smoking room before coming out to see what was going on. A sensible precaution – until someone else got their hands on it.

Neither man moved. On the ground Percy Slater started to snore. The sound was incongruous in the circle of Hogg's Corner.

'See,' said Adam, 'no harm done. He's sleeping sound as a nipper. Now, Seth Fawkes, you go and pick up the spade and you get digging. Otherwise I swear I'll let loose with this. Not at you, maybe, but at him.'

He waggled the shotgun in the direction of the snoring man.

Seth knew he was defeated, for the time being. He turned round and began to cast about in the dark for the spade. He couldn't find it straightaway. He went across to pick up the lamp and search for the spade. He swung the light from side to side. The spade was lying a few yards off. Seth had just picked up the spade when it happened. The snoring ceased and there was a scrabbling sound. Seth turned back, to see Percy in silhouette sitting up and then rising unsteadily to his feet. Brother Adam was standing a few yards off, cradling the shotgun. He did not hesitate but swung the weapon towards the staggering man. There was a flash of light and a ringing report, which stunned Seth.

Afterwards Seth could not decide whether Adam had deliberately fired or whether the gun had discharged by accident. Either way the result was the same and Percy Slater lay stretched out in the middle of Hogg's Corner with a dark hole in his chest.

Nor did Adam seem overly troubled. 'Should have rapped him a little harder in the first place,' was all he said.

'You bugger,' said Seth.

'Give me the spade,' said Adam. '*I'll* dig if I have to.'

'Come a step nearer and you'll get your head stove in. That gun is empty. It's only got the one barrel. I've got the spade and a longer reach than you.'

Seth swung the spade towards his brother's head. It made a whooshing sound in the air.

'Not very fraternal, Seth.'

Nevertheless, Seth's tone and behaviour together with the disastrous turn the night had taken must have persuaded Adam that he was going to get no further. He dropped the shotgun on the ground.

'All right,' he said, 'all right. Hold your horses. Here's what you're going to do. You're going to give me a few hours to get clear of this place and after that it's up to you. Whether you bury this big bag of bones or whether you go running off to the peelers with some story, it's up to you, brother. But if I get taken, I'll make sure you get taken as well. And if I swing for it, I'll make double sure you swing alongside me. I saw a public hanging once, in Aylesbury many years back, a Quaker who'd gone bad and poisoned his fancy bit of stuff. It went bad for him at the end too. He died hard, as they say. Course, we don't hang people in public now, we're too civilized for that palaver. But there's still the scaffold and the rope and the drop, and you will be there with me to share it, indoors or out. Got that?'

He did not wait for a reply – anyway, what was there left for Seth Fawkes to say? – but seemed to drop into the darkness beyond the edge of the mound. Holding the oil lamp and the spade, Seth went over to Percy's body to confirm that his master was dead. Then he retraced his steps across the field and scrambled up the ha-ha and so round the side of the house and back into his eyrie in the stables.

Seth didn't doubt that his brother meant what he'd threatened. That if he was apprehended, he would do his worst to ensure that the blame and the punishment for Percy's death were shared. Seth felt a touch of grief for Percy but, much more, he felt angry with Adam. His immediate concern, though, was to preserve himself and to stay where he was. He did not want to live the life of a fugitive, let alone face the scaffold. His position at Northwood House should be secure. The master might be dead but there were others with a legal stake in the place, Percy's wife and that clergyman son of his.

Seth Fawkes did not sleep that night but, as soon as first streaks of grey were showing in the east, he went back to Hogg's Corner. The crows were circling above the mound. Percy Slater's body lay where it had fallen, arms and legs outflung and a great red tear in the centre of his chest. The corpse was stiff and cold. The shotgun was a couple of yards away. The spot in the middle of the mound, where Seth had been directed to begin his excavations with the spade, looked untouched. There was no visible evidence as to why Percy Slater – or anyone else for that matter – should have been out at Hogg's Corner in the middle of the night.

Seth had thought hard in the last few hours. Although he was not as quick-witted as his brother Adam, he was no fool. He realized that the death of the owner of Northwood House would have to be reported to the law, and sooner rather than later to avoid arousing suspicion. He also realized that his first idea, that Percy's death might be made to look like a suicide, would not hold water. The fatal wound was in the wrong place. Seth contemplated spinning some yarn about spotting a band of gypsies in the neighbourhood of the estate, or seeing thieves being pursued from the house by Percy and then hearing a single shot. But he decided to keep things simple, he decided to stay close to the truth. Spinning a story meant getting tangled up in lies, and remembering what was true and what was false. Ignorance was the best defence.

Accordingly Seth Fawkes alerted Nan to what he'd found. The woman, who was as tough as old boots, tottered out to Hogg's Corner and saw for herself. She seemed perturbed by the sight and wrung her hands but she asked no questions, as if the discovery of a body was an everyday event. When she returned to the kitchen, she settled down to a bowl of porridge while Fawkes took the carriage to Downton and then on to Salisbury.

Now, several hours later, Seth was striding up and down the weed-strewn terrace while Nan, indoors, was fussing over the corpse of Percy and assisting the local doctor. Meanwhile the sergeant and the constable were tramping over Hogg's Corner as they examined the scene of the crime, stroking their chins and looking wise and coming to the conclusion that a crime had been committed.

The sergeant had asked Seth and Nan a few questions. When had they last seen Percy? Had they been disturbed in the night? Was there any sign that the house had been broken into? Did they hear the sound of a shot? That kind of thing. Nan had professed genuine ignorance while Seth pretended to his. The old woman had prepared some supper for her master early the previous evening and then left him to his own devices in the smoking room, as usual. Seth said that he'd seen his employer at some point in the previous afternoon, which was true enough.

In the hours since the murder of Percy Slater, Seth's feelings had not abated but grown stronger. He was still half afraid of his brother, and did not doubt Adam's threat to tell tales on him if caught, but the anger almost outweighed the fear. Percy had been a decent enough cove in his way. He'd been a toper and a gambler and had allowed the estate to wither away, but he had made few demands on Seth. Now he was dead, murdered, and a basic sense of justice in Seth demanded that someone should pay for the crime.

Tom's Room

The autumn afternoon was drawing to a close. Tom Ansell was about to go into his room to write a note to David Mackenzie, from whom he had received a letter that morning, lamenting the 'misfortune' which had landed him in gaol and asking to be kept informed. Meanwhile Helen was waiting for him downstairs in the snug of The Side of Beef . They had been invited to dine with the Selbys that evening.

Jenny the chambermaid was at the top of the stairs as Tom arrived on the first floor. She drew aside to let Tom pass and, as she did so, gave an almighty sneeze.

An unthinking 'Bless you' was on Tom's lips when something made him pause. The maid had already mumbled an equally automatic 'Sorry, sir.' She drew out a dirty bit of cloth from her sleeve and wiped her nose. Tom couldn't help noticing her hands. She had long, bony fingers with reddened tips.

'Jenny, is it?' said Tom. 'Can I speak with you a moment? Speak in my room?'

The chambermaid looked taken aback but nodded. She followed Tom into his bedroom and remained by the door, which she left ajar.

Tom stood still for an instant. He wondered what to say next and was given his cue when the girl sneezed again.

'That's a nasty cold, Jenny. Who did you catch it from?'

'Dunno, sir,' said Jenny, bafflement replacing the slight apprehension on her face. 'One of my nieces, I 'spect.'

'And I wonder if anyone has caught it from you in turn.'

Jenny glanced over her shoulder at the partly open door. Obviously, she was dealing with a guest who'd gone a bit soft in the head. Should she humour him or make a dash for it?

She should have made a dash because the strange young gentleman crossed to where she was standing in a couple of strides and, before she could react, seized her left hand and held it up in front of her face.

'Where did you get this? This ring? Who gave it to you? Or did you steal it?'

Jenny shook her hand free from Tom's grasp. 'Steal it! I never . . . he . . . said . . .'

'Yes? He said. *Who* said? What did he say?'

'It was given me by – by a friend.'

'When was it given to you? A day or two ago?'

'Maybe.'

'Then you had better tell me who your friend is, Jenny. The last time I saw that ring it was inside a glass case in a house belonging to a dead man. You've heard of Canon Slater, you must've heard about his murder?'

Jenny turned pale. She staggered. Afraid that she was about to faint, Tom put an arm round her and guided her towards a chair. He wondered whether he should go and get Helen. He wondered whether he was making a terrible mistake. Yet even as he looked again at the ring on Jenny's finger while he was helping her to sit down, he was certain that it was the very one which he'd glimpsed in Felix Slater's study. The ring was tarnished, yes, but what really distinguished it was the irregular zigzag pattern, incised into the soft metal not using a modern implement but something which was primitive and ages-old.

Tom knelt down in front of the chambermaid. She shook her head when he asked if she wanted a glass of water. She wouldn't look at him. He stood up once more.

'Listen to me, Jenny,' he said, striving to keep his voice low and even. 'I believe that you accepted that ring in good faith, as a token from an admirer perhaps. You've more or less admitted that you were given it only a day or two ago. Now, I don't know where your friend got the ring from. Perhaps he received it in good faith also. But I need you to tell me about it, because I think that this – what you are wearing on your finger – has come from the house of a dead man. I recognize it.'

At this, Jenny extended her left hand, palm outwards, and stared at it as if it belonged to someone else.

'He said it was like an engagement ring, only not official,' said Jenny. She spoke even more quietly than Tom had, as if she was talking to herself. 'He said it was old, and said how it had been a whatd'youcallit? – a hairloom – passed down through the generations. He said I must wear it in private where only I should be able to see it . . . and I didn't wear it private and look what has happened.'

'Are you engaged then?' said Tom. He was waiting to work round to the identity of the man who'd given her the ring.

'Not official engaged,' repeated Jenny, still staring at her hand, now curled up in her lap. 'I think he must've been joking with this ring. He's give me joking presents before, toasting forks and such.'

'I don't understand,' said Tom, but remembering the inexplicable burglaries in the cathedral close.

Jenny looked up at Tom for the first time. There was a shrewdness in her look now, a shrewdness and something else besides. 'He give me the ring 'cause he was paying me back. He got something beforehand.'

Tom felt uncomfortable. Perhaps sensing this, Jenny continued, 'It's not what you think. I already give him what you think, and give it him for nothing. And do you know, mister, here's a funny thing . . . '

'Yes?'

'I didn't mind giving it him for nothing.'

Tom saw that they were getting bogged down in detail. 'I don't care very much how you came by the ring but I believe it to be the property of a dead man,' he said.

Jenny turned her gaze from him. 'I'm sure it's an honest gift,' she said after a time.

'So where did the ring come from?'

'I don't know *where* it come from, mister, but it was Adam gave it me.'

And she went on to explain that Adam – a quite well-spoken chap rather older than Jenny and one who'd knocked about the world a bit, by his own account – had tipped up in the city a few months ago out of nowhere. Now he did some unspecified job in another part of Salisbury. A labouring job, maybe, because he had scratched and dirty hands often. Though he seemed to be too clever to earn his living with his hands. He was a bit mysterious, didn't give much away. He befriended Jenny after drinking one night at The Side of Beef, he soft-soaped her.

When they'd got more confidential (which was Jenny's word), they'd sought out places where they might . . . you know. Adam claimed that he couldn't risk his reputation with his employer by taking her back to where he worked and lodged while she, Jenny, was accommodated on the top floor of the hotel when she wasn't staying with her sister and innumerable nieces. So they had to look out for open-air spaces, for cosy nooks or flowery meadows. Luckily it was summer and there were plenty of both to choose from. Then, with the cooling of the weather, came a cooling in the friendship. Until a few evenings ago when Adam appeared in the back yard of The Side of Beef, with a particular request.

Here, the bravado which had been in Jenny's tone up till now dribbled away. Eventually Tom got her to admit that Adam's request had been to tell him the floor and number of the room occupied by a visitor from London, a young lawyer. Also, she was to turn a blind eye during the next few minutes while he went and had a poke around. In fact, instead of turning a blind eye she might keep watch for him. In double fact, if he could borrow her pass-key for an instant he could slip in and out, and no one the wiser. He meant no harm, he said. Just wanted to have a peek at the gent's room. In return, he promised Jenny that she would receive something . . . a present . . . a surprise. And it was true, wasn't it, no harm had been done to the gentleman's belongings, only they were left somewhat disarranged.

'S'pose you're going to tell Mr Jenkins, sir?' said Jenny after she'd finished her recital.

Tom shrugged. He didn't know. He ought to inform the landlord about the chambermaid but at the moment there seemed bigger fish to fry.

'Well, go and tell him then,' said Jenny with a return of the old defiance. 'Mr Jenkins asked me for what I give Adam and I couldn't abide the thought of him even laying a hand on me – which he's tried to do often enough. He's had a down on me ever since. Go and tell him and see if I care.'

'Go and tell who what?' said Helen.

She was standing at the door to Tom's room.

'I grew bored with waiting, Tom. I was starting to think you'd found another dead body or drowned yourself in the bath or something. And I have had an idea about Atropos. But first, who's telling who what?'

'It doesn't matter,' said Tom. 'I'm not going to tell anyone anything, Jenny, as long as you tell me a single thing in exchange. This fancy-man of yours. Is he just Adam to you or does he have another name?'

'Why, yes, he is called Eaves,' said Jenny. 'Adam Eaves. Which I thought was funny, if you think about it. Adam Eaves.'

'The gardener at Venn House,' said Tom. 'The man with the shears.'

'Atropos,' said Helen.

'Atropos who cuts short the thread of human life.'

'What are you talking about?' said Jenny.

Later it struck Tom as odd that in all the time he had been asking Jenny about her fancy-man, she had not sneezed once. If she had caught the cold from one of her nieces, he knew now the person she'd passed it on to: the gardener who'd sneezed violently before giving them his lopsided grin. The gardener who'd certainly been responsible for thieving innocuous kitchen items from the other houses in the close and who had, with an almost equal certainty, thieved away the life of his master, Canon Felix Slater.

Tom ran out of the room and clattered down the stairs to the lobby of The Side of Beef. Helen raised her eyebrows at Jenny in female commiseration or incomprehension before following him, calling him to wait. She caught up with him on the pavement. The sun was beginning to set, a glaring red descent through the chimney smoke and the mist starting up from the river.

'Where are you going, Tom?'

'The cathedral close.'

'I'm coming too.'

'No, do not. I think that Eaves is a murderer.'

They stood there an instant, undecided. Helen glanced up at the sign which hung above the hotel porch. The carcass of beef which advertised the place was glowing red in the late afternoon light.

'Then we should go and find Inspector Foster. If you're right then this Eaves is a dangerous man.'

'Yes, yes,' said Tom. 'But in the meantime the fellow may be making his escape if he hasn't already done so.'

Helen saw the hectic look on Tom's face. He nodded at her and then set off at a smart pace down the crowded street. She had no choice but to pursue him.

* * *

Henry Cathcart was going to make a confession to his wife. He walked wearily down the stuffy passage leading to her room and knocked on the door. It was late afternoon, a time when Constance was usually lively (by her standards) after her nap. In fact, Constance had been more alert recently. The murder in the close had given her zest. Even the 'Come in' that answered Henry's knock was firmer than normal.

He was not pleased to see that Grace was in the room, fussing around the table on which were displayed his wife's various remedies. Not pleased, but not surprised either since Grace spent most of her waking hours with her mistress and some of her sleeping ones too.

'I should like to be alone with Mrs Cathcart,' said Henry.

Grace's gaze flicked towards Constance, who was sitting up in bed with a copy of the *Gazette* in her lap. The maid's look seemed to say, *I will leave the room but under duress and only if it is all right with you, Mrs Cathcart.* Or perhaps she meant no such thing and it was only that Henry was sensitive to Grace's looks. She left the room with little fuss, however.

'Shall I draw the curtains, my dear?' said Henry when they were alone. A spectacular autumnal sun was brushing the rooftops of the houses on the other side of the street.

'Leave them, please, ' said Constance. 'It is nice to see the outside world from time to time.'

Henry stood indecisively near the window. Eventually he came to sit on the edge of Constance's bed. His wife shifted her attention away from the newspaper. Perhaps she sensed her husband was about to say something significant. He was wondering where to begin even though he had already told the story, or parts of it, to the Inspector earlier in the afternoon.

'Constance, I . . .'
'Yes?'
'I have been behaving rather foolishly, weakly, if you like . . .'

And Henry Cathcart went on to describe how he had allowed himself to entertain occasional visits from Mrs Amelia Slater. Of how he had perhaps been more encouraging of them than he should have been. Of how, from the outside, such things might look compromising. Of how, in fact, he had compromised himself in a more dangerous sense by visiting Venn House on the very evening of the Canon's murder. Had discovered the unlocked front door and paced up the silent passage and paused outside the closed door of Felix Slater's study.

(He did not mention to Constance that he had dropped his monogrammed handkerchief somewhere near the study door – the handkerchief which was speckled with blood actually from a shaving-cut and no more sinister source, and which had been seen by Bessie the maid and retrieved by her mistress.)

Henry said that he had slipped out of the Canon's house with the sense that something indefinable was wrong, only to be drawn back a few minutes later by the brouhaha surrounding the murder. He was as amazed as anyone else to see that the haplesss individual being ecorted away by the local police was Tom Ansell, the son of his late comrade-in-arms. Henry hadn't informed the police that he himself had walked into Venn House since he had seen nothing inside and didn't want to muddy the waters of the investigation. Of course he did not believe that Ansell had committed the crime – what would be his motive, for one thing? – and assumed that it wouldn't be long before the unfortunate young lawyer was released.

(Which assumption was correct. Cathcart neglected to say, though, that his first thought on hearing that the Canon had been murdered was to imagine the wife doing the deed. Hadn't she talked, almost fondly, of widowhood?)

Now, however, things had taken a peculiar and even darker turn with the death of Percy Slater at his estate in Downton and the disappearance of Walter Slater and the hysterics of Mrs Slater. It was as if the whole family was labouring under some curse, like characters in an ancient tragedy. Accordingly, he had decided to tell the Inspector what he knew – which wasn't much – and had referred to his visit to Venn House on the night of the first death. He wanted to have everything clear and out in the open.

(Or almost clear and out in the open. Cathcart had been frank with Foster, up to a point. He'd hinted, man to man, that he had a partiality for Mrs Slater, a partiality which had always stayed strictly within the bounds of respectability. He described how he had paid her the occasional visit, or she him, to discuss the stock in his store and the clothing catalogues, for he valued a lady's perspective. He mentioned that he'd dropped a personal item in Venn House on the evening of the murder, a handkerchief which had subsequently been returned to him. He admitted this only so as to guard himself against further . . . insinuations from Amelia. If the police were aware of the full story, then the widow could not exert any pressure on him. In truth, Foster had not been very interested and listened to Cathcart with scarcely concealed impatience. He had bigger business to attend to.)

Finally, Henry Cathcart described to Constance how he had 'seen through', as he put it, Mrs Amelia Slater. She was a – he hesitated before saying this – an unstable woman, perhaps a dangerous one. He had witnessed for himself her hysterics earlier that day. She seemed to be obsessed not so much with her dead husband but with her absent nephew. He didn't know what to make of her or of the situation in general.

(Which was more or less true.)

Constance heard him out. It did not take very long, for Henry had not a great deal of substance to say. Her great eyes grew wider and she nodded once or twice as if what she was hearing wasn't much of a surprise. Then, looking more animated than Henry had seen her in many months, she leaned forward and patted her husband's hand where it lay on the bed-cover.

'There, there, my dear,' she said in a tone which suggested that he rather than she was the invalid. 'I perhaps know more about what's been going on than you think. Long ago I concluded that Mrs Slater was the kind of woman that you have just discovered her to be for yourself. I'm glad your eyes have been opened. Now perhaps we can talk about making that trip to London to see Mr Moody and Mr Sankey . . . '

Cathcart sighed, whether with relief or vexation he couldn't have said. He half expected her to make some comment about there being more joy in heaven over a single sinner that repenteth, etc. Instead Constance glanced at the *Gazette*.

'The authorities do not seem any nearer to discovering the murderer of Canon Slater.'

'No. It is a mystery still.'

Although for Tom Ansell and Helen Scott, the mystery was almost solved.

The Spire

Tom and Helen were witness to a peculiar sight as they approached Venn House at a brisk walk. Far from having to search out Adam Eaves in his lair in the garden – as they expected to do if they were to find him at all – the very man appeared before them. He burst out of the gate in the wall when the couple were a hundred yards or so away. Instinctively they halted and Tom flung out his hand as if to protect Helen. Tom wasn't quite so hot on the chase as he had been when he'd first grasped the gardener's secret from what Jenny had revealed. The few minutes which it had taken him and Helen to cover the distance between The Side of Beef and the West Walk had given Tom the space to think of Helen's warning of danger. Yes, it was dangerous. This was a likely murderer they were seeking. Yet, Tom told himself, the man had probably fled in the interim since they had glimpsed him that morning.

But, no, he was fleeing now, at the very instant when Tom and Helen arrived at the place. Another figure rushed out behind him, looking to neither right nor left but intent on the man in front. There was fury in his every movement. He was waving an arm in the air, almost shaking his fist. This person too looked familiar. It was – although this was hard to explain – the coachman to Percy Slater. Fawkes, he was called.

The two ran across the secluded lane like men in a race who are nearing the finishing line and putting on a final spurt. They were black shadows in the red twilight. Both men wore the little caps known as billycocks, which somehow added to their malevolent, pantomime look. Tom recalled that scene at Salisbury station on his arrival a few days earlier. Two figures, silhouettes in the fog, playing some peculiar game on the plaform, the way one of them had toppled on to the railway line while the other merged into the shadows. He couldn't explain this either but he was convinced it was these two, Eaves and Fawkes, that he'd seen.

A low wall separated West Walk from the great stretch of lawn which fronted the western end of the cathedral, and this wall Adam Eaves now vaulted. There was something animal-like in his speed and agility. But the man at his heels was only a little less quick and lithe. He, too, cleared the wall and soon both men had the look of malevolent children cavorting on the lawn.

'What is happening, Tom? I recognize your gardener but who's the other one?'

'It looks as though someone has got to Eaves before us. Percy Slater's man, in fact. Perhaps the gardener is looking for sanctuary in the cathedral. I'll see where they're going while you get help.'

'There must be people in the cathedral. They could help stop them.'

Tom visualized a clutch of ancient reverends and canons raising a hue and cry. 'No,' he said, 'you go to the police house while I try to keep track of Eaves and Fawkes. Don't worry, I will not go near them.'

Helen saw the sense in what he was saying but she put her hand on Tom's arm and told him to be careful, before walking back down West Walk at a rapid pace. There was a handful of other afternoon strollers further up the road but none of them appeared to have noticed anything odd about the sight of two men running in the cathedral precincts.

Tom Ansell didn't have to leap the boundary wall since

he was standing conveniently near a gap in it which opened on to one of the several gravelled paths criss-crossing the lawn. By now the figures of Eaves and Fawkes were black specks against the immensity of the west facade, which was receiving the full force of the setting sun. The clerestory windows burnt like fire and left red spots dancing in front of Tom's eyes.

He started to run across the grass and the effort and excitement of the chase drove all caution out of him. He observed the two in front veer to the left as they neared the steps leading to the double doors in the western porch. The doors were shut fast, presumably locked. No entry or escape that way. The man in front – gardener Eaves – rounded the north-western corner of the church and vanished from sight. Something about his movement suggested that he knew where he was going, that he had a particular destination or bolt-hole. His pursuer – coachman Fawkes – was only a few seconds behind him and he too slipped round the corner.

Tom was able to save time by changing course and going on a diagonal across the grass after the first two. He ran towards the northern flank of the cathedral and halted when he had a clear view of most of that side. The area lay in the shadows cast by the great bulk of the building and it took his eyes an instant to adjust to the change of light. There was no one to be seen lurking among the buttresses of stone soaring above him, no one moving on the open lawn that lay on this side too. No shelter or hiding place apart from a fringe of trees and a scatter of houses and gardens which were several hundred yards off to the east and north.

That left the cathedral itself. There was a porch just beyond the north-west corner, providing a more convenient and less imposing access to the interior than the main doors. Tom went warily towards the side entrance, conscious that someone might be lurking in the gloom of the porch. But that too was empty. The door was ajar. He pushed his way inside, still with caution.

Once there he moved quickly into the open spaces of the nave, away from the shadows of the great pillars which stretched towards the east. He paused again. It was the first time he had entered the cathedral. Despite the circumstances he stood still for an instant, overwhelmed by the airy spaces of the vaulting above his head, the vista along the nave. A few candles twinkled in the distance at ground level but they were feeble by contrast with the shafts of red-gold sunlight that came through the clerestory. A voice from the region of the choir was intoning something – a prayer perhaps – but Tom could not distinguish the words. There was a scattering of people down there too, but no one at this western end.

If an evening service was in progress, then perhaps Eaves and Fawkes had concealed themselves among the congregation. But there were other, more immediate places for desperate men to hide. In the shelter of the pillars which were thick as tree trunks or in the depths of the side chapels. And there must surely be further exits on the south side of the building and elsewhere.

Casting his eyes around, Tom searched for some hint, some clue as to his quarry. And found it almost straightaway. He heard a groan. A dozen yards behind him a body lay slumped against a low outcrop of stone which ran into the narthex and supported the base of a lone pillar. The body was garbed in black and at first he thought it was one of the men he was pursuing. But as he drew nearer he realized that it was a cathedral official. A verger probably, to judge by his dark clothing.

The man was moaning and clutching at his head with a bloodstained hand. He was elderly and almost bald, with a few strands of white hair. The blood came from an injury to his scalp. Tom crouched down on his haunches.

'Are you all right, sir?'

The verger took his hand away from his head and looked at it, puzzled. The injury was not so bad, more of a scrape than a deep cut. Tom assisted the old man to climb to his feet. He stood, propping himself against the pillar, and gazed around as though the place was as unfamiliar to him as it was to Tom Ansell.

'Have you seen two men?' said Tom.

'What do you say?'

'Men running.'

The verger dabbed at his head and examined his hand once more before replying, 'One of them pushed me in his rush. I fell and hit my head.'

'Where did they go? Did you see?'

The man did not answer but sank down until he was sitting on the stone surround of the pillar. Tom did not think he was badly hurt but merely shaken up. He sensed rather than saw someone to one side and spun round. But it was only another verger, a younger man hastening to the aid of his fellow. Tom did not want to stay to explain what had happened. Every moment's delay reduced the chance of finding the two fugitives. Or rather, one fugitive and one pursuer.

'If you see them, give them a piece of my mind,' said the sitting man. 'I do not know what they expect to find in the triforium.'

He gestured behind him and Tom, glancing up, noticed a wooden enclosure that formed a kind of internal porch in the north-western corner of the building. There was a door, slightly open. Tom might have suspected a trap but he reasoned that men in such a hurry that they shoved aside a harmless old verger would not take time to close doors after them. By now, the younger verger had reached the injured man. Tom nodded to him and moved away before he could be asked any questions.

He stepped through the door of the enclosure and shut it behind him. He was standing in a stone-flagged lobby which, through a vaulted opening, showed the beginning of a flight of spiral stairs. There was no other exit, no different direction in which Fawkes and Eaves could have gone. Tom took the stairs two at a time, but the tight turns in the staircase and the smoothness of the old, worn steps caused him to lose his footing more than once. A little light came squeezing through slit windows.

He reached the top and paused to catch his breath and work out where to go next. But, again, there seemed to be little choice. A narrow passage led off to a railed gallery overlooking the nave. Was this what the old verger had called the triforium? After the dimness and constriction from the ascent to this level there came an abrupt burst of light and space. To his right the sun streamed through the windows, some of clear glass, some stained. To his left were the airy upper reaches of the nave. A small part of him that wasn't preoccupied with keeping his balance – the guard-rail was low – was aware that the sound of prayer had been replaced by singing which was thin and distant.

At the far end of the gallery was another lobby and a second spiral staircase. Tom halted for an instant. Each time he was listening out for sounds coming from ahead or above. Scuffling steps, the noise of a struggle perhaps, for he was convinced that Fawkes intended to do harm to Eaves. But there was no sound.

On the next level, Tom found himself above the vaulted ceiling of the nave. By now he was well out of the public area of the cathedral. The light, strong at this western end, was swallowed up among the massive timber frames that receded into the depths of the roof. It was like being inside an upturned ark. The wind, more evident at this height, rattled at the myriad of small panes in the west-facing windows. There was a walkway along one side of the roof, stretching above the pale domes of the vaults. Tom couldn't be sure but he thought he detected a flicker of movement at the far end.

He started off along the walkway. It swayed slightly underfoot. This, and a rope strung between timbers which provided the only handhold, reinforced the feeling of being aboard a ship. It grew darker as Tom got closer to the end of the roof of the nave and he had to stoop slightly to enter a short passage where the walkway finished. This time he emerged into a large white-walled chamber which, he realized, formed one of the floors of the tower. A loud click startled him until he saw its source was an arrangement of wheels and cogs and cords that stretched through holes in the ceiling to the next storey. Above him must be the bells of the cathedral clock.

Tom was about to give up his quest, wondering whether Fawkes and Eaves had eluded him and taken an altogether different path through or out of the building, when he heard a distinctly human sound from the staircase which led to the floor above. It was a shout of alarm or a loud curse – he could not decide which – muffled but also magnified by the twists and turns of the stone spiral. Not the sound of an elderly verger or a discreet keeper of the bells. Tom approached the staircase, which was contained within one of the four great columns that ran up the corners of the tower.

He wished he had some object with him which might be used as a weapon. Even an umbrella would have given him confidence. But he had nothing. He could have gone off to get assistance or at least waited for it to arrive: Helen must have reached the police house by now. He might have delayed at the bottom of the spiral stairs, to intercept whoever emerged. But suppose there was some other route down from the tower?

Tom, torn between retreating and advancing, couldn't recall a time in his life when he'd so consciously put himself in danger. There was a killer up the tower, there was another man (with God knows what driving *him*) on his tail, and Tom behind them both.

He took the next set of stairs, passing an entrance to a second white-walled chamber which, a brief glance was enough to tell him, contained nothing except a set of bells, and so continued up an even narrower stone flight. He must be nearing the top of the tower. He slowed, partly because his breath was running short, partly because he could hear voices.

He rounded a final twist in the spiral and his head came level with a floor which was of wood not stone. This was the topmost point of the tower and the base of the cathedral spire. If Tom had looked up he would have seen a central wooden column from which sprang a branch-like jumble of scaffolding and small platforms, used for repairs to the inside or access to the outside of the spire. The column soared up straight as a tent-pole and as thick as the main-mast of a ship. Near it was a great treadmill-like wheel which must have once been used for hauling blocks of stone.

But Tom did not look up to where the inside of the spire disappeared into dizzying darkness. Instead his eyes were fixed on the two men who stood facing each other a few strides away from the place at which his head protruded above floor level. It was Eaves the gardener and Fawkes the coachman. They were panting, both of them, and glaring at one another. Luckily for Tom, they were so busy breathing and glaring that they were quite unaware of him.

Fawkes was holding something in his hand. It might have been a knife. Tom could not tell since the light was poor up here. But, as if conscious that he was playing to an audience, Eaves said when he'd recovered his breath, 'You won't do much harm with that, Seth. It's only a trowel.'

'I grabbed it from your store,' said Fawkes. 'It's got a pointy tip. You come near and try it, Adam.'

'It's not the pointy tip, Seth, it's the mind behind it that counts. The mind and the will. Have you killed a man before? Have you?'

The silence from the other was answer enough.

'*I* have,' said Adam Eaves.

'I know. You killed my master Percy Slater. I was there.'

'Poor old Percy Slater. Well, he shouldn't have come out the house at that inconvenient moment.'

'And you did for his brother too, didn't you, Adam?'

'We've been through that already, Seth. You know it doesn't mean much to me, this killing lark.'

This was a shocking confirmation to Tom Ansell as he stood below the topmost steps. He remained very still.

'So I say to you, Seth, that if I can deal with the two Slater brothers just like that –' and here the gardener snapped his fingers – 'then I can deal with my own brother.'

Brothers? Eaves and Fawkes, brothers? Tom remembered that there been something faintly familiar about Fawkes the first time he'd seen him. A likeness to Eaves?

'I'll keep you here, Adam,' said Fawkes. 'I'll keep you here until justice comes. I will prevent your escape.'

'Oh, bugger justice,' said Eaves. 'You mind what I said to you earlier. If I swing so will you.'

'I'll take my chance on that. I've had enough of you and your tricks.'

There was a pause as if this was an answer that Eaves wasn't prepared for. Tom heard the wind whistling through gaps in the fabric of the spire. Then Eaves said to his brother, 'I suppose you think there's no way out of here 'cept down the stairs.'

'There is not,' said Fawkes, but he did not sound altogether confident.

'Have you heard that tale, matey, of a sailor who was so glad when old King Charles came back to rule this happy isle and called in on Salisbury town, that he went and capered up the spire and did a handstand on the very top? Have you heard that tale of a sailor?'

'You go capering up the spire then, Adam,' said Fawkes,

'and I'll say goodbye to you when you're on the way down.'

'Or p'raps I'll just caper in your direction instead.'

And at that, Adam Eaves did a queer kind of dance towards Seth Fawkes, who continued to hold out the implement – was it really a trowel? – in front of him. Tom involuntarily started up the steps until he was almost out in the open. And down below he heard, yes, the the thud of boots and the sounds of voices. Voices calling out – calling his name. 'Tom!' or 'Mr Ansell!'

Eaves seemed to halt in mid-spring, at the sight of someone emerging from the staircase, perhaps at the sounds coming from below.

'Up here!' Tom yelled. 'Here!'

The gardener changed direction and darted beyond the massive wheel that stood like some treadmill in a prison of nightmares. He fumbled at a door on that side of the spire, the southern aspect. But the door was locked or it stuck fast and he abandoned the attempt after a couple of seconds and scrabbled towards the western wall, on the opposite side to where Tom had appeared.

Meanwhile Seth Fawkes, who was slower than the other man and had started back in shock at Tom's presence, now resumed his pursuit. There was a clanging sound and a sudden gust of air and a blaze of red light from the setting sun as Eaves managed to wrench open the west-facing door which, once released, slammed back on its hinges under the force of the wind. Tom scrambled and ducked his way through the jumble of beams and struts which occupied the central area of the base of the spire, ignoring bruised shins and a knock to his head. As he neared the door, the rectangle was darkened for an instant by a shape. It must be Fawkes, reaching the entrance before Tom, following his brother out into the open.

The sun was directly in Tom's eyes. Standing on the threshold of the door, he was aware – without being able to see anything clearly – of a mighty stone spire and infinite acres of space above his head, of the cathedral roof and the grassy close and the fringes of the town below. Of the glint of the river beyond. Of a great orange-red ball blurring a distant line of hills. No noises that he could hear, apart from the rushing of the wind. Then he took a deep breath, and stepped out on to the ledge which fronted this angle of the spire.

The ledge or viewing platform was scarcely a yard across and little more than half a dozen yards in length, broken up by buttresses which turned the spaces in between to small bays. There was a parapet of stone but it was less high than a ship's rail. Tom, his eyes still dazzled by the light, instinctively grasped at the parapet. He glanced to left and right from his vantage point in the middle of the ledge. He could see nothing, and believed for an instant that the two men, Eaves and Fawkes, had somehow effected a miraculous escape.

But no. From behind one of the buttresses to his left there came thumps and groans, and two black-clad figures fell writhing to the ground in a curious, sideways, rag-doll fashion. One of them – Tom could not discern which of the two, since the man's back was to him and he was still wearing the billycock hat – scrambled to his feet and started to kick at the other. The space was so limited that the kicker could not get much force or swing behind his attack. Then there was a swiping arm, a flash of metal in the sun, and the kicking stopped. Tom guessed that the weapon was the trowel which Fawkes had been wielding. Now the one on the ground dropped the trowel, grabbed hold of the other's legs and clasped them to him, causing the upright figure to fall back against the parapet.

Tom's attention was distracted for an instant by a clattering in the chamber behind him. The sounds of panting, of voices straining to call out his name after the rapid climb to the top. He twisted his head and shouted out into the darkness over his shoulder, 'Here we are!'

When he turned back, he saw that the figure who'd been on the ground and grasped the other by the legs was now rearing up. He was still holding his opponent's legs below the knee. With a great heave, by bracing himself against the wall, he pushed himself fully upright and seemed to pour – there was no other word for it – seemed to pour his opposite over the parapet, as if he was tipping liquid out of a jug.

In a single, fluid motion the other man pitched over the edge and tumbled outwards into space. With all sense of himself suspended, Tom was barely conscious of what he could see: amid the sun-spots that danced in front of his vision, there was a collection of black rags and sticks (the limbs, he realized, yes, the arms and legs) which grew smaller as it fell towards earth. Or not the earth, precisely, but the sheer flank of the cathedral roof.

Then he felt hands grasping his shoulders and pulling at him and he was afraid that he too was going to be thrown off into nothingness. Automatically he gripped the sides of the doorway. But the hands went on dragging and a voice said, 'Come inside!' and another said 'Get out of the way!' and they were different voices, neither of them belonging to the two men who'd been struggling on the parapet.

Tom fell back into the chamber at the bottom of the spire. He lay there, as several shapes crowded past him and out through the doorway. His confused state was worsened by several great blows struck on a giant gong, sounds which it took him a moment to identify as the cathedral clock. Then he felt his head being lifted gently, almost cradled.

'Are you all right, Tom?'

It was Helen. She was kneeling on the floor. He felt the softness of her hands, the fabric of her coat brushing his cheek. He was going to tell her to stand up, otherwise she'd get her clothes dusty and dirty, but instead he said, 'What happened?'

'I was going to ask you that,' she said, leaning forward and kissing his forehead.

Then the crowd who'd gone out on to the viewing platform returned. Only three of them, as it turned out. Inspector Foster, Constable Chesney and another policeman whose name Tom didn't know.

'Nobody there,' said Foster.

Tom stood up. He gripped one of the scaffolding beams, not so much for help in staying upright but so as to hold on to something solid.

'But I saw them,' he said. 'They were fighting.'

'I mean there's nobody up here,' said Foster, pulling on his side-whiskers for emphasis. 'Down there –' now he jabbed with his forefinger towards the imagined ground many hundreds of feet below where they were standing – 'down there's a different story, and not a very pretty one either.'

And, standing next to his superior officer, Constable Chesney rammed his fist into his open palm to simulate the sound of bodies striking the ground.

Salisbury Station

Or the sound of a body, rather than bodies, and one striking not the ground but a lower roof.

A single corpse was recovered that afternoon as the sun fell and darkness rose in the cathedral close. It was badly battered and disfigured, like a mariner thrown from a ship and tossed among the rocks before arriving on shore. The damage to the mortal remains of Adam Eaves – or Adam Fawkes as he should more properly be called – had been caused by the force of impact against the stone outcrops, the buttresses and finials, in the lower stretches of the cathedral. The black shape which Tom saw plunging to its doom had soared outwards as it went down and then must have bounced and tumbled like a climber falling from a precipice, before landing finally on the roof of the cloisters.

There could not be much doubt that the remains were those of the gardener to Canon Slater. There was Tom's evidence, that he had seen an improvised weapon (the trowel) in the hands of Eaves's assailant, and that it was those hands which were responsible for throwing the other off the spire. But, more conclusively, there was a statement, almost a confession, which was found in a pocket of the dead man's clothing.

It was brief and ill written but clear enough. It told how he, that is Adam Fawkes (also known as Adam Eaves), had murdered both the Slater brothers. Felix had been killed when Eaves had been surprised in the act of stealing the papers from the chest in the Canon's study, searching for documents and plans which would show the whereabouts of a supposed hoard of ancient treasure buried in the Slater estate at Northwood House in Downton. Slater was sitting down, about to write a note of dismissal, unwisely taking his eyes off the gardener. Then a few days later Percy Slater, the owner of Northwood House, had died not by his own hand but killed by Adam as he was attempting to dig up the place where this treasure was rumoured to be, a spot known as Hogg's Corner.

There was no mention in the confession of the so-called Salisbury manuscript, whose disappearance (in Tom's eyes at least) might have been a motive for the murder. But the handwritten memoir of the Slater brothers' father was discovered among various items in the queer little lodging occupied by Adam in the garden of Venn House. The lock which secured the book from prying eyes had been forced by Eaves. The other items in his stash included bits and pieces of tarnished gold – rings, bracelets, brooches – which had undoubtedly been excavated from burial sites around the town.

With the discovery of Eaves's body, it was equally beyond doubt that the gardener had been responsible for the death of Andrew North, the sexton. If North had been seized by the mania – which he'd caught from Felix Slater -for digging up old items, stealing them if necessary, then Eaves had obviously seen a way in which he might take a short cut, by thieving from the thief. Even if he had to commit a murder in the process. North, who'd worked for Felix Slater, must have encountered Adam Eaves, must have grown to fear him and to identify the gardener with Atropos, the wielder of shears.

And more bizarrely, the stolen hoard found in the gardener's lodge also contained toasting forks and jelly moulds together with other kitchen implements which dated back not thousands of years but no further than a few months.

Inspector Foster scratched his head and tugged his side-whiskers over this but he was able to offer some explanation to Tom Ansell and Helen Scott while he was bidding them goodbye on the platform at Salisbury station.

'It seems to me,' he said, 'that this Eaves fellow was a thoroughly bad lot and had been ever since his birth. A walking example of Original Sin, if you like. We've established that he was born at Downton to a God-fearing family and that he was brother to Seth Fawkes. He ran into trouble early on in Salisbury – one of the men in the police house has an old cousin as remembers him – and then he disappeared God knows where. To foreign countries maybe. God knows why he came back here either. But he got himself a job as a gardener at Venn House. He enjoyed dressing up and playing a part. And all the time he was on the lookout for ways to make mischief and mayhem.'

'Mischief!' said Helen. 'I'd hardly call murder mischief.'

'No more would I, miss. But he liked causing trouble and he liked murdering, did Mr Adam Eaves, liked the thrill of it. Mr Ansell here has confirmed he said as much when he overheard Eaves and his brother exchanging insults up the tower.'

'I don't know about the thrill of it,' said Tom, 'but it didn't seem to hold terrors for him as it would for most of us. Yes, he probably enjoyed it.'

'It's my belief he liked the thrill of thieving too,' continued the Inspector. 'It was him as broke into those other houses in West Walk and stole small items that were almost worthless, and he did the robberies just for the hell of it – begging your pardon, Miss Scott.'

Tom nodded. 'That's why he didn't trouble to conceal the burglaries. Wasn't one of the householders actually woken up by the clatter of pans being dropped in the kitchen, as if the thief wanted to alert everyone to his presence?'

'Just so,' said Foster. 'Mischief and mayhem, you see.'

There were still some mysteries attached to the business. The principal object which Eaves had been seeking in the mound in the grounds of Northwood House had apparently been a solid golden torque or neck-piece. Tom recalled that Felix Slater had made some passing reference to it at their first meeting. But it transpired that it was all moonshine, and well known to be moonshine in the locality. The piece never existed or, if it ever had, was thieved long ago. There was a mention of it in the Salisbury manuscript, which Tom had had the leisure to look through more carefully and which was now safe inside his valise, to be deposited in accordance with the dead man's instructions at the London office of Scott, Lye & Mackenzie.

Old George Slater described how he had even done a bit of digging himself, and turned up nothing. If Adam Eaves had perused the manuscript more carefully, he might have realized this. But perhaps he *had* read about it, as he skimmed the stories about Byron and Shelley, and refused to believe that there was no treasure. Eaves had also stolen from the Canon's study some papers and plans which he believed would guide him to the precise spot. Plans which Felix had retained from his own younger days of fossicking about in the family grounds.

A greater mystery was what had happened to Seth Fawkes, once he had succeeded in throwing his brother from the heights of the cathedral. If apprehended and tried, he might have been found guilty of manslaughter or perhaps acquitted because he was acting in self-defence. Who could say? But the coachman to Percy Slater had not been apprehended. Indeed, it was as if he was gone from the face of the earth. Had Tom Ansell not seen with his own eyes the struggle between the two brothers – and had other people in and around the cathedral precincts not also testified to the presence of a pair of men, one seemingly in pursuit of the other – he might have believed that Adam had flung himself off the tower, by himself.

This was the story as reported in the *Gazette*, that the gardener to Canon Slater, overcome with guilt and remorse at his prior acts of murder, had done away with himself in the most public and dramatic fashion. He had conveniently provided a written account of his crimes, as discovered in his clothing. It was the simplest version to credit and it was enthusiatically peddled by Inspector Foster. It wrapped everything up nicely, it accounted for two killings (three, when you included the sexton Andrew North) and it brought the murderer's own tale to a satisfactory resolution.

There was a rumour to the effect that a second man had been up the tower but when questioned by the newspaper the Inspector cast doubt on it, without going as far as an absolute denial. As he said to Tom later on the evening of the events on the spire, 'I take you at your word, Mr Ansell. You are a lawyer, after all. But the fact remains that there was no one to be found up aloft apart from your good self. Oh yes, there were two men chasing each other all round the houses, we have other witnesses to that, but the cathedral is a big place with many holes and corners. Who's to say that this Seth Fawkes did not sneak off into one of them?'

'In that case, where is he now?' said Tom.

'He may turn up and then we shall see what is to be done with him,' said the Inspector. 'But remember that if he has killed his brother, as you believe, he may have gone on the run. He may even have done away with himself as well.'

But Seth Fawkes did not turn up, alive or dead. He had not returned to Northwood House nor was he discovered in some ditch outside the town. And Tom was happy to leave the matter there. Privately, it was his belief – no, his conviction – that Seth had battled to the death with

Adam, and then managed to escape from the spire. Either by somehow hiding himself in the shadows of the viewing platform even as the police were out there or, more daringly, by climbing round to one of the other faces of the tower. It could be done. There was that story of the sailor who'd climbed to the very top and performed a handstand. All one needed was the steadiest of hands and nerves, and great foolhardiness – or despair.

Other aspects of the Salisbury business had come to a slightly happier conclusion. Walter Slater had emerged again, now cleared of any suspicion of the death of his uncle or father, whichever of the two Slater brothers was credited with whichever role. (The true facts of his parentage remained a secret.) The curate had never returned to Venn House that night, despite his assurances to Canon Eric Selby, but gone back to the shelter of St Luke's and the ringing room.

The poor young man was badly shaken and his whole life turned upside down. But he was being comforted by Miss Nugent, and in time might reconcile himself with his mother, Amelia Slater. He would inherit the Northwood estate once the legal process was complete – was due to inherit it anyway, regardless of who exactly his father had been – but Elizabeth, Percy's wife, had the right to dwell there in her lifetime if she chose. Mrs Slater, informed of Percy's death, was imminently expected from London for the funerals of her husband and her brother-in-law. Her attitude to his death was not known though, given the estranged nature of the lives they'd been leading, she would perhaps not be too distressed.

But in the meantime Walter, perhaps to distract himself from the tragic tangle of recent events, had absented himself officially from his clerical duties and gone with Miss Nugent to busy himself at Northwood. He had made clear his intention to put the place in order, had taken on fresh help from the town of Downton as well as a neighbouring village to start setting the house and grounds to rights. The aged Nan would be left as she was, to live out her days at Northwood dowager-style. It was an open question whether Walter Slater would return to the Church, or whether he might combine his vocation with that of a landed gent. Too early to say yet.

So Tom Ansell and Helen Scott made their goodbyes to Inspector Foster on the up platform of Salisbury station. The train was waiting its moment to depart on time, puffing smuts of smoke into the grey light of the November morning. Tom could see the cathedral spire above the station buildings, seemingly much closer than it really was. Strange to think that he had lately been witness to a life-and-death struggle up there. And it was at this very station that he had glimpsed the earlier tussle between Seth and Adam Fawkes on the fog-bound evening of his arrival.

Inspector Foster was saying something and he had missed it.

'Sorry?' he said.

'The Inspector was wishing us a happy future together,' said Helen.

Perhaps noticing the look on Tom's face, Foster said, 'I hope I have not spoken out of turn, but I am right in thinking that . . . '

'Someone has yet to ask the question,' said Helen.

'And someone else has yet to make the reply when the question is asked,' said Tom.

And so they boarded the train.

I suppose it is possible that Tom Ansell might have proposed to Helen Scott there and then on the train, since he had already been frustrated or intercepted in his intention on two or three occasions and had almost given up the search for the propitious moment. The compartment floor was a little dusty and greasy but he might have crouched down in a gingerly fashion rather than kneeling properly, and asked her for her hand. He might have proposed like that and she would almost certainly have accepted, if they had had the compartment to themselves.

But they were not to be alone. At the last instant, as the train was about to pull out of the station, the door was opened and an oldish lady was almost pushed inside by a porter who deposited a capacious bag immediately afterwards on the floor of the compartment. She was wearing a large hat which would have flown off with the speed of her arrival, had she not clasped it to her head with a black-gloved hand. Tom, who was sitting on the other side of the compartment with Helen opposite him, stood up and hoisted the lady's bag on to the rack above her head. She thanked him, *sotto voce,* and then, without more than the swiftest glance at the young couple, produced a small, serious book from somewhere in her voluminous dress and proceeded to study it as intently as if it were the Bible or a devotional volume.

Tom was disappointed. He'd hoped to be alone with Helen. Even if he wasn't to propose to her, they might have enjoyed chatting about the events in Salisbury and talking about what the Inspector had told them. But it did not seem appropriate to discuss their part in an exciting drama when there was company. He remembered that when he'd been travelling down to Salisbury, his compartment had been occupied by an old lady whom he'd also helped with her luggage. Was this the same one? He did not think so, but there was a symmetry to this absolutely meaningless coincidence.

Tom settled himself into the seat next to the window and smiled at Helen. Prepared for the train journey, she already had a book to hand. It was titled, Tom could see, *The Shame of Mrs Prendergast*. Another sensation novel, no doubt, to judge by its title and enticing cover, which showed a woman with a low-cut dress and necklace of pearls glancing in apprehension over her shoulder at a man who stood in the doorway to her room. For himself, Tom had nothing to read apart from Baxter's *On Tort,* which he had considered discarding in The Side of Beef in Salisbury for Jenkins to ponder over but which some last-minute scruple had caused him to pack after all. There was also the Salisbury manuscript in his case, which he would certainly not have got out and opened in a railway carriage. So he had to content himself with looking out of the window at the bare, wintry landscape of the plain.

From time to time – very often, in fact – he glanced across at Helen. At first she returned his looks and smiles but then he observed that her attention seemed to be distracted away from him or from her book and towards the old lady who was sitting in the diagonal corner. Tom glanced sideways but the woman with the hat, which obscured most of her face, seemed to be absorbed in *her* book.

He returned his gaze to the dreary view from the window. When he next looked towards Helen, it was to see a change in her expression. Her mouth was open in surprise and she was shaking her head urgently, not at him but at the other occupant of the compartment. When Tom twisted in his seat, he saw the old lady was staring straight at him. The hat had been pushed back on her – or rather, his – head. She – or rather, he – was holding a gun, a small gun, snug in a fist.

It was, he realized with a rush of terror, no old lady but Adam Eaves, garbed in black and disguised as a female. It would have been absurd, unbelievable, if it hadn't been for the deadly earnest expression on Eaves's small face. The glint of his eyes. The weapon in his hand. The devotional book thrown on to the floor of the compartment.

'What's the matter, Mr Ansell? You're looking at me as if I was a dead man.'

Tom opened his mouth but no words came out beyond a gargled croak which he turned into a cough. Helen, who'd had little more than a glimpse of the murderous gardener outside Venn House, was quicker to recover.

'We thought you were dead,' she said. Her voice was quite steady in the circumstances.

'Being dead is convenient, I've found,' said Eaves. 'I've been dead before. It enables you to pass unseen. Like being an old lady, when nobody notices you either. That's true, isn't it, Miss . . . Miss . . .? Not that you'd know, because everyone's certainly going to notice *you*. Is it Miss or is it Mrs . . . I can't see a ring on account of your gloves, and I haven't had the pleasure of an introduction.'

'Miss Scott will do.'

Helen said this coldly, and Tom didn't think he'd ever admired or loved her more than he did at that moment. He spoke, more to distract attention away from Helen than anything else.

'The body which fell from the cathedral was your brother's, then. It was Seth's?'

'Course it was. He didn't have a head for heights like me, poor fellow.'

'But there was your confession,' said Tom.

'My confession?' said Adam Eaves. 'Oh yes, I read about that in the paper and had a good laugh. But it was none of mine, Mr Ansell. It was Seth as wrote it out and brought it to me just as I was leaving Venn House for good 'n' all. He got upset when I wouldn't sign it. Why should I put my monicker to a document like that, eh? You're a lawyer. Tell me, would you?'

'Probably not,' said Tom, wondering whether he dreaming this whole scene.

'But Seth, he thought he could make me sign and turn me in or some such nonsense. He got into a right state when I disagreed with him, he tried to attack me, chased me all about the place. I believe you saw us, Mr Ansell.'

At this, Eaves stood up. A ridiculous figure in full skirts of some cheap material and a great-brimmed hat tilted to the back of his head like a cowboy in an illustrated magazine. He swayed slightly with the motion of the train but the gun was steady in his hand. It was a little gun, such as a woman might carry concealed in countries where women did carry such things. Tom thought of the United States.

'Why don't you leave us alone?' he said. 'Why don't you make your escape instead of causing more trouble?'

'I could do, couldn't I?' said Adam Eaves, as if the idea was occurring to him for the first time. 'Why don't I? Because I'm not minded to is why.'

'There is a station soon,' said Helen.

'Is there, Miss Scott? No station for a fair few minutes yet. I know this line better than you, see. What I am going to do is fire this weapon a couple of times because this model is special, it has two barrels. I will do harm to you – the both of you – kill you, perhaps. And then I am going to pull what they call the communication cord. Have you noticed that, Mr Ansell and Miss Scott, the communication cord? It's quite the new device and hangs on the outside of this carriage, just above the window. It rings a bell in the driver's platform and when it rings he says to himself, oh there's trouble, I wonder what, maybe a passenger taken sick of a sudden, and he puts on the brakes, and so this train draws to a standstill and so I make my escape over these fields, leaving you two here groaning and moaning. Or making no noise at all maybe, because you can't. By the time anyone finds out what's happened, I'll be over the hills and far away.'

'In God's name, why?' said Tom.

'Why? I've always wanted to pull the communication cord on a train.'

'Why do you want to harm us, I mean?'

''Cause I can,' said Eaves. ''Cause you got in my way.'

Eaves raised the gun and wavered in his aim, angling it first towards Tom then Helen. And back again towards Tom. Helen, who was still holding her sensation novel, threw *The Shame of Mrs Prendergast* at Eaves. He was taken by surprise. The book – it was a thick volume, full of incident – struck him in the chest and the gun flew out of his grasp and landed at Tom's feet. Without thinking, he scooped it up and pointed it at Eaves.

'It's not loaded,' said the gardener. 'I was only joking.'

'Try me,' said Tom. The gun, a woman's weapon undoubtedly but small and potent, was in his hand. It had two barrels, one on top of the other. It was not cocked. Tom put one hand on the trigger, set far back in the handle, and the other on the hammer. He heard a thudding in his ears, over and above the clacking of the train. There was a kind of red mist before his eyes. He scarcely recognized the sound of his own voice.

'Try me,' he said again. 'I would as soon kill you as look at you.'

'I believe you would, Mr Ansell,' said Adam Eaves.

With a swift movement, encumbered as he was by his female clothing, Eaves swung round and put his hand on the door handle. The train was travelling at speed on an embankment, and there was a drop on either side. 'No time for the cord but *c'est la vie*,' said Eaves, and he opened the door.

Once he'd opened it a fraction, it slammed back against the side of the carriage, propelled by their forward motion. The smoke from the engine entered the compartment. Adam Eaves half jumped, half threw himself outward into space. Later Tom was reminded of the way in which Seth Fawkes had been cast from the cathedral spire.

By the time Helen and Tom had recovered themselves sufficiently to pull the communication cord – moving warily towards the gaping door, watching the countryside whirr past their feet, Helen holding on to Tom while he fumbled on the exterior of the carriage for the cord – the train had moved on at least a couple of miles.

Mackenzie's Castle, Again

'Tell me again,' said David Mackenzie. 'You two seem to have had a very exciting time of it while I have been laid up here.'

Tom and Helen were taking tea in the Highgate house with Tom's senior. They had been greeted enthusiastically by Mrs Mackenzie. That mannish lady had embraced Helen and winked, actually winked, at Tom. Outside the window of David Mackenzie's room the weather was the same as on Tom's last visit, with the fog licking at the window and a general gloom descending. Inside, the fire was slumbering and Mr Mackenzie was sitting in the same armchair, puffing at the same pipe, and wielding the same back-scratcher to reach the tricky points on the leg which was encased in plaster. Perhaps in deference to Helen, he was drinking tea rather than brandy. Otherwise it was as if he hadn't moved in the several days that Tom Ansell had spent in Salisbury, witnessing murder, being nearly accused of it, and then seeing the demise of the real villain.

Tom had given his account of everything which had happened. He described his one meeting with Canon Slater, his glimpses of the Salisbury manuscript, the journey to Northwood House, his brief sojourn in Fisherton Gaol, the tangled affairs of the family, the true relationship of Walter Slater to Felix and to Percy, and so on. Tom no longer felt under any obligation to keep things secret, now that both the Slater brothers were dead.

Most of this was new to Mackenzie, and he listened with profound interest.

At one point he said, 'Well, there is no telling with people, is there? They are not what they appear to be. It's like the Tichborne Claimant. No doubt if any of our affairs were examined in the harsh light of open court, all sorts of inconsistencies and impostures would be revealed. Felix Slater seemed to be the respectable one while Percy was the wastrel of the family. Yet it was Felix the churchman who caused his wife to disown his son, and Percy the gambler who agreed to take him as his own. There was perhaps more kindness in Percy than there was in his brother, even if there was no love lost between them.'

They weren't the only unloving brothers in the business, thought Tom. There was also Seth Fawkes and Adam Eaves.

When Tom reached the final encounter with Adam Eaves on the train, he brushed over it, perhaps out of reluctance to relive the dangerous moment. He had been talking for the best part of an hour, and through several cups of tea. But David Mackenzie said, 'Tell me that part again,' so now Helen took up the climax of the story and repeated it in more colourful and vivid language than Tom could have managed. She stressed the murderousness of Eaves, their hair's-breadth escape. Tom wondered, not for the first time, whether the episode would find its way into the novel she was composing.

After Tom had tugged on the communication cord – a small part of him being curious to see whether it would work, and the bell ring in the driver's cabin and the train come to a halt (which it did) – there followed a period of confusion.

The guard arrived outside their compartment together with other interested passengers, and Tom explained how they'd been attacked by a fellow traveller, who had made his getaway as the train was moving. He did not mention the gun, which he had slipped into his pocket, or that he knew the attacker's identity or the fact that he had been disguised as a woman. The story was far-fetched enough as it was. But the presence of Helen and her own words, together with the evident respectability of the couple, and the capacious bag (belonging to the 'old lady') which was still in the luggage rack, was sufficient to convince.

The train could not stay blocking the line. The fireman had already placed a red light on the rear carriage to warn any approaching engine on the up line, and the driver was agitating for them to move on. So they chugged on to Andover. From there, the Salisbury police house was telegraphed, and Helen and Tom were left to await the arrival of Inspector Foster while the train proceeded on its way.

Foster arrived with Constable Chesney, also by train from Salisbury. For the second time, Tom and Helen told their tale. He handed over the little gun, which Inspector Foster declared to be 'not of English manufacture'. The large bag which Eaves had abandoned when he quit the train was opened and found to contain a peculiar assortment of clothing. 'Looks like disguises, guv,' said Chesney. The sight of an elaborately embroidered tunic-like garment, definitely not of English manufacture, prompted the constable to add, 'Do you suppose he was going to pass for a Chinee next?'

By now, a couple of hours had elapsed and it was at least another hour before a search of the line several miles down the track could be instituted by the police and employees of the railway. Tom and Helen, who'd spent the time in the station refreshment room, were convinced that Eaves would never be found, living or dead. The man seemed to bear a charmed life and there was no reason to believe he wouldn't be equally charmed in death.

In due course, however, Inspector Foster announced that they had discovered a body at the bottom of an embankment, in roughly the place where the murderer had leapt from the carriage. Tom's first thought was that this must be another sham. But, no, it seemed not. The body was that of a man garbed in woman's clothing. It was not in such a battered condition as the corpse of his brother retrieved from the roof of the cathedral cloister, since it had not fallen so far or met with such rough obstacles on the way down. Eaves was identified by the Inspector, who had seen the gardener on more than one occasion.

For the second time that day, Foster bade them goodbye. But it was a temporary goodbye. Tom and Helen were told they would have to return for the inquest, which would not be held for a week or two. They were allowed to travel on to London, where they arrived at Waterloo, weary, as it was getting dark.

Tom escorted Helen back to her Highbury home and left it to her to explain their adventures to the formidable Mrs Scott. He'd already had a twenty-minute conversation with Mrs Scott, while Helen was changing out of her travelling clothes upstairs, a conversation in which he had to tread the line between informing her of something and requesting it of her. He was conscious of being tired and haggard, of having escaped a murderer and spent the day waiting for news of a body. Yet something carried him forward. And he'd been agreeably surprised by Mrs Scott's response. The lady had gone so far as to give him a sort of smile and to say that the news he brought was no real news to her and that any fool might have seen it coming. Tom wasn't sure about the 'any fool' bit but he supposed that this was the closest he would get to assent and congratulation from Helen's mother.

On the way up to London Tom had asked Helen to marry him. They were alone in their compartment, and were not interrupted by murderous gardeners disguised as old ladies or by police inspectors or anybody else. Tom asked, not on bended knee but sitting next to her on the buttoned carriage-cloth of the seat and holding her warm hand (she had removed her gloves), and Helen said yes, she said yes. Her hands were shaking slightly. So were his. Tom did not know whether it was the excitement of the proposal or the shock of the morning's adventure. Both probably.

The next day they went together to see Mr Mackenzie, once Tom had deposited the Salisbury manuscript at the office. Some word of what had been happening in Salisbury must have reached old Ashley, the clerk with the corrugated forehead, because he actually expressed his pleasure at seeing Mr Ansell again and took personal charge of the manuscript. Tom wondered whether he would flick through its handwritten pages and be shocked by the contents, but Ashley was most likely beyond shock.

David Mackenzie too expressed his relief that Tom and Helen had returned unharmed.

'I feel that I failed though,' said Tom. 'Our client is dead and the maunscript which I went to get was stolen.'

'But the murderer has been found, and the manuscript recovered. And you have achieved one distinction which I think no lawyer in our office has yet managed.'

'Oh yes?'

'You have spent a night in gaol. You wrote to me about it.'

Tom had almost forgotten the letter. Looking back, his gaol experience seemed quite a minor event.

'Tell me, Tom, did you have a chance to look inside it? The Salisbury manuscript.'

'Just a glance.'

'And?'

'There were one or two encounters in it,' said Tom

uncomfortably, 'which you would not want your servants to read – or the ladies for that matter.'

'Tom!' said Helen, clattering her cup into her saucer. 'Never let me hear you say that again. I do not know about servants but whatever is fit for you to read is also fit for me.'

'I'm sorry,' said Tom.

'Ah,' said David Mackenzie, 'my wife has heard from her good friend Mrs Scott that you are to be married, and I see that it's true.'

'How so, Mr Mackenzie?' said Helen.

'Only a couple who were married or were very close to it would talk to each other in that way.'

So, the Salisbury business appeared finally to be over. And was over, when the couple journeyed once again to that city on the plain for the inquest on Adam Eaves at the beginning of December. The gardener, who had been erroneously identified as the corpse found in the cathedral close, was found to have killed himself while the balance of his mind was disturbed. Conclusive proof of this was to be found in his female disguise.

Train suicides were not unknown. There had very recently been one off the Blackwater Viaduct in Truro. This case, though, was dramatic and tortuous enough not merely to fill the pages of the *Gazette* but to excite the interest of the national papers, whose reporters could scarcely make sense of all its twists and revisions as to who had killed whom, and why and when and how. Well, could you?

However, the young couple, who'd given evidence at the inquest during a brief visit at which they stayed at the house of a delighted Eric Selby and his quiet wife, were more interested in another newspaper feature in which they figured as protagonists. They did not make the headlines this time. In fact, they had had to pay (at the rate of sixpence per line) for another item – it was a smaller, more discreet item – in which was announced the imminent marriage of Mr Thomas Edward Ansell and Miss Helen Georgina Scott.